DUST AND DESIRE

Also available from Conrad Williams and Titan Books

SONATA OF THE DEAD (JULY 2016)
HELL iS EMPTY (NOVEMBER 2016)

CONRAD WILLIAMS

DUST AND DESIRE

A JOEL SORRELL NOVEL

TITAN BOOKS

Dust and Desire
Print edition ISBN: 9781783295630
E-book edition ISBN: 9781783295647

Published by Titan Books
A division of Titan Publishing Group Ltd
144 Southwark Street, London SE1 0UP

Previously published as *Blonde on a Stick*.

First Titan edition: November 2015

1 2 3 4 5 6 7 8 9 10

A CIP catalogue record for this title is available from the British Library.

Printed and bound in the United States of America

For Rhonda, Ethan, Ripley and Zac. Always.

"Man the sum of his climatic experiences Father said. Man the sum of what have you. A problem in impure properties carried tediously to an unvarying nil: stalemate of dust and desire."

WILLIAM FAULKNER

PROLOGUE

He arrived on the Euston Road just as it was getting light, one cold morning at the end of November. He had spoken maybe six words on the way down from Liverpool. The canvas holdall remained in his hands at all times, even though it was large and cumbersome. He shook his head – a single violent jerk – when the drivers who picked him up suggested he sling it in the back. In the tension that followed, he could tell that they considered it a mistake to have stopped for him. They gripped the steering wheel too tightly, or struggled to make conversation. They turned the radio off, or on.

He didn't want to make small talk. He just wanted to arrive. London was at the end of this road. Everything was at the end of this road. His own doorstep and everyone else's, linked by miles and miles of tarmac. Just one road, going everywhere.

As the driver of his final lift sped away, leaving him outside the Shaw Park Plaza Hotel, he knew that this place could become as much his as Liverpool had been. The city was dirty and ugly. It had no favourites. It pretended it did, but you'd eventually be found out. At its best, the city tolerated you. And that suited him fine. He listened to the traffic stutter along Euston Road, until the cold made his eyes water. He squeezed the handle of the holdall, its worn grip moving into his fingers, moulding to their shape, comforting him. It was like holding his mother's hand: something that must have happened once, he knew, although he could not remember it. He watched some of the passers-by, the way their hands were naturally curled in towards their bodies as they walked, hopeful or ready – maybe instinctively ready – for another hand to join theirs.

His fingers itching with ghosts, he broke into his final ten-pound note to pay for breakfast at a cafe off the main drag. There was a *Sun* lying on his table but, although he tried to read it, his mind wouldn't settle on the words. His bacon sandwich was dry and difficult to chew, but it was hot and he ate it all, his first meal in over eighteen hours. Food was merely fuel, and he had little time for it. It just got in the way. He sipped his coffee until its tasteless heat had dissolved the cold, hard knot in his belly. Slowly, exterior sounds and smells began to break down his barriers. He was too tired to try to stop them. He sat back in his chair and ordered another coffee.

Outside, a tramp walked past the window, a blue hand outstretched.

He pushed his unfinished drink out of the way and wrestled his bag past the early-morning suits queueing for their toast and tea. The tramp was dipping into a rubbish bin now, seeing what he could unearth from the discarded *Metro*s and drained cardboard cups. The man's face was so gaunt, the inside of his cheeks looking as if they were about to touch each other. His cardigan was shredded: it seemed to cling to his body by dint of gravity, or sheer bloody-mindedness.

Turn and face.

Gradually, his breathing evened out. The casual impingements of madness retreated. This was only a tramp. Nobody he knew or had once known. Everything was cool. There was nothing to fear. It was time to get to where he needed to be. From his back pocket he pulled out a small, pink diary, very worn, with illegible gold initials embossed on the front cover. He flipped it open and scrutinised the photograph clipped to one of the pages. He wondered how she might have changed over the years, realising he must allow for the differences that might have visited her. He must try to pin her to the there and then, even if, in the here and now, she appeared to be a totally new kind of person.

It started to rain; umbrellas went up around him and the passing throng became like a formation of soldiers with their shields up, marching turtle fashion. Needles of rain bounced off the impervious black canopies, slanted across a hundred inscrutable faces. He managed to dodge them and the traffic, hurrying along Pancras Road to the entrance to St Pancras International Station, where a dozen suits without protection from the rain tutted and stamped, consulting their watches, gazing up at the sky.

He had been here once before, he thought, many years ago, when he was little more than a toddler and the station was not so expansive. On a day out, it had been. He remembered a stall where you could get warm almond croissants. That was gone now, it seemed – or maybe not gone but lost to the glut of shops that had sprung up in the hall beneath the platforms. Now it was like being in a glass shopping mall. Upstairs was a champagne bar where, if you bought a glass of bubbly, you could have some complimentary oysters to enjoy alongside it. That seemed almost preposterously decadent: a long way from the dollop of gravy Marge would decorate his chips and peas with at the fish bar in Anfield.

You could live here, he thought, with a sudden thrill, as he wandered from shop to shop. People streamed by him, stared straight through him, lost in the subtle panic of needing to be elsewhere, their minds filled with platform numbers and departure times and nothing else. He was invisible. Back home, people said hello to him in the street. You couldn't walk into a pub or a café without someone knowing you. But here, everyone wore the same countenance, as if the face was shocked that it possessed eyes, as if looking at others was too aggressive an act and the expression was its own apologist. People were stone, here. They were as cold as the concrete they walked on.

He bought another coffee at the Cappuccino Bar, and drank it in a fenced-off area reserved for patrons only. People were forming huge queues at the newsagents to buy reading matter for their journeys. In the distance, beyond the outer edge of the curved platform canopy, he could see the cement-coloured sky teeming with rain. The silhouettes of trains waiting to depart were slowly being erased by their own fumes. The place smelled, not unpleasantly, of scorched diesel.

Opposite, a woman on a stall selling smoothies was busy wiping down her counter. He watched her hull strawberries and feed crushed ice into a row of blenders. She worked diligently, never once looking up unless it was to serve a customer. He guessed she had been in this job a sufficient while for the novelty of such a busy place, with its people-watching, to have grown stale. She had alluded to her job before, on the message boards at skoolpalz4eva.com, but only mentioned that she worked mornings, and enjoyed it, and that it got her out of the house while her husband, a musician, taught guitar to a steady stream of bored children.

After an hour, a young man arrived, and they chatted behind the counter for a while until the woman took her apron off and patted him on the shoulder. The young man assumed her place, took up a knife and turned carrots into coins, ginger into pins and needles.

The woman retrieved a magazine from behind the counter and carried a plastic cup of frothy, shocking-red juice directly towards him. She pushed a current of air before her. He drew the smell of her into his lungs, a mix of fresh fruit, soap and recently laundered clothing. He thought he could smell something of the past, too, on her: bitterness and regret, maybe, but he was guessing.

'Mind if I park here?' she asked him.

He shook his head and withdrew into his space, wishing she had chosen a different table, despite his pursuit of her. There were plenty of unoccupied seats, but they were at tables being used by people with piss-off amounts of matching luggage, or newspapers that were spread out like territorial markers. She dunked a straw into her drink and spread her own magazine – one of those weekly celebrity-obsessed glossies – in front of her. He glanced at her while she pored over the photos of Posh and Kim and Miley before alighting on a crossword and pulling a cheap Bic pen from her pocket, its end chewed to opacity. She wore a fur-lined denim jacket, jeans and a pair of dark-blue Acupuncture trainers: the kind with Velcro straps, no laces. Her hair made her look like some kind of spaniel: centre parting, flattish on top, soft brown curls down to her shoulders.

It was her, after all. No question of it. Her hair was maybe a little longer, but there was no doubting she was the same girl. A woman now. Wide eyes. Nice, friendly mouth. Little rash of freckles across the bridge of her nose. That she was in his sights within a couple of hours of landing, without any problems or inconvenience, infused him with confidence. The pall of fear and uncertainty was pushed even further away. The sky began to clear.

He said, 'Mask.'

'Excuse me?' The woman lifted her head. He couldn't take her scrutiny and looked away.

'*Mask*,' he said again, more quietly. 'Cher film, 1985.'

'Really?' she said, filling in the letters. 'Thanks. You seen it?' she was looking at him properly now, taking him in.

He shook his head. 'Cher should stick to what she's best at.'

'Singing?'

'No, plastic surgery. She's had more stitches than Roger Bannister, that one.'

The woman laughed and he thought: *In the bag*.

'What's your name?' he asked. She looked at him for a moment, the slightest shadow of concern darkening her face. But then she smiled and, as she opened her mouth, he thought: *Linda*.

'Linda,' she said.

'You're not from around here, are you?' he said. 'I mean, originally. I can tell from your voice.'

She had come to London four or five years previously to try to get some production experience at a film company, or in television. He knew all of this from the message boards. She now relayed it to him in almost the exact same words.

They chatted casually, as strangers sometimes do when

they have time to kill and nowhere else to kill it. She looked at him for long stretches, her fingers twirling the pen. She was gazing at his muscles, her eyes lingering on the biceps filling the armholes of his white Gap T-shirt. She seemed confused, as if uncertain that such a young-looking boy should be so toned, so swollen.

Presently she went back to work, and he dawdled over his cold coffee, writing in a battered journal, the words going down hard and black, scoring future blank pages with the jags and slashes of his memories. Before she finished her shift, he moved away and watched her from behind a stall selling London souvenirs: T-shirts with supposedly funny slogans and Union Jack underwear and catatonic Beefeater dolls in clear plastic sleeves. Eventually she gathered her things together, waved goodbye to her colleague, and headed for the tube station at nearby King's Cross. He followed her to Soho, where she shopped for shoes and had a late lunch with friends at Café Pasta, until it grew dark. Then, behind Holborn underground station, down a narrow alleyway called Little Turnstile, as she waited for someone to answer the doorbell she had just rung, he crept up behind her and slit her throat with a knife that was flesh hot from lying against his thigh all day. Her bag was on his shoulder, the purse from her front pocket in his, and he was across the main drag and into Procter Street before her mind caught up with what had happened to her body, and spilled her to the pavement.

PART ONE
LASCAR
ROPE

1

I came out of the Beehive on Homer Street and trod on a
piece of shit. Big surprise. I'm always doing it. It was the
end of a pretty rough day, and the noble gods of misery
obviously didn't fancy me toddling off to bed without
pissing in my pockets one last time. I looked down at my
shoe. The piece of shit said: 'Can you get off my face now?'
I lifted my foot and let him stand up.

'Barry Liptrott,' I said, 'you're looking well.'

Liptrott straightened his collar and, with a grubby
handkerchief, did what he could about the muddy cleat
marks from my size 9s on his cheek. 'You didn't need to do
that. I didn't do nothing to you.'

'Force of habit,' I said. 'Last time we bumped into each
other, you were carrying a knife, in a decidedly unfriendly
way.'

'I'm straight now, Sorrell. Straight as arrows.'

'Yeah, right,' I said. 'Straight as fusilli, more like. Straight
as da Vinci's perfect fucking circle.'

'I mean it.'

19

'What are you doing around here? This isn't your manor.'
I was thinking of bed, and Mengele. I was thinking of that
bottle of Grey Goose all cold and lonely in my freezer.

'It's a free country, Sorrell. A man can take a gentle stroll
of an evening, can't he?'

'Just get out of my sight,' I said. 'I don't want to see
you around here again. You walking down this street, it's
knocking thousands off the value of my flat.'

'I've been looking for you.'

'Christ. After "Brand-new ITV comedy", those are the
words that make my blood run cold the most.'

Liptrott spat grit on to the pavement. 'Just listen, will
you, for a fucking change.'

He told me then, and I played nice all the way through it.
When he was finished, I nodded, smiled and said: 'Fuck off.'

'What *is* your problem?' he said. 'I'm doing you a favour
here.'

'*You* are doing *me* a favour? Why? Last time we met, you
didn't even speak because I'd spannered your mouth off,
remember? While we were waiting for the coppers to turn up.'

'All right, then, I'm doing it for her. But I know you could
use the work.'

'I do okay,' I said, a little too snappily.

'I don't mean nothing by it,' he said. 'We all need a bit of
work, 'specially at this time of the year. And anyway, I know
you, and she's looking for a good man.'

'Yeah, Lippy, we're the best of friends, you and me. Who
is she, this girl?'

'Her name's Kara Geenan. Nice girl, but desperate.'

'She'd have to be if she counts you as one of her mates.
How do you know her?'

The lights in the pub behind us went off. I nodded in the

direction of Old Marylebone Road. I didn't like talking to Liptrott anyway, and I certainly didn't like talking to him in the dark. We stood at the corner and watched the office workers coming out of the Chapel, the wine bar across the road. They had a Christmas menu going already, seventy quid, all in. I was well up for it myself, but my wallet wasn't. I listened carefully to Liptrott. I wanted some work, but I wasn't going to let him know how badly. He told me that he had got chatting to her when he happened to be in the block of flats where she lived, doing some rewiring for a relative. He gave her his number, told her to give him a call if she needed any electrical stuff doing. She had called him last night, pissed and hysterical, convinced that her brother had been murdered.

'Give her this,' I said, handing him one of my cards.

'Wouldn't it be quicker if you gave me your address? I know it's round here somewhere.' He glanced back along Homer Street as if his hunch might reward him with a neon arrow flashing on and off above my window.

'I'd rather give my cock to medical school at this very minute than tell you my address. Now, fuck off.'

'She needs to see you, Joel. Tonight. She's desperate.'

'Fu. Ck. *Off.*'

I print out a batch of those cards, about fifty of them, every night. In the daytime, I put half a dozen in my wallet and distribute the rest. *If you are desperate. If you can't go to the police. If the police won't help you. Then maybe I can. Private investigations. Discreet. Effective. I get results. Write, in the first instance, to Joel Sorrell...* I then walk all over London, dropping cards in phone boxes, in pub toilets, on cinema seats, buses. Once a week I collect my mail from a post office box at the newsagent's round the corner. There isn't usually a lot. Sometimes there's dog shit in the envelopes. One time there was a photograph of a topless woman who had undergone a double mastectomy. Clipped to the pic was a marriage proposal. Another time there was a cheque for three hundred pounds and a note written in blue crayon: *SEND ME HI-HEELZ, BEE YA TCH.* No return address. Not that I had any high heels to send. I tried cashing the cheque but it bounced like a Spacehopper on a pogo stick. Yet I can manage that. Better than leaving a phone number. Better than leaving my address. I don't like strangers in my home. Not any more.

When I got back to the flat, I poured myself a drink and turned on the radio. I don't have a TV. Get away? No, really. Get away? No, *really.* I prefer *Late Junction* on Radio 3. They have some weird shit on there – warbling Finns and people who pluck and bow the inside of grand pianos – but it helps me to relax.

Mengele deigned to lift his head from his favourite bit of rug and blink at me with his amber eyes. Mengele is a silver tabby Maine Coon cat, and he is a big bastard, a stone and a half. I swear he looks at me sometimes as if to say: *I could take you... I know I could take you.* I feed him tuna on Saturdays and some dry stuff called Fishbitz throughout the week. Dry stuff is better for his teeth and his pisser, apparently. In return he dumps half his body weight into his litter tray every night, and uses my legs as a scratching post. Otherwise he sleeps and that's it. That's cats for you, I suppose.

I opened the back door and stepped out on to the balcony.

I'm on the top floor, so it's an all-right view. I can see the roof of the Woolworths building on Marylebone Road, and the clock tower at the Landmark Hotel. If I crane my neck to look past the chimney pots on Seymour Place, I can see the top of the BT Tower. Directly opposite me is the back of the Stanley Arms. Sometimes I can see a young girl who sits in a room and plays guitar. Or a plump, middle-aged woman who cleans like she's sold her soul to the Devil in order to be allowed to do so. Sometimes I watch the guy who does the lunches preparing sandwiches and jacket potatoes and shepherd's pie. I don't eat at the Stanley Arms.

I drank my vodka and thought about Barry Liptrott. I didn't like the way he had tracked me down like that. I must be getting old. Getting careless. Back when I brought Liptrott down for selling knives to kids involved in some nasty school wars, I was on top of my game. If he could nose me out – and Liptrott was not a player; in fact he wasn't even worth a place on the bench – then presumably the more dangerous people in this sordid city could do the same. That wasn't good. I wasn't up to it. I took another gulp of Grey Goose, and that helped a bit. Poured some more: easy way out. This was what was slowing me down, taking away my edge. I had never been much of a drinker, previously, and I prided myself on that. I'd loudly order a glass of orange juice when everyone else was getting the pints in. But that was before a lot of stuff happened, stuff that I found I didn't like remembering too clearly. Booze is instant fog for the brain. Booze is great in that way. Booze is just great.

Christ, why did he have to use that word: *desperate*. I'm a sucker for desperate people. Perhaps because I'm one myself. In helping them, perhaps I'm hoping that I might find the key to how I can help myself.

When it grew too cold to stand outside, I came indoors and took off my jacket. Quick thumbnail now of the flat, and it won't take long. One small bedroom with a sofa-bed permanently extended. One bathroom. One kitchen that is visited occasionally by a family of oriental cockroaches. A living room. No pictures on the walls. Bare floorboards. A couple of shelves with a couple of books. My trusty old radio. Mengele's rug. Mengele. A yucca. The view. A vodka bottle. Me.

I woke up smartish, found it was still dark. The Grey Goose had stripped the insides of my mouth away; it felt raw, tender. The bottle was still in my lap. I stuck it back in the freezer and turned off the radio. Now I could hear what had disturbed me: voices were steadily rising from next-door west. I hardly ever hear anything from next-door east, and I don't know if that's worse, but the guy there lives on his own so what can you expect? Westside, when they aren't screaming at each other, they're fucking each other senseless – either that or they're playing their BBC wildlife videos at full whack; I can't tell the difference. Now it sounded as though they were in fighting mode. From her – pure Estuary English – I heard: '...*I've had to put up with free facking years of this*...' His voice was lyrical Highlands, impossible to goad, and he was going: 'If you'd just sit down and let me explain...'

At midnight. Christ. I took a shower and put on a fresh shirt. I chucked a handful of Fishbitz into Mengele's dish and grabbed the car keys. Then I left them to it.

* * *

It's a Saab V4, since you're wondering. Maroon. K reg. I bought it in 1985 for three hundred and fifty pounds and it's been in constant service ever since. It's seen some action, this car. It's been driven to places I will never take it again. It's been pushed more than a car of this age and class ought ever to experience. But there have been some good times, too. A lot of them on that back seat. It's been to Dungeness and Durness, known fresh air and foul, but it's never let me down. The steering wheel knows my hands so well, I'm convinced it's altered its shape over the years to accommodate them more comfortably.

I started her up and took her along Crawford Street, first left into Seymour Place and then left again up on to the Westway. I love driving at night. Obviously, the traffic's pretty much non-existent at that hour, but that's not the main appeal. London, for me, comes alive at night, seeming to breathe and seethe with possibilities. It flexes its muscles, this city, when everybody is asleep, perhaps working out the cramp from the previous day, with so much filth clogged in its airways, so many dirty feet shuffling along its streets. Regenerating itself, sloughing off its outer skins, the dark is this city's friend. They feed off each other, London and the night. As do the few who emerge at this hour, who know how to read its secrets.

I drove the car hard until I reached the White City turn-off. Then I eased her down to forty and cruised to the Holland Park roundabout. A minute later and I was in Shepherd's Bush. I parked the car on Lime Grove, outside the house I used to live in – *we* used to live in – when everything was all right. *Do you remember?* I wondered. *Do you think about this place, Rebecca, from time to time?* But, of course, she didn't. The house was dead, just like her. Venetian blinds kept whatever now went on inside there a secret from me. We had built a den for Sarah in the cellar, painted its walls in bright colours, to be her own little place. The nicks on the wooden supports would still be down there, ticking off the inches as she grew taller. Sarah, giggling, as I tried to hold her still, while Rebecca reached up with a penknife.

I sat in the car looking up at the windows while my breath formed some more ghosts to keep me company. Then I gunned the engine and eased out into Goldhawk Road. By the time I got back to my flat, there was silence from the flat next-door. I had another drink, took another shower, and got my head down. Kip was what I needed: a long, hard, X-rated session of hot kip.

Yeah, right.

2

I don't remember the last time I had an unbroken night's sleep. Sometimes I can blame it on Mr and Mrs Decibel next door; sometimes on Mengele, who sings in the night, or claws at the closed windows (I don't let him out – he cost me two hundred and fifty quid for Christ's sake, far too much money to just let him end up as cat jam on the road), or else likes to sand-dance in his litter tray. Mostly I have to blame myself: drinking too much, thinking too much. Once I grasp the tail of a thought that's slinking out of view, I can't let go. It's like a crocodile; if I let go, it will turn around and bite my hands off. So I mull stuff over until it starts getting light, and then it's too light to sleep and I get up, not having resolved anything, really. I've resolved to murder the cat a few times, but how could I when he looks at me like that? Should have got myself a fucking lizard instead.

She needs to see you, Joel. Tonight. She's desperate.

Liptrott told me she'd be in Old Compton Street, in one of the all-night coffee bars. He said she'd be there for as long as it took. If I showed, I showed: if not, big coffee bill. I walked it, needing the spank of cold night air to clear my head, and wondered, not for the first time, about how many desperate people there were out there. It almost made me want to stick my name in the *Yellow Pages* and have done with it, come over as a proper outfit instead of a cheapo prick with a printer, on a par with those kids selling lemonade from their front gates at twenty pence a pop. But I like my privacy. Jesus, I *love* my privacy. I love it so much I want to marry it and provide it with children. The stuff that turned up in my PO Box told me I was doing the right thing.

She was the only *she* in the place, and she was sitting by the window, watching everyone who walked past the entrance. When she saw me come in, her face was so expectant it might have given birth to quins. She asked me if I wanted coffee and I said no, I wanted sleep.

'There's no need to be snippy,' she said. 'You didn't have to come.'

'I came because I don't want Barry Liptrott staining my doorstep any more.'

'Barry's all right.'

'Define "All right". He's a fucking man-frightener of the first order.'

'He's *all right*. He's okay.'

'He's not when he's skulking round your bins at midnight.'

'Can we talk now?'

'How do you know Lippy?'

She was wearing a hooped rugby top with the collars turned up, a black tulle skirt, leather leggings and biker boots. I can only surmise that she'd got dressed in the dark. Her make-up was sparse, which was good, as she didn't need much with such clear skin. The mascara emphasised her blue eyes, which were her best feature. She hardly blinked. In her right hand she clasped a clutch bag. Or clutched a clasp bag.

Whatever they're called. No handles, no straps. You know, helpful things that can carry maybe a single spring onion, or three carefully folded tissues. In her left hand she held a mobile phone, which she put down whenever she took a sip of her drink. When the sip was finished, her hand was back on the phone.

'I'm a freelance journalist,' she explained. 'I got talking to him one time when he was doing some work round at my flats, and I asked if he'd mind being included in a piece I wanted to write on small-time crooks. We got on.'

'Really? Either he's been to charm school recently or your judgment of people is seriously knackered.'

She sighed theatrically. 'Look… I need to talk to you.'

I shrugged. 'Maybe I'll have some coffee now, after all. Actually, would you mind if we went somewhere else? I need a grown-up drink.'

The pubs were shut, of course, so I took her to an unlicensed bar off Cambridge Circus. A black guy on the door took a ten-pound entry fee off me and shepherded us inside. A girl behind a plank of wood resting on two stacks of telephone books charged me a hilarious amount for a can of Tennant's that she wrested from a carton bound in shrink-wrapped plastic. It was warm but when has England ever done cold? Ice bucket? Ice, fuck it, more like.

A couple of staggeringly pissed guys were seated on empty kegs at the back of the room, having an argument that consisted of them swapping increasingly voluble 'No's. There was nowhere else to sit, but she was into her story by then. She wanted me to find her missing brother. Missing? Great. My fillings reacted as if I'd just chewed on a bit of tin foil, but I got a grip on myself. After all, a job was a job. In my line, all jobs are shitty. It doesn't matter what amount of

29

shit is involved; the fact is that somebody else's shit is just the same as any shit of your own, and you come out of it at the end smelling exactly the same.

My alcohol levels were edging towards the red zone, and I was super-tired, but I was on top of it enough to pull on her reins when she came out with a little piece of nonsense.

'Just rewind a little bit, sorry, what's your name again?'

'Geenan. Kara Geenan.'

'Okay, Kara, just rewind that segment and turn the volume up a little.'

'I said, he seemed okay when I dropped him off at home last night.'

'Funny, it still sounds like you said he seemed okay when you dropped him off at home last night.'

'That's right.'

'So you saw him last night?' She was okay-looking, this Kara Geenan, I had decided: nothing to write home about but maybe worth a postcard to a mate. Big blue eyes. Really, quite magnificent eyes that bored into you, sucked you in, chewed you up and spat you out. Caramel hair cut short, lots of shape, lots of body to it, like hair out of an advert. The rest of her was as plain as the packaging on an economy-price bag of plain flour. What elevated her from the ordinary, of course, was the fact that she was crazier than a purse full of whelks. And did I mention her eyes? Bloody good eyes. They didn't stop doing what they were programmed to do.

'Yes,' she said, showing me now how exasperation ought to be done.

'So how do you know he's missing?'

'I called him this morning and he wasn't there.'

'Shit,' I said, 'that's serious. Maybe you should get a

stakeout at his place of work. Jesus, what if… Oh God, if he went to the newsagent's, then that's it, he's toast.'

'Are you trying to be sarcastic?'

'No. I *am* being sarcastic.'

'Barry was right. You *are* a cunt.'

'Yep, I'm with Barry on that one, too.'

'Look, I *know* my brother. He's missing. You have to believe me.'

I finished my beer, and took out a second mortgage while I ordered another. 'Go home. Check out the places you'd usually find him. The pub. The footy. Pat yourself on the back when you track him down after one nanosecond.'

'I can't. I don't like the places he goes to.'

'Kara, this is madness. He is not missing.'

'He is.'

'Look, everyone goes missing at some point in their lives. You don't even have to go anywhere to go missing. Me? I don't know *where* the fuck I am half the time.'

'He's in danger, I know it.'

'Then explain it to the police.'

'I can't go to the police.'

She was scared rigid of cop shops. Apparently a little matter of ripping off a plod who got frisky with her one night. Drugged him with some Rohypnol and pocketed his fat wallet. She was convinced she was on their shit lists, public enemy number one. I checked that my zipper was done up tight.

She was looking at the floor by now. Her hands wormed across the mouth of her clench bag. 'Please,' she said, 'prove to me I'm only being hysterical. You'll get paid for it. What risk is it to you?

'Name.'

'Jason Phythian.'

'How old is he?'

'He's eighteen.'

'Eighteen?'

'Please.'

I looked at her. I wanted her to say please again.

'*Please*,' she said.

'Okay,' I said. 'Okay, I'll find him.'

She looked up, her face like something you might see on Christmas Day. I told her my daily rate and, credit to her, her eyebrows stayed put.

I finished my beer and was about to stand up, when she put on a few extras: a smile, a huskier voice, and her hand, on my thigh. She suggested we go back to her place. It wasn't so much a mood swing as a mood tsunami. 'I've got a bottle of wine that needs drinking. Filthy night like this, why not?'

I said, 'You're nice-looking, and ordinarily I'd be up for it, but I don't fuck my clients, Kara.'

'Come on,' she said. 'I'm lonely and scared. I need some animal comfort. What's wrong with that?'

'I don't do comfort.'

'You're a hard bastard.'

'I need to be. And you'll thank me for it, before long.'

'Just a drink, then?'

'I've just had a drink. I'm tired now. I want to go home.'

'I'll come too, then.' Another glimpse of that smile: that same smile that suffered a heart-attack and keeled over before it reached her eyes.

Jesus Christ, I thought. I said: 'No.'

'Where do you live?' she asked.

Again, I said: '*No*.' A little more forceful now.

'Okay, okay. You don't know what you're missing, though.'

'I'm missing a whole barrow load of strife, Kara,' I said. 'You're very sweet, but I'm not interested.'

'All *right*,' she snapped, and her eyes lit up as if they'd been splashed with petrol. I backed off and shut my mouth.

She opened her clamp bag and pulled out a purse that was only slightly smaller. She handed over the first day's wad, and promised me a week's pay in advance once she could get to the bank the coming morning.

'Tell me, what's his weakness?' I asked, cautiously.

'His what?' Her temper had abated, it seemed, the spunk gone from her eyes.

'His weakness, what is it? Women? Men? Drugs? The horses? Macramé?'

'Women? That's not your weakness, is it?' she replied.

'We're not talking about me.'

'He likes a drink, I suppose,' she said flatly, back to her straightforward, businesslike self. I'd blown my chance, so now it was polite talk with Ice-woman.

I nodded. 'We all like a drink. Do you know how many pubs there are in this city?'

We stood on the street corner looking dumbly at each other. 'So tell me where he lives,' I said. 'Tell me about these places he goes to that you don't like.'

I went home. *What risk is it to you?* I thought.

What risk? Plenty. Plenty fucking risk.

3

I was going to call Kara in the morning but I find that in order to do such things you have to get up before noon. I got up around 4 p.m. I then called her but there was no reply. I don't know what I intended to say, probably something along the lines of an apology for the way things had gone the previous night but, sod it, what did I really care about people's opinions of me? I thought about having a shower but realised I'd have to get out of bed first, and I really didn't want to do that yet. The flat was cold and my head was treacly with vodka and beer. I lay there wishing I smoked, and wishing that Mengele could fix his own fucking breakfast. He was at the end of the bed, stabbing at my toes with his claws and trilling like some magical bird.

In the end it was either get out of bed or face the rest of my life with whittled feet. I poured him out some fresh water and a pile of Fishbitz, and pulled on a shirt that didn't have too many stains on it. The arse of my jeans was so thin I was in danger of losing my cheeks through osmosis to the outside air. My boots could have passed for two cowpats. I stood in front of the mirror, wishing I'd worn some shades first because – whoah, watch out, London – the world's most stylish walking cadaver was about to hit the streets.

But I'm not that bad. At least, I hope I'm not. I *will* be, no doubt about it. Another ten, fifteen years and my face will look like something that's been knitted from a heap of overcooked noodles, but for now, well, I'm bearing up. The mirror shows a guy in his mid-thirties with good hair, if a little unkempt, bluey-greeny-grey eyes – good eyes, if a little hunted – and a mouth that, in a novel, would probably be described as cruel. In a certain light I can look gaunt, but maybe I'm doing myself a disservice; it might just be that I've got a pair of killer cheekbones. I always wanted a scar, you know, like the one the eagle-eye Action Man had – a slash down the cheek, probably from a dagger, or a bayonet – but the only scar on my face is a three-stitch job sustained when I fell over against the rear end of my dad's Morris Minor van, aged four. It's a younger-looking face than it ought to be, considering all the vodka and sleepless nights, never mind the smoky death-pits I patronise. It doesn't look lived in yet, but it will. It will all catch up with me in the end.

Outside it was cold enough to freeze the juice in the corners of my eyes. It was depressing to be going out when it was dark again, thus not seeing a moment of daylight for over twenty-four hours. I pulled my jacket – a black, nubuck job that's on its last legs but still able to keep out most of the bad weather – more tightly around me and stuffed my hands in the pockets. Then I headed off in search of hell.

You don't need a map for hell, I suppose. I think that, to know it, you just have to have lived it a little at some point in your life. London knows hell so well, it might be asked to be godfather to its child. And it isn't necessarily always in the places you'd expect, although a lot of it is. You can find hell in the most exclusive parts of the capital, if you know which streets to cut down, which doors to knock upon. So it was, tonight. Some of the places on Kara's jolly little list I knew already: the strip clubs, the pubs that were so violent that the management served beer in plastic glasses, the amusement arcades and the snooker halls. But here was one little corner of Hades I had yet to patronise: Stodge, a restaurant in inoffensive Hampstead. I took the car round, and parked it on Gardnor Road, between an Aston Martin DB7 and a Porsche Boxster, where I'm proud to say, though it didn't gleam quite as much as its neighbours, it did not look out of place one bit. I walked up to Heath Street and hung back from the restaurant a little, just watching for a while who was going in and coming out.

Stodge is one of those new restaurants that is unashamedly British in its outlook, professing to have been at the vanguard of British cookery's reinvention and offering a menu larded with pies, puddings and rib-sticking dumplings. The guy who runs the place is called Danny Sweet, an ex-boxer who had brought his pugnacious attitude into his kitchens. He's in the Sunday supplements now and then, apparently, spouting off about how he hates to be referred to as a celebrity chef, and then a week later he's on *Celebrity Masterchef*.

What the public don't know is that he's still into boxing, but not the friendly kind with padded gloves and Queensberry Rules. What is even more incomprehensible, considering his clout in the industry, and his media exposure, is the fact that he hosts bare-knuckle bouts in the cellar of his restaurant.

I strolled up to the nosh shop, gave the menu some attention, and clocked the beanpole doorman, his eyes so hooded he made Salman Rushdie seem startled.

'Hi, how are you doing?' I asked. 'Don't tell me, I should have booked in 1903 if I wanted a bite to eat tonight.'

'Private party, anyway, sir,' he said, turning said hoods in the direction of a sign in the window that said just that. 'By invitation only. Unless you know the password.'

'Monosodium Glutamate,' I said, trying to make out some of the shadows that moved behind the glass.

'Spot on, sir. May I take your coat?'

We looked at each other for a long time, my watch-it gland reacting in extreme spasm. '"Monosodium Glutamate" isn't the password,' I said.

'No, sir. But I'm feeling charitable. I've been opening doors all day for stiff collars who didn't even thank me for doing it. At least you had the basic human decency to say hello.'

I stared at him a while longer, wondering if he was someone I'd helped to put away in the past, but I'd recognise a basketball player like this. 'Okay,' I said. 'What kind of private party is it?'

'Swingers,' he said, giving birth to a smirk. 'You look like you could do with a little fun.'

I let that one glide by me and went inside. There was a table with a bunch of leaflets for something called *The OneOnOne Club*. Next to it was a small photocopier and a girl with a Polaroid camera slung around her neck. There was a loose dress slung around her boobs and bum, and she was slinging wine down her shouter with the kind of enthusiasm you just can't fake.

'Ickle piccie,' she said, as I made to walk past her. 'Gotta have a ickle piccie.'

'No thanks,' I said.

'So we can circulate it. Anyone likes your face can write their number on the back, and you get your ickle piccie back at the end of the night with lots of lovely dates to look forward to.'

'I'm not a swinger,' I said. 'I'm a plumber. There's a blockage in the pipes.'

'Oh,' she said, then took a fucking ickle piccie anyway.

It was pretty busy. The tables in the dining area had been pushed to the perimeter, and a mass of people, who had clearly spent for ever getting ready, were demonstrating the admirable skill that is standing the maximum distance from everybody else in a confined space. No milling, no mingling, just lots of people looking as though they were at an audition for a new play called *Rabbit in the Headlights*. At least the lighting was subdued, so the sweat of fear didn't show up too much.

I grabbed a glass of champagne from a stooge with a tray and found a quiet spot against the wall that gave me a good vantage point over the fun and games, as well as a view of the staff door which I guessed was the entrance to the cellar.

I wondered what Geenan's brother did here. She hadn't expounded and I hadn't pressed her on it, but now I wished I had. Maybe he worked here, maybe he swung here, but I doubted it. If anything, I reckoned he scraped his knuckles off on other people's faces in Danny Sweet's bear pit. I was itching to get down there for a look around, but it looked as though match-making alone was on the menu tonight so I relaxed and sipped my champagne.

Gradually, the alcohol did its work and the gaps between the assembled loners shrank. Soon the restaurant was filled with the cacophony of people asking 'What do you do?'. The photographs soon followed: Xeroxed copies of faces in various degrees of mortification. There was one that didn't look at all bad, although she was probably only here because she had false teeth, or was married to her job, or she shat herself when she humped. Emboldened by another glass of Piper-Heidsieck, I scribbled my name and my mobile phone number on the back of it and dropped it in the large glass bowl where everyone else was now feverishly doing the same.

I made the mistake of smiling at a woman who was on her way to the toilet. She banked hard left in my direction and sucked the oxygen from my immediate vicinity with a ferocious air kiss.

'What do you do?' she asked.

'I make jewellery,' I said.

'Wild,' she said. 'Silver? Gold?'

'Human bone,' I said. I was just spouting now. I didn't mean to shut her up, but I'd just seen Danny Sweet leading a posse of phenomenally ugly men around the outside of the flirtathon and through the cellar entrance. I forced my eye to fall on each and every one of them, and wondered which one was Geenan's brother. What was their fucking problem? Wouldn't Kara be embarrassed when I turned up with her brother, who would be perfectly within his rights to tell her to bugger off out of his life until she stopped behaving like a first-class arse?

'I... I wouldn't mind seeing some of your jewellery,' she was saying.

I lightly squeezed her arm. Another snap-happy dolt took a photograph of me over her shoulder. 'That's awfully sweet of you,' I said. 'You don't have to try that hard, though. Believe me, save it up for someone who deserves a woman who will delay taking a piss for him.'

I left her and ambled over to the staff door. Someone had put on some suitable music. Suitable for the fucking grave.

Chris de Burgh. A woman dressed in red is doing *what* with you, Chris? Yes, because she's deaf and blind and quite possibly brain-damaged. I was happy to leave them all to it.

Stone steps. A bare 100-watt bulb. The sound coming up from the cellar was like a sledgehammer being repeatedly introduced to a mound of watermelons.

I hesitated at the swing-doors at the bottom of the steps. Testosterone alone promised to push them open, and not from my side, either. My testosterone was trying to put its belongings in a handkerchief and slink away. I composed myself and slipped through.

Mayhem. Around twenty beery, sweaty bodies were packed in a tight circle around a knot of flailing limbs. I was bemused by the lack of cheering. Apart from the occasional hiss of someone wincing at a punch, the shuffle of footsteps as the scrum watched the scrap, and the sounds of fist on meat, it was relatively restrained. Obviously because Sweet didn't want to draw any undue attention to his private club.

I caught glimpses of the two shirtless men hammering each other's faces. They both wore masks of blood. One guy was gradually gaining the upper hand, though.

'Rather them than me,' I said, and one of the guys in the audience gave me a look that told me to hurry it up and get on my way. I circled the group, keeping back in the shadows by the wall, and checked faces, looking for someone who resembled Kara Geenan. When one of the men at the back of the crowd broke away for a breather, I collared him and asked him if Jason Phythian was in, tonight. Another ugly look.

I was about to cut my losses and get out of this stifling, violent shit-hole when I noticed that my route back to the door was blocked. Intentionally blocked. The scrum had lost interest in the fight now that it had become so one-sided. A metronomic pulpy slapping sound indicated that the contest was over.

Danny Sweet stepped forward as I tried to make myself look less isolated. Everyone was staring at me.

'New boy,' said Sweet. 'All new boys must fight.'

'I'm not that new,' I said. 'I've been around the block a few times.'

'Well,' he said, 'that block is about to be knocked off. Choose your foe.'

'I don't fight.'

'You do if you're in here. So, you will.'

'Look, I was with the party upstairs. I thought the toilets were down here.'

'Take your shirt off,' he said, 'and pick your fight partner.'

'All right, how about you?' I said.

'Fuckhead,' he said, 'I don't fight. I ref. These hands' – he held up his mitts for me to see – 'are my prize possessions. They're insured for half a mill. I'm not going to be knocking up any lamb and flageolet-bean stew with chunks missing out of these beauties, am I?'

'Is Jason Phythian down here? I'll fight him.'

Nobody came forward.

Sweet turned to face his cronies. 'He's making names up. He's too shy to pick someone. Who'll have him?'

'I'll have him.'

A walking argument for the introduction of eugenics shambled out of the throng, pulling off his T-shirt as he did so. He had a tattoo on his chest of a naked woman on all fours, her backside raised at an anatomically questionable angle. Underneath was the word LADIEKILLER. He had the face of something that should have been sitting in a bush picking its arse and eating soft fruits. While he flexed his arms, I turned to Sweet and asked him if there were any rules.

'No rules,' he said.

So I turned and kicked Ladiekiller's bollocks into orbit. Then I was pushing through the bodies to the door, before anyone could argue that what I'd done was really rather unpleasant. Ladiekiller's mewlings drifted after me up the stairs, along with some raised voices. There were going to be some feet following mine pretty soon.

The swingers were pairing off like it was a chromosome lookalike party. I slalomed through them and was hauled back by the beanpole just as I was about to make it on to the street.

'You forgot something,' he said, wagging his hoods over to my right. The woman with the Polaroid camera was tottering after me, a clutch of photographs in her hand. I pocketed them, thanked them both, and ran all the way back to the car.

4

Although it was an easy drive home from Hampstead, I dumped the Saab at Belsize Park and caught a tube to Archway. Another of Phythian's so-called haunts was in N19, a good old-fashioned public house where you drank till you made yourself ill. None of that fannying around that was going on at Stodge. I imagined the most fannying that went on at the Lion was up against the wall outside, at chucking-out time. The excitement of the last hour had made me a bit jittery and I wanted a drink. Scratch that, I wanted several drinks. And I was going to offer a black little toast to Kara Geenan before each one.

Part of what she'd told me the previous evening – hell, earlier that morning – kept rolling around in my mind like a pebble in the drum of a washing machine. Not the lunacy about her brother going missing mere hours after she was with him, but more the detail that she fed me regarding who he was. She hadn't sounded to me like someone listing the aspects of someone she cared for. There were no little embellishments when it came to describing his face, for example. He was just: brown hair, blue eyes. In my experience, it's hard to get such a belt-and-braces sketch of a missing person. The client will twat on for twenty minutes about how glossy her hair was because she brushed it morning and night with a Charles Worthington vent brush, or his eyes were grey or green depending on what colour top he wore and the light in the sky just made his eyes come alive... So it concerned me that Kara's facts should be so naked, so cold. It didn't sit nicely with her rushing out at midnight, fit to shit with panic about her baby brother.

But I wasn't too concerned. I really couldn't care less how weird their relationship was if it meant my bank balance was about to turn a pinker shade of red. I would either find him, or I wouldn't. I'd get my cash and could forget about missing persons for a while. Or I could forget about *other* people's missing persons, at least.

I emerged at Archway into that astonishing horrorfest that is the collision of a number of main roads. It seems that all roads lead to Archway. And then they die there. Archway could be the place where old roads come after they have enjoyed their youth as edgy country highways or suburban dual carriageways. They come here and they just go 'fuck it' and coil up in weird spaghetti shapes and expire then make the cars grind to a halt. It had been a while since I was last in N19, and I was pretty certain the traffic was the same. All the drivers' faces look like: 'Bollocks, I had a choice, but I decided to drive through Archway.' You can see them, almost physically wrestling with the compulsion to weep.

I crossed Junction Road, averting my eyes as one does at the scene of an atrocity, and breezed into the Lion. According to Kara, her little brother had a flat a little further north, on St John's Way. But I needed a pint before I tackled Roadkill Central.

'Kronenbourg,' I said, as I sat on one of the stools at the bar. The barman went to it without a whimper: just the kind of barman I like. I took a slow look around the pub, guessing which of the half-dozen beer-nursing thugs might be villains and which mightn't. By the time the barman had delivered my pint and sorted out my change, it was six-nil to the cons. I asked him if he knew someone called Phythian.

'That his surname?' he asked. He had something rattish about his face: it was pointed and twitchily interested in what I was questioning him about.

'Yeah, Jason Phythian. Know him?'

'Can't say I do,' he said. 'Lot of people round here aren't so friendly as to give their names up when you pull 'em their pints.'

I described Phythian and expected a shrug from the barman, as if I had just described thirty men who used this pub on any given day.

'What are you?' he asked. 'Copper?'

I shook my head and sank a third of the lager. It had a sour aftertaste: there aren't that many boozers around these days that look after their pipes too well. 'Just helping to track down a friend for a friend.'

He nodded and moved away to serve one of the grim-faced regulars, who would no doubt still be in the same position at the bar come closing time.

He's making names up, Sweet had said. Maybe I was. Maybe Jason Phythian wasn't his name, or maybe they were just protecting such a young man from his big sister, who might be angry to discover that her brother was mixing it with the missing links down at the fight club.

I was almost finished with my drink when somebody else walked through the door. Somebody I knew? I fished about in my memory for a while, until the name came to me. Whitby. Neville Whitby. Freelance photographer of some repute, although he had no formal training. While most pros were busy with their light meters and flash indexes, playing who's got the biggest lens, Nev was busy taking photos, solid quality stuff that regularly found its way into the papers. I had crossed his path a few times in the past few years, and liked his blatant disregard for his profession, and the prima donnas who worked in it. He had a hard and fast rule when it came to taking pictures, as I remembered him telling me when we were standing in the rain, waiting for some nugget of information at some outdoor press conference ages before. He took his photos in the morning or in the late afternoon; the light was crap at any other time of day.

I watched him shrug off his coat, and hailed him as he headed towards the cigarette machine.

'All right there, Joel?'

'Not so bad, Nev. Let me get you a pint.'

I bought him a Guinness and got myself another pint of lager. We sat by the window, one of those thick glass affairs with lots of flaws and ripples in it, so you can't see clearly in or out. Weird figures wobbled past beyond the glass as they stalked up and down the Holloway Road.

'What brings you out here?' I asked him. 'You live down in Oval, don't you?'

He nodded and unwrapped his pack of Embassy Regal. 'I'm supposed to be covering an eviction, but I don't know if I can be arsed. Got a tip-off that some crusties are about to be forcibly removed from a derelict flat in Fitzwarren Gardens. Unofficial job, apparently. Some real bruisers involved. I thought it would be fun to snap some kid being hurled out of a top-floor window but I'm not so sure now.

I just don't seem to have the appetite for it any more. I haven't taken a picture of a cheque presentation for fifteen years, and I'm actually beginning to miss it – the humdrum. You need a bit of humdrum in your life. And, anyway, your modern student type doesn't seem to have the heart for a battle these days. Too cosseted, obviously.'

He contemplated his cigarette as though an upsetting message were written on it. 'I'm supposed to be cutting down,' The light gleamed on his scalp, visible through his sparse, dirty-blond hair. 'Look at that,' he said, pointing at the warning that covered two-thirds of the packet in bold, black lettering. *Smoking Kills*.

'I know,' I said. 'They might as well use bigger letters and just print the word *DIE* on it.'

'Want one?' he said, more brightly, as if my joining him would lessen his guilt. I shook my head. He sighed. 'You can't not smoke when you're drinking. It's the wet and the dry. It's magical. It's like having a cuppa without a biscuit. Anyway,' he said, 'what are you up here for?'

'Missing person,' I said. 'Woman who lost her brother yesterday, thinks he's dead or murdered, or kidnapped.'

'Yesterday? Sounds like a nutcase,' Neville said, then went outside to suck in some carcinogens. And have his fag.

'You've been watching too many Humphrey Bogart films,' I said, after he came back inside, 'but, yeah, she's fruitbats.' I gave him a quick description of what had happened, while he extracted a second cigarette and rolled it around his fingers.

'Maybe she's lonely. Maybe she does this to get involved with someone. It's easier than chatting up a stranger.'

'I don't know,' I said. 'There's something really not right about this. Something in her voice, in the way she looks at me – something not right, something edgy. She never blinks either. It's like talking to a fucking owl. It's making my shit hang sideways.'

'Have another drink, then,' he said. 'It's my round.'

Another drink or two with Nev was important, I felt. He was a good contact and he needed to be cultivated. We staggered out at a little before 10 p.m., both of us cultivated to arseholedom. The sky was the strange undark that you find in well-lit cities, a kind of white haze just veiling the limitless black beyond. The street was like the Olympia Car Show. I was trying to stop the tears from coming, but it didn't seem to matter so much out here, in a biting December wind.

'Christ, my eyes are watering it's so fucking cold,' I said, convincingly. Nev was fiddling with his camera bag.

'Bollocks to the crusties,' he said. 'I'm going home. Hey, do you fancy a curry?'

I pointed at my watch and shrugged, then I slipped off the curb and went sprawling in front of a 2CV, the driver of which leaned on his horn despite his speed being exactly 30 mph below the legal limit.

I waved Nev goodbye and funny-walked through the mired traffic, angling up Sandridge Street and into St John's Lane. The cold was making my cheeks numb, and my hands couldn't get warm in the pockets of my jacket. I needed a piss and I was this close to turning back to the pub, intent on getting medievally trousered, when the tears got serious and I had to stop.

Have you heard from Sarah?, Nev had asked. That was all. Five little words that knocked me back further than any punch or gut-kick I've received in the past three years, since she disappeared.

No I haven't heard from Sarah. Nobody has heard from Sarah. Because she's dead. Everyone knows that, but they keep asking. They keep ripping me open.

I told Nev what I knew. The police, as far as they could be bothered to look into a hopeless missing-persons case, had come up with no clues. My own hunt had reached plenty of dead ends, but I was always on the job, always sniffing her out. It was the longest case I'd ever undertaken and I was paying myself a piffling amount, but I would never stop. Even though she was dead. Especially as she was dead.

'She's not dead.' I stopped on the pavement, half suspecting that it hadn't been me who said the words. It was beginning to snow. I blew my nose and wiped my eyes. Astonishing what a sob can do to your drunkenness. I breathed in deep some of that shockingly cold, polluted air and crossed the road, trying to rub some feeling back into my face. Number 13, St John's Way, this guy Phythian lived at, according to his jelly-head sister. Thirteen was how old Sarah was when she went away. It seemed I had thought about the events of 16th August 2012 for more time than I had ever actually spent with her, but that couldn't be the case. Not yet. She would be sixteen now, and a young woman. She should have been in her first year at college, studying A-levels... Art maybe, or Music. Or maybe she didn't fancy academe and was starting work instead. Or maybe she'd taken a year off, gone travelling, picked up a few skins and tried them on for size, tried out some different people, seen how her edges fitted in with those of the world. She might have done that... but not if she was dead. I couldn't work out if I wanted her dead or not. It all got too much. If she wasn't dead, she surely would have called to let me know she was all right. I wasn't so bad a father as not deserve at least that. If she was dead, and I didn't know about it, was that any better? I'd be searching for the rest of my life, but at least she'd be at peace, that was what was important. I'd rather not know. I'd rather keep searching, but maybe not too hard, in case I actually found her. In case I found her and she was dead after all.

I crossed the road and thought about how it had gone, that day she had disappeared. Or I might have done, were it not for the fact that a light had come on inside the house.

I tried to see in through the window of the ground-floor flat, as I swung the gate open, but there was a slatted blind concealing the front room. Maybe I should just ring Kara, I thought, tell her to come round, because her brother was home, presumably bored already of running away, and I was suddenly angry at being jerked about like this, money or not. I rang the doorbell. The light went out. Something smashed. I cupped a hand around my eyes and leaned against the door to try to see through the stained glass into the hallway. When the door swung inwards, almost causing me to trip over the threshold, I found myself in a deeply unusual situation.

I have only ever been scared – really, truly, hey-there-go-my-nuts scared – maybe three times in my life. Two of those times were when I was around seven or eight years old, and I had suddenly discovered that the dark was a pretty unpleasant place to be, especially when you were certain that something with big teeth was living inside the lampshade. The third time was when I went with a married woman whose husband found out about me, and he kept me awake all night with a phone call in which he detailed very specifically what he was going to do with my head once he'd cut it free of my shoulders.

And here was that old feeling again: my tongue and lips like a few curls of used sandpaper.

I stood in the hallway, listening for the other guy. For Phythian.

'Jason?' I called out. 'I'm here to help out a friend. Your sister, Kara Geenan, she's worried about you. Thinks you've gone missing.'

How crazy it can be, doing these private jobs. How fucking *out there*. It dawned on me that all my life was made up of standing in the dark, trying to make out the shape of whatever was up ahead. I wished I'd taken up Nev's offer of a curry. I'd rather a chicken jalfrezi was now responsible for my runny guts.

' I reached for the light switch but there was no bulb in the socket. I had better luck once I reached the living room, where the light had been only recently doused. I spent less than a second in there, but long enough to know that the occupant wasn't too keen on decoration but liked skin mags, Pot Noodles and Heineken beer. There was also a cot with a cheap paper mobile hanging over it. Kara had said nothing about her brother being a dad. A recent dad, at that. Further along the hallway, my boot crunched on to what had smashed earlier: a white plate. I bent down and picked up a few of the larger pieces: just pointlessly cheap china, of the kind you find in a Poundstretcher. He'd scarpered, it seemed.

The kitchen smelled of nicotine and old bacon, the open back door swinging on its hinges, plastic streamers swishing around like some exotic dancer's straw dress. I flicked the light on and looked around. If pigs ever evolved to the point where they started using kitchens, this is what they'd look like. Every pan was thick with half-moons of solidified lard. The washing-up bowl was rammed full with crockery. I moved to the door and looked out at the amorphous reaches of the garden, a scrubby mess filled with the skeletons of old bicycles, a washing machine, an upended wheelbarrow lacking its wheel.

I stared down at the pieces of china in my hand. Spotlessly clean. Maybe the guy had dropped it in shock at how spick it was. But what was he doing running around in the dark with a dish in his hands, for God's sake? I was about to answer my own question, one of those questions that has an answer so simple that you smack your head with frustration, when you realise it. Too much to drink, Joel, far too much to drink. You're slowing down. I actually thought that: *You're slowing down, you sitting duck, you no-mark wanker*, in the moment that he surged up behind me, wrapped his gloved hand around my throat, and started hammering open my skull.

5

Maybe it was a warning. A friendly warning.'
I looked at Neville, really gave him one of my best Paddington Bear stares, but he wouldn't let it go. I was lying in a hospital bed in a ward with five other pyjama cases. I had been 'very lucky' according to the nurse who swept by about half a dozen times every hour, her nylons shushing like a cineaste with hearing difficulties. Everyone who survives a murder attempt seems to be 'very lucky', but I begged to differ. I would have been 'very lucky' if I'd decided to wear my Kevlar bobble hat before I'd gone out. I would have been 'very lucky' if my assailant had developed a fatal allergy to coshes a second or so before he stuck it on to me. Or decided that he didn't want to hit me after all, but shower me with kittens instead.

'I mean,' Neville was continuing, 'if he meant to kill you, I'm sure he would have done a better job on you. Used a knife, a gun.'

'Nev,' I said, 'he smacked me twice on the braincase with what felt like a steel bat. Surely, if it was a warning, he'd have just shown me the cosh, said something a bit sinister like, ooh, I don't know, "This is a warning".'

But I knew he was right. He would have finished the job off if Neville hadn't reappeared. He'd had a change of heart about the crusties and hurried after me to ask if I wanted to go and join in the fun. The guy then ran off and Nev found me dragging myself back on to the pavement, calling out for someone called Melanie, while painting the pathway with my own blood.

'Who's Melanie?' he'd asked me, soon after arriving for his hospital visit. I didn't say.

Nobody brought me grapes or chocolate or disappointing flowers from a petrol-station forecourt. Nev very kindly agreed to feed Mengele for me while I was out of it.

When the police came to question me I didn't mention anything about Kara Geenan or her brother. I recognised the prick who sat at the end of my bed. We'd been at training college together, up in Bruche, and his name was Mawker. When he'd made it to plain clothes, he took it literally: you've never seen a more depressingly grey individual. He could wear blinding red with acid-lime polka dots, and after a while the pattern would disappear and slowly turn into something the colour of porridge. He wore a side parting that looked as if it had been applied with a set square. His moustache had a bit of previous and was to be found in the mugshot folders. His eyes were so close together that they probably swapped tears whenever he looked in the mirror.

'*I* think,' Mawker said, rotating his pencil between his fingers, 'that *you* know who attacked you. *I* think that *you're* protecting someone.'

'Interesting methods I deploy, losing all that blood to protect someone. Your hunches aren't fit to sit on Quasimodo's back.'

'Gary Cullen,' he said.

'Or his,' I said, thinking *Who?*

'It was his flat you broke into.'

'I didn't break into any flat, Mawker. The fucking door was open.'

'What's the story with you and Cullen? Why did you want to see him?'

'I didn't want to see him. I don't know who he is. It was a mistake. It was just bad luck.'

'As liars go,' Mawker leaned forward, giving me a kipper whiff of what he'd had for breakfast, 'you're about as bad as they come.'

'Am I coming or am I going?' I said. 'As grammarians go, you're a cock-end.'

'Gary Cullen escaped from Summerhead eight weeks ago. We've been trying to find him ever since. The man is dangerous.'

'Nooooo shit,' I said.

'His wife has gone walkabout, too. They used to live in the flat on St John's Way but she, her two nippers and now Gary Cullen have all disappeared.'

'He got a sister?'

He frowned. 'Not that I know of. Why?'

I shrugged. I was trying to put it all together in my head, but my head needed putting together first. I needed some bastard-strength painkillers and some decent kip. I needed some vodka, too. Hang on, I'll make a list...

'You doing all right, Joel?' he said. I was taken off guard. All this sledgehammering about, and I wasn't ready for the little stiletto slipped between my ribs and finding the coldest part of me.

'What do you mean by that?' I asked, hating the hunted whine in my voice.

'Just that you seem a bit pale.'

'So would you if you'd just had someone use your nut for a gong.'

'No,' he said, and he moved his face closer, as if he was seeing something beneath the skin that he couldn't quite make out in this light. 'The other stuff, Joel. I mean Rebecca, Sarah. How do you feel?'

I wanted to lean over and bite his nose off, spit it back in his face. But I sucked all the rage back in and just stared him down. He wasn't a bad man, Ian Mawker, but when he tried to be one, he just became something to be pitied. Keep hold of that thought, I thought. Even if... *especially* if your head is filling with snapshots of Rebecca in every different shade of dead.

'Working much?' he asked, breezy as you like.

I put up with it, joshing him about his inferior marks during training back in the late '90s, and the time I walked in on him in his room while he was trying to persuade a girl, visible through her bedroom window opposite, to take her top off for him. He left, but not before comically warning me to think twice about 'leaving town'. I could still hear him tapping his pencil against his teeth long after he'd taken himself and his grubby Columbo mac outside.

I dialled Kara Geenan's number and got a long, uninterrupted tone. I don't know what was worse: wishing that the guy had hammered me another five times and done the job properly, or realising that I was going to have to speak to Barry Liptrott again. I swung my legs out of bed. Not too shoddy. I stood up. Pain crawled up and down my back but it was manageable.

'Where do you think you're going?'

She must have put a silencer on those nylons. 'Nurse

58

Ratched,' I said, 'what a pleasant surprise.'

'It's Nurse *Rasheed*,' she said flatly, not getting it at all. 'Get back under that blanket.'

'You'll have one hell of a bedbath on your hands if you don't let me go where I need to go.'

'We have special implements for that.'

I eventually talked her out of it, but she accompanied me to the toilets and told me to hurry up. I was about to announce that I was going to discharge myself, but behind her, standing on the other side of a pair of swing-doors, I saw that Mawker had left behind a police guard. I wouldn't be able to fart without him making a note of it.

I looked out of the window. There was a drop of ten feet or so, but it would be into a drift of snow. I couldn't see how thick it was, but it was better than nothing. I squeezed out through the gap and jumped into a patch that looked the most forgiving. What could be the worst that lay under that white blanket? It wasn't as if hospital security had planted landmines.

I disappeared up to my knees in water.

It's not the easiest job in the world to flag a cab when you're dressed in pyjamas, less so when those pyjamas are sopping wet and streaked with mud. Eventually though, a taxi driver pulled up in front of me and took me home. He was violently anti-hospitals, due to his mother having to wait for a replacement hip that was inserted the wrong way round, so he had no problems about me trying to escape. When we arrived at my flat, I nipped inside to get some money to pay him. I found the door was hanging off its hinges. Just outside the front door is a hatch that leads into the attic. This too was gaping. Inside the flat there was a hole in the ceiling and a pile of plaster and floorboards on the floor. The footprints from a pair of trainers were smeared on the wall where the burglar had reached to gain purchase as he dropped in from above. Because the door had been locked from the outside, he'd had to break *out*; so a number of knives, including my favourite – an eighteen-inch Japanese vegetable knife that I used for chopping everything – had been snapped in his desperate attempts to get the door open. Mengele was nowhere to be seen. Nev, when I called him, was as shocked as I was. The place had been fine when he came to feed the cat as recently as the previous afternoon. I thanked him and rang off, grateful, at least, that he hadn't walked in on the loonies while they were redecorating.

Although there had been quite a bit of stuff shifted around or knocked over, there didn't seem to be anything missing. Maybe the burglar had been freaked by the lack of televisual booty.

'Jesus Christ.'

The taxi driver crunched his way into my flat, his mouth sagging as if his chin had been swapped for a ten-kilogram weight.

'Don't step on anything,' I said. 'It'll all have to be dusted for prints.'

'I thought you'd forgotten about me,' he said.

I gave him his fare but he was reluctant to leave. I ventured into the kitchen. The drawers were hanging open like thirsty mouths, their contents junked on the floor. I saw Mengele's tail whipping about outside, and opened the door on to the balcony. He was sitting on the roof, having presumably escaped through the small sash window above the sink once the ceiling had begun to be smashed open.

'Good boy,' I soothed, looking up at him. However, he was intent on a pigeon that was rooted to a single spot up on the chimney. The bird was eyeing Mengele as if it couldn't quite believe the size of him. I left him to it and went back inside. The cabbie was putting down the phone.

'Just called the police for you, mate,' he said, in his best 'tip me' voice. I thanked him, forcing a smile, and ushered him out, then I sat on the sofa and tried to force some thoughts. I had to get out before the plods arrived. It was unlikely that Mawker would look upon this as leaving town, but you never knew.

I got dressed, packed a small rucksack with some clothes, and dragged Mengele off the roof and into his cage. I made sure I had my keys and my wallet, before I went to the freezer and rescued the bottle of Grey Goose. Then I called a handyman mate of mine, Jimmy Two, and asked him to come round soon as he could, to board up and padlock the doorway. I went downstairs and stood on the pavement for a long time, wondering where the hell to go to next.

When a police car turned into my street, I made a decision. Away was good enough, for now.

6

Barry Liptrott worked lunchtimes at Lava Java, a club in Vauxhall, pulling pints, mixing margaritas, watching pissed office types try to salsa. That was what he did when he wasn't holding up old age pensioners or shoplifting, trying to impress someone in the underworld, trying to get a leg up to the rarefied climes of... I don't know, maybe twocking tricycles or beating up blind septuagenarians who had been unfaithful to their partners.

I got there at around 1 p.m., long before the joint started kicking, and found my entry barred by a phenomenally ugly bouncer. He was so ugly it was like he was really trying at it. He'd have frightened chimps out of a banana factory.

'Hi,' I said. The bouncer seemed put out by monosyllables. He leaned against the door and crossed his arms. Well, I say arms but they were more like legs. His legs were like legs too, but the kind you find on a rhino.

'Is there an entry fee?'

He looked me up and down with the speed he might read *The Very Hungry Caterpillar*. My hair went grey waiting for him. 'You ain't comin' in.'

'I need to speak to Barry. Barry Liptrott.'

'Oh, really, what about?'

'I wanted to ask him where he buys his shoes.'

He actually gave my feet a look.

'What are you?' I said. 'A bouncer, or his secretary? Or his bumboy? What, exactly?' I wasn't altogether sure he was human, but he had opposable thumbs, so I was ready to give him the benefit of the doubt.

His face collapsed like a pie crust with too much air underneath it. 'You say one more thing, I'll fucking wear your face for a mask.'

'I just–'

He had a good punch on him, I'll give him that. I landed on my arse and rocked back till I could see the coils of rust swooping across the sky, where exhaust fumes were reacting with the sunlight. I stayed there for a while. It was quite pleasant, until blood began to leak down the back of my throat. I sat up and felt my teeth. Still there. My lip was split, though, and the pain was so sharp, so intense, that I could feel it a couple of feet in every direction from the epicentre.

Just then, Jonathan Dayne swung into the car park in his Jaguar XJS. A sticker on the boot read: *How's My Driving? Dial 0-800-EAT-MY-SHIT*. Jonathan Dayne, aka Knocker, owned Lava Java. And he had more form than the Inland Revenue.

'Knocker,' I said, jovially, as he stepped out of the car, the cheeky glottal part of his name helping to pebble-dash my shirt with blood. I was almost happy to see him.

'What do you want, scummo?' He slammed the door and the car rocked unsteadily on its ancient suspension.

'I want you to call off this no-necked bison-fucker and then invite me in for headache tablets and vodka.'

'I don't work here any more, dickhead,' Knocker said. 'I sold it last year. I'm just here for a salsa lesson.'

I groaned and drew myself up to my intimidating five foot nine and a half as the single-cell organism in a suit came at me.

'It's okay, Errol,' Knocker said, holding up his hand. 'I'll deal with him.'

'You're such a good Samaritan, Knocker,' I said, 'but I can take care of myself. Muscle-bound fuckers like that, they go down easier than perished elasticated knickers on a skeleton.'

'Comedian,' Knocker said, entering the club and not hanging around to see if I was following. 'Always so fucking quick, no wonder someone gave you a pasting. I'm surprised it doesn't happen more often.'

'Touché,' I said, and decided to stop talking for a while, at least until I got some eighty-proof analgesics down my neck.

I waited at the bar for him to finish his lesson. They had Grey Goose, which was a surprise, so I ordered a vodka martini. I stared at my bloody mouth in the mirror, and got the first one down me quick. I like it in a chunky glass with two blocks of ice and a sliver of lemon peel, if I'm not drinking it straight from a shot glass, but here I was glad to have it how you're supposed to have it.

I checked out the other frugger-buggers who were gearing up for their dance lessons. Some of them even wore the proper shoes. There were a couple of nine-to-fivers reading their newspapers over a beer and a sandwich, before heading back for another four hours of Rich Tea, Facebook and group memos. Not the kind of place that actually needed a bouncer, but after midnight anything was possible: fights, bloody dance-offs, salsa slayings…

'Another?' the bartender asked. I nodded, to save my mouth, and he mixed the drink. He gave me a napkin for my mushed-up mush, and I nodded again. Good bartenders don't just serve you drinks; they're all about comfort. They know the right things to say, they know never to say too much, and they do the right things.

This bloke was a good bartender.

I sipped my second VM of the afternoon and watched him work, preparing a Bloody Mary mix that he stored in a two-litre plastic bottle; making sure there was enough ice – more than enough ice – in the buckets; slicing lemons and limes; arranging his bottles so the labels faced towards the customer. He had a well-stocked cocktail bar: liqueurs (maraschino, crème de menthe, framboisette and so forth) on the left hand side of the cash register; syrups (grenadine, falernum, orgeat, etc.) and cordials on the right. Up above, on glass shelves in the centre, was the hard stuff, none of it, I'm glad to say, in optics. These bottles were flanked by a huge number of cocktail glasses, some 2 ounces, most 3 or 3½ ounces, and all of them with long stems. You drink certain cocktails without a long-stemmed glass, you'll fuck up your cocktail. They have to be cold from first sip to last, and that isn't going to happen if you've got your clammy mitts wrapped around a beaker. I recognised some of them: Pousse-Café glasses, Delmonico glasses for Sours, a couple of Julep mugs, and the straight glasses for Highballs and Collinses. At one end of the bar were the glasses he used for Old Fashioneds, the chunky ones, 4 or 5 ounces. I keep a couple of cocktail glasses at home, for when I can be bothered. Seven-ounce bastards. And one fifteen-ounce behemoth for when my intention is to rip my tits down to the bone.

All of this guy's glasses, his pitchers, stirring rods, strainers and shakers were so clean they could have passed for mint. I sipped my drink and nodded some more. This bar was a nice bar and I was enjoying sitting here and admiring a man who liked his work.

A woman came in wearing a smart black dress. She ordered a glass of Chardonnay and opened her purse. She smiled at me, said something about the weather, about not knowing what it was going to do, or something; I wasn't hearing her too clearly because the smart black dress and the Grey Goose were kicking around in my head, and I was thinking, *no, please, no, not now*, but you can't push it away. You must never push it away, not when it wants to come so strongly, not when, some day it might never come and you'll wish for it to come back so hard that you'll pull a muscle, and so:

It was the best day we ever had. And for no crazier reason that everything between us clicked. There was no cinema, no special meal, no day out at the beach. It was just an ordinary day, an ultra-ordinary day, but it was the day that bolted her incontrovertibly on to what it then meant to be me; bolted her so securely that it seemed she had never had a past of her own, never been anything other than mine. The day that, for the first time, I realised I was dumbly, joyously, cripplingly in love with her.

I'd known Rebecca what? A couple of weeks? We'd clashed together a few times after drunken pub nights, or visits down to the woods with bottles of wine and ghetto blasters playing, Christ, what were we listening to back then? In 1994. *The Holy Bible, Grace, Hips and Makers*. And this particular night we'd been on the cheap Bulgarian red since the afternoon had withdrawn into one corner of the sky.

We'd been talking about culture: it had been the buzzword of this particular day. We didn't get past a couple of sentences without crowbarring it in. We decided we needed to improve ourselves with a bit of culture, so we dressed up. Shirt and tie, smart black dress... Jesus, Rebecca. Jesus Christ.

It begins.

On to the stage, to the understated applause that only gatherings of this sort can produce, comes a kind-looking man and a wolfish woman wearing a red dress. She sits at a grand piano. He takes an age over the position of his cello before smoothing his hair and taking in the audience while exhaling levelly. Then, with a disconcerting flurry of movement, the instruments find their voice, driven by manic stabs and jerks of arms and hands. I can't equate the disarray of their employ with the sublime rapport of their strings.

Their sound creeps around the slotted pine panelling, stealthy as oil, settling against the skin during slow phrases, spirited away like a rising helix of bubbles during the fast ones. In this moment there are only two spheres of being: the music, and your presence; a silent proximity exerted by the loose arrangement of your clothes, the way your leg climbs over its partner, your left hand gently grips the right. I can smell your perfume (and, if I turn my head a little, I see the wet flash of your eyes and the threaded chunk of metal jolted by your pulse in the gulley between your breasts).

After Barber, after Bach, the musicians play Debussy's 'Sonata' and you shift slightly, the hard edge of your forearm meeting mine on the intervening rest. The playing of music evolves on the stage in several layers, like cells in an animation: the man turning pages of music, the pianist, the cellist. The cello. I see details that might have eluded me at other times, but with this heightening of sensation it does not appear strange that I should notice the cellist's hand: a white spider fleeing up and down the cello's neck. Or the polished part of his knee where the bow brushes it at the limit of its stroke; filaments of horsehair; the muscles in the pianist's arms.

Back home, you set about making tea. I riffle through your CD collection till I find Borodin's 'String Quartet No. 2 in D Major'. Lighted by candles, your room looks austere without being imposing. The first night I spent here, you and I looked at each other from opposite sides of the room for an age before you came to sit by my feet and hold my hand. This is what you do now, after placing the tray with the teapot and mugs on the table. I slip down on to the floor and you move between my legs, lying back so that your head finds the dip of my right shoulder. We don't say anything.

There is a beautiful, haunting phrase that Borodin uses over and over during the *Notturno*. The cello's voice is plaintive and hopeful, rolling around the other three string instruments like an invocation. Although you don't move against me, I feel a settling of your weight, as if your muscles and bones have slipped beyond the threshold at which they find their usual repose. I become aware of your heartbeat and the measured journey of your breath. Everything is right for me in a way it hasn't been for years. Slowly, with as much tenderness as I can muster, I place my hands on your shoulders and squeeze, allowing my fingers to work their way across your arms and the flat gloss of your chest. Your clavicle, the cob of bone at the back of your neck – I touch it all, trying to pass on something of my need for you: all my warmth and good feeling for you. Nothing is so important. Can you feel this? Eyes closed, I move my hands to the swell of the music, following the ebb and flow of the cello's ache. In my touch is all the tenderness we've shared before. The raw centre of you is where I'm trying to reach, softly plucking and drawing upon the area that remembers the good times and knows there will be many more. I know this can work. Can you feel? I know this can work. This is love. Along with the charity of my hands, I send a message, forcing it through my fingertips and into the knot of pain and confusion we all carry at our centre. *I won't let you down.*

You stay my hands. Bring one to your mouth and kiss the palm. This is love.

The first time: on the heels of a dovetail kiss, you moved over and sank upon me till I had no measure of where I ended and you began. The soft curtain of your hair moving pendulum slow above my face; the sound of the fountain outside the only thing pinning me to reality...

I was deciding whether to ruin my day with a third martini, when finally Knocker deigned to give me a nanosecond of his time.

'So,' he said, ordering a white-wine spritzer, 'what are you up to?'

I told him.

'Found him yet?' he asked. He made himself comfortable at the stool next to me.

'We might have had a coming together of sorts.'

Knocker took a lighter out of his jacket pocket, started rotating it between his fingers. 'So what are you doing here?'

'I like the cocktails. And I was thinking of signing up, maybe doing a few classes. We could enter competitions, be a team. Shit, you can even lead. What do you think?'

'What is it you want, scummo?'

'The woman Liptrott introduced me to, Kara Geenan. I wonder if you know where she is?'

'How the fuck should I know?'

'Okay, let me put it another way.' I grabbed hold of his hair, snatched the lighter from his hand and set fire to his tie.

'You fuck-me brainwank,' Knocker said bizarrely, trying to back off.

'Where is she, Knocker?' The flames were tucking in and I reckoned his shirt would catch fire before they reached his throat. 'You and The Lip are tighter than a gnat's chuffpipe. You always know what he's up to, who he's up and by how far. Tell me, quick mind, and I'll put you out.' I turned to the barman. *Glass of water*, I mouthed. He didn't bat an eyelid.

'Last time I saw her,' he said, 'she was at a pub in Westminster. She was friendly with the landlord, some guy called Nathan. He'd know where she is.' He was squawking like a wronged parrot by now. I was smelling burning hair. His chest wig was going up.

'Name of the pub,' I said.

'Fuck it, Sorrell, come *on*!'

'Name.'

'The Paviours Arms,' he said. 'Page Street.'

I doused him and threw him back off the stool. He landed on his arse and looked up at me, blinking a slice of lemon from his left eye.

'What was in it for you, Knocker?' I said. 'Couple of K? Blow-job? Leg-up to the next broken rung on the ladder? Who is she? What does she want?'

Every time he breathed, he sprayed a little bit of water like some fucking porpoise. 'I don't know,' he said. 'Me and

71

Barry were delivering some watered-down booze for an outfit I'm in with, up Stanford way. This woman, she was waiting for us in the gaffer's office one day. Said she needed to find some guy called Sorrell, an ex-copper. Said she heard we knew who she was talking about. Told us that if we gave her what she wanted, she'd well, let's just say she was nice to us. Been a while since anyone was nice to me.'

'What are you talking about?' I said. '*I'm* nice to you. I like you enough to sort out your wardrobe for you. You look much better without that tie.'

'You watch yourself, scummo,' Knocker sprayed again out of his blowhole. I should have thrown him a fucking fish.

I thanked the barman and left before the bulging suit arrived to make me kiss his knuckles some more.

Though my flat is pretty spartan, even more so now since it's been burgled, I've always made sure I had some other stuff locked away in a storage joint called Keepsies, which is round the back of the police station at Paddington Green. Special stuff. Emergency stuff. Stuff that you just shouldn't have lying around the flat. I nip over there and pick some of it up when my life starts filling up with warning signs.

I know Keith, who runs the place, from way back when I first came to London in the early noughties. When I went solo, one of my first pay packets was courtesy of him, after I'd provided the evidence he needed that his wife was cheating on him. What he paid me was a fair whack, but nothing compared to what she had been siphoning from his bank account over the years.

He gives me fifty per cent off the monthly rate for the smallest of his lockers, which is still big enough for, say, one of the larger widescreen TVs on the market, and thirty quid a month is no great drain.

I was early – the place only opens after lunch on certain days of the week – so I sat in the Saab drinking illegally hot coffee from a cardboard cup, waiting for Keepsies to open. I asked myself some tough questions, there in the car, while I blistered the pulp of my lip. Chief among them: Joel, what the *fuck* is going on? I asked that of myself a few times, with increasing volume, but I didn't scare any answers out of myself. A goodish-looking woman, a cry for help, a missing brother, a botched cosh job, a burgled flat, and a goodish-looking woman vanishing into thin air. She was the key, I reckoned. If I found her then everything would slowly unfold like a scrunched-up ball of cellophane. I hoped.

I was startled out of my thoughts by Keith tapping the plastic stirrer from his own cup of coffee on my window. I got out and we shook hands. He asked me – through mouthfuls of his chicken and mayo sub, as we crossed the road to his warehouse – how things were going, and I said fine. He nodded grimly. He knows exactly what I've got locked up at his place, and it's all credit to him because I could probably get him closed down if the police ever found out. I signed his register and left him at reception, telling him I'd only be a couple of minutes. Then I wandered off to find my cubicle, fishing the unmarked key from my pocket.

In the cubicle was a scuffed brown-leather briefcase and a larger container, one of those solid Samsonite suitcases from, I believe, their Silhouette range. Very attractive silvery appearance, like brushed steel. I used another key to unlock this and took from it a paper envelope that contained three hundred pounds in twenty-pound notes. I skimmed off a hundred and folded it into my wallet. Replacing the envelope,

I turned my attention to a soft canvas bag. From this I retrieved a gun, a 9mm Glock 17, the kind of weapon used by the police, and a box full of shells. After a long deliberation, I put the gun and the bullets back. Guns scare the shit out of me.

Then I thought about the bashing I'd been given and took it out again. I had never fired it in my life. In fact I don't know much more about that gun other than it makes a loud noise and kills people. I don't know its history (I don't want to know its history) but it has probably a very ugly past, since I came across the weapon in the bedroom of a teenage runaway who had overdosed on pure heroin. I thought the mother of the boy would be shocked enough by his death and his habit without discovering that he was carrying firearms around with him, too.

There's other stuff in the bag. Things I wouldn't get shot at or arrested for. Pictures of Rebecca and me. Pictures of Sarah and me. Pictures of the three of us together, looking happy. I inspected one of them before I locked the cubicle and went back to Keith at reception, to sign out. Three smiles, all on the same 6x4: me, Rebecca and Sarah sitting in the garden in Lime Grove, just as the sun was going down. I can almost smell the buddleia, as well as the perfume on Rebecca's throat. But whenever I see these photographs, whenever I think about those times, I'm not smiling.

I motored over to York Road, stopping off at my flat to check that Jimmy Two had done the work I needed. The makeshift door and padlock combo now looked more secure than what had preceded it.

Inside the vet's were three women, all of them collecting age hard, as if it was a hobby, and holding toy dogs on their knees in various states of tartan and shiveriness.

'Morning, ladies,' I said and, leaning on the receptionist's desk, asked if Dr Henriksen was in.

'I'm in, but I'm busy,' she said, stepping out of her surgery. She was wearing a pair of surgical gloves which makes sense. But I wouldn't have said anything either if she'd come out with a pair of goalkeeper's mitts on. You don't question the methods of people in medicine. Somehow, you just don't. She was also wearing a short black skirt and a pair of barely black nylons that made a noise when she walked, which entered both ears simultaneously and came together in a hot melted knot at the centre of my head.

'Hi Melanie,' I said. 'How's Mengele?'

The varicose jobs behind me audibly sucked in their breath at my mention of that name, and for the nth time I asked myself just what had been going through my head when I came to name my cat. Bitterness, probably – and the fuck-you bug that I'd been infected with since my teenage years.

'Your *cat*,' Melanie said, steadfastly refusing to acknowledge the animal's name, 'is fine, as you well know. And he's ready for you to pick up now.'

'Ah,' I said, 'slight problem.'

Dr Henriksen gave me a look over the oblong frames of her Calvin Klein glasses. A blade of brown hair swung out from behind her ear and hung alongside her deep red mouth. With a face like hers, who needs Zebra crossings?

I could feel the wattles on the old dears behind me quiver as they strained to hear what I had to say.

'Can I speak to you in private for a second?' I said.

I think she's keen on me. I hope she's keen on me. Sometimes she strikes me as someone who is merely humouring me, using me as a benchmark by which she can measure her connection to the human race, a way of keeping her oar in until such time as she feels she has spent too much time chasing the rewards of her career and decides to knuckle down and swap rings. Other times – just slivers of time, but slivers worth waiting for – she's warm to me unlike any other woman I've known, including Rebecca. We've never made love. We've never even clashed teeth after a few too many Stellas at the Marylebone Bar and Kitchen. But there's a change in her voice, her smile, the heart-stopping moments when her bottle-green eyes get tired of looking at mine and slip to check on my mouth for a beat or two. There's some electricity between us: enough to keep me interested.

I closed the door behind us, once she'd ushered me into her surgery. I could imagine the ecstasy of rolled eyes as I ducked past her to enter. On the operating table was a tortoise. We regarded each other for a moment – the tortoise even nodded – before it went back to looking sullen and daydreaming about lettuce, or roller skates, or whatever.

'Go through to the back,' she said. 'My office.'

'I'm in a bit of a tight spot,' I said, as I pushed on through to a tiny room that, until Mengele had been deposited there, had been dominated by an ancient IBM computer and a pot plant.

'Oh dear,' she said. She plugged in the kettle and raised her eyebrows at me. 'Tea?'

'I'm fine, thanks,' I said. Mengele hissed at me, then looked up at Melanie Henriksen for approval. 'Anyway, yeah, a tight spot.'

'Mm,' Melanie said. I had only known her for six months, but it was enough for her to have learned to grade my bullshit. If there were Pyrex containers for it, mine would be in one bearing the label: *Very poor*.

I blew out my cheeks and widened my eyes to illustrate just how very tight my tight spot was.

'The answer's yes,' she said, 'but you'll have to ask me.'

'Okay,' I said, 'would you be kind enough to massage my buttocks? With olive oil?'

'Try the question that was on your mind first.'

'Believe me, that *was* the que–'

She gave me a slow blink. 'The other question. Try the other question.'

'Well, I was burgled and the flat's in a state and I just need you to look after *Der Todesengel* for me – just for a few days.'

'Okay,' she said, 'happy to. What about you?'

'I'll muddle through.'

She shook her head. She looked pretty disgusted with me, but in a nice way, if you can believe it.

'I have enough space at my flat. I have a very large sofa.'

'I couldn't impose–'

'You are imposing, so you might as well take advantage. It's no problem.'

She jotted her address down on a pink Post-it and adhered it to my nose. 'I'll be in after seven tonight.'

'Melanie–' I began. I must have been getting a bit gooey-eyed because she shooed me out, and quite right too. I gave Mengele's chin a rub first, and I nodded at the old dears and their shivery dogs. Then I got in my car and drove to Westminster.

It started to rain on the way but I wasn't too bothered about that. I was busy thinking, why couldn't I have been burgled before now?

7

I parked a little way up the road from the Paviours Arms. I don't like situating myself directly outside the building I'm aiming for. Even my own gaff, I park a hundred metres or so further along the road. Things shouldn't be too cosy, too convenient. Even when it's chucking it down. Things are too sweet, you start to ease off. You find, when you need it most, your edge has turned into a curve, and a big soft one at that.

It was busy in the pub, but then it was getting on in the afternoon, on a Friday, and the suits were in a rush to get slaughtered. You could see the ones who had been here since lunchtime as they'd taken over the sofas, and their tables were audibly complaining under the weight of so much glass. I pushed past the acres of cheap jackets and women in black (why is it so many women in offices wear black, and nothing but? They must curse Marlboro for not doing black packs, or pray that John Player might become trendy some time soon) and, using two portly men at the huge bar as a mangle, fed myself through to the weary barmaid. I ordered a pint of Stella and, shielding my drink as best I could, jinked slow-motion over to the one space in any pub where you are unlikely to find anyone standing: the square inch by the gents' toilet. Behind me was a space dedicated to food, and I sneered at the ranks of loosened ties as they tucked into their fish and chips and shepherd's pies. A pub was for drinking. It ought to smell of spilled beer and urinal pucks, not of vinegar. Crisps, pork scratchings, peanuts: fair enough, because you need something salty to help your beer down. But meals? In a pub? Christ, it brings me out in hives.

I forced my attention back to the scrum to see if Kara Geenan was around, but that would have been just too dashed lucky. A guy with a bunch of keys as big as a football attached to his belt appeared behind the bar and spent some time chatting to another guy at one end, who was sipping a pint of Guinness. I was about to set off on another life-threatening trek to the north face of the bar, when Big Keys disappeared into the back. Nathan, I thought and, by way of congratulating myself for such sterling deductive reasoning, drained my glass and went in search of another pint.

I took my time with that one, because I could feel the buzz from the cocktails getting their second wind. I watched the various pockets of execs and secs and no-necks flirt and argue and play their little power games, all the while grateful that I'd bailed out of the great career jet just after take-off. I was no more a true policeman than a badger is an Olympic-class ice-dancer. It didn't help that the helmet was an embarrassment and the pay – for wandering around in a uniform that might as well have had the words 'HATE ME' daubed on the back – was staggeringly awful. At least now, although my money situation was even more staggeringly awful, I could wear plain clothes, fall out of bed on my say-so and swear 24/7 at the boss. I had to make a go of what

I was doing and, to a certain extent, I did. Fear drove me, more than anything else. Fear that I'd end up in an office wearing Homer Simpson ties and emailing the guy sitting two inches to my left to ask him if he had any spare paper clips I could borrow.

When Rebecca died (when Rebecca was killed, when she was killed), a couple of months before Sarah went missing, it made it all the easier for me to hand in my notice at the Met. If they hadn't accepted my resignation they would have sacked me within six weeks, because I had gone into something of a decline. I drank a lot, I stopped shaving, I stopped washing. I stopped caring. Because what I cared about wasn't there any more. And maybe that thought, filling my mind like a black sun, blinding me to anything else, meant that Sarah's leaving became inevitable. She must have noticed how much I marginalised her when I was trying to deal with what had happened. And I was writing on a very small page, so of course she was going to fall off the edge. What I cared about, a big chunk of what I cared about, *was* still there, but my wallowing wouldn't allow me to see it like that. How must she have been feeling? I never asked. I still don't know. I'm too scared, too much of a chicken to even begin to guess. Instead, I tried to find other Rebeccas in bars so dark that even a passing resemblance was enough for me. When I woke up next to them in the morning, I left before they could ask me if I really meant what I'd said, and if something that happened so fast really could be *it*. And Sarah witnessed it all. I wasn't The One for anybody (I should have been, first and foremost, to my daughter) and I felt like that for a long time, until Keith pulled me out of the mire and asked me to spy on his wife.

Since then I'd done some gritty, shitty jobs, but every one

of them rates a ten next to the zero involving cheap, crease-free shirts and an hour for your lunch. I'd done mobile, static and covert surveillance; traced witnesses, fleeing debtors and missing persons; investigated insurance claims; executed company searches and pre-employment checks. I've proved infidelities. I've been punched, shot at (admittedly with an airgun), run over, and now I've been clouted around the loaf with a cosh. I've waded through each and every different type of manure, and at the end of it I've taken my shoes off and cleaned them without a peep of complaint. The worst thing about this type of work is the hanging around, and following that is having to listen to the inane gas that flies out of people's mouths while you're hanging around. You have to listen to a lot. And I was listening to it now.

Two gym-slim blokes. One in a green woollen three-piece, one in a navy pinstripe silk-mix, a pair of Loewe shades resting on his head. Both of them, you could tell, played squash, or badminton, every lunchtime and the sense of competition was deep and hot inside them, like bile eating up their insides. They were now playing *I've been to more places than you*, and each sentence, more or less, began like this: 'When I was in Mogadishu…'

The jaw-clench-per-minute ratio was sky-rocketing.

'If you're ever in Warsaw,' Silk-Mix was saying, 'you have to stay at the Hotel Bristol. How could you not? I mean, it was opened by Maggie Thatcher, but don't let that put you off.'

Three-Piece took a big, punctuative swallow of his Strongbow and, nodding, replied: 'I won't go to Nigeria again, no way. I got shot at. That really put me off the place. Billy clubs studded with nails. People carrying them in the street.'

Silk-Mix: 'You know, some years ago I was in Sierra Leone. Believe it. The most dangerous place on Earth. The

82

front line was between two villages and they're called, you'll never guess, Somerset and Winston. Believe it. That's why there were British troops over there. That's the only reason.'

Nathan appeared at the bar again. I think he had added to his keys in the hour or so since he was gone. He was walking with a fucking *list*. I pushed unsteadily past Three-Piece and said to them: 'In Morecambe they've got this pub with a sign that says "No nuclear weapons", yeah. No, *really*.'

God, I was more pissed than I'd given myself credit for. 'Nathan,' I called out, approaching the bar. 'Nate. Nat. *Natters*.'

He was looking at me as though I had just sold his grand-mother for a handful of turds. 'Do I know you?' he asked.

'No, but you know somebody who knows me – which makes us virtually related. Let's go on holiday.'

'I think you've had enough to drink. Why don't you put your pint down and leave.'

'Kara Geenan,' I said.

There might have been the slightest hardening of his stare, but he handled it beautifully.

'I said you're drunk,' he said. 'Leave. Now.'

Punters were now clearing a space at the bar. Maybe they'd seen this kind of thing in here before. What was he going to do? Lash me with his Chubbs? The gathering silence helped clear my head a little. He was coming around the bar and, up close, I could see he was no slouch. What I had perceived as flab was really part of a very hard gut. There was no give anywhere on him. He didn't try to look dangerous, like the soft ones do. He looked laid-back and affable. Which obviously meant he could twist me into pretzel shapes without breaking sweat.

He took my hand and very gently manoeuvred it up my spine until I was bent double with pain. He got down low too, and murmured something in my ear. Then he let me go and I acted like a good boy and went outside. Five minutes later he was where he promised me he'd be.

The taxi rank on the corner of Regency Street and Horseferry Road was quiet at this time of night, this no-time in between people going out after work and stumbling home once the bars and clubs are closed. A couple of cabbies were taking advantage of the slow period to catch up on their red-tops or their zeds. A fine rain had begun to fall, and was misting the scuffed cellulose of the taxis like hoarfrost. Nathan was standing with his hands in his pockets, looking up at the moon as it skidded along the roofs of the apartment blocks on Victoria Street. I stretched, feeling blackspots of pain break out all over my body, and waited for something to happen.

'She's nothing to do with me,' he said at last.

'Why so defensive?' I said.

'I'm not being defensive. I just don't want any trouble.'

'Come on,' I said, 'she's plenty to do with you. She's a looker. She's been seen at your boozer, stuck to your arm like a plaster cast. I don't want the sticky details. I just need to find her. Is she at your place?'

'Why do you need to find her?'

'She owes me money, and an explanation. In that order.'

Nathan sighed. He dropped his gaze and stared at me. I must have been a bit of a come-down compared to the moon, but I was touched. 'I haven't seen her for a couple of days,' he said, and he sounded like someone glad to get it off his chest. 'She was staying with me. She got a job here first, serving behind the bar, and we hit it off. Couple of weeks later she had an argument with her landlady about rent, and I said she could stay here. We've got some spare rooms. But

84

she didn't end up using any of them, if you get my drift.'

I nodded. 'Where was she before she turned up on your doorstep? Did she say?'

'Liverpool. She wasn't shitting me, though she'd have been wise to after what she did, little bitch. There was a ticket from Lime Street Station in her bag. And some of the numbers on my phone bill were 0151 jobs.'

'When was this?'

'She got a job with me tail end of summer, about three months ago.'

'And she's moved out, has she?'

He nodded again, his jaw firm. 'Without telling me. And she took the folding stuff from the safebox, too. About four hundred pounds, the little cunt.'

I thanked him and tapped on the window of one of the cabs, feeling too drunk to drive. 'Maida Vale,' I told the taxi driver, and crawled into the back seat. My head was at that precarious state where only sleep or more booze would placate it. And my cheek was hurting where I'd bit it at the mention of Liverpool. *Liverpool, for fuck's sake.*

'Hey,' Nathan said. 'You find her, you let me know where she is, okay?'

'Of course,' I lied.

Dr Melanie Henriksen lived in a split-level flat in a smart Victorian terraced house on Oakington Road. The blinds on the front window were shut when I got there, but a pleasant honey-coloured light was edging them and I could hear, as I reached for the doorbell, music playing through a partially open window. As the cabbie pulled over, I looked down at the £3.99 bottle of plonk that I'd bought on the way over. It sat in the plastic carrier bag smirking at me. Fuck, *and* it was a screw-top. I gave it to the driver – some tip – and got out.

'Hi,' she said, after she'd buzzed me in. 'I was just about to get ready for bed. But, now you're here, how about a drink?'

Though I was eager for sleep, I said I wouldn't say no to a vodka, and she went off to the kitchen at the rear of the flat. I followed her languidly, checking out the place as I did so. The living room gave on to a study with a mezzanine sleeping area. There was a tiny Sony Vaio on the desk, and a potted plant that might have come straight out of the Amazon rainforest. There was a window looking on to the sunken garden where a fountain gurgled, but it was too dark to see anything out there. The hallway had a framed print of Simon Patterson's 'The Great Bear' and an arresting painting in sombre oils, by some guy called Walkuski, of Icarus before his feather-duster impression came a cropper.

Mengele was sitting on a large, sumptuous cushion beneath a couple of bookshelves filled with old Penguin crime novels, the ones with green spines. He broke off from cleaning his toes to give me a contemptuous stare. The kitchen was comparatively small (that said, you could have fitted my entire flat into it), but all the cons wore fishtail coats and rode around on Vespas. Boffi units, some very nice Fritz Hansen chairs, and a Barber Osgabi dining table. I was scared to put down the glass she handed me, since there was nothing so retro as a coaster. Maybe she had some courtesy-bots that would scuttle out from under the sink to hold your drink for you when you needed a rest from holding it.

'Nice pad,' I said, trying not to sound too impressed. 'Vets, they earn a wad then, or what?'

'It can be very rewarding financially,' she said, over the rim of her glass. 'I've worked hard for what I've got. And I'm not wasteful with money. I like nice things.'

I liked nice things, too. And she had a very nice thing

leaning against the back of a chair as she sipped her drink. She was wearing a cream Armani trouser suit over a simple white cotton vest top. She was barefoot. She had let her hair down, too. Earlier, it had been kept back off her face by a leather thong; now it hung in brown undulations around her jaw line. She didn't look away too often, which was fine by me; it meant I got to enjoy those dark green eyes for longer.

'Where do I sleep then?' I said, draining my glass.

'The sofa. You can turn it into a bed.'

'Get many visitors?' I said, wanting to push my luck just a little bit.

As she finished her own drink she sucked an ice cube into her mouth. Her red lips were very moist. She was looking directly at me, so draw your own picture as to how you think my face appeared.

'I like to make my guests feel welcome,' she said. 'And comfortable.'

'How comfortable?' I asked, feeling about as comfortable as a peeled baby in a bag of salt. My clothes were suddenly too tight. I wanted to slip into something more comfortable. Like her, for example.

'Are you flirting with me, Joel?'

'I am if you hope I am,' I said. 'If not, then no, I'm not flirting with you, I'm just seeing what your resistance level is, what load you can take before your temper snaps.'

'Well, I'm not put out by your little game,' she said. 'Carry on testing my resistance.'

If brains were wool, I wouldn't have enough to knit a Smurf's scarf, but I'm not colour blind and the only light I could see was green. I went over to her, pressed my thigh between hers, and put my arms around her.

'This is most unprofessional,' she said, in a voice that was suddenly thick and lacking its earlier assuredness.

'I've never been accused of that before,' I said, ladling on the irony.

'No, me' she said. 'Getting involved with a patient.'

'It's not quite the same, is it?' I replied. 'I mean, I'm hardly going to start coughing up fur balls.'

'Your leg's trembling,' she said.

'That's not my leg.'

I kissed her before she could try to get any more smart remarks out of me. She stayed with it for a couple of seconds, then broke off, moved away.

'Not yet,' she said, with a little smile. It was still maddening, but I could live with that. I didn't realise just how beautiful the phrase 'not yet' could be. 'Not yet' was a 'yes' wearing a skimpy negligee and sucking the tip of its finger. She squeezed my hand as she went by me and told me to sleep well, and that there were sandwiches in the fridge if I was hungry. I poured myself a nightcap and sauntered into the living room, with the plate of ham-and-cheese. Mengele had moved to the sofa and I let him stay there. I switched on the TV, pushing the mute button on the remote, and watched BBC News 24 in the dark, while behind me I heard the maddening sounds of clothes coming off and deep duvets being drawn back. As I kicked off my shoes and lay back against the cushions, I wondered if she slept in the nude. Her perfume was on me, and so were Mengele's eyes.

'Jealous?' I asked him, and fell asleep.

'Joel? Joel?'

I struggled out of sleep and found it was dark, very dark, but I saw her in the doorway, pale and naked, her arms raised slightly, palms resting on the architrave. The lemon from my spilled drink was perched on my crotch. How classy. But she didn't seem to mind. She came to me and reached for my hand, and drew me up towards her. She kissed me gently at first, and then more deeply until we found a tempo that was more like desperation, and that didn't stop until we had stumbled through to her bed, and I was naked too, and inside her, and *inside* her, and then the panting and the sweat and the soft weight of her breasts on my chest and sometime before it was over I was crying and she shushed me and I don't know how I returned to sleep but somehow I did and it was good, it had all been good, even the tears.

Harsh morning light, a cat and a note sitting on my chest. There was about three litres of drool on my shoulder and my hair, when I reached up to scratch my head, feeling as if it had morphed into something worn by the lead singer of A Flock of Seagulls. No wonder she didn't wake me up. Maybe she was on the motorway by now, in her Audi TT, toeing it for all she was worth in an effort to get as far away from me as possible, while begging for a trans-Atlantic flight on her Motorola. I couldn't blame her. I unfolded the note:

Couldn't bear to wake you – you looked so sweet. Help yourself to breakfast. There's a spare set of keys on the kitchen table. I'll be home around 8. Maybe we could go out for dinner? Last night was… interesting. Mx

Interesting. I thought about how she had looked rising above me, her head flung back, her mouth open, *interesting, very interesting*, but I decided thoughts like that could wait.

I didn't want to start getting aroused with Mengele still slouching on top of me.

I booked a table at a smart pizza restaurant on Formosa Street and took a shower. I thought about leaving a note for her as well, but decided that it would all seem a little too cute and cosy, so I simply tickled Mengele under the chin and went out.

It was cold again this morning. The sky was slate-grey, and, on the fringes of the city, huge boulders of cloud were piling up. The wind slashed in under my jacket and made my nipples feel like a couple of scabs.

I caught a tube at Warwick Avenue and headed back to Westminster to pick up the car. Luckily I got to it before the traffic wardens did. I dropped it off back at my flat and caught another train at Edgware Road, stopping by at a sandwich bar to buy a couple of pastries and a coffee. On my way out, on Chapel Street, I thought I saw the actress Rachel Weisz hefting her shopping towards the bus stop, but that very scenario disproved it. It was a tortuous journey to Archway, via the underground, but I didn't want to put the poor Saab through a fate worse than scrap heaps.

While I was sitting there, in-between a man trying to do the day's *Guardian* crossword and a girl in a flowery frock and black biker jacket playing Fifa on a DS, I mused on the fact that I had never seen anyone famous while I had been here in London. I thought I had spotted that guy Foxton, the bass player from The Jam once, on a Northern Line tube train, wearing glasses and a bushy hairdo (Foxton, not the train), but I couldn't be sure. And in Selfridge's, a couple of years previously, I thought I saw Helena Bonham Carter in the Food Hall, checking out the fish while picking her skirt out of the crack in her arse. Neither sighting had been confirmed. Jimmy Two was always seeing celebrities. Within an hour on one occasion, Hugh Laurie had asked him the time, and Mariella Frostrup had apologised profusely to him for stepping on his foot as she came out of Rasa on Charlotte Street. It made me wonder if I was lucky or not.

Daylight made St John's Way appear more agreeable, but not by much. I located the house and stood outside for a while, checking the neighbouring curtains for twitchers. There was no blood on the paving stones where Nev had discovered me. The rain, or maybe someone worried that the value of their flat might nosedive, had cleaned it away.

I went up the path and tried the door. It was locked. I rang the bell but nobody came to answer. Round the back of the terrace, I picked my way down an alleyway that was remarkably free of rubbish, but for a supermarket shopping trolley and a punctured football. It was almost tear-inducing not to see a stained mattress or a television with its cathode tube punched in. I had a peek over the wall and saw that the rear door of the flat belonging to this so-called Gary Cullen was swinging open on its hinges. I forced my way through the flaky gate and beat a path to it through the brambles, sun-bleached plastic toys and forgotten, mildewed washing hanging on the line in his wasteland of a backyard. Ancient plastic cider bottles were grouped together next to a bundle of sodden *Mirror*s tied up with string. Gardening tools leaned against the wall – a hoe, a rake, a spade with a deep crack in its blade – and all of them had seen more rust than soil during their lifetimes. There was also a stubby little garden fork with some nasty-looking tines, which I picked up, and a few lengths of rotten timber with bent, badly hammered nails sticking out of them.

I cupped my hands and, pressing them against the

window, stared into the kitchen; it was looking much as I'd left it the last time I was here. I could smell Melanie on my fingers, an emboldening fragrance, so I closed the door behind me and called out hello. No answer. Well, I'd had no answer last time, and paid for relying on the silence. Gripping the fork, I padded along the corridor, where there were still some fragments of crockery from the plate that had been dropped, and poked my head into the living room. The same nest of Pot Noodle cartons and copies of *Swank*. Maybe a few extra Heineken empties. And there were some nappies, some used, some waiting to be used, in a pile under the window, which I'd either missed last time or had recently been introduced to bolster the grime factor. I went to the window and checked outside, then shut the curtains, switched on the light and gave the room a full cough-and-drop examination.

The sofa was fucked. Even a throw couldn't disguise the slashes in the cushions and the monumental stains – paint, foodstuffs, any number of bodily fluids – that had Jackson Pollocked it to kingdom come. The carpet was pockmarked with threadbare patches, some so pronounced that you could see through to the floorboards. The wallpaper was rearing back from the walls, and who could blame it? A cupboard yielded a few cans of lager and a maxibag of Walker's salt-and-vinegar crisps, a chipped mug filled with screws, nails and washers, and a couple of Scart leads and aerial cables wrapped in polythene.

Out in the hall, the stairwell led up to a black throat. The doors to the other flats failed to lock in the stale stench of fast food and booze they contained. Whispers of it came down to me from the landing. There was a door under the stairwell with a padlock on it. I tried it anyway. The door rattled in its frame, and a dead echo fell away into the cellar.

My mobile chirruped in the stuffy closeness of the flat, causing me to jump. My voice sounded too surrounded, too hemmed in.

'Sorrell? Is that you?'

'Detective Inspector Ian Mawker. You know that an anagram of your name is *I'm a Wanker*?'

'Don't think you're the first to fill me in on that little gem, Sorrell. It's not clever. What are you doing out of hospital?'

'Freeing up a bed for some poor sod who needs it more. But I'm touched that you're checking up on me.'

'I'm doing anything but checking up on you. I want you somewhere – like, here. And now.'

'What if I'm busy?' I said.

'Put it off, Sorrell. I'm serious.'

He gave me an address in N16, adding, 'Be there within the hour.' And then he killed the line.

I went for a cup of coffee at one of the less offensive fast-food dives on Junction Road, then I had another. After that I strolled down Holloway Road and waited ten minutes for a 253 on Seven Sisters Road. The bus dropped me off on Amhurst Park, opposite a natty little terrace called The Trees. It had a gravel forecourt and mock-brass plaques announced its name. The other houses and synagogues and blocks of flats sneered at it. Mawker was leaning against the bonnet of a squad car, pouring coffee from one of those super-sleek brushed-steel flasks. Yellow police tape blocked off both the entrance and the exit to the parking area, and a police constable stood guard at one of the large red doors leading into the terrace. As I crossed the road, three men in white lab coats came out of the same door.

'I told you to be here within the hour,' Mawker said. I put

on a horrified expression and pointed at the roof; when he snapped his head that way, I plucked the cup out of his fingers.

'I did everything I could, everything, to make sure I was here later than you asked,' I said. The coffee was weak, and what flavour it might have had was now masked with too much sugar. I handed it back.

Mawker was wearing the same coat and tie as when he'd been to visit me in hospital. The collar of his shirt was fraying, and shadowy with sweat and grunge. He looked irritated by me already. 'Where are you living these days, Ian?' I said.

'Ealing,' he said wearily. 'Right, now that we've enjoyed our cosy bit of chit-chat, come with me.'

The PC stood to one side to allow us in, and we went up the stairs to the third floor. The smell hit us on the first landing. At the top of the stairs, another PC was standing just outside the only door, doing his best potted-plant impersonation. He was sucking extra strong mints to keep the smell from getting to him.

It was a small flat, but there was a lot of blood. Most of it was confined to the bedroom, although whoever had begun spilling it had walked it into the bathroom, the kitchen and the living room afterwards.

'Why am I here?' I said.

Mawker cocked his head at the bedroom, so I went to have a closer look. The body was still there, naked, erupted, strewn across the sheets like something from Professor Gunther von Hagens' shed.

'You know him?' Mawker said. 'Name of Liptrott.'

'Not sure,' I said. 'He seems to have lost a bit of weight.' Mawker looked at me with a pitying expression, as if I was a kid showing off at a party.

Liptrott had been unzipped. His face meanwhile bore the

expression of someone who has just been given a key to the room marked *Hot Pussy* only to find a cat in a microwave.

'How long's he been dead?' I asked.

Mawker looked at one of the lab coats. The lab coat said, 'Two days.'

Mawker said: 'Two days.' Then he said: 'Where were you oh, I don't know, let's say two days ago?'

'Fuck off, Ian,' I said. 'Doesn't he smell a bit rank for a two-dayer?'

'Heating's been on full blast,' the lab coat remarked.

Mawker pulled out his notebook and made a great play of opening it to the relevant page. 'We've got a statement from an Errol Bewsey, who works as a doorman at the Lava Java Dance Club in Vauxhall. Said you turned up looking for Barry Liptrott, and that your attitude...' he paused to consult his notes '..."minged".'

'So lock me up and throw away the key.'

'Why did you need to see Liptrott?'

'I wanted him to be best man at my wedding. He could still do it, if he likes.'

'Sorrell,' he warned, hard and cold. I was almost impressed.

'Okay,' I said, 'I'm trying to find a MisPer for a woman called Kara Geenan, probably not her real name. Lippy put her in touch with me. And then she disappeared right after someone tried to brain me, which I thought was interesting, as she gave me the address in the first place.'

'Go on,' Mawker prompted, as if I had a whole bunch of similar stories to tuck him into bed with.

'She claims that the guy I'm looking for is her brother. Says he's eighteen years of age.'

'Did she report him missing to the police?'

'Oh, I doubt it,' I said.

'Why?'

'A, because she reckoned he'd gone missing a mere matter of hours after her seeing him last. And B, because I think it was all a set-up. A trap.'

'For you?'

I smiled at him. 'What is it you're at now?' I said. 'Detective Inspector? What is it you have to do to get Detective Chief Superintendent? Put a ball through a hoop? Find your bollocks while blindfolded?'

He ignored me, which was the best way to deal with it, I suppose.

'So you went up to Lava Java to elicit her whereabouts from Liptrott?'

'Yeah, but he wasn't in. I talked to a friend of his, guy called Dayne. Used to own the place. He didn't know where Kara was, and he didn't know where Liptrott was. He was a veritable font.'

'Why you?'

'Why me what?'

'Why do you think this guy wants you dead? Apart from the obvious?'

'I don't know,' I said.

'Really?'

'Really.'

'I think the chap who did this tried to do you.'

'Gary Cullen? What's the link? Why would he suddenly start wanting to go on a killing spree like this?'

'You tell me.'

'No, *you* tell me. What's Cullen's form like?'

Mawker consulted his notes again. 'Petty crime, mostly. And then a bit of nastiness five years ago when he bit some guy's nose off in a brawl.'

'But nothing on this scale?'

'Not till now, no. However, it's not unknown for bag snatchers and petrol siphoners to graduate to this kind of bad.'

'Well,' I said, 'it had crossed my mind, although if Cullen did me, he seemed to a bit rushed, a bit amateurish. I mean, he twatted me and fucked off before I was even seeing stars. Doesn't compare to the character who did this. The cunt who did this hung about to make sure, and then hung about a bit more to admire his technique. If it was Cullen, he's come on a bit. And fast. But I don't reckon it was.'

'So what else do you know?'

'I know that Geenan was staying at the Paviours Arms in Westminster for a couple of months, pulling the landlord's pump, and I also know how to play the theme from *Bullitt* on a Jew's harp.'

I didn't tell him about her coming from Liverpool, because there was no point in having him wiping his dick all over the curtains in two cities. There was enough going on for him to fuck up down here.

Bloody footprints had been walked across the floorboards, but it looked as though the killer had been wearing slippers, or polythene bags over his shoes, leaving no prints, only patternless smears. All you could tell from those marks were the size of his feet.

'Been any others like this lately?' I asked.

'No,' Mawker replied. 'But I'm as eager to find this Geenan woman as you are. Perhaps even more eager.'

He looked tired. I wondered if he'd been on holiday at all in the last five years, and I doubted it. He was one of those men who took his work home with him, drank with it in the evenings and slept with it in his bed. Mawker lived alone. All of his thoughts were focused on crime and trying to stop it, or on cleaning up afterwards. There was nothing left for fripperies such as new suits, fresh razor blades, holidays. Or women. I'd asked him once, when he was a few pints into an evening, if he was seeing anyone. He looked at me as if I'd offered him his mother in a sandwich. I don't think he found a spare moment in the day to even begin to consider what he was missing out on. Which I felt sorry about, if only because it meant he was constantly hanging around like a fart in a sauna.

'Well, I'll make sure I let you know when I find her.'

'You do that,' he said, tediously.

I left just then, before he could think of anything to keep me there longer. I would have liked to have mooched around in the flat on my own for a bit, see what I could have turned up, but there was no chance of that. Mawker and me had never really clicked at Bruche. He had been to university and went in on accelerated, became a textbook copper, did the exams, moved into CID and rose rapidly. I followed my nose a bit more, and I made more collars than he did, but they were messy collars that usually ended up with innocents and back-up getting hurt. After the nth carpeting and the business with Rebecca, I got out. I didn't see my police career as political; I wasn't about to become a pawn for the top ranks to play around with. I wasn't interested in arresting shoplifters who were too skint to buy themselves or their children a bottle of milk. I couldn't care less if someone was nicking CDs and video games from the local HMV. I merely wanted the hard cases done over: policing was a war as far as I was concerned. There was a lot of scum in the city and I wanted to get it skimmed off.

Top brass didn't like that. I was too rough for them. I was dangerous. They were scared that someone might get killed if I went after a villain, thus bringing down a huge pile of shit on to their desks. So they gave me a desk job, too, and the guy who gave it me is still picking the splinters from it out of his arse.

Before I reached Seven Sisters Road, I got the shakes bad and had to sit down on a low wall hemming in one of the numerous estates that muscle on to the road leading down to Manor House tube station.

Where's your smart mouth now, Joel my lad? Where's the quipping and the lipping and the gypping now?

My fat mouth was staying tight shut, because otherwise it was likely to spit my breakfast and a litre of coffee all over the shop. On the food chain, Liptrott might have been several links down from a bucket of runny shit, but he was essentially harmless, and he had died badly. Very badly. I didn't like to witness death in any of its forms, but I didn't like to see anyone suffer a violent death, no matter how unpleasant they were. Mainly because it was not nice to look at, but also because it was – strange to say this, but I can't think of a better way – *disrespectful*. Violent kills showed a complete disregard for the most basic human connection. One person doing that to another person, it beggars belief. How could you want to unshackle mortality like that, drag it out in the open, steaming and red? How could you yourself face up to that unless you were as far away from being human as it was possible to get without being a different kind of animal?

I also didn't like it because it reminded me of the day I'd walked in on my battered, gutted, *emptied* wife.

I clutched hard to that wall and quelled the nausea,

fought back the hot tears, and watched my hands carefully until they stopped shaking. Resorting to the mouth, I knew, was bad sometimes, but it was my way of dealing with it. Mawker had his treadmill, a routine of steadfast plodding after clues, which reminded me of a machine part performing the same, monotonous act day in, day out. Some people relied on drink or drugs. Some people drove it out of themselves with sport. I had my mouth. My mouth got me into trouble sometimes, too many times, but every time I opened it, it saved my life just a little bit.

Feeling better, I set off walking, and I discovered two things by the time I reached Finsbury Park. One was that Mawker had dispatched a tail, and two was that the guy was as raw as they come. The thing about following people is that it's tough to do it well. The best pursuits are all about anticipation. They can even follow you from the front and second-guess your moves. They sense you're going to hang a left into the shopping precinct, or a right into the car park, probably before you do. But this clown...

I stopped at a coffee shop across from the park entrance and took the only space that was left by the window. Finsbury Park is one of those parts of London that nobody goes to during the day. It's an in transit place, so nobody hangs around on the streets, unless it's a tramp with a can of electric soup and the need to shout a lot at his invisible friends. There were no other free tables in the coffee shop, but he gamely followed me in, knowing at least that to hang around outside was to expose himself even further. He stood at the counter with his coffee while people craned around him, to give their 'to go' orders to the flustered staff.

I took my time. After I finished my cup, I borrowed a newspaper from an off-duty garbage-disposal guy and flicked through it in a leisurely fashion. By now my shadow had been sipping from the same coffee cup for the last thirty minutes. A small cup, so what? Hot coffee? Yeah, right. He was starting to look around into the corners of the ceiling now, as if he was some amateur room designer with new ideas for the place. He asked an Italian girl, who was filling a tray of mugs with stewed tea from an urn, what colour the walls were – 'Is that sunset pink?' – and was given a look that said 'No, it's fuck-you red.' When he tried to borrow a paper, the builder slid it away from him, saying he hadn't finished it yet, before going back to a conversation with his companion.

After that we went on a long walk south through the crumbling roadside houses of Holloway. I had a long chat about Liptrott's death with an off-duty forensics guy I knew called Fentiss, who was trying to flag a cab on a street corner while my tail spent so much time looking into the window of a dry cleaner's that Fentiss eventually noticed him too. We both turned to watch Mr Green as he rubbed his chin in front of the *3 suits cleaned for the price of 2* deals. Fentiss informed me, on the q.t., that everybody down at Scotland Yard was wetting his pants over Liptrott because Merseyside police had an unexplained death on their files, from five years ago that bore the same MO. Great, I thought, fucking Liverpool again. Of all the cities in all the world, it had to be that one that dunked its chips in my gravy.

I ended up losing the tail by hopping on a bus as it was about to depart from the bus stop. I blew him a kiss from the rear window as he stood at the same stop, before he checked his watch and then glanced back along the road. There was another bus coming along. I shook my head: *Follow that bus.* He was out of sight by the time it arrived, so I got off at the next stop, walked behind a wall and waited for his bus to drive by. He was standing by the driver, peering out into the distance.

I caught another bus and followed his bus into the terminus at Euston. He was nowhere to be seen as I hopped off. I sent Mawker a text message: *th@ ws an inslt, knbhd*, and then I went into the train station and booked a ticket to my past.

8

I didn't want to travel up north for any number of reasons. Mawker had warned me not to leave London, so I didn't want to incur his wrath... nah, only kidding. I didn't know how long I'd be gone for and it would mean that Melanie might go off the simmer for me. Also, I needed to get to Kara Geenan and her so-called brother – Phythian – before anybody else ended up like an entry at a blind butchers' carving competition. I was pinning my hopes on this Phythian fucker, even though I had yet to be convinced that he actually existed.

Cullen didn't sit right with what had happened so far. Mawker had said he'd done a runner from Summerhead, a relatively low-security mental hospital that was based, coincidentally (I hoped), in the north-west of England, which was another reason to head up that way. But what did that mean? How many nutcases slipped their handcuffs and wandered off in search of a bit of fun? If it could happen in *One Flew Over the Cuckoo's Nest*, it could happen in Summerhead. So I didn't want to go, but there seemed to be more reasons for me to go than there were keeping me here in the Smoke.

Kara and her brother would be down here while I was up there, however, and although visiting Liverpool might give me some idea as to why they were in London, it wouldn't provide me with a map to their front door. But, mainly, going up to Liverpool was also going home, and that was the grit in my Vaseline. It was like continually ripping a plaster from a cut only to find that it just isn't healing.

I hadn't been back to the north-west since coming down to London in 2001. I realised, after buying the ticket, that more than anything else it was because getting out of the big city would be tantamount to marooning Sarah here, although there was no logic to suggest that this was where she actually was. Just because she went missing here didn't mean she was still missing here. I forced myself to accept that this journey was something I was going to have to do. I thought it was marginally crucial in order to try to save my own life, though many might have disagreed. *Listen*, I instructed myself, *it isn't London where Sarah's missing from; it's somewhere inside you.* And that place was always going to be with me, no matter where I went.

It was getting on for late afternoon, but I didn't want to go back to Maida Vale yet. I walked down Tottenham Court Road, past all the electrical goods shops with their displays of gadgets that were getting so small you were given a complimentary magnifying glass with every purchase. I had a half of lager at the French House on Dean Street, standing outside because the place was stuffed full of people with portfolios and surfer beards and mobile phones that played the theme tune from *Coronation Street* in an ironic way.

Liptrott had been *slaughtered*, yet there were no signs of a struggle. I think I myself might have put up a bit of a fight

104

rather than just stretch out on the bed and let it happen. That meant he must have known his murderer. Either that or Cullen, or whoever, was in the flat before Liptrott got home. I explored that avenue a little further and – as insane as it sounded because presumably the killer wouldn't have known how long he would have to wait there, maybe hours – it tugged on my handle more than anything else. He possessed Grasshopper's stealth; could walk on rice-paper without tearing it, but that didn't tally with the clumsy approach of my guy in St John's Way. So what did that mean? An off day, or two men involved?

The other option, that Liptrott already knew him, surely couldn't work. Why would Liptrott pretend to me that he was acting as go-between for Kara, if Kara and he both knew that Phythian wasn't a MisPer? Unless I myself was the point of the whole thing, and they needed Liptrott to be offed because he might become my way in to their world. Liptrott couldn't have realised that I was in that kind of danger. He was a crim, okay, but he wasn't hardcore. Violence was to him what a steak pudding is to a vegan's shopping list.

If Kara and Cullen were from Liverpool, then it might make sense that they were in it simply to get me, although I couldn't think of anybody who had held any grudges against me from my days as a trainee copper or, before that, as taxi driver shuttling clients along the East Lancs Road and the M62. Not grudges sufficient that they'd wanted me dead, at least.

I decided it was time to go and check out my flat. A couple of days had passed since the burglary, and if anybody had been sitting outside in a surveillance car they'd have an arse like two pieces of frozen ham by now, as well as a severe dislike of coffee. Back on my road, I dawdled by the awning of the wine bar on the corner and gave the street the once over. A skip was sitting on the roadway, its tarpaulin cover failing to conceal a riot of broken office furniture, lumps of plaster and an enamel bath. The cars parked along the street were dark and apparently empty, but no, there was a scarred little Golf opposite my door, with a large shadow in the driving seat. I hung back a little and rubbed my mouth. A couple of days' beard growth rasped like indecision made audible. Then I remembered, with some surprise, that I had a killing machine down the front of my jeans. As well as a gun. I palmed the Glock and edged down the blind side of the row of cars. The driver was kind of hunched over on his side, his head resting on the window. Maybe he was asleep.

I opened the passenger door, got in and pushed the barrel of the gun into his 'nads. I said, 'What's your fucking door policy on that, fat boy?'

The bouncer sat up quick and straight, like a classroom pupil hoping to be picked to wipe the blackboard. His eyes were as wet and large as would be the wound in his groin if he didn't start talking. I said as much.

'Knocker sent me,' he said. 'He wanted me to beat some info out of you.'

'Why?'

'Liptrott's dead.'

'I know that.'

'Knocker wants to know if you had anything to do with it.'

I shook my head. 'Do I look like a killer? I mean, do I? Christ, everybody wants to know if I had something to do with it.'

The bouncer was looking at the gun nestling deep in his pods. 'I didn't know you had a gun,' he said.

'No,' I said, 'I hate guns. So if you're nice to me, I'll put it away.'

'I'm just doing my job.'

'No,' I said again. 'Errol, isn't it? Your job is to punch the spines out of people who try to get into Lava Java wearing trainers. Your job is to lift weights all day until you look like you put your jacket on but forgot to take the coat hanger out. Your job—'

'Oh, for fuck's sake,' he said, relaxing now that he knew I wasn't the hard case I was making out. 'Shoot me. You'll be doing me a favour.'

Just then I saw a shadow fall across the oriel window set into the top-floor landing where my flat is. There was a wink of light, a cigarette maybe, and then it was all back to normal.

'How long have you been here?' I asked Errol, withdrawing the Glock from his sack and pushing it back into my waistband.

'Off and on, about twenty-four hours. With piles.'

'I'll send them a Get Well card if you do me a favour.'

'Why should I do anything for you, other than stave your face in?'

I licked my lips. I could feel my mouth going dry, the way it always goes when violence is only minutes away.

'Somebody wants me dead,' I said. 'And I think the person who wants me dead is in that building, waiting for me to come back.'

'That sounds suspiciously like your problem,' Errol said, getting cockier by the second.

'Yeah, well, I think he killed Liptrott, too. And if we get him, then that's a new puffa jacket and steel toecaps for Doorman Number One, don't you think? See it as a career move. And anyway, I've got a piece. How bad could it go?'

He thought about it, his face taking on the intensity of a mathematical theorist grizzling over a four-pencil problem. 'We nail him,' he replied, 'I take him.'

'I get to talk to him first,' I said.

'Deal,' said the bouncer, the dumb, trusting A-wipe.

We got out of the car and hurried over to the front door. I said, 'Go upstairs and knock on my door in five minutes. If he gives you any grief, tell him you're a bailiff coming to secure chattels or something. Just stand in the doorway. You'll know what to do as soon as I open it.'

He looked at his watch as I nipped over to the communal door of the next terraced house, which formed part of the same block of flats. I rang every doorbell in turn, and a couple of seconds later a woman answered.

'Cockroach man,' I said.

'Not for me,' she said.

I said, 'They will be. They're coming up through the basement, big as mice.'

She buzzed me in. I ran up the stairs two at a time and thanked God the layout was exactly the same as my own gaff, only mirrored. I unbolted the attic hatch at the top landing and lumbered my way up through there, wishing I had a torch instead of a gun. I resolved to start smoking immediately, if only because it would mean I'd have matches in my pocket all the time. I shuffled to my right in the gloom, trying not to make any noise to alert the flats directly beneath me. My neighbours wouldn't have heard me anyway; they were arguing with each other over an unpaid phone bill that contained '*abaht firty facking pahndswuff of facking chat lines, you cant!*' The hole that the burglar had kicked in, in order to get down into my flat, was faintly visible just up ahead. Empty storage boxes barred my way, but it was a

108

relief to find that was all there was, and that there was no dividing attic wall.

I hung over the lip of the hole and the mess inside my flat gradually emerged from the darkness. I swung a leg over and dropped to the floor as quietly as I could, which wasn't very. Then I tiptoed grittily over to the door where it slouched on its hinges and peeked out through the crack between it and the jamb. Errol was coming up the stairs, and I could see the shadow of the guy on the landing jittering around as if he was made of candle flames. Then Errol's head rose into view and the other guy was jabbering questions at him, warning him, but in an uncertain way, as you do when about seventeen stones of meat joins you in a confined space.

Errol now blocked out all the light. I saw the edge of his coat, and a drawn look on his face, which was probably not wholly the result of climbing three flights of stairs. He knocked three times on the door.

I heard the nervy guy: 'It's padlocked from the outside. The *outside*. Fuck's sake, what are you? Dense or something?'

I teased the muzzle of the gun through the gap and against the padlock. I squeezed the trigger. The lock spun off and hit Errol in the hand. He spun away with a grunt and tottered backwards on his heels, as I swung the door open. The guy was shrieking and he kept ducking in and out of view, keeping Errol between me and him while he wrestled to pull something from his pocket. He looked as comfortable as a hedgehog born with ingrowing prickles. Sweat lashed off him and turned his bad haircut into something intolerable. His tiny eyes flashed unhealthily like the gleam you see on blobs of tar. On his throat was a black tattoo: a cobra's head, all fanned out ready to strike.

I kicked Errol in the chest to hurry him up and he went

over on to his back, cracking the balustrade with one foot and putting a dent into the plaster of the wall with the other. He piled into the little wanker, who folded over on top of him. He continued scrabbling in his pocket, even when I pressed the hot mouth of the gun against his cheek. My hands were shaking and the sweat was dripping off my face.

'Who are you?' I demanded, my voice trembling, but emerging harsh as hell. I didn't know which way this was going to go. Errol was trying to get up; he was moaning about his hand and the fact that I had kicked him down the stairs. All the while, I kept my eye on the little wanker's pocket, and repeated the question, my voice sounding a little more unhinged. I could barely hear myself above the throb of blood in my head. I was now roaring in every possible way. Doors were opening, and then rapidly closing again.

Under the probing muzzle of the gun, I could see how his skin was in poor condition. It wrinkled away from the metal, but didn't snap back with the kind of elasticity you'd expect from someone who appeared to be in his late twenties. It also seemed his teeth were doing all they could to say cheerio to his gums: there were a lot of black joins in his mouth. I reckoned, if I pulled back his sleeve, there would be a lot of black marks up his arms too.

He pulled out a long-bladed knife. And that seemed fine. I expected that from a low-life grunt like this. He brandished it and, yes, that was what people with knives often did. I wasn't so happy about his apparent disregard for my gun, however, and I was even more appalled when he drew the knife across his own throat, painting the walls, Errol and myself in what seemed like an endless hot tide of his own blood.

9

You ever try going for a nice, chatty pizza when that kind of shit has gone down?

Give me credit, I had a go. But first I spent a lovely part of the evening down at Marylebone Police Station, giving statements and being mercilessly grilled. They were at least nice enough to get me a fresh change of clothes so I could walk the streets of London without resembling a vampire with a drinking problem. All I could think about – as the burly BO magnets at the nick were leaning over me and playing bad cop, badder cop – was how controlled, how graceful the little wanker's suicide cut had been, when prior to that he had been moving like the jags on an oscilloscope.

When they finally let me go I phoned Melanie to tell her I'd be a little late, but she was okay about it, told me she was reading a medical journal over a G&T at the restaurant. She asked me if I was all right, and I said sure, even though I knew the tightness in my voice must be giving me away. I liked that she was waiting for me, trusted that I was going to show up, but a part of me wished that she had thrown a strop and gone home, vowing never to grant me a second of her non-professional time again. Things were going very bad, very fast and I was scared that I was bringing too much naughty into her life. I was glad of Mawker's new tail, who was even more cack-handed than the previous one, so I went out of my way to make sure he didn't let me give him the slip on the way back to W9.

At the restaurant I immediately told Melanie what had happened, and that I couldn't stay at her place any more if I was to feel secure in the knowledge that she would be safe. She was a little shell-shocked by my news, which I had expected, but I wasn't expecting her to say that it was all right, she'd be all right, it was okay for me to stay.

'I can't… I won't have what happened at my flat happening at your place,' I said.

'How can it?' she said. 'It's Maida Vale. Where newspapers are ironed and underwear changed twice a day. People go out for weekend breakfasts in a *suit*.'

I told her I had to leave London anyway for a few days, that it would be for the best if I took a little heat away from her front door. Until everything was sorted out.

'By that you mean until you're dead?'

'Anything but that would mean sorted out, in my book,' I said.

'But it's a possibility.'

'It was damned near a fact earlier today,' I said, knocking back half a glass of chilled Chardonnay and wishing I'd ordered something stronger.

'Where are you going?' she asked. The question was intoned neutrally, but there was the slightest tilting of her eyebrows. Our relationship had shifted. There was a degree of concern trying to melt away the ice at her edges, and it touched me. Except I wish it had happened at any other point but now. I'd never been brilliant when it came to…

'Where will you stay in Liverpool?'

…timing.

'That part of the world, the north-west, it's my old stamping ground,' I said. 'I've got plenty of contacts up there I can depend on.'

'Old girlfriends, you mean?'

'Not necessarily. There are some, but they'd sooner fry my arse off with a bit of garlic than give me a sofa for the night.'

'Popular with the ladies, were you?'

'Notorious, more like,' I said, and tried to divert the evening in other directions because faces were trying to push through. There'd be time enough for memories once I stepped off the train, but not now. Not with this woman.

We finished our drinks and pushed our empty plates away. I paid the bill, and felt guilty when I wished that she'd offered to deal with it. I needed to get hold of some cash from somewhere soon – my stash at Keepsies wasn't going to last for ever – or I was going to find myself visited by some real hard men, bailiffs bigger than Errol, with sledgehammer fists and back-brain sensitivities.

It was unseasonably mild as we walked the pleasant streets back to her flat. At the corner to her road, I stopped her and said goodbye.

'Come inside,' she said. 'Just for a little while.' The backs of her fingers pressed against my stomach, slid a millimetre down behind the waistband of my jeans. 'Just so I can say goodbye.'

I kissed her on the forehead and stepped out of reach. 'It isn't safe,' I said. 'Look after Mengele for me. I'll call you. And if you feel lonely or scared or anything, give Keith Bellian a ring.' I spelled out his surname for her. 'He's in the book. Tell him I told you to call him, and he'll come and get you.'

'Keith Bellian,' she repeated. I nodded and walked away.

I turned back once I heard her footsteps making their way to the front gate, and I watched until she was safely behind the closed door. Still I remained, watching the street, looking for any signs that there was someone wise to her involvement, but the street was quiet and, like me, sleepy.

I headed back to the tube but paused to tie a bootlace in a drive on Chalcot Crescent. 'Evening, PC Subtle,' I said, addressing the shadows.

'Bastard,' came a voice from the azaleas.

'The girl I was with, you'd be better off keeping watch over her,' I said. 'She's worth more than a dozen of me.' And then I was away.

PART TWO

WiRE

Wire pocketed the money from her purse – a matter of twenty pounds and a handful of shrapnel – and with it he bought himself dinner: pasta, lean chicken, steamed vegetables, a bottle of mineral water. No wine. No dessert. Keep control. Know your body. Your limits and levels.

She had a little label tucked into the side of the purse: *If lost, please return to… a reward will be given.*

He caught a tube to Tufnell Park. The woman had lived in an attractive Georgian house on Dartmouth Park Road. Leafy. He liked streets with trees on them. He liked trees. He had no compunction about giving trees a hug.

He watched the house for hours. He did this safe in the knowledge that neighbourhood awareness was not as honed locally as it was back home in Liverpool. There was much more of a serve-yourself attitude here. He knew about London. He wasn't stupid.

Once it was apparent that there was nobody at home, he slipped in through the front gate and kicked in the basement window. He slid through it into a room with a sofa and a desk with a computer on it. The room was very white. Even the computer was white. The only things that weren't white included a potted plant and a bowl of Granny Smith apples. A white guitar, a Les Paul, hung on the wall, and it was the only thing that did. He moved up the steps to the ground floor, where a piano stood in the hall. Pages of sheet music, basic children's stuff – 'If I Had a Hammer', 'Little Boxes' – rested on the music stand. An empty Ski yogurt pot had been left on the stairs, a screwed-up tissue and a clog of hair stuffed inside. In the kitchen, a casserole sat in the centre of the table, with a pink, heart-shaped Post-it note tacked to its lid: *H. Lamb stew… middle shelf @ 180, soon as you get in. Love you, Lx*

Messy, bright pictures – unrecognisable daubs of paint that might have been dinosaurs or flowers, or pictures of Mum and Dad – were fixed to the fridge with magnets.

He climbed the stairs. First floor: two bedrooms obviously belonging to children. Toys all over the floor. Characters from *Thomas the Tank Engine*, *Toy Story*, *Ben 10* on the walls. Second floor: bathroom, Mum and Dad's bedroom. She was an untidy woman, in private: jumpers and jeans and cargo trousers lay around like deflated bodies. He went through her stuff in a desultory fashion, and he did not flinch when he heard the front door creak open, and noise instantly filled the house.

He went up to the third floor even as he heard the trampling of footsteps and the shriek of laughter, as the children ascended. Further away, he heard car keys drop on the kitchen table, then music – Radiohead, he thought it was – and the clink of cutlery as dinner places were set.

The third floor was a work area: two studies, a small bathroom with compact shower, toilet and sink. Her study faced the same road that he had just been watching from. No computer in here, just a desk with a large notebook on it, a simple wooden chair with a blanket over the back, a bookcase that held lots of gardening and cookery volumes. At the back of a drawer in the desk he found a large tin which yielded a Jim Crace paperback, a carton of Colgate dental gum, two tampons, two plastic wallets containing handwritten notes, phone numbers and contact names, an old diary, a tube of Smarties and a Siemens mobile phone with a cracked screen.

He flipped through the diary and found photographs of Linda looking much younger. Most of them were of her and some guy called Si, to whom she had written little messages of love on the rear. In one of the photos she was baring her breasts and blowing a kiss. In another, she was sucking the thumb of the person taking the picture in a lascivious fashion, her eyes half closed. Apart from three ten-pound notes hidden inside the paperback, he found nothing else of interest. He put everything back in the desk. Then he lifted his holdall on to the desk and shoved his knife into a side pocket. He didn't need to wipe it clean, because it was so sharp that it cleaned itself on the way out of whatever it had been stuck in. ok.

From the bottom of the holdall, under an oil-stained towel, he pulled out a plastic carrier bag. He unwrapped the gun as if removing some kind of binding from an item of religious treasure. Show respect. Show dangerous things respect, and they won't bite back. The butt was wrapped with masking tape, and the registration number had been filed off. He stared at the silver plating and curled his finger around the trigger. A .38 snub-nosed Smith & Wesson with the cylinder loaded and ready to do what it did best. It was a revolver, so the shell casings were retained within the gun, which meant that there was less evidence for forensics to work on should he ever be obliged to use it. He had bought it in the Old Swan for two hundred pounds from a guy called Ryan. He never even asked if it had been used to kill anybody, since he was too together for that kind of paranoid chat. That kind of chat could get around, and he didn't want to become known as someone whose lips were always on the flap. Someone who was borderline shitting it.

A young voice calling down the stairs: 'Dad, can we watch *Flapjack*?' Not yet, according to Dad, who then turned up the music a notch to drown out any more requests.

Wire tucked the gun back into its hiding place and stepped over to the window. He jabbed his fingers at the numbers on the dead woman's phone. Wherever you may be in London, he had heard, you are less than eight feet away from a rat. Maybe the same could be said of weapons, too. Everyone seemed to be carrying these days. On the Wire's own patch in Liverpool, he didn't know anyone who didn't carry a chiv or a cosh or a gun. One guy never went out without a pair of Bowie knives hidden down his trousers. It was even worse in London, from what he'd heard. But he didn't like guns, considered them too much of a liability. Knives were the craftsman's tool. But, then, this was the Smoke and you had to have a gun to get ahead. No time for craftsmen down here. Well, maybe he'd show them how to think differently.

Now he heard 'Who?' The voice was flat, disinterested. It sounded too cultured for the number he had dialled. This number was supposed to be his *in*, his friend in the big, bad, bloody city. Maybe he had misdialled.

'This is Wire,' he said, his voice soft, like a child's voice still. 'This is the Four-Year-Old. How are you? It's been a while. Did you…?'

The voice was back again, cutting through him – naughty, naughty, but let it go. 'There's a phone booth corner of Seven Sisters Road and Woodberry Grove. Be there in an hour.'

The Wire wanted to ask questions, but instead he pressed the 'call end' button, knowing that the voice had done just the same. He had learned quickly that patience meant everything in this business. The lack of it undid you, put you inside. Wire checked his *A-Z* and figured, yes, he could be in Manor House in half an hour. But first, but first...

On one wall the dead woman had hung a cork board. Photographs, theatre tickets and letters from friends were pinned to it. He reached into his pocket and pulled out a small plastic box filled with self-adhesive gold stars. In each picture of her, he concealed her face with them. While he worked, he found himself thinking about his mother, something he did more and more these days. The redness of her lips. The way her clothes hung on her. The blonde hair.

He was still thinking of her as he slipped down the stairs, with his holdall over his shoulder, not checking to see if the children had spotted him, because of course they hadn't; not checking to see if the father was likely to walk into the hall, because why would he? He was the Wire. He was invisible. He was out in the street once more, and turning his face to the sky, fighting the tears, and he always won. He always beat the tears back, but there was only one person who ever threatened to draw them out of him. And she was nowhere now. Like him. Like him.

It might be sunny outside, but to us there's shadows and rain all over the fucking place. Me ma came in just now and asked us what I wanted for me tea. I goes shepherd's pie, peas, chips, bread and butter. She said right, buckethead, that's your starters sorted, so what do you want for your mains? Least, I wish that's what happened. I can make them come to me, the daydreams, if I close me eyes and I'm alone in a silent room. Everything's clear in me head, what she smells like (she wears this perfume called Charlie), what she's wearing – sometimes she's got a button missing on her cardi or her necklace has twisted, the one she liked best with all the tiny conch shells on it – and the way she's got her hair; but her voice and her face won't form. I look at it and it kind of mists over, as if she's too shy to let us see it. I know why that is. It's not 'cos she's shy or me imagination is letting us down. I know what Ma looks like. I carry her with us wherever I go. It's because she… it's the way she…

Turn and face.

Mr Tones' voice in me head. Good name, Mr Tones, for a PE teacher. I liked him. He was a Scouser like us. Was. What a divvy. Still is. Once a Scouser, always a Scouser. I bunked off whenever we did cross-country or 1500 metres. If you're fourteen, you shouldn't be doing cross-country. And I was only two at the time. That kind of lark is for spindly old bastards with digital watches and beards wearing shiny shorts that go right up your crack. I think he knew, but he never said nowt. Everything else I liked. Football most, of course. There's a bit of football in every Liverpudlian's blood. Tonesy said to us once, he said, 'If I had your left foot, I'd be playing for Manchester United.'

'I'm not that shite, am I, sir?' I said and everyone fell about laughing.

I played left-wing, John Barnes, me. I took everyone on, made them look like cunts. Tonesy said I could ghost past players. I liked the sound of that. But I could move, too.

'Skin him,' Tonesy would shout if I just had the right back to beat and press on the gas and, see yer mate, have a nice time down there on yer arse with all the other worms. Then cross the ball in with the sweet left foot for Connie or Wez or Warbo to nut in. Either that or bury it meself. Leather it. No chance, 'keeper. Pick that one out.

End of every attack, Tonesy calling out to us, Turn and face, and as one we'd twist round so we were facing the ball, back-pedalling, keeping our eyes on the ball every moment. A new start, a new play. Find your man. Mark him. Keep your eye on the ball. Never look away.

I don't know what her voice was like. I lie awake at night sweating over that. I wish she could have recorded her voice for posterity. It kills us to think that I'll never know how her laughter sounded. Looking at her picture, well, you just can't tell from the look of her, can you?

If I'd been old enough to go to a school where the kids were old enough to know how to be cruel, I'd probably have been called Dads, 'cos I seemed to have had more than me fair share of them. I don't remember any specifically, but Ma's diaries say it all. She wasn't a slut, me mother, and anyone says she was'll find themselves grinning through a second gob, she was just a lonely mare in search of company. They flitted in and out of her life like restless cats, staying for no longer than a few months. Her emotions were all fucked up, though. She was clingy, making demands that they couldn't deal with. She recognised this and wrote about it in her diary. The entries start off neatly enough, the handwriting resting on the faint lines on the paper, but it isn't long before the words start jagging about, becoming crushed just to fit on the page, the margins crammed, the sentences loaded with swear words and question marks. It's *hard to believe that she would go to work and spend the day with a classroom of kids, like a completely different person, being as breezy as I know she was, open and friendly to her pupils and colleagues. I've seen the cards they sent her, wrapped up in tissue paper and tied off with ribbon. They all loved her. There wasn't a single person who came into her life who didn't love her, for a while, for at least a little bit. Except...*

Turn and face.

He made it to the telephone kiosk at Manor House a couple of minutes before the appointed time. The night had further defined itself during his journey underground; only a palest stripe of dark blue under the black indicated that daylight had ever had anything to do with this broken place. The traffic on the Seven Sisters Road was ugly and fast: grubby white vans; sleek, executive cars driven by scowling faces, erratically steered Volvos. The cars slowed down for the speed cameras, and then tore away. It was a relief to get away from the sound of howling engines when the phone in the kiosk rang. He closed the door behind him and picked up the receiver. –'Don't talk,' the voice says, the same voice, 'just listen. I am not happy about your being here. I don't think it's a good idea. I know you believe you're up to it. You're clean, simple and fast. And I like the sound of that. I know you've grown. I know you're impatient. But I can deal with this. I don't want you harmed. I will not allow that to happen, my sweet. But, for now, I have something for you to do. I have someone.' She passes on an address and the name of the target. –'I'll watch you every step of the way.' And then the line goes dead. The Wire – the Four-Year-Old

– steps into the noise and chill once more. He's feeling the gentle curve of the combat knife against his thigh and can almost imagine the quilted Micarta handle in his fingers, so familiar that it's like a part of his hand. He feels clumsy without the weapon. He can't remember a time when he didn't own one.

Me memories feel false, as made-up as the words in a book. But they say that even the most wildly imagined novels have a bit of truth in them, bits of a lived life tucked in by the author, little grains that give the feeling of truth to the whole thing. I was four when she died (no, I was one, remember, I was only one when she died) but, through the diaries and the few photographs of her that I've got, I feel as if I've known her for much longer.

We lived in a quiet little two-up-two-down. She looked after us well. I know this because I've still got all the clothes she bought us when I was a baby. Ironed, folded up and stored in a big suitcase. They have me name stitched into the collars and waistbands. Also, in her diary, during calm times, she wrote notes to us, or else poems. On the date of me birth – 29th February 1996 – she'd glued a picture of us, a few days old, and drawn a big red love heart next to it. When I got older, old enough to start looking after meself, I met up with a few of the men who spent a little time with her, got to know her through them. I never held a grudge against them. It wasn't their fault they couldn't bear me ma's strange moods.

One of them I got on with all right. His name was Neil Lever, a bloke who used to work in a chip shop in New Brighton when he was seeing her, the last person to be with me mother before she topped herself. He thought I'd tracked him down because I wanted to kick his head in. He cowered away from us in this little Wirral pub, where they served beer called Wobbly Bob and people sat outside eating lunch: plates of what the menu called chilli con carne but what I knew had come out of a tin and had a bit of curry powder mixed up with it. I'd seen their kitchens, and nothing gets past me.

Lever thought I thought he'd driven her to it. I liked the feeling that gave us, his cowering away from us, but I told him I wasn't there for any aggro. I just wanted to hear about me ma. Once he could see I didn't want any money out of him, and that the only thing I was happy banging on the counter was an empty pint glass, he opened up a bit and told us about the few months he'd spent with her.

The target was within walking distance: Amhurst Park. It was a large road, but it seemed to be used as little more than a rat-run. Cars screeched along it from the Seven Sisters Road, or Stamford Hill, and bombed past squat blocks of flats masked with scaffolding and brick nets, crumbling synagogues and masses of fat black bin bags. He walked quickly past a large queue of people at the bus stop, who were more interested in what might or might not be coming along the road than noticing who he was. And that was good. He felt comfortable among people, in the thick of them, because they tended not to pay him much attention. He had something grey about him, something bland, despite his physicality: he could blend into his background. The address emerged among the hedges on his right, a Victorian terrace set back off the road. A gravel forecourt was packed with a variety of cars: a Ford Cougar, a Rover 25, a Golf GTi plastered with dead leaves and sap from the lime trees, a black and red TVR that looked as if it hadn't been driven for years. He skipped up the steps to the front door and casually glanced around at the main road and the people on the street. There was a fat guy washing a Citroën Xsara but, bar the speeding cars, the rest of the street wasn't too busy. Kids playing with a wheel rim in a vacant parking space. A dog checking out the smells in an overgrown garden. The Four-Year-Old was protected by the screen of hedges, and by the trees, ready to do his best, and his worst.

He pressed the button for Number 18, but there was no reply and that was good too; that made things that little bit easier. He tried the buzzer to the ground-floor flat, the curtains of which were twitching. A woman with a scratchy voice answered. –'It's Dave,' said the Wire. 'I locked myself out. Can you let me in?'–'Dave? Hang on.' He watched the woman unlock her door and peer out at him from the communal landing. He smiled and shrugged, all sweetness and light. She was wearing a threadbare dressing gown with more stains than material on it, and her hair was mussed and matted. She moved slowly towards the front door, her limbs swollen and bent like a child's drawing of an old person. But this woman could not have been that old. She moved into the light and he saw she was quite young, perhaps only in her late thirties. Her back was hunched and her legs moved stiffly, as if she was walking on stilts. She fumbled at the lock with pink claws. Seriously, seriously fucked. –'What flat are you?' she asked. –'Nineteen. I moved in a couple of weeks ago.' –'Oh, right. People move in and out here so quickly these days,' she droned on. 'I've been here ten years, and I won't be going anywhere else.' She got the door open finally and he pushed past her towards the stairs. 'Listen,' she continued, 'if I gave you something to sign, a petition for a handrail to go outside, would you sign it for me? I've got MS. It's a swine getting up them steps. They'll do it if enough people sign.' –'No problem,' said the Wire. She smelled of sour alcohol and stale cigarette smoke. Lipstick made her look tragically clownish. He said: 'You wouldn't have a metal coat-hanger by any chance, would you?'

On the top floor, there were two flats. He listened at the door of Number 19 for a moment, but there was only silence, nobody home. It took just under a minute, with the coat-hanger through the letterbox at 18, before he caught the latch. Inside, he allowed the flat's smells and sounds to sink into him. He stood at the doorway of each room, assessing their contents, memorising them: the kitchen with its piles of dirty dishes and takeaway food cartons. The Jordan calendar on the wall above an empty bottle of Woodpecker cider and an ashtray crammed with scorched roaches. The living room with its battered La-Z-Boy, the 36-inch Mitsubishi widescreen, the pile of videos: *Dr Fellatio's Marathon Suck-Off*, *Bukkake Blow-Out*, *Ring Driller 2000*. The deck of cards on a coffee table sticky with beer and grease. The bathroom with its unflushed toilet, its veins of green, cracked sinks and dripping taps. He worked out the routes that its owner might take every morning, trying to absorb the sordid rituals that took place here in the flat. He became the flat. He became the ghost of the person who moved through it.

After an hour, he shifted to the bedroom and peered under the bed. Porn magazines, football boots, a wedge of fossilised mushroom pizza. There was a thick layer of dust under there too. He found the Hoover and cleaned it out. Then he slid underneath and waited. On a job, he always wore soft leather trainers with a specially softened sole, the cleats melted smooth with a cook's blowtorch. He never wore jeans because the rivets might scratch against the wood on bare floorboards, like the ones in here. Moleskin trousers instead. Soft cotton or woollen jackets. No nylon. No leather. To be dangerous, you had to dress like a baby; you had to be soft.

He stared at the underside of the mattress for seven hours, thinking of the voice, of the woman. He thought of how she had promised him protection, when he felt he could offer her the same thing, even though he was ten years younger than her. Yet he was no child, and he did not want her to deny him the reason for his coming here. Not when he had waited so long, and channelled his every waking moment into preparing for it. He supposed she played this game because, deep down, he needed her to. He needed that game to make him feel as though he wasn't really there, as though he were a character in a film: real, but imaginary and therefore untouchable. She had played it with him since the off, and she played the game well. He didn't know her real name. And he half suspected that she didn't, either. He has always had to find one for her. It helped. It helped that he was involved in the issue of her identity. Again, it made him feel less there. Like a spirit. A ghost. And now, listening hard, there came the key in the lock. He didn't move for another three hours while his target heated something that shivered in plastic in the microwave, then watched the blunt, brutal sluicings of hard inside soft on his TV. He remained a statue, the Wire, for an hour after the target slipped into bed. Had a wank. Swore at some guy who made his day go badly. Winding down. The weird unquiet of sleep. And then the Wire moved. In the darkness, he moved with the speed and grace of something that has never known anything but.

The men in her life. All the fucking men. The sounds I had to put up with, the banging and the moaning and the pillow-screams. All of it coming through that thin wall like remembered nightmares. They never fucking stopped an all, even if I went in to her to tell her I was scared, or couldn't sleep. The men would look round at me from where they had her jackknifed over the corner of the bed, and they'd mouth at me to fuck off away. Naked bodies glistening with sweat. Tattoos that looked glossy with it, as if they might just slide off their skin. Red faces and bunched muscles. Pudding guts. Gritted teeth and stubble. Grunting. All this grunting. Sounds of pain. The eyes narrowed and furious. And they call it making love? Making hate more like. I'd go and pour meself some milk and I'd hear them blow their wads and then the jangle of belts soon after, as they hurried to be dressed and out of it. No cuddles in the moonlight. No 'There, there'. No breakfast in bed for these cunts. The slam of the door and the moans didn't stop. It was like listening to a hard wind testing the weak spots of a house, trying to find a way inside. I'd take me milk into her room and she'd be this pile of tits and tissues. How do you come back from all that? The numbers of men increasing but the need for affection never going away, never having its edges rubbed smooth. Where do you turn when what ought to be working doesn't? What else is there but the need to try to find an echo of that first one: the man who planted the seed of love in her heart. The bastard. The fucking bastard. At least the cunts that followed were honest enough. All they wanted was a bit of slit. No promises. True grit. Kitchen sink. Not him, though. Not that sorry twat.

Where are the real men? *she'd ask me, her eyes glassy with gin. I could see him in their wetness, a memory she clung to like a wish never shared. He'll come back. It was all over her expression. He'll come back.* Where have they gone? Or are they all just hiding from me?

He was sitting on a bench, playing the game, trying not to look at too many people but trying to guess which one it might be. It was a bright afternoon, very cold, with the sun pale and unformed in the sky, struggling to gain altitude. He rubbed his hands together to keep them warm, to keep them ready, always ready, and took in the scene unfolding around him. There was a number of office workers in their suits and smart skirts, trying to fit their mouths around overloaded sandwiches while reading magazines, *Heat* and *Look* and *Now*, or broadsheet newspapers that were like origami tests – papers you needed a map to help you read. A woman in a tracksuit, with an orange sweatband keeping her hair out of her eyes, leaned against the park railings, her hands behind her back, face tilted up towards the sun. A man in a yellow reflective bib swept up dead leaves and litter from the pavement, nudging people's feet aside so he could get at the crap under the benches. As he did this to the Four-Year-Old, there was no accompanying eye contact. So did that mean he was actually the one, or not? Wire waited, but the dustman moved on. He didn't mind that much. It was important that such episodes were subtle. He was the blunt end, the inflicter of damage. The woman had to be the cunning one, the sweet, cool and calculated one. It wasn't all about putting your target down. The planning had to be keen and correct; he himself merely signed off the blueprints. He rolled them up and put them into a tight tube and sealed them away for ever.

'Is anybody sitting here?' The woman startled him, and that wasn't good. He had to make sure that never happened again, but he chewed hard on his panic and tried to gather some control.

'You,' he said, chummily, 'if you get a wiggle on.' He waited for her to say something, offer him something more but, after sitting down, all she seemed interested in was her apple and her book.

He watched a group of schoolgirls move across the square, awkward and gangly in their grey jumpers and black skirts. At the same time, a man carrying a Budgens shopping bag emerged from Conway Street and approached him. This time; it had to be this time. How long must he wait? His view of the shopper was intercepted by the schoolgirls as one of them leaned towards the bin to drop in an empty crisps packet. The Four-Year-Old kept his beady on the man, craning his neck to see around the girl, but he had already strolled on, swapping his shopping to the other hand, then dragging a handkerchief from his pocket to blow his nose. The Wire looked down at his hands and, there was an envelope resting on the bench, by his thigh. The schoolgirl didn't look his way again until she and her friends were almost on the other side of the square. By then her face was nothing but a pink blob framed by light brown hair, a ponytail coming to rest on her shoulder. Nice. Clever. He liked it. Subtle.

He picked up the envelope and wandered back towards Cleveland Street, where he paused to rip it open and check the contents. There was a thousand pounds in fifty-pound notes, and a phone number. He stuffed the cash in his front jeans pocket and shredded the telephone number with his remarkable nails once it was snagged in his memory. On the one hand he was happy about the money and his success so far – he must have impressed the woman – and he liked the thrill of the game, not knowing who was who, liking the sheer anonymity, the delicious dislocated feel of it all; but the fact that she was reluctant to speak to him after so much shared experience, the fact that she had sent a child to act as courier, was disappointing.

Where was the respect? How was he to make progress if the woman who could give him the job he needed most refused to meet him? The woman who was at the same time pushing him, drawing out the perfection that sat at his centre, just anticipating its moment? She talked of protection, but nothing could save him now. If he didn't do the job – if she took it away from him and executed it herself – then he was finished; he became a husk for the rest of his life. And if he did end up doing it, then once it was done he knew he would turn into a pillar of stone. There was nothing to come afterwards. Happiness would arrive and depart at the precise moment that life fled the eyes of the man who occupied every second of the Wire's existence. Future had no meaning. It was true, that old saying, especially for him: Tomorrow never comes.

Then I had us one of those days that sticks in your memory as if it existed better there than in real life. Everything about that day was super-real. The colours that filled in the shapes surrounding us, from getting out of bed to getting back into it, could have been borrowed from a cartoon.

It started without a plan. I went round to see if Rob and Dave were coming out. I'd vaguely thought about cycling to the reservoir and titting about there all day. But they were helping their dad build a stone wall in the garden. Rob asked if I wanted to help, but I thought, fuck that, and went off by meself.

'Try Gavin,' Dave had said as I was leaving. 'He lives just round the corner.'

So I did. I didn't know Gavin James – Jamzy – that well, had been a little in awe of him, in fact, because he was a couple of years older. He was the captain of the school football team, and he was popular with girls, but he didn't have any of the arrogance of some of the other lads in his year.

When I knocked on his door, his dad answered. I was made to wait in a tiny hallway while Jamzy was fetched. When he arrived, he looked puzzled. He smelled of dubbin, as he had been cleaning his football boots. After every match he stuffed his boots full of newspaper and, once they were dry, he brushed the soil off. Then he rubbed dubbin into the leather. They were old boots, his Patricks, but they looked beautiful.

'What do you want?' he said.

'I was just on me way up to Walton Reservoir,' I said. 'Want to come?'

'Nah,' he said. 'I'm playing football this affo.'

Maybe he saw how pissed off I looked, because he then asked us if I wanted to play too. I said yeah, trying not to come over too keen like, and he told us to be at the gas fields with me kit within the hour.

'Red shirt,' he instructed.

I went home and changed into me kit, giving me boots a quick polish with the Kiwi so they'd look a bit like Jamzy's, and cycled over to the gas fields. The fields were a fucking mess, but they had real goalposts on them. They were on the edge of the town, in the shadow of a couple of gasometers. Nobody knew what the fields were really called. Everyone knew them as the gas fields.

When I got there, there was half a dozen lads playing three-and-in. I hung back and waited for Jamzy to turn up. I was startled by the green of the grass which, from the road, had not seemed as bright or as, well, green, even though the sun hadn't come out. There was a guy hanging around near the pitch. He was a scruffy-looking twat, and I'd seen him before, sitting on the benches in town, or trying to get into pubs that he was barred from. I'd never seen him sober, and here he was now, pouring Carlsberg Special Brew down his neck, red-faced and muttering. He was Irish – Tavlin, I think his name was. At least, that's what the kids who taunted him in town called him. 'Up the IRA, Tavlin,' they used to say to him, and they'd get a mouthful of abuse in reply.

The girl from the previous night was there too, standing by the touchline. She looked fucking fine. She gave us a little wave and that made me face burn a bit, and I felt bad about how things had gone between us. She didn't seem to be holding a grudge though.

Jamzy turned up not long after, and Rob and Dave were in tow. I felt a little annoyed that they'd obviously agreed to come out with him, but had refused me own invitation, but that resentment didn't last. Partly because they're such good company that you forget pretty quickly any disagreements you might have had with them, and partly because loads more boys turned up within the space of a few minutes and teams were being picked, and partly because of what happened when Rob saw Tavlin stumbling around the goalposts, trying to unzip himself for a piss.

'Are you all right, with him being here?' he said to us.

'Why shouldn't I?' I said. 'No harm. He's just a pissed old bastard. He's never done nowt to us.' Rob had the look of someone who's said too much and only just realised it. He knew there was no point trying to laugh it off. He watched Tavlin pissing into the grass, warbling some tune or other, and said:

'Well, no, but he did something to your mam, didn't he?'

Rob told us, as we were lining up for the start of the match, that his dad had heard that Tavlin had gone into a pub one night when me ma was singing. He had waited till she came off the stage, bought her a drink and, as she was taking it off him, he slid his hand up her skirt and shoved his fingers into her knickers.

It felt as though the colour from me shirt had leaked into me eyes. When I looked over towards the girl, she seemed to have frozen as if someone had replaced her with a perfect cardboard replica, but her eyes bored into us, and there was knowledge there, it seemed like, and understanding. If you could have hardened the rod of air that connected our eyes and examined it in a lab, you'd have seen nothing but me and her linked, combined, mixed up so much that it would be impossible to tear us apart. It give us a punch in me guts, but it also focused me anger, turned it into something white-hot. I took it on to the pitch with us and almost got into a fight when I scythed through the opposition's centre forward, leaving me stud marks on his legs and tearing his shorts.

Every time I passed the ball, or the action switched to the other side of the pitch, I turned me attention back to Tavlin. He was performing a Mexican Wave now, on his own. He was on the second of his tins, the empty having been thrown on to the pitch. He was wandering along the touchline towards the halfway line as I got the ball. I dribbled with it in his direction, then purposefully gave the ball away. When the winger who I'd passed to was three feet away from Tavlin, I steamed in, taking the ball, the winger, *and Tavlin with it. He didn't know what hit him, but as he lay there with beer foaming all over his stinking, gnarled face, I leaned over him and hissed: 'That was us.'*

But it wasn't enough. I felt empty as the game wore on, me anger given a direction, but no real result. The girl had gone and I felt like a bee that had lost its sting. I felt gutless, without direction. Tavlin struggled to his feet and staggered away across the field, the incident already forgotten, any pain he might have felt dulled by the beer he was constantly sinking.

'Take it easy,' Jamzy said. 'It's just a knockabout. It's not the Cup Final.'

When I could see Tavlin just as a speck against the horizon, vanishing amid the collapsed, cement-coloured rows of the housing estate that noses on to the gas fields, I told the boys that I had to get going but I'd come back later if the game was still on. It wasn't unusual for football matches to last eight hours, dwindling away to a five-a-side or becoming engorged by passers-by into a full-on war but never breaking for anything so lame as half-time.

I got on me bike and set off after Tavlin.

I thought I'd lost him, at one point. The estate stretched out before us, one long avenue of boarded-up windows, burnt-out cars, and kids smoking fags while passing around a two-litre plastic bottle of sweet cider. A dog scurried past, eyes enlarged by the thinness of its body. Then she came out from the blind side of a hut on a patch of wasteland. She had a look on her that was as naked and pure as a one-second-old baby. It told us that I was hers and she was mine. It told us that we were as integrated and as inseparable as Siamese twins sharing one heart, one brain. I looked at her and there I saw a mirror.

'He's in there,' she said, her voice forcing every other fragment of sound into the background.

Me mouth filled with saliva. It felt as though me prick had been swapped for a broom handle and, even at the feeling of it, she looked down at me crotch and smiled. When I tried to look into her eyes, my focus slid away and fell on her hair, or the curve of her waist, or her tits, perky and tight, cupped in their white bra that was visible through the sheerness of the blouse she was wearing.

She asked me: 'Will you see this through?'

'Yes,' I said.

'I know.' She was nodding. 'And I knew you were always going to say yes to me. And you will, won't you?'

'Yes,' I said. I'd have said yes to any question that popped from that soft, teasing mouth of hers. I'd have said yes if she asked us to get into a bath of petrol and play with a disposable lighter.

She said, 'I will take care of you, if you want it.'

'Yes,' I said.

She said, 'I'll help you find your mother – if you want it. I'll help you destroy what makes you unhappy.'

'Yes,' I said.

She said, 'Trust me always. Do as I say and you shall come out on the other side happy.'

'Yes,' I said. 'What's your name?'

She smiled. 'I haven't got one. You'll have to find one for me. And you will.'

'What do you want me to do?' I asked.

She said, 'He'll go in there. He's pissed and clumsy and he might do himself an injury – or worse. Imagine, being pissed and trying to get warm when you've got nowhere to go. What might you do? How wrong could it go?' Then she *walked off around the back of the hut.*

Then I saw him, draining a can as he appeared from the hut's blind side. Just as she had a minute ago. It was as if, in the second of her disappearing, she had miraculously turned into this fuck-up of a human being. It was like being tricked in a magic show and I couldn't see the join. When I dashed around behind the hut, she was nowhere to be seen.

Tavlin had been for another piss; a large black stain now covered the crotch of his trousers.

'She said you'll go in there,' I said.

Tavlin looked at me unsteadily. 'Warra fogn hell?' he said.

God knows what the hut was. I think maybe it was a relic from an old car park that had once stood here, one of those unauthorised jobs that looks the part because of some wanker in a cap handing out tickets at a fiver a go. It had always been called 'The Tramp's Hut' because a tramp had been found dead from exposure inside it one winter, trying to find shelter away from the cold.

I cycled closer to him and asked him for a drink of his beer.

'Fogn bazd,' he said. 'Sog may fogn dog.' His eyes were this weird blue, like a swimming pool: bleached and wet but almost frying with hot colour. I kicked the can out of his hand and moved away on the bike before he had a chance to grab us. He reached into his jacket pocket and pulled out another gold tin. He was swearing non-stop now, although I couldn't tell where one word began and another ended.

'All right, Tavlin?' I said. 'You stupid fucking bastard.'

He blazed at us. He threw the can and it caught me ear, making it burn, before landing and splitting on the kerb, jetting fizz all over the place.

He ran at us and I almost fell off me bike, but he was only trying to rescue his lager. He knelt on the kerb and supped at the split in the tin, as if it were venom he was trying to suck out of a snake bite. The crack of his arse rose from his shiny, paper-thin keks. I felt the world go away for a second and the unreal colour of everything turned a dirty, dishwater grey. When it rammed back into us, Tavlin was upright again, mumbling unhappily and trying to unhook the latch on the tramp hut.

'I'll do that for you,' I said. I got off me bike and kicked the latch free.

'Thanz,' he said. 'Yuh fogn cont.'

Inside the hut was a bucket full of cigarette ends and an upturned plastic milk crate. A wank mag, with all the colour sucked out of it by the sunlight, lay open on the floor. A blonde woman held her greasy snatch open for the camera. He sat down on the crate and poured some more beer from his split tin into his mouth and across his shirt.

His tongue lolled in his mouth.

She glistened in too many places at once.

I felt sick… felt the hut start to sway.

'Have you got a match?' I said.

He said, 'Fog.'

I kicked the door shut on him and slotted the latch back in place. He didn't say nowt. I cycled half a mile to a corner shop and bought a box of England's Glory and a can of Coke. By the time I got back I could hear him snoring inside.

I took a match and struck it. When the flame had settled, I set fire to the cardboard box and tossed it through the window. The box landed on the wank mag, obscuring the blonde's snatch. I felt enormous relief and a sudden sense of utter correctness. Of poetry.

The box flared up and the mag caught fire. Tavlin didn't move a muscle.

I cycled away. I was maybe a hundred metres away from the tramp's hut when I heard the first shouts.

'Fogn helpuzz,' I whispered. 'Fogn bazd.'

I was nearly home when I heard the sirens. He was on the news that night, Tavlin.

I went to sleep and I dreamed about him coming out of the hut. When he opened his mouth to speak, fire flew from between his teeth. His clothes were burnt off him and he had the girl's body. I went to him and twisted his head off, as easily as loosening the screw-cap on a bottle of pop. Inside his head were the words MADE IN CHINA. When I looked at his face, he was the girl from the wank mag. She winked at us and peeled herself open. I stepped inside her and fell asleep for a thousand years.

When I woke up in real time, in real life, I realised what the smell of blonde was. But it was gone just as quickly. I didn't see the girl again for a long time, but it didn't matter. I was getting into other things then. I was growing up.

He stopped now in front of an Indian restaurant and looked at his reflection in the window. He noticed that he was idly stroking the small diary in his chest pocket. He got it out and flicked through the pages almost tenderly, his fingers soft and delicate, not wanting to damage the paper, tracing the patterns worn into its leather covers. The names written in here were added many years before, and his handwriting reflected that: it was the handwriting of a child, of someone who was just learning to join his letters together. Three of the names – there were thirty in total, the size of her class – had been neatly ruled out, but the pencil that had scored through them was recent, its lead shiny across the old, dull names. Putting a new layer on top of those names was like closing an electrical circuit; he felt a jolt leap through his head as if he was at home again, a child in those lazy, hot days in a Liverpool classroom as the summer holidays chased him down.

Some of the names he could put faces to, some he had trouble remembering at all. But it didn't matter: those names would continue for as long as he kept his book. It was the names, not their owners, that justified him. He had already put a line through the three names that had conspired to take his mother away from him, and the most important name of all didn't need to be written down. It was so well known to him, it might as well have been carved into the meat of his brain with a knife. That name sat on his tongue every minute of every day. The shape of its vowels and consonants were as well known to him as those of his own.

He bought a ham-salad roll from a sandwich shop – no mayonnaise, no salt, a multigrain roll, extra tomato for the antioxidants, the lycopene – and ate it on the way back to his secret hideaway. Once he arrived, he spent ten minutes picking the blood from under his fingernails. There was a lot of it, dried and black now, and removing it was a sad job. Getting rid of any trace of what he did upset him, because then it felt as if it never happened, as if he was never involved. Rubbing away the signs of his work was like rubbing away the work itself. Sometimes it was an effort to convince himself that he had ever killed.

It was Jamzy got us into body-building. He told us that birds wouldn't look at you unless you had some meat on

142

your biceps, a six-pack under your shirt. I told him I didn't like beer and he looked at us as if I was joking. But I don't like it. I don't like any alcohol. I wasn't interested in birds either, apart from the girl I'd seen at the footy that time, but I didn't dare tell him that in case he thought I was queer. I wanted to improve meself, make the best of us that there was. I wanted to find the full capacity of the power in me arms and legs. I wanted to reach that brink, and stay there – go beyond it if I could. I wanted to be a mirror to all that compacted violence I saw leaning over me mam. I wanted to reflect that go away in their eyes. I wanted to return a little bit of the fear they'd put up me.

We went to a gym called O'Riordan's one night, when it was teeming, cold winds tearing up and down the streets like invisible drag racers made of winter. I was wearing a torn grey T-shirt and jogging pants, a pair of weight-lifting gloves. The T-shirt flapped around us like a sail that was going to take us off into the sky if I wasn't careful. I tucked it into me waistband and bent me head against the wind and rain.

O'Riordan's was just a couple of hundred square metres of a warehouse up Prentiss Lane. The rest of it was closed, windows boarded up, falling to shit. Used to be a wire factory; there was a lot of that round here, a big industry in these parts. The entrance was up a fire escape. The girl on the reception desk didn't say one word to us, just pushed a clipboard at us for us to sign, and pointed at the entry fee, which was laser-printed on a sign behind her chair: £1.50 per hour. We gave her three quid each and moved into the gym proper. A short, bullish guy, whose neck was disappearing into the ledge of muscle rising from his shoulders, gave us our induction lesson. He was all right, as it turned out. Name

143

of Bobby Jepson. What was left of his hair was dirty blond, cropped short. He made up for that with a thick moustache. His skin was dark from the solarium, his eyes blue as the stone on me mum's engagement ring. He showed us the free weights and the bench presses, the exercise balls, skipping ropes and treadmills. We warmed up with a fifteen-minute ride on the exercise bikes, and then worked our way around the machines.

'What is it you want from this place?' Bobby asked us.

'I just want to get fit,' Jamzy said.

I said, 'I want to build up me body and get strong. But I don't want to lose any mobility, like you have.'

Bobby looked at us hard, and I smiled as if to show I was joking.

'Okay,' he said, slowly, not taking his eyes off us. 'Okay.'

He taught us how, if you want to build up mass, you do lots of reps at a low weight. If you wanted to improve your strength, though, you had to up the weight.

'There's no point doing lots of reps on a high weight,' he said. 'What you're looking to do is put lots of little tears in your muscles, and you can get that from one set of 15 reps. When the tears heal, it forms a new layer of muscle. That's what body-building is all about: doing yourself damage.'

So that's what I did. Jamzy stuck to the treadmills to build up his stamina and try to burn off the beer belly he was getting. The gym started filling up after half an hour, as workers came off the 6–10 shift. The air was filled with the clank of iron and the grunts of men, and a few women, pushing themselves through the resistance of the machines.

About fifteen minutes before the gym was due to shut at 11 p.m., a man in a smoky-grey suit came through the doors. One or two of the men on the machines nodded to him as he strode right through the gym towards the door at the back with a sign that said Staff Only. He flashed his teeth at them. Bobby cut him off as he was about to open the door, and they shook hands, swapped verbals for a few minutes. The man in the suit then clapped Bobby on the back and went through into an office.

We left soon after, and I could hardly walk. Me legs felt as weak as a foal's and me chest burned where I had been using the bench press. We went to the pub across the road for a couple of glasses of water, and necked them double-quick while the staff were emptying ashtrays and putting stools up on tables. I felt amazing. I felt cleaned out, reassembled.

'That was fucking brilliant,' I said. I couldn't stop feeling me arms. They felt thick and powerful, pumped up as though someone had been inflating them on the sly.

'Yeah, let' s go again tomorrow.'

'Day after,' I said. 'You have to go every other day, because you need to let the muscle recover.'

Jamzy didn't come with us, next time I went. He was seeing some girl he'd chatted up at the bus stop. Fair enough, so I went on me own. I was aching something chronic by then, but I went. And I kept going. Every other day. Couple of miles on the bike. Stretching. And then I zoned in on various areas of me body. One day I'd work just on me arms. Next time legs. Next time back and chest. Next time abs. Moving the weights in different directions to draw the potential from me body. I put on weight. I started eating lots of carbohydrates the night before a training session. I ate steak and eggs for protein. I ate so many greens, I thought I'd start shitting pure spinach.

'You're looking all right, Wire,' Bobby said to us one night, maybe six weeks after I'd started. Blokes down the gym started calling us Wire because I was thin and full of sinew. And tough. I was getting on all right with everyone because I kept me mouth shut unless I was talked to. There was Bobby, who I could call a mate now. And Fivesy, who lived round the corner and bred pedigree Burmillas. And Colin 'Garden' Rakes, who ran a taxi firm and would give us a lift home in his Lexus. I still saw the man in the suit, either the smoky-grey one or a black number. Always with a white shirt, and a tie in a solid colour, no patterns ever. Turned out he was O'Riordan. He was built like a brick shithouse, very thick through the chest, a face like a block of wood, heavily tanned, and lots of lines but it looked good like on an actor, a little bit like Willem Dafoe maybe.

The torn grey T-shirt was filling out. It no longer flapped on us when I walked to the gym in the evening. I started spending days in the woods, driving my fists, and the edge of my hands into the gritty loam, toughening them up. From a standing start, I'd take off through the wet, getting up to sprint speed as soon as I could. Then I'd stop. Short sprints, quick turns, again, again, till I was moving so quickly it was as if it was happening before I even decided to do it. I was bulking out, but the running and the bikes and the sprint work kept me lean.

I was working the rope one night when Bobby came over and said that O'Riordan wanted a chat with us.

I went up to his office and walked in without his say-so, but he didn't mind. Said he expected it. He told us he was shutting the gym for the weekend for refurbishment, but he wanted me to come in and use the machines for free, as long as I'd make a cup of tea for the workmen, let them in and out, that kind of thing.

'Why me?' I said.

He was looking at his nails, which were buffed to a high shine, nicely shaped like a lass's. 'Because I don't trust any of the other cunts in here,' he said.

'Why don't you do it yourself, then?'

He stopped preening and looked at us. He had hard, grey eyes. He also gave us a look at his gnashers. They seemed bigger than they ought to be. 'Because I run this outfit. And because I'm asking you to do it.'

'What if I say no?'

'Find another gym.'

'There in't another gym.'

'Then say yes.'

I said yes.

I came in the next morning in my kit, letting meself in with the key O'Riordan gave us. I brewed up in the staff room and listened to the radio for a bit, then did some stretching. I was twenty minutes into a bike ride when the door opened, and Boardo come in. Paul Boardman worked on the wagons, driving freight up and down the motorways. When he wasn't on a job, he was in here, pissing everyone off with his pushing in on equipment when everyone else was waiting patiently, or banging the gear around, no respect for the weights. But he got away with it because he was O'Riordan's minder. He talked to you while you were concentrating on your reps, telling you in detail about the birds he licked out in his cabin the night before, picked up from some service station or other: how he had to clamp his hand over their lipstick because his prick was so big he made them scream, and he didn't want people thinking he was killing tarts inside his rig.

He didn't look at us once as he walked over to the free weights and started curling the kilos. Which told us plenty: he

147

knew I was going to be here. O'Riordan hadn't let on about Boardo being around. So I kept vertical, working on the chin-up bar and the bike and the rope, waiting for him to make his move. There were no refurbishments taking place today. No cups of tea to make. No banter with the carpenters.

He took his time about it, sidling along the workout mats, checking himself out in the full-length mirrors, till he was close enough for us to smell the sweat off his armpits.

'All right, Wire?' he said, voice low, his back to us. I tensed up. It was coming.

When he twisted around, quicker than a man of his bulk deserved to be, I was ready. He had a Stanley knife, the handle wrapped in insulation tape. I watched it move past the spot where me cheek had been a second earlier. I stepped back and passed the handle of the skipping rope into me right fist, freeing me left, me best hand. He launched himself at us and I stepped aside, sweeping the loop of the rope under his foot and tugging hard. He went down awkwardly, his ankle folding under him, and he shouted. He rolled on to his back, the Stanley knife pointing at us all the time, and rubbed at his ankle. His face was very red. I put the rope down and picked up a dumb-bell, about twenty-five kilos piled on to it. The weights chinked and clinked on the bar as I moved towards him.

He levered himself upright and slashed out at us as I broke into his space. I met the blade with the weights, knocking his arm to one side. Unbalanced, he put out his other hand to stop himself from going down again, and I sent me left foot steaming into the centre of his chest. His face went pale. He knew it was the beginning of something very bad. Twenty minutes later, when O'Riordan and three of his cronies were pulling us off him, I couldn't see any expression on his face

any more because most of it was dangling between me teeth.
One of his ribs was poking out of a hole in his vest and he
seemed to be breathing through it. The top of his head had a
dent in it you could have filled with a large apple. I thought
it was an improvement.

'He looks much better, doesn't he?' I said, and the cronies
backed off. One of them was swallowing against a tide of
vomit that kept surging into his mouth. He gave up fighting
it and sprayed over one of the treadmills.

'The cleaning bill for that comes out of your wages,
Eddie,' O'Riordan said. When I was calming down, the
cords on me neck going back to sleep, O'Riordan told the
others to fuck off. He got bored waiting for Boardo to snuff
it, so he cut his windpipe open with the Stanley. He kept
saying, 'Your hands... your fucking hands.'

He told me what to do with the body and I followed his
instructions to the letter. When I came back, he had us in his
office again and he told us he had a job for us, if I wanted
it. Shadowing him in the clubs. Chauffeuring for him. Being
the bite to his bark.

I said, 'Yes, I' ll have your job, but if you set us up like
that again, I' ll give you cause for concern.' I said it just like
that, as calm as you like, something I heard on the telly. He
wasn't expecting it, and it took the tan out of his face for a
few seconds. And then he said: 'Deal.'

A neutral voice answered when he rang the number in the
morning. It was raining heavily and it was difficult to hear
what the voice was saying. Buses and taxis were turned into a
blurred mess of reds and blacks, through the foggy windows
of the phone booth. –'I did what you asked,' he said. 'Can't

we meet?' –'Very soon,' the voice said. 'I'm happy with the way you went about your business. There'll be another job for you.' – '*The* job?' –'Maybe, but darling, I am so worried about you.' –'When?' he asked, hating the wheedling tone of his voice, hating that he cut across her while she was speaking from her heart. –'You will be contacted. You will have the details. Cold now, distant.' –'When? When?' The line died in his hand. She must have many contacts, the Four-Year-Old thought, and some of them must be watching him, to see how he conducted himself. He must keep himself calm and focused at all times. He mustn't give her cause to doubt his ability.

He dashed across the street, fast and light, powerful and invisible, hunching away from the deluge, feeling so nimble that he might have dodged each and every drop of rain. He bought a newspaper and took it inside. It was less busy, it seemed, today. The coffee bar where he had found Linda – where Linda had found him, where he had drawn her to him – was very slow; three or four customers sitting at tables, sipping from their cups. Her smoothie stall was now closed, while the flowers, the croissants, the handkerchiefs on the other stalls were for the benefit of nobody but the staff today, it seemed. The platforms were populated by people who didn't appear to be getting on or off the trains. It could have been a tableau of pointlessness and apathy, arranged specially for his eyes.

Wire watched some of them as they strolled around the concourse. He bought a cup of coffee and sat at the counter, blowing on it till it was cool enough to drink. His eyes settled on the scars on his arms. He flexed his muscles slightly and the scars writhed like livid snakes.

* * *

I worked on me third birthday. My last birthday before I decided it was time to make me move down to the Smoke. O'Riordan needed some help in dealing with an ex-colleague called Wilkes who was muscling in on the club scene, offering his own bouncers, what he called 'professional, no-nonsense doormen', and undercutting O'Riordan something mental. That way we'd already lost our business with Echoes, and Flight, and Mirrors. We'd had word Wilkes was going to be at Blue Storm on this particular night, and we got in O'Riordan's Merc, just me and Fivesy with O'Riordan himself driving like a mad bastard, running red lights, clipping kerbs. He was frothing at the corners of his mouth, swearing constantly; you could just about hear it under his breath: cunt... cunt... cunt... cunt... Me blood was up, too. I was thinking, I become a man tonight. I prove to meself, and I prove to the girl, that I can cut it. I would reach a new gear tonight.

O'Riordan wanted us tooled up for the evening, but I said no, I didn't want anything that was going to slow us down. Fivesy had a compact hunting knife he'd bought in Kentucky on holiday the previous year which he'd smuggled in to the country in a giant jar of Smucker's peanut butter and jelly. O'Riordan had his piece on him, a Derringer with a pearl handle – a lass's gun, but nobody was going to tell him that. I didn't want nothing, because I wanted me hands free. Me hands could do more damage than Fivesy's knife or O'Riordan's toy shooter. What was the point of filling your hand with something that your hand could do itself anyway?

We get to Blue Storm at just gone midnight, and the place is humming. Cudge and Dobbo on the door, as usual, and we give them the nod from the Merc as we cruise into the car park and find a dark corner. Come 2 a.m., kicking-out time, we see Wilkes turn up in his gunmetal Lotus, followed by a black BMW. He gets out of the Lotus with a tall red-haired slut in a glittering, tight green catsuit. Four of his no-nonsense doormen get out of the car too, and I think: in the bag. They're soft fuckers: all buffed fingernails and cleanse, tone and moisturise. I bet they wore gloves in the gym. I bet they took bottles of Powerade in with them. Spent more time waxing their French-crop hairstyles than they did pressing metal.

We saunter over, while Wilkes is amiably chatting to Dobbo, maybe trying to get him to turn coat. Smiles all round. Bigger smiles when Wilkes sees O'Riordan. But not when he sees us. That smile dims a bit, the way the reflection of bright sunshine on a wall will fade suddenly when thin cloud passes in front of it. It was the look of someone who recognises madness when he sees it. He'd heard talk of what I could do. He had an inkling that the rumours of what happened between us and Boardo were anything but. He had a feeling that, were he to take a spade to some of the soil around Alderley Edge, he might find Boardo or at least pieces of him.

Wire, he says quietly. There's none of that shouldn't you be in bed shit. Shouldn't you be doing your homework. Nineteen or ninety, it makes no odds in this business. Violence couldn't give a toss how tight your skin is. Wilkes' boys are looking us up and down like a bunch of farmers at a meat auction. I don't blink. I don't smile. I don't say a word. I don't meet anybody's gaze. I slowly flex me fingers, that's all. I've got long fingernails, like a classical guitarist. I soak them in vinegar every night. I can puncture the top

of a tin can with them. Click-click-click they go now, as I
stretch and massage each one against its neighbour. Click-
click-click.

O'Riordan says: Let's go inside, shall we? Let's all have
a drink.

We file in. I take up the rear. I don't want them to see us.
I just want their sense of something animal padding after
them. I want hackles rising.

The club is still emptying. Staff dip into shadowy booths,
first asking, and then telling the pissheads to drink up, let's
have your glasses. The music's stopped playing, but the
system hasn't been switched off yet; the hum and crackle
might easily be the tension leaping off our little posse as
we head to the bar. Everyone orders bottles of San Miguel.
O'Riordan pours tequila for him and Wilkes. I shake me
head. I don't want nowt. I'm assessing the lie of the land:
how the stairs down to the dance floor are edged with
protective metal strips. I'm looking at the brass rail running
the length of the bar. Me eyes are assessing this grainy club
light, getting chummy with its shadows. I see the booth with
the bottles that have been missed by the barmaid collecting
empties. I see the cigarette in the ashtray that hasn't been put
out properly. I see a thousand things that I can maim you
with, a dozen things that will kill you. I slow me breathing.
I feel me heartbeat levelling out, so it would keep time with
the second hand of a watch. I wait for it. I wait.

The suits unbuttoning. Laughter. Wilkes saying, This
town can be big enough for the both of us, Walter. We could
clean up if you throw your cap in with us.

O'Riordan: If I throw in with *you?* How about the other
way round?

Some of Wilkes's puppies joking now, relaxing. Wilkesy

and O' Riordan getting on like best mates. No *bloodletting tonight. Take advantage: have a few beers. Enjoy yourselves. Think Liverpool can win the title this season, now they've got a bit of width? How's the car? Seen the new de Niro film? Flirting with the women cleaning up behind the bar.* Look at the Tangas on that. *And Fivesy joining in, but tipping me a look every now and then, his hand in his pocket. Me, I'm waiting, eyes on O'Riordan.*

Sometimes I wonder what I would look like if I let this rage inside us take over for good. Would I have fangs? Red eyes? Would me hands twist into claws? The hate fills me every waking moment so that I have to force meself to calm down before I let fly on the first fucker to cross me path.

Waiting.

One time, sleeping rough in Stanley Park, this old woman grabbed me toe to wake us up, and I had her down in the grass, throttling her, roaring in her face before she'd had chance to blink.

Waiting.

I've often wondered why the blood I've tasted is so sour, and I think it's because the meat of the men who carry it has been spoiled by fear. I saw this programme once about abattoirs where pigs were slaughtered unprofessionally; where they were aware of their fate and ruined themselves with panic. PSE, they call it: pale, soft, exudative meat. Where the meat is lighter than normal in colour, with a sludgy texture and wet surface, often with high drip loss, and a pH below 5.6.

O'Riordan turns to us and says: 'What about you, Wire? You ever thought of running a club?'

Unleashed.

I turn to one of Wilkes' puppets. I say, 'What's your pH?

154

Lower than 5.6, you reckon?'

He goes: 'You wha–?' And it's the last sound he'll make without some kind of synthetic assistance, because click-click-click *me forefinger and finger-fucking finger disappear into his throat up to the first knuckle.*

He's out of the game, so it's just three left and Wilkes, who's already backing off. Fivesy's got his blade out and it's stuck in the guts of another stooge who's looking down at it and he's got his mitts around Fivesy's and it's like he's trying to help Fivesy as he slowly hoists it north, ripping a line through him that turns his crisp, white shirt into a very noisy red.

The buzz fills me head, as if me brain has been replaced by a nest of angry wasps. It's the sound of violence. The oldest sound there is.

The stragglers have seen what's happening and some of them are screaming, heading for the doors without any encouragement at all now. The staff have frozen, watching us with mouths open, thinking, 'Do I wade in and try to stop this? For minimum wage?'

I'm standing over one of the two poor saps that are left, and somehow I've transferred a great patch of his face on to me fists. I pick him up at the waist while he babbles at me about his girlfriend being pregnant, please, please, and he's light, so criminally light it's almost not fair, and I swing him round and down, and the back of his head cracks against the bar rail, right where there's a lovely couple of nuts securing it to the wood. His chin snaps into his chest hard enough to give him a bruise, and I leave him on the floor where he twitches, eyes flickering, losing blood through every hole he was born with, and some new ones too.

The last one I punch once, hard, right in the solar plexus,

155

*while he's busy throwing kung-fu shapes and warning me
about what colour belt he wears. During his fish impressions
I donkey-kick him down the steps. He lands nastily on the
dance floor and stays there, and I think he's dead because
there was one mighty snap when he landed, and I don't
think it was the sound of O'Riordan tucking into the free
Twiglets at the bar. It's all taken less than a minute. Fivesy's
cleaning his knife against Wilkes's jacket. Wilkes's crying,
saying to O' Riordan through great bubbles of snot and
spit:* What is it you want? Anything, I'll sort it. I promise.

And O'Riordan, soothing him, saying, Come on, Peter,
let's all go for a ride. *And Wilkes begging now, but nobody
likes a cry-baby and we get him outside and into the Merc.
We're out of the car park and heading up the Chester Road
even as the first of the blue lights comes stuttering on to
the scene. Couple of minutes later, O'Riordan parks up by
a gate in front of a field. A pale track leads into it a few
feet, and then gets swallowed up by the dark. We ignore
that and invite Wilkes to walk across the road towards a
wall. Beyond the wall is the golf course. We scramble over,
Fivesy getting a laugh from O'Riordan when he says we
wouldn't have this problem if you was a member, and we
push through the trees and the rough and find ourselves on
the fairway of the first hole. The sweep of grass looks as
smooth as soap.*

*O'Riordan takes a hip flask from his jacket and offers it
to Wilkes. Wilkes shakes his head, but then grabs the flask
and has a hard drink out of it.*

What are you going to do? *Wilkes asks, and then answers
his own question.* I don't want to die.

We have to make an example of you, Peter, *O'Riordan
says.* If I let a cunt like you piss all over my operations, well,

that's just going to give the green light to any other Joe who wants to come and steal a bit of my land.

I won't bother you again, I promise, *Wilkes says.*

O'Riordan: I know you won't.

He looks at me and I take Wilkes by the arm. Fivesy hands me his hunting knife, and I pause for a moment before accepting it. O'Riordan starts screaming, but I give him a slap and he shuts up fast. He's looking at me as I drag him along the fairway. He's looking at me, and looking at the green, and looking back at O'Riordan and Fivesy who are sharing the hip flask and looking up at the stars.

Wilkes licks his lips and turns his black eyes on me again. How do I get out of this one, hey, Wire? Name your price.

I don't say a word. Me at work, I make Marcel Marceau seem gobby. But as we get nearer to the green and the bunkers that surround it, I'm thinking about the way things have gone tonight, and starting to worry.

What if I have a glass jaw? *I think.* What if I'm unable to take a hit. One day I'll come up against someone as quick, or as hard, or as nasty. And if I can't sustain an injury, I'll be in danger. I'll be bound for the cemetery. Tonight you come of age, *I thought.* Tonight you reach a new gear.

He's getting wobbly on his feet, now, knowing what's coming, so it comes as a surprise to him, I'm sure, when I goes: Here's your price. Here's what it will take to get out of this.

And he's all, What? What? Anything. *And his eyes are big and round and interested.*

Me: I want you to show us what pain means.

Silence from Wilkes. He thinks I'm pissing with him, pissing on a dead man.

I say: Can you do it?

He goes: Yes.

I take me jacket off, then me tie and me shirt. I hand him Fivesy's knife and he unsheathes it slowly, as if he still can't quite believe what's going on here. I tell him to hurt us. I tell him to slash at the biceps of me right arm. I tell him to not get any funny ideas about trying to kill us, because I will know. I will know instantly, just by the positioning of his feet, and his angle of attack, and I will stop him.

He hacks at the muscles for thirty seconds until he's out of breath and we're both covered in me blood. I gritted me teeth for what I thought would come, but it didn't grow beyond a manageable heat.

You call that pain? *I ask him, and it's nothing. He's nodding desperately, but what does he fucking know?* What do you fucking know about pain? *I demand. But he's not speaking. He doesn't have a clue. I goes,* I'll tell you about pain. *And I tell him about me ma and her dying and how much that hurt, how it felt like a million scissors being opened and shut inside us all at the same time. I talk and I talk, and Wilkes doesn't say a thing. I'm so enraged that I don't know what I'm doing with the knife, or Wilkes, until I'm no longer sitting in sand, but a kind of gritty black mud. His head flops against us, looking up at us like some doting lover dozing on me lap. He's still listening, even though is ears are no longer attached to his head. I keep talking, I keep telling him about pain until O'Riordan and Fivesy turn up, and they ask us very gently to put down what's left of him, it's time to go.*

Neil Lever said, 'She had a song, your mum, she used to sing in the pubs when they had open mike sessions. She didn't *have much of a voice, but people stopped yakking in order to listen to her, maybe because she sounded so genuine. It was her own song, her own tune. It was the only song she knew.'*

A part of us remembers that, or wants to remember. She used to take us to the pubs in a basket and put us on the table among the pints, while she got up to sing Sorry Boy. Some pisshead would look after us for three or four minutes, give us a stout-soaked pork scratching to suck on, until Ma returned, the place roaring. I do remember the applause, if nowt else.

Where have you gone? My sorry boy, my sorry boy?
How can I go on? My sorry, sorry boy?

Lever met her at one of them pubs. She was damaged goods by then, putting on weight from drinking too much, face bloated and bloodshot. She was taking pills to get her to sleep at night, and pills to keep her awake during the day. The school where she worked had sacked her. Some of the pupils had complained about the way she nodded off during classes, or her mood swings which could turn her from the placid creature she was into somebody who snapped and glared. I read about it in her diaries. She made a list of the girls who had gone to complain to the head about her. I've got that list now.

'We didn't do anything that normal people do when they get together,' Lever explained. 'No cinema or restaurants. No take-outs in front of a video. It was as if I'd come into it a couple of years after the start. We sat together in silence mostly. I went to all the pubs with her when she was singing. I picked up her prescriptions from the chemist.'

Lever had left the chip shop and was working as a rides

operator at a shitty little theme park off the M62, called Wowland. Once we'd got to know each other, I used to pick him up when he'd finished his shift and we'd drive around, visiting all the pubs and clubs where Ma used to perform, or other places of note. Sometimes I'd get there early and watch him from the fence as he pressed a big green button to get his ride started – some feeble roundabout of spaceships with chipped paint and slashed seats – and a big red button to stop it. Every four weeks, the staff were rotated. The worst job was in the mere, helping the punters get started in their pedalos, and then parking them after they returned. Lever had to wear thigh-length waders, and the water was never anything other than dead cold. He had to smile like a madman whenever the kids splashed him, which was all the time. The best job was driving the miniature train around the perimeter of the theme park.

There was a gap in the fence at the top end of the grounds, and I'd nip through it and hop into the cab with him. He had a hip flask and a small FM radio to make the journey even better. I found meself wishing that he had been around when I was growing up, then. Things might have turned out different.

Trundling along under giant plastic dinosaurs turned white from years of sunshine and bird shit, the excited giggles and yelps of the kids in the carriages behind, he told us how he'd found her hanging from the ceiling light in her bedroom, six feet of copper wire wrapped around her neck like one of them fancy African necklaces. I had been in the room next-door, playing with a toy, reading a book, crayoning on the windows. I must have heard her kick the chair away, then her frantic efforts to rescue herself when the brain's instinct for self-preservation was triggered, the choking sounds in her throat as she strangled. They were there somewhere in me

160

head, and I never wanted them unlocked.

I felt sorry for Neil Lever, finding her like that. After a couple of weeks, I ran out of things to ask him and he ran out of things to tell. Except, on the last day I saw him, he took us to one side and looked at us for a long time.

'You look like her, you know,' he said, 'same eyes. And you both have this... sadness about you. Don't be sad. Don't be bitter about what happened. She needed something that nobody could give her.'

'One person could have,' I told him. 'There was one, but he fucked off out of it not too long after I was born.'

He also said that there was something else there, too, a desperation in me eyes that also haunts every photograph that features me ma. A hint, perhaps, of something hideous: a craving, famished aspect. 'Yeah,' I said, turning it on for him now, making him look away under the intensity of me stare. 'There's a word for that, mate. Love.'

He couldn't come back with anything, so I said goodbye.

I did try. I did try to hold back the sadness and the anger. But she had been driven to kill herself, being rejected by the man who she had invested so much time and money in. Someone who had just walked, who started her on her path into that dark little area of the garden that nobody comes back from. The tangled area that doesn't smell too good, where the cats go to die. Where the footballs vanish and nobody wants to go and retrieve them. The bastard who did that, legging it after I was born, because he couldn't hack it: he couldn't hack all the responsibility because he was so young. And, all right, he wasn't me proper dad, but me ma needed him and he fucked off. Too young. Needed his freedom. Didn't want to be tied down to an older woman with kids. Well, boo-hoo, fuckhead, I want you. Because *you sent me ma over the edge. I want to take you down to the shattered little corner of the garden and force you to have a fucking good, long look at it. I want you to fucking move in there, permanent.*

See her now, I can, in her pressed jeans and a chocolate-brown pullover fraying at the sleeves. The clearest image I will ever carry: grey morning, dew on the grass. Everything soft. A mug of coffee in her fist. A ciggie in the other. Smoke ghosts. She moves across the overgrown lawn so smoothly she might have been gliding. She's talking to me but her voice is all wrong. It's full of blood and gristle. Air is squealing out of her. A drag on the fag, and smoke escapes from the gashes in her throat. She tosses me the copper wire, hacks up something about not needing it any more. She disappears into the fog.

I've still got that wire.

He closed his eyes and listened to the platform announcements. The voices from the tannoy were soothing somehow. He liked it here, liked its anonymity and lack of character, he liked it much more than the pissy little room in that brown house, in the endless row of brown houses, where he was staying in Liverpool; the house which was much too small, and smelled of clothes washed with cheap detergent that hadn't dried properly. Waiting to grow, waiting for the accretion of years. For maturity. –'You'll need to get a job,' she said, and this time he wasn't startled, even though he wasn't looking her way. He sensed her nearby, that was always the case, even when she was miles away. Sometimes he looked at her, or thought of her, and it was so much like looking at himself that he didn't believe he could be who he was. But that was good. That was okay. Because if even he wasn't sure, then what chance did anyone else have of working him out? He looked up now, straight into those dizzying eyes of hers. –'I don't understand. I have a job. I have *the* job.' She was carrying a mug of coffee and she made a gesture with her hand, maybe to see if the seat on his table was free. She sat down before he could say anything. –'Don't look so pained,' she said, and sipped at the froth on her coffee. –'Who are you?' he asked.

He knew very well, this woman who talked to him on the phone, this woman who had saved him from himself all those years ago, but whenever she was there in the flesh, it made him feel awkward, on the edge of being lost, a child again, and he was crushed into his seat by something close to guilt at the knowledge that she knew who he was and the terrible things he had done. He had to retreat into the game, and she understood that. She knew it protected him. And she wanted nothing else but to protect him. She'd promised that half a lifetime ago, it seemed. She promised it to him again now, as she reached out to stroke his forearm, to hold his chin with her small, gentle hands. He stole glances at her through the steam coming off their cups. He wished he smoked, so that he might have something else to do with his fingers.

She was wearing large glasses, tinted burnt-orange, a beige corduroy skirt, a boatneck top and a brown, cropped leather jacket. Every time he saw her in his dreams, or like now, she looked different, but enough like his mother that he wanted to cry out and lift his arms to her, as he must have done in the cot when his mother came to him at the peak of his nightmares, or when hunger upset him. She watched him for a second, then quickly turned away. She didn't look at him again. –'You have to get a job,' she said again. 'It won't do, you moping around, waiting for something to happen.

Waiting for a signal that might never come. We have to pretend we don't know each other. You might think you're blending in but you're not. You're like blood on a wedding dress. If I'm found out, then you'll be found out. We have to put some distance between us.' –'But it's all I know,' he said. 'It's all I can do.' She nodded slightly. Lipstick scalloped the rim of her cup. –'I know someone.' She slid a piece of paper across the table. He didn't pick it up immediately, but instead watched her hand retreat like something startled. 'He'll give you work, and in time I will get messages to you, when I feel it's right. When the time is right for you to make your move. I'm doing this because I love you. I love you.' –'But I don't have an address. No references. Nothing.' The wheedling tone was returning to his voice. He was small again, frightened, alone. –'It doesn't matter. I'll sort it,' she said. 'Do you understand what I'm saying to you? You need to fade away for a while. You need to step back.'

He waited until she was ten minutes gone before opening the piece of paper and reading the address written on it. He pushed back his chair and walked over to the steps leading to the Underground, wishing that he had told her that he loved her, too.

Anyone watching him from by the platforms would have seen a young, fit man, perhaps an athlete, pause at the top for a few moments, looking down into the tiled throat as if composing himself for a long, unpleasant journey. Then they'd see him straighten slightly, and run a hand through longish black hair that was in need of a wash, before sinking slowly out of view.

Turn and face. Turn and face.
Find your man.
Mark him.

PART THREE
INFANTICIDE

10

She came to me in a dream I was having, in which I was eating a plate of roast lamb in a meadow filled with violently red poppies. She came to me and hijacked my dream. That was her way. She could inveigle her way into your life, anything you were doing, until you were suddenly doing something else, the thing she wanted you to do, and you couldn't see the join of where or how it had happened, only her impish grin as she celebrated another victory over her gullible dad.

We sat among the poppies, and she occasionally reached out to hold my hand. She always held my hand when we sat together, whether it was to watch the football on the telly or having lunch in town, or at a film at the Odeon. I said to her, Sas, you know I love you, don't you? And I turned to find she was gone. And I wasn't holding her hand any more: I was holding my own. I started looking for her among the poppies, worried that in telling her I loved her I had chased her away from my life. And I saw something in the field, something redder than the flowers, if that was possible, and I ran towards it, knowing that it wasn't just that I loved her, *it was that I hadn't loved her enough during the awful time when we were trying to get back on track after Rebecca had been killed. And before I reached the red, before I could determine its shape and its meaning...*

I was shaken awake by a guard at Lime Street Station. It was getting on for ten in the morning, and I shivered on the platform, wiping my eyes, wishing that there was a bar or a pub open at this time of day. Wishing that I'd packed a jumper. Wishing that I'd even packed. Wishing that my mind wouldn't betray me like that whenever I was asleep. Most of the people from the train had already disappeared through the ticket barrier, and the train was cooling on its tracks, catching its breath now the journey was over. Exactly what I should be doing myself. I'd had to leave my car at home because it would have stood out here and I also didn't fancy coming back to it to find a solitary wing mirror remaining.

I stalked up to the concourse by the entrance to the station and looked out at Lime Street itself. Liverpool was wadded in mist. St George's Hall, across the way, looked like a ruin from a ghost story, its exhaust-darkened columns failing to look real, as did anything – cars, buses, people – that streamed up and down the arterial road.

I went into a café built into the containing walls of the station and ordered a bacon-and-egg sandwich and a mug of coffee. I sat by the smeared windows and watched the buildings slowly reclaim themselves from the mist. It could as well have been the previous night, which I'd spent most of in a horrendous grease pit by Euston Station, nursing mugs of tepid tea and watching the cockroaches leave in droves, kvetching about the filth.

By the time I'd had my breakfast and another cup of coffee, I felt as if I might be fit enough to play a more prominent part in the morning. I walked down to the easyCar rental place on Paradise Street, and picked up the A-class Merc that I'd booked at the same time as buying my train ticket. Then I drove through the rush-hour traffic to a B&B I'd found out about on Marine Crescent, in Waterloo, a couple of miles north of the city centre. The woman running it, an old and starchy hen called May, seemed happy to see me even though I'd interrupted her in the middle of filling glass jars with what looked like raspberry jam. She scampered up three flights of stairs to show me my room. It was the usual B&B nightmare: florid pink wallpaper, threadbare moss-green carpet, knick-knacks strewn all over the place (plastic dogs next to a brass alligator nutcracker; a ceramic plate of Princess Diana opposite a framed mirror etched with the Coca-Cola logo). She gave me the rundown on breakfast and checkout times, then bid me a good day and went back to her preserves.

I stretched out on the bed for a while and thought about Melanie. How her body had moved under the dress she wore as she walked back through the shadows and lights to her front gate. I thought about how much I'd have liked to further explore what that body moved like when it was dressed only in me. I wanted to call her but I didn't want to appear too possessive. Instead, I wandered downstairs to the hallway and checked in the phone book for a name that I knew I wouldn't find.

But there was a Geenan there. *Geenan, J.*

Whoever it was, they lived in Hope Street, back in the centre of town. I rang the number, unsure as to why my heart was beating so hard. A man answered, who sounded tired and broken. Like a man who has received too many kickings in his life and never known what it feels like to dole a few out instead.

I said, 'Is Kara there, please?'

'You cunt,' he said. 'You fucking cunt, leave me alone,' and put the phone down.

I tried the number again but Geenan, J., just let it ring. I dialled the number of an old journalist friend of mine who worked on the *Echo*, a guy called Mike Brinksman, and arranged to meet him – late on, as it transpired, because he was up to his nuts in a red-hot story about a city councillor and an underage schoolgirl. The traffic had eased, and it only took me ten minutes, but by the time I got to Geenan's address there was nobody in. The cathedrals at either end of the street seemed uncertain about how they should look; the remnants of the mist still clung to them and softened them into childish sketches.

I went round the back and looked through the window, but no luck. I knocked on the door next to his, and a fat bloke with white flesh wearing an off-white vest and a pair of blue tracksuit bottoms answered it. One hand was clamped around a pear, and his fingernails were crammed with filth. A dead cigarette was jammed in the corner of his mouth as he ate around it. The smell of hot fat and boiled vegetables breathed its way past him.

'Do for you?' he asked.

'Next-door,' I said. 'Do you know where Johnny's gone?'

'Jimmy,' he said.

'Yeah, of course, I was thinking of his brother.'

'I didn't know he had a brother.'

'Anyway,' I said.

'He'll have gone to work,' he said.

'On a Sunday?'

The other guy took a bite out of his pear.

'Quickest way there?' I said. 'What is it, do you reckon?'

'The Docks? You're having a laugh, arntcha?' he said. 'Not from around these parts, then?'

'Used to be. Long time ago.'

'Try the Mersey, then. You never know, you might find the Docks down there. Now, d'you mind, only I'm missing the footie.'

'Which one is it? There's bloody hundreds of them.'

'Princes,' he said, or I think he said, because the door was closed by then.

I found a car park on St Nicholas Place, in the shadow of the Royal Liver Building, and sauntered down to the riverside just as the foot ferry bound for Seacombe was puttering away from the landing stage. To my right, a path swept into Princes Parade, a sad, broken-down stretch of water surrounded by a great deal of dead land where once a number of unloading sheds and residential buildings had stood, all confined by the crumbling remains of the granite-rimmed dock wall. It was hard, as I walked down to the blasted industrial estate that existed there now, to imagine ships of any description inching in towards the jetties. A rowing boat would seem too grand for this place now, let alone the New York packets, or the cotton ships and traders that had swarmed in during the 1800s.

Someone was walking towards me, a man in a yellow reflective coat and a hard hat. He held a clipboard in his hands, but he obviously didn't want to conduct a survey.

'You, piss off. Now,' he said. He had a face like Punch. His nose and chin were so close together I supposed that he had to push his mouth out to the side in order to kiss his boss's arse. He got close enough for me to see the little bits of dried egg on his tie. He smelled faintly of Dettol.

'I'm here to see a Mr Geenan.'

I find that if you slot that indefinite article in before a name, it gives your manner the kind of professional gloss you might otherwise be missing. Here's me in jeans and a badly scarred leather jacket, hair needs cutting and a pair of suitcases under my eyes, but because I say '*a* Mr Geenan', Eggy Tie's on the back foot. He thinks I'm an undercover cop. Thinks I'm Inland Revenue. Health and Efficiency.

'Jimmy?' he said. 'Jimmy's busy. I'll deal with it.'

'No,' I said. 'No you won't. It's a delicate matter. Personal. I need to discuss it with Mr Geenan privately.' I began to get my wallet out, to show him the unforgivably poor warrant card I'd made with a few crayons and a photo, but Eggy was already making cut-it-out gestures with his clipboard.

'It's okay,' he said. 'Jimmy's over by the warehouse. He's on the forklift. Tell him I said it was okay to take a break. If there's anything I can do to help, I'll be in the Portakabin over there.'

He went off, mincing prissily, his too-fat thighs rubbing together in a way that must generate too much heat, making you think he'd go up in flames if he wore the wrong kind of fabric or put on a burst of speed. Presumably thought he'd helped the cogs of justice to wheel around a little more freely. He'd soon be sitting in his Portakabin, studying his clipboard, while stewing in his juices over why I'd come to talk to Jimmy Geenan. I hate clipboards. Give someone a clipboard and they can't help but start acting like an officious twatter. Even if the clipboard has nothing clipped to it but a piece of paper that says *Don't forget: bananas, dry cleaning*.

The warehouse seemed to be void of anything that might need a forklift to deal with it. A few men in luminous yellow coats and hard hats sat around drinking tea, clipboard-free.

You could feel the liberty, the goodwill. A couple of them smiled and nodded at me, but you could tell the ones who were obviously up for a clipboard soon. They scowled, their top pockets brimming with pencils. They played with their tape measures in a menacing fashion.

Jimmy Geenan looked as depressed as the buzzer on the reception desk of a hotel run by deaf people. He was wrapped in a heavy donkey jacket as he manoeuvred his forklift into position in front of a sad pile of pallets in one distant corner. Their cargo was obscured by thick layers of plastic wrap. Geenan's hard hat, his thick black beard and unnecessarily large-lensed glasses gave him the air of someone trying to conceal himself from the public, as if all three belonged to a mask that he took off once he got home of an evening.

'Mr Geenan?' I said, as I approached, but either he was ignoring me or he couldn't hear above the electric whine of the forklift's engine. I stood in front of the forklift and raised my hand.

'Excuse me, Mister,' he called out, 'but I'm trying to work here.'

'My name's Joel Sorrell,' I said. 'I rang you earlier. About a Kara Geenan?'

The indefinite article wasn't impressing anybody this time. He moved the forklift forward, its tines extending on either side of me, until I was pressed back against the pallets.

'I told you to leave me alone,' he said.

'Kara's in London,' I said. 'I think she's got something against me. Has she mentioned me to you at all? Joel Sorrell? Said anything to you about me? Why she's got such a pain in the arse about me?'

What little I could see of his face was screwed up with

173

either rage or incomprehension. He killed the engine and got down from his seat. He was a good three or four inches taller than me and his hands were balled into fists. The breadth of his combined knuckles could probably have been measured in feet.

'I don't want any trouble,' I said. 'I just want to find Kara.'

'Yeah, well it's too late for that. I don't know who the fuck you are, or why you're doing this to me, but I'm going to put a stop to it right now.'

He waded in, but it was fairly easy to step back, ducking under one tine of the forklift and keeping some distance between us. I showed him the gun and he went limp, his hands unfolding at his sides. They were shaking.

'Why don't you fuck off out of here, you little bastard,' he said, and his voice was shaking too. He seemed close to tears.

'Look, Mr Geenan, maybe I've got the wrong end of the stick here. I don't mean to annoy you, and I'm sorry if I've upset you.' He gave a short, desperate bark of laughter. 'But I really need to find Ka–'

'Kara's dead,' he said, and the words dropped between us like tiny frozen fledglings falling from a nest. His face opened up, even as he said them, making him appear surprised. Maybe he was. It looked as if he had never uttered the line before. Footsteps behind me: half a dozen of Geenan's workmates sloping over. No clipboards in sight. One of them was carrying a large wrench.

'I'm sorry,' I said, 'but I'm in trouble. I'd like to talk to you about it. If you feel you can. I'm staying at the Seahorse Inn on Marine Crescent. Come and see me. I don't mean you any harm, believe me.'

I started to move away. I don't know if he'd caught any

of what I'd said, because he had covered his face with his hands. His workmates were picking up the pace. One of them said, 'Oi, wanker, come here,' and I considered it for about as long as it took for a message to fly across my synapses to get the fuck out of Princes Dock.

11

I waited at the B&B for a few hours, but realised he wasn't coming and who could blame him? I ran a bath and soaked for forty minutes, then I thought about changing for dinner and thought, *sod it*, and put on the jeans and shirt that I'd been wearing for the last week, and which were currently considering filing a formal complaint with social services for my maltreatment of them. I went out and found a chip shop and ate fish and chips at the dockside, looking out at the Wirral peninsula. If I was a poetic man, I might have said that it was being gradually flattened under a great convoy of black clouds that were shedding their load. But I'm not a poetic man, and it all just looked like a great heap of shit pressing down on another heap of shit. I wondered about Kara and why, if she was going to take an alias, she should take the name of a dead girl. It couldn't just be a coincidence. I mean, how many Kara Geenans are there in the world? I reckoned maybe just the one. I only hoped that my Kara had known the real Kara personally. Less attractive was the prospect that she'd read about her death in the papers and just liked the name enough to pinch it for herself. Whatever, the Kara I knew was becoming less and less savoury in my eyes. In fact I was looking forward to seeing her again and finding out just what her fucking problem was.

Dinner over, I decided to leave the car in the car park near the B&B and walk back into town to shed the mega-calories I'd just taken on board. The gun was left in my bed, keeping it cold for me. When I arrived, I went for a cocktail in the basement bar of a big hotel and gave the brush-off to the prostitutes who latched on to me as I entered, complimented me on my jacket and asked if I wanted some company. They went away when I said, sure, but do you mind if we just talk? About my father? And his special needs? There were plenty of other poor dinks for them to work on.

There was some kind of science-fiction convention going on at the hotel, and everyone was wandering around saying 'Klaatu' to each other and comparing home-made phasers made out of dead Persil washing-up bottles. They wore name tags that said stuff like *Epididymus, from the planet Vas Deferens*. I finished up and got out quick, before I was energised into one of their bedrooms for some kind of anal-probe experiment.

It was still cold but the vodka martini had taken the edge off the chill. I went on a crawl through the pubs in the town centre, trying to work out how things had changed since my last visit here. I wasn't due to meet up with Mike Brinksman for another couple of hours.

It was a little depressing to find that some of the pubs I'd liked, such as the Swan, had been closed down and earmarked for demolition. And drinking in the Grapes or the Vines proved a grim experience. There's nothing worse than having a pint in a pub for old times' sake only to find that it's now just a pub, without any of the magic it contained when you were sitting around a table there with your best friends or a woman who was making the back of your neck hot. A pub you love isn't so attractive when there's nobody in it you recognise, beyond lots of other sour-faced thirty-somethings flailing around for the same thing.

At ten I made my way to the Philharmonic at the junction of Hope Street and Hardman Street, not a million miles away from Geenan's place. I was determined to have another crack at him at home, without his hard-hat hard mates to back him up. I was a fifth of the way into a pint of lager when Mike came in.

I'd been at school with Mike Brinksman. He'd kicked further education into touch when he failed his A levels and got himself a job as a trainee reporter on the *Runcorn World*, a Mickey Mouse free weekly rag that wasn't even based in the town it represented, but ten miles away. He'd spent two years there, earning eighty-five pounds a week, before lucking into a job at the *Warrington Guardian*, and thence to the *Liverpool Echo*, where he'd been ever since, apart from the occasional casual shift for one of the daily tabloids.

He looked tired. I got him a whisky and patiently listened to him outline the story about the councillor, while inside I seethed with the need to plug him about the killing in Liverpool. Once he'd got it off his chest, he relaxed, taking off his coat and losing some of the tension in his shoulders. He had very small, very blue eyes that appeared permanently surprised, in a face that was childishly round.

'What brings you up here?' he asked.

'Rafa sees me as the new Luis Suarez,' I said. 'I've resisted up till now, but then Roy got on my case and told me I'd need a few matches to prove myself for England.'

179

'Thank God for that,' he said. 'I thought you were after information.'

'Actually, now you mention it…'

We had another drink. I told him about Liptrott and the suspicion that it was linked to a murder committed five years previously in Merseyside.

'Cause of death?' Mike asked.

I shrugged. 'I never got that far, but I saw the body. It looked as if he'd been opened up like a toddler's Christmas present. I'd say loss of blood, but I couldn't tell you which the fatal wound was.'

'Knife, then?'

'Yes,' I said. 'Oh yes.'

'I'll ask around. I don't remember it off the top of my head, but I'll check the filed copies and talk to a few plods I get on with. Might be a bit tasty for me up here, anyway, if they're going to reopen the files on it because your lot have got a hard-on for the killer.'

He gave me one of his cards, and rejected my suggestion that we move on to a club. Mojo's, an old favourite of mine, was on Hope Street, a hop, skip and piss against the wall away.

'I'm shagged,' he said. 'I'm off home. How long are you in the 'pool for?'

'Another day or two. Depends what I dig up.'

'I'll talk to you tomorrow then. Give us a call round lunchtime.'

Mojo's was the kind of place you only find out about through a mate. You could wander up Hope Street during the day and not realise that one of its terraced houses concealed a three-floor club with bars, dance floors and the kind of interior decoration that made Laurence Llewelyn-Bowen look as outré as a Mr Byrite cardigan.

I found a table and sat down with a pint. It was a bit early for Mojo's, but then I knew how packed this place could get once the pubs reached chucking-out time. Which was not to say that the club was filled only with lonely echoes when I got there. There was a good crowd in, and the music was loud, some drum 'n' bass track that made your lungs vibrate. I people-watched for a bit, enjoying the currents that pulled the girls and boys this way and that. The way they moved to the music, even though they weren't dancing: the little tics and twitches of those who were trying to impress, the opening and closing of posture depending on who was nearby, the eye contact. Everyone was fluent in body language in here, it seemed. Apart from one or two mutes who continued disrupting the whole, beautiful rhythm.

Like this guy, sitting next to a woman who was saying no to him every which way but verbally. Everything about him was a bit of snot in your ice cream, from his too-shiny bouffant hair to his no-need-to-iron shirt and knitted tank top, his white trousers and slip-on shoes. He was walking a coin across his knuckles, a large one, that looked like one of those commemorative jobs they'd handed out at school for the Silver Jubilee. Some people, I understand, think that looks cool. Nothing that obviously took years of hardcore practice, at the expense of a normal, healthy existence, is cool. And this guy clearly must have spent aeons in front of his mirror, walking that coin, knowing that to perfect it was to unlock the door to an embarrassment of female riches.

Wrong, minge-wipe.

A middle-aged woman was on the prowl, trying to crash drinks from the students sucking their alcopops at the bar. Some mother high on a night out with her mates, maybe tickled by a compliment or two from some pissed lads earlier on, thinking she could cut it with the foxes in here. She had good legs, I'll give her that, but they were only good for a hippo. Her boobs were situated where they ought to be but her black bra, visible through the sheer white top she was wearing, wore a sign that said Hardcore Scaffolding Ltd. The less said about her arse the better, but she made two stools groan when she spread it across them.

I was groaning, too. She'd picked my table.

'Well,' she said, 'fuck me ragged with a cricket bat.'

'Sorry,' I said, trying not to linger too long on her Maybelline mask.

'I'm waiting for someone.'

'If it isn't Joel Sorrell.'

Christ. Please, God. Please, *God*, if I never have another drink and promise to apply for a place in a monastery, please tell me that I've never porked this Certificate 18 non-special effect.

'You don't remember me, do you?'

The people who ask that question get it slightly wrong every time. They should try inserting a 'want to' in between the 'don't' and the 'remember'. I studied her eyes, for as long as they stayed in one place, and gritted my teeth. I was in a club that I liked and the last time I'd been here, so had she, but she and I had been fifteen years younger, and then free of an amount of excess fat that could have gone to create a third person.

'Hello, Annie,' I said.

'Are you married?' she asked.

'Yes,' I lied.

'Liar,' she said. 'Where's your ring? Or maybe you're on the pull tonight? Naughty boy.'

'Annie, if there was ever a time when I was not on the

pull, it's tonight. I'm so much not pulling that I'm actually pushing. I'm pushing so hard.'

'You always were a weirdo,' she said. 'Nice arse, though, as I remember.'

'Yes, well that was yesterday. And today is today and we've all moved on, haven't we?'

She asked me if I was going to be a gentleman and buy her a drink, and I said no. 'Then I'll buy you one,' she said.

She got me a pint of lager, and while she was at the bar I almost made a break for it, but I wasn't going to let her spoil my night and, anyway, I'd have to wait outside in the cold for Geenan to get home. I thanked her when she came back and then spent some time studying the knots and wormholes in the wooden table. When I looked up again, she was crying.

I felt like all men do when a woman starts to cry: guilty, shitty and confused.

'I'm sorry,' I said, although I wasn't sure what I was apologising for. It seemed to work, though, and she sobered up a little.

'It's okay,' she said, dabbing at the panda-esque horror that her eyes had become. 'I'm just tired and drunk. I was only being friendly.'

'I know,' I said. 'It's me. I'm no good any more at recognising *friendly*.'

'You sound like a bitter old man,' she said.

'Bang on the money,' I said, and dumped a few big mouthfuls of lager down my neck.

'Do you remember–'

I touched her arm. 'Please, could we not play that game?'

'It's all I've got,' she said.

'I remember everything. So no point carrying on.'

183

'You still live in the area?'

I shook my head. 'I ran away years ago. Went down south.'

'Why?'

I smiled, or tried to. All I could feel was a cold worm trying to move around where my mouth ought to be. 'I could tell you but it would mean nothing to you.'

She didn't say anything. For the first time that night, I wished she would.

'Look,' I said, 'I moved away because I felt I was getting dragged down. I felt smothered and I didn't want that.'

The club was getting busier and I glanced at my watch. The pubs were closing and hundreds of people had now realised they were wearing their beer-heads and needed to fill them. Images from my past in the north-west were queuing up like surly youths outside a chip shop, fired, feisty and ready to visit actual bodily harm on me if I so much as dared look at them.

'I went to hairdressing college when I left school,' she said. 'And then, after I dropped out there, I got a job in a baker's. Hair today, scone tomorrow, that's what my husband always says.'

I could believe it. I bet he said it every day.

'I met my husband the day after me and you... you know.'

'Really?'

'Yes. I had a hangover – as you know. And I was out in the garden getting the washing in. He was next-door, cleaning windows. We got chatting.'

She lifted her glass, which was empty, then returned it to the table. I didn't offer. I had now changed my mind and decided I was getting out the moment she turned her back. 'Did you ever get married?'

'Yes,' I said.

'Kids?'

'Annie.'

'I'm sorry. I'm just being friendly.'

'So you keep saying. I wouldn't bother about that. I had my friendly gland removed in a special operation.'

'When we, you know... weren't you seeing someone? Teacher wasn't she?'

I got up too quickly and knocked our glasses to the floor. I think I turned her chair over too, while she was in it. I can't be sure. Because I was moving fast then, barging through the students and their trendy oblong spectacles, their tiny rubber handbags and two-storey platform trainers. The bouncers were thinking about pinching me, but whether they thought to let it go because I was leaving anyway or because there was something in my eyes that gave them cause to back off, I couldn't say. Either way, they were wise to.

I got out on to Hope Street and sucked in the cold air hard until my lungs caught fire and I started getting a headache. The wind dragged its icy nails up and down my spine. I tugged my jacket close and jammed my hands in the pockets, stalked over to Geenan's house. There was a light on in the front window.

I knocked on the door. He still wasn't answering. I knelt on the doorstep and pushed open the flap on the letterbox.

'Jimmy,' I called out. I thought I heard a television. 'Jimmy? It's me. It's Joel Sorrell. I talked to you today. I didn't mean to upset you, but I need your help. I know it's eating you up. But my girl is gone too. My little girl is gone, too, Jimmy. I'm in the same dirty bathwater as you. I know–'

The door opened and he was standing above me, his face twisted up as if he'd just eaten a forkful of shepherd's pie

185

only to find that it was shepherd's shit. 'You don't know a fucking thing,' he said.

He went back into the house, leaving me to get to my feet and follow him.

12

I woke up wearing my clothes. 'You shouldn't have done that, Jimmy,' I said, which was also the last thing I remember saying from the previous night, before I reached that point of drunkenness that ensures you remember nothing else. He'd just opened a second bottle of Jameson's. I'd had one more drink, the whiskey tasting like water, and must have passed out. He then either put me in a taxi or I recovered sufficiently to do it myself. Crucially, though, I remembered pretty much everything that was said up until that point.

I'd slept too late for breakfast, but I wasn't up to it anyway. I had a wash and scooped up my keys and wallet, then went downstairs. Outside was wetter than a Conservative back bench. I ran through the rain to the rental car and started her up, flicking on the headlights and the wipers as I nosed out of the car park. The intense fragrance of the interior, something rose-based, was so cloying that I almost threw up. I wound down the window a little and chewed on the damp air. By the time I hit the A562 going east, I felt a little better, but every time I thought about Annie, or the way she'd tried to jemmy a way into me, I felt my gorge rising.

I was in a fury for allowing Annie to infect me with the past, after I'd left the north-west to get away from all that hurt. That I'd acquired a great pile of new hurt – deeper, nastier, insidious hurt – down in London had no bearing on the matter. It was a different hurt, a hurt I thought I could cope with more successfully because I was older and wiser and more cynical. And I must have been doing something right, because I wasn't running away any more. Maybe that was what separates adults from children: the direction you take and the speed at which you take it when the monsters come looking for you. But Annie wasn't to blame, especially not after what Jimmy told me.

More fool me for thinking I could dodge my demons.

I followed the Speke Road out of Liverpool, stopping off at a drive-thru McDonald's for a large McCoke and a few McNurofen cadged from the McGirl at the service hatch. I was about to leave, when Mike gave me a call. He'd spent a few hours in the archives and had found a reference to the murder I'd asked him about.

'August 2005,' he revealed. 'Woman by the name of Georgina Millen. She was twenty-nine years old when she was killed.'

She'd been opened up with the kind of frenzy a thirteen-year-old boy affords a copy of *Playboy*. The MO didn't resemble anything that Merseyside's CID had seen before. The prints they took at the scene came up with zero matches when they were fed through the computer. Despite the public's near-rabid demand for an arrest to be made, and one of the largest man-hunts in the north-west's history, nobody was nailed for it. Now I could remember the panic that had flowered in the subsequent weeks. Everyone seemed tensed for a follow-up death, as if someone with such anger in them, such a propensity for murder as violent as this, could not surely have spent himself on a single victim. All over the area, schoolgirls vanished from the streets, confined to their bedrooms, and ferried to and from school by fathers who regarded each other with suspicion in the car parks. But then someone else was killed in a different way, in a different place. The tabloids foamed about other things, attention shifted, interest dropped off. As it always does.

Mike gave me the name of the murder site, and a couple more bits and pieces including the name of the school that the girl had attended. I thanked him, promising him a pint and a Chinese next time I was round his way. Before I rang off, I asked him to hang fire on any follow-up stories about the possible connection between this death and the one in London. He gnashed at that for a while, but eventually caved in. 'Just till I've had a bit of breathing space on it,' I confirmed. 'A week, perhaps. Certainly no more than two.'

'I'll be all over it then, Joel,' he said. 'So don't go asking me for any more time.'

Which meant I had a week, ten days tops, to finger the bastard. Otherwise, what with the heat the papers would bring to the situation, he'd go to ground. And Mawker would throw me in a cell and have my balls rubbed non-stop with a cheese grater.

Another twenty minutes and the A562 became Fiddlers Ferry Road. I followed it through its regeneration into Widnes Road and turned off at the Penketh roundabout, on to Stocks Lane. I turned right on to Meeting Lane and drove down to the end, bearing down on the waves of *déja vu* that were threatening to make me lose control and pile the car into one of the neatly clipped front lawns. I must have weeded and mowed a fair few of the gardens along here in my time, back when I was casting about for something to do. I did all kinds of odd-jobs: gardening, furniture removal, digging up potatoes, picking raspberries. About a year before I joined the police, I got the taxi-driving job, and also a few stints as a security guard through a friend whose father was the regional inspector for a nationwide security firm. Of all the jobs in all the world, that one stunk like a skunk with halitosis living on a sewage farm. I used to spend sixteen-hour shifts, 8 a.m. till midnight, sitting in a Portakabin on building sites, chasing off kids who wanted to play in the sand. I couldn't bunk off the patrols and read or get a suntan because there were checkpoints at various areas around the site that I needed to punch in at certain times throughout the day, just to prove I'd been doing the job properly. Now, instead of chasing off those kids who wanted to play in the sand, I was trying to find them.

I parked the car on the road outside the primary school and walked through the playground to the main entrance. There were kids all over the place, pretty much what might be expected, I suppose, although this was a new strain of kid – an überkid. I was accosted by a couple of them who asked, in basso voices, if they could look after my car. I told them no, and that it didn't matter if they did anything to it because it was a rented car and was thus insured against damage.

'How about if we do something to you instead? Are *you* insured against damage?' This from a boy who couldn't have been any older than ten with, I swear, a furring of pseudo-moustache on his top lip. He must have topped five foot six.

'Which failed experiment produced you?' I asked him, feeling cheap at having a pop at a child but, well, he started it.

'Come again?' Bumfluff said.

'Are you one of the teachers here?'

Some of the other kids laughed. Bumfluff didn't say anything, but he didn't have to. He was turning red, his hands balled into fists the size of Puerto Rican mangoes. I was impressed, but I moved on before he did something to get himself expelled.

Inside the entrance hall was a small, presently unmanned, reception desk. The walls were filled with collages of winter scenes, lots of glitter and tinfoil and clear plastic glued on to black backing paper with Uhu. Another board contained words describing winter. To the usual ones someone had chalked – without any of the staff noticing, it would seem – the words *Miss Hicks's tits*. From the assembly hall came the sound of someone playing the piano astonishingly badly.

A cough, one of those questioning hacks used by people who can't be arsed to try out their manners, made me turn around. A woman who looked as if she was put on the earth to wear shawls scurried into the entrance hall. She was thinner than the plot of a TV movie and bore the ingrained expression of all teachers who wish to instil terror into their charges: a kind of hawkishness that comes with true dedication and practice. It wasn't something you could wash off easily. She couldn't be all bad, though: she had cat scratches on her hands.

'Yes?' she said, in precisely the voice I expected. Borderline shrill.

'My name's Joel Sorrell,' I said, then added, in a voice filled with urbane ennui, 'Can you help me?'

My dad had given me this little trick when I was young. He said, whenever you're talking to a woman, before you say anything, ask her if she can help you. And say it in a little-boy-lost voice. I've always followed his advice. It never works.

'What do you want?' she asked, her tone brittle.

'I need some information,' I said, ditching the little-boy-lost and trying the wolfish admirer of older women ploy. I gave her a smile. 'Got cats?' I asked, nodding at her hands and revealing my own scars.

'Gardening,' she said. A disappointment, but it was an in of sorts. 'Are you from the police?'

'No, I'm representing a client who has a missing relative. Possibly abducted from this school.'

'We have nobody missing from this school. We have excellent security measures here.'

'Which is why I was allowed to get in without anybody checking who I was.'

This seemed to bring her up short. Any chance of her being my ally was now as likely as Osama Bin Laden appearing in a Wigan panto.

'I can assure you,' she said again, 'that our security here is excellent.'

I didn't really care. I said, 'Two pupils from this school were murdered. Did you know that?'

'That's complete non–'

'No, it's true. Two girls. One called Kara Geenan and another, Georgina Millen. Both killed in the same year, 2009.'

'Those names don't ring a bell,' she said, but nothing more, clearly expecting me to take that as my cue to leave.

'Who are you, by the way?' I asked. 'Cleaner?'

'I'm the Deputy Head,' she said, firmly.

'Oh,' I said. 'You wouldn't be Miss Hicks, by any chance?'

'How do you know?'

I smiled. 'One of the boys outside told me your name.'

Get that 'Miss' – I could buy it. She was all Vosene and Pontefract cakes, spending long nights in, listening to Radio

2 and thinking of a man called Gerald who had once volubly admired her hibiscus.

'I'd like to see the headmaster, if that's okay. This is a pretty serious matter.'

She left me there with the ice thesaurus, and I decided against freaking her out any further by going for a wander along the school corridors, just to show her just how excellent the school's security was, and instead waited by the staffroom, which was as full of furtive bitching as the bike sheds or the patch of spare wasteland behind the gym.

Presently, a rotund guy appeared through the swing-doors leading to the assembly hall. He and Miss Hicks scurried towards me like the Number 10 made flesh. His hair was receding and his dark suit was dusted with dandruff from the remnants. He had sad eyes, but who wouldn't, being in charge of a shower like the ones I'd met outside?

'Banbury,' he said. 'Don Banbury. Headmaster.'

I told Banbury what I'd told Hicks, and he was in the middle of saying the same thing she'd said when he cottoned on that I wasn't talking about now.

'Hang on,' he said, and pinched his lower lip between his thumb and forefinger. 'In 2009? I wasn't here then.'

'I didn't say you killed them,' I said.

He kind of half-laughed at that, as if I'd made a joke but he couldn't quite enjoy it as much as he wanted to. 'Come with me,' he said, in that *don't you dare deny me* kind of headmasterish way.

We went through a large door into what I supposed was his office. There were no canes or slippers lying around. They did it differently these days, the old violence. It was all psychological now – much more effective. Maybe they went on courses for it.

Hicks had vanished, glad to get shut of me. Banbury gestured at a chair and I sat down. He then got on the blower to someone called Ollie, and asked to see the registers for the year in question.

'Tea?' he asked me.

'Coffee, if that's okay,' I said, and he nodded, relaying the order through to Ollie.

We played verbal tennis with the weather and the football, and then he served me something with a bit of topspin.

'I'm not at liberty to tell you who I'm working for,' I said.

'But you're looking for one of our ex-pupils. Someone you say is already dead?'

'No,' I corrected him, 'I'm looking for the person who killed them.'

'You think the person who killed them was a pupil here?'

'It's an eyebrow-raiser, I admit, but no less possible because of that.'

'Mr Sorrell, this is a good school in an improving area. I'm not sure I'm happy with your theory that we nurtured a murderer here.'

'I'm not saying you did. I'm saying it's a possibility. And, anyway, it would have been before your time.'

He smarted at that, and might have come back at me were it not for Ollie coming through the door with our cups, a plate of biscuits and a couple of large folders.

I sipped my piss-weak Nescafé while he fingered the buff suspension files and pinched his bottom lip again. 'Can I see some identification?' he said.

'I don't have any,' I said. 'I work on my own. I used to be in the police force and I can give you some people to contact if you need references, but it will take time and there's a man on a slab in London with his tripes hanging out of him, thanks to this bastard. Another murder occurring isn't that far-fetched and this is my only lead. If it works out, you'll be fêted. If somebody else dies because you were too busy playing red-tape fannies, then my mate Mike Brinksman at the *Echo* will be up your nose faster than a Vicks inhaler.'

'There's no need–'

'There's every need, Banbury. Now, come on, get shuffling.'

He went through the papers so slowly that I dragged my chair over to him and started giving him a hand. I asked him if there were any teachers still around from five years ago, someone who might shed some light on the girls who had gone missing, but he was shaking his head even before I got to the end of my sentence.

'It's not the most prestigious of schools, I have to admit,' he said. 'There's rather a rapid turnover of staff here.'

He gradually got chatty again, giving me information about registers and photographs that I wasn't asking for, but I was glad that he was cooperating – if only because he thought it might mean his becoming a local hero.

A knock at the door. A kid with hair like a twelve-inch record that had melted over his head entered the room. His glasses had little bits of Band-Aid on the hinges. He looked a feisty little twat.

'What is it, Jeremy?'

'Miss Sharples sent me, sir. I put a drawing pin on Tim Raines' chair.'

'Did he sit on it?'

'Yes, sir.'

'Wait outside,' said Banbury, ladling on the menace. I was starting to enjoy my day at school. But that didn't last long.

I was still ploughing through the custard creams when he passed me a class photograph that I had seen before, many years ago. I knew it was the same picture, for a number of reasons. There was a kid on the end of the middle row, pulling a face, his lips drawn back from his teeth and his eyelids screwed up. Another had stuck his tongue out. At the front, in the centre, sat Miss Blythe – Gemma Blythe. I knew Gemma Blythe. I knew her very well.

'Why are you showing me this picture?'

'The girls,' he said. He pointed at two faces, then showed me the corresponding names on the back of the photograph. 'You've got to be fucking kidding.' My head was swimming. I hadn't realised this was Gemma's school. And I hadn't realised that the two dead girls had been in her class. But on the back of this photo, the names were there: Kara Geenan, Georgina Millen. They were some years away from their deaths, and looked about as happy as two kids unaware of that fact could be.

'Unlucky year,' he admitted. 'I wasn't aware.'

'Did you know Gemma? Or was she before your time, too?'

His eyes widened. '*You* knew Gemma?'

'Yes,' I said. 'We were an item for a while.'

'I'm sorry,' he said, and the hairs at the back of my neck started to prickle.

I said, 'It wasn't that bad a relationship.'

He half-laughed again, as before, searching my face as if for permission to do so. He started shaking his head slightly, like a foreigner who isn't quite following the thread of a conversation. He cleared his throat and stared at his empty teacup. 'Tell me you know.'

'Know what?' I said.

'Shit,' he said, and carried on talking, but I didn't listen for a while because I was still shocked at hearing a headmaster come out with a word like that. I finally zoned back to hear: '... why she committed suicide. She had a baby to support. Oh, God, it wasn't...'

'No,' I said. 'It wasn't mine.'

The baby was partly the reason I'd called it a day on our relationship. I was too immature to take on a woman and her child. I thought that leaving her would make it easier in the long run. It was certainly easier for me. There was no way I could possibly have known that she'd crack, as she hadn't come across as one of life's capitulators. Turned out that she killed herself, a couple of years later.

I felt exhausted all of a sudden, fed up with the musty old documents and depressed about my pending drive back to Liverpool. I wanted to be in London, teasing the cat and sitting with Melanie on her big sofa, stroking her ankles. But then part of me railed against that, throwing up images of Gemma, impossible images of her dangling from a flex in a cold room while her kid cried over a congealed plate of food in front of a TV that wasn't working. Nobody had told me about her death – but then nobody knew me. We'd had what, six months together? Hardly enough for someone to feel combined with another, but obviously enough for her. I remember her pleading with me to think about it, to change my mind, but all I could think of was the terror of responsibility.

'I've seen enough, I think.'

Banbury stood up and walked to the door. 'I hope you found what you needed.'

'More than enough,' I said, and looked away. 'Sorry for coming on like an arsehole, earlier,' I added. 'I'm desperate to get hold of this bastard.'

'Yes, well...' Banbury said.

'The photograph,' I said. 'Can I have it?'

Jeremy was now trying to pick a hole in the grouting between the wall tiles. Banbury growled at him to get into his office. As he did so, Jeremy turned to me and mimed a wank. Outside, the bell had gone for the afternoon's classes to begin, so the playground was empty. I walked through the swirling crisp packets, the bubblegum and the spittle to the main gates. Someone had written the words *Your a fuccking bellend* on the car windscreen, in indelible pen. I didn't disagree.

13

I sat in the visitors' car park at Summerhead Hospital, listening to the tick of the Merc's cooling engine, and studying that photograph for maybe ten minutes while everything outside its white border shrank away, turned dim, diminished. Including myself.

I stared so intently at her face that I thought I may have somehow affected the pearl surface of the paper, bruised it, worn it away slightly. Aside from the occasional memory – the bubble unlocking itself from the muddy depths of my mind and rising, unbidden, to the surface – I had not seen that face for almost twenty years. But, as the real world impinged again in the nearby sound of tyres on gravel, I saw that the photograph was still fine but for a few creases and a minute tear in one corner. It was me who was damaged. I had aged a little more, while she remained young and beautiful, and always would.

I put the photograph in the glove compartment and opened the car door. The vehicle that had just pulled up was a handsome, olive-coloured Stag. A middle-aged guy with silver power streaks in his hair got out, with a tan that made

George Hamilton IV look peaky. His trophy wife followed him, quite a bit younger. Maybe she wasn't his trophy wife, perhaps she was his trophy bit-on-the-side instead. Maybe they were going to visit his trophy wife in hospital. She was holding flowers and a smartly-wrapped box that might have contained chocolates. We all nodded at each other with flatline mouths, the kind of greeting that only ever happens in hospital car parks. I watched them leave the gravel and follow a white flagstone path up to the entrance to the psychiatric wing. Behind me, a great swathe of green stretched out to the edge of a small wood. A cricket pitch had been marked out on the grass, its wicket protected by lengths of carpet and a rope marching around its perimeter. The pavilion on the far side was boarded up for the winter: it looked pale and listless, as if it was made from the same stuff as the sky. To my left, the land fell gently away to a level, grassy area dotted with weeping willows. To the right of that, and behind the main hospital building, a steep hill carried a road up towards a lodge house and the hospital's catering facilities: you could smell bleach and cabbage water drifting down. To my right, the road that I had followed through the hospital grounds ambled away through pleasant overhanging trees and squares of light green, that looked like the dry tablets in a box of watercolour paints. Birds tossed chirrups to each other through the soft Cheshire air. A fresh wind rustled the few leaves that were left on the trees, then rolled across the meadows beyond the hospital grounds, creating hypnotic currents through the tall grass.

All in all, a splendid place to be if you were seriously fucked in the head.

I followed the same path the trophy couple had taken, and pushed through a couple of heavy glass-and-brass doors into a faux-marble interior that was dark and cold and smelled antiseptic. That description went for the receptionist too: a starchy hen in a tweed suit and one of those white blowsy blouses with about an acre of soft collar that looks like a meringue gone wrong.

I slipped on a pair of reading glasses that cost a couple of quid from Boots, and went over to her, mussing up my hair and trying to look agitated. The receptionist was signing some stubby book of chits for a guy in royal-blue overalls, who was chewing gum and absently rolling the end of a pencil in his earhole. He was telling her about his day at the races, and she was either ignoring him with the effortless panache of the professionally aloof or she was stone deaf.

'...came in at 10-1, can you believe that? I put a tenner on it, just to show off to her really, like you do, but I didn't in a million years think it would romp home like that. I only picked it because its name was like hers, only a bit different: *Tarte aux Pommes*. Her name's Pam, you see?'

I waited impatiently for him to shut up and for her to finish signing the receipts. I rubbed my hair some more, and shuffled my feet and whispered to myself: *Shit, shit, oh, bother and blast.*

Eventually she deigned to look up and ask me how she could help. I was knocked off balance slightly, because now I could see that she was really rather young, and not unattractive. I instantly ceased with the scatty-old-gent disguise and leaned against the counter.

'Hi,' I said. 'I'm in a bit of a pickle.'

'I'm sorry to hear it. What can I do?'

Christ, she was what? Twenty-two, twenty-three, going on fifty. *What's with the tweed?* I wanted to scream at her, but maybe such an ascetic get-up had been forced upon her by her superiors. Maybe, back home, she showered off this dour exterior, poured herself into skin-tight leather and burned bras all night.

'I had a friend here. He… left, unexpectedly, shall we say?' I raised my eyebrows and looked around me, leaned in a little closer. I was pleased to see her mirroring my actions. A fragrance came off her, something sultry, almost feral. She was no member of the knitting circle, this one. She didn't even know how to eat a Victoria sponge, let alone make one. I felt I should wink at her, just to let her know that I knew. 'Name of Cullen. Gary Cullen.'

'Ah,' she said, and sat back in her chair. 'We've been told not to talk about Mr Cullen until a full investigation has taken place.'

'Yes, but I've driven all the way up here from London. He had a mistress and, well, she's pregnant and only a few weeks away from giving birth. She's not well.' I was thinking wildly now, trying to come up with something that would get her to lean forward and create that little pocket of intimacy again. But I was losing her: the tweed was creeping across that gap that contained her heart. She actually fastened one of the buttons. 'I just need to know if he had any visitors before he took off?'

'I'm sorry, sir, but we've been given express orders not to talk to anyone about this.'

'Not even a chap like me who would like to whisk you off for dinner later…' I smiled, lifted the glasses, had a long look at the name tag pinned to her left breast, '…Sonya?'

I might as well have shown her a dead rat in a shoebox. I thought, *How come Mickey Rourke managed to land none of this crap in* Angel Heart?

The shutters went down in her eyes. I was dismissed.

A couple of overweight security bods in matching black serge stepped out from behind an arch that would have led me deeper into the hospital. I pretended not to notice them, nodded my thanks to the receptionist and went back to the car park. I waited for the guards in their itchy suits to step outside, and then I ostentatiously revved the engine and steered the car on to the road that led to the exit. In the rear-view mirror, I saw one of them speaking into a walkie-talkie. By the time I got down to the exit, three more puddings in half-mast trousers were waiting for me. One stood in the road, preventing my progress; another one approached me revolving his finger. The other stood there with nothing to do, fighting the urge, no doubt, to rescue the yards of serge that his arse was slowly eating.

I did as No. 2 was requesting, and wound down the window. He sank his head into view. He was wearing the kind of buzzcut and clipped moustache that you find on hard bastards in edge-of-town pubs. I bet he wore Fred Perry shirts and owned a Staffordshire bull terrier. I bet his best mates were only ever referred to in abbreviated form. I bet he saw them only on Friday nights, because Saturday nights was quality time with his girlfriend.

'Afternoon,' I said. 'Problem?'

He wouldn't fix his eyes on mine, which I didn't like one bit. In my experience, that's shorthand for *I'm going to hurt you very badly*. He was polite, too, which only tweaked my watch-it monitor up an extra few notches. I kept my foot hovering over the accelerator, and left the handbrake off.

'Could be,' he said. 'Would you mind switching the engine off, sir?'

He invested the word *sir* with the tenderness with which Harvey Keitel says *cunt*.

'I'd rather not.'

He was nodding, as if to say to himself, *We've got a clever swine here*. 'I hear you've been making enquiries about Gary Cullen,' he said. 'Could I ask why?'

'You certainly could,' I said.

Time passed. His astringent aftershave muscled its way through the off-side window and stuck its thumbs in my eyes. His mates were strolling after him, looking this way and that, affecting nonchalance while their knuckles turned white.

No. 2 stepped back slightly and played charades some more: *Get out of the car.*

I smiled at him, quizzically.

'Could you get out of the car?' No please, no sir. Three bags full of edge and irritation. He was eager for violence now. He was bouncing lightly on the balls of his feet. I've seen that before, too. Right before the blood starts flying.

'I could, yes.'

Instead, I floored it and traversed the fifty metres or so to the exit with No. 3 gurning against my windscreen. He slid off as I turned the Merc on to the main road, but his greasy expression of astonishment remained until I parked up in a lay-by, half a mile further along the road, and wiped it off with my handkerchief. I changed out of my Merrells into a pair of waterproof Caterpillar boots that I keep in the back of the car, and slid down the embankment to a barbed-wire fence. Once I'd picked my way gingerly through that, I found myself in a field populated by a piebald horse watching me in the good-natured way that horses do. I took my bearings and angled through the field. Ten minutes later I saw another fence, this one wooden, painted white. Beyond that I saw the tip of the pavilion. By the time I'd climbed over the fence, I could see the edge of the main hospital building.

I reached the rear of the pavilion and checked my watch. Night was due to start its shift here in a couple of hours. Till then I had the crude graffiti scrawled on the back of the pavilion to keep me company. That, the cold, and the grumble of hunger in my belly.

Becs came to me, during those cold two hours, after I had given up trying to break into the pavilion to see if there were any barrels of biscuits from the previous summer's afternoon teas. She sat with me while I huddled against the back wall, under the red words SHAZ SUX COX, looking out over the field I had trudged across as it turned dusty, its white fence growing ghostly in the gloaming. I didn't turn to look at her, in case that meant she would go away. I stared straight ahead and we talked in low voices, about Sarah, mostly, but also about Melanie. When it was time to get up and turn my thoughts to other things, I could remember nothing of our chat apart from the way she had said it would be all right, really, if I wanted to be with someone else: *Being with someone else doesn't mean that you're not with me as well.*

The cricket pitch had meanwhile become a black hole separating me from the hospital. Lights now punched through the blocks of brown stone. I saw silhouettes in the windows, figures looking out at the screaming miles of darkness and seeing nothing but a mirror for their own minds. I wiped away my tears and began to walk the boundary that would take me along a line of tall, slender cypress trees, keeping me hidden until I reached the forecourt. As I got nearer, I checked for possible ways in to the building. The visitors' car park was still being used, which was a relief: it would mean I probably wouldn't be stopped if I was spotted wandering the wards. To bolster my chances, I snatched up a handful of irises from a flower bed at the edge of the car park, and returned to focusing my scrutiny on the doors. My best choice, I decided, was not one of the orthodox entrances that might be manned by security muppets looking out for me to return. Instead, my attention was drawn to the fire doors, and one in particular, since it seemed to provide unofficial access for admin slaves who needed to pop outside for a cigarette break. To facilitate ease of passage, a brick had been placed against the door to prevent it locking and thus stranding poor, freezing nicotine addicts on the wrong side of it. I watched while a group of three women shivered there and turned the air blue, then hurried back inside. As soon as they were gone, I rushed out of the shadows, across the road, and in through the same door. Wisps of smoke hung around the chilly interior, along with the dulling echoes of heels on stone steps, the chatter and laughter of colleagues well known to each other.

I hesitated in that alcove by the steps, suddenly cowed by the enormity of the building I now needed to search. I didn't have a clue where to head for. What got me moving was more footsteps descending: the next wave of lung-abusers.

I headed along the passageway to the main ground-floor corridor, tastefully decked out with mushroom-coloured paint on the walls and a carpet that was a kind of creamy, broad-bean green. I spent the next five minutes or so walking along it while the irises spilled crumbs of soil from their exposed roots. I must have looked suitably visitor-ish, however, because the white coats, starched skirts and blue overalls didn't stop me to ask where I thought I was going.

I experienced a bit of a heart murmur when I stumbled upon the reception area and, although Sonya had clocked off, No. 1 and No. 2 were still spoiling the scenery, as unpleasant as their toilet-task namesakes.

Just to the side of the reception area I found a little map of the building that showed me exactly where I was, but where precious little else could be learned. A squeak of leather on the marble floor warned me that YOU ARE HERE might soon become YOU ARE HERE, HERE AND HERE, so my eyes fell upon the large space that was the recreation room, and I decided that would have to do for now. I hurried along as the serge uniforms turned on to the corridor. I felt their eyes on the back of my head, maybe beginning to recognise the battered leather jacket, and it was all I could do to stop myself from breaking into a sprint.

' I turned a corner and felt some relief that they hadn't shouted out for me to stop. A minute or so later, I was standing by a large wooden door with a plastic plaque affixed to it: REC ROOM.

I went in. Thankfully, although I had suspected so, the recreation hall turned out to not be for the use of staff.

The air was thick with illicit cigarette smoke. Through it drifted patients in varying modes of what looked like catatonia. They all wore pyjamas and slippers, or bathrobes. A snooker table stood at the centre of the room, with a yellow lamp spilling low-wattage light over it. On the far side, a soporific game of table tennis was taking place. A bunch of unmoving heads watched a film on a television that rendered all colour as an eerie mix of green and blue. The lazy slam of darts into a cork board. Sticky trays bearing plastic cups of orange squash were doing the rounds, along with plates of bourbons and ginger nuts. One of the guys with a tray offered me a drink and I took it, along with a couple of biscuits, which I snaffled.

'Do you know Gary Cullen?' I asked him, before he could move away. He shook his head.

I moved deeper into the torpid mass of bodies. A couple hunched over a chess set might even have been asleep. A guy leaned over a cue to try for the blue into a centre pocket as a great spill of silver drool spun out of his slack mouth.

Medication time had come and gone at the zoo.

I took my time and spoke gently, not wanting to upset anybody's narcotic tranquillity. But after half an hour I was beginning to get impatient. I sat next to a woman in front of the television, where a green Roy Scheider was talking to a blue Meryl Streep across a green-blue desk. 'Do you know Gary Cullen?' I asked her. I had said nothing else since I got here, and I was starting to feel very weird, as though I might say nothing else ever again. As if I had taken some medicine, too. My words were even slowing down to match the pace of theirs.

She shook her head.

Christ. 'Does *anybody* in here know Gary Cullen?'

A *no* chorus.

'He used to be a patient here. He was a little violent, I think. Messed up. He sneaked away without asking permission. About two months ago. Surely one of you knew him?'

A *yes* chorus.

'You *all* knew him?'

I couldn't have wished for more yeses if I had been at the antonym club and had just asked if anyone knew what the opposite of *no* was.

I collared the guy with the tray just as he was taking the empty cups back to the kitchen.

'You knew Gary Cullen?'

'Yes,' he said.

'But I asked earlier and you said– '

'You asked me if I *know* him. No, I don't *know* him. He's gone now, but I *knew* him.'

Great. I fall into a room full of basket cases only to find they're playing semantic jokes. Fucking wonderful.

'Okay,' I said, trying to swallow my anger. 'Can I talk to you about him? Just a few questions?'

We were in the kitchen by now. A woman was kneeling in front of the guy doing the dishes and fellating him with the kind of energy you might find at a narcoleptics' sleepover. He was as flaccid as his dishrag. It was all too appallingly bathetic.

'What do you want to know?' he said.

'I'd like to know about his visitors,' I said. 'One in particular.'

'He never had visitors.'

'Never?' I asked. 'Are you sure about that? Not *one*?'

'No, not even his wife. She couldn't afford to come up here from London. Nobody came to see Gary. Nobody came to see a lot of people.'

I must have looked distraught, because he asked me if I was all right.

I nodded and then, moronically, asked him again: 'Not one visitor?'

'No, it's not as if he was alone. Don't think Gary Cullen was a sob story. He had plenty of friends. One in particular.'

'Who?'

'A woman.'

'Did his wife know?'

'She wasn't that kind of friend.'

I said: 'Do you know… *did* you know her name?'

He shook his head. The guy at the sink was starting to laugh in a way that put me in mind of a car with a small engine starting up on a very cold day. 'That tiggles,' he said.

'Look, can we go back to the other room?'

He introduced me to Paul after we returned to the snooker table. Paul had slept in the bed next to Gary's. Paul's place in the queue of players had been jumped by a small, stocky scowl called Ronnie. To pacify him, Ronnie was allowing Paul to chalk his cue after every couple of shots.

'I understand you were quite close mates with Gary Cullen,' I said to him. Paul didn't say anything. His arms moved ceaselessly inside his voluminous silk nightgown. A red serpent crawled up the back of it.

'Blue tip?' he asked Ronnie, and Ronnie bowed his lips, shook his head. Then, as if his thoughts had caught up with what I asked him, Paul said, 'He used to give me his dessert whenever we had rice pudding or semolina, or any of that stuff. I love that stuff.'

'Yeah,' I said, 'like I say, close mates. So were you around whenever he was chatting to this best mate of his, this female friend of his?'

'Sometimes,' he said. 'Oi, blue tip?'

He went off and chalked Ronnie's cue and I chewed my lips. One of the nurses had come in and was giving everyone half-hour warnings that it was time to start winding down and think about heading back to their beds.

Paul was back, blowing chalk dust off his fingertips. 'No miscues, not with me around,' he said.

'Where can I find her?' I asked. 'It would be really helpful to have a chat with her.'

'I bet it would,' he said. 'Why do you need to know?'

'She's my wife,' I said. 'She was cheating on me.'

'Ouch.' Paul waggled his hand, said: 'So why didn't you come and visit her?'

'Who says I didn't?'

'If you did, you'd know where to find her now.' People laughed at that. He laughed too.

I ignored him, and pressed on. 'What did they talk about when they were together? Do you know?'

'I've no idea. I was always sent away when she was around. He always wanted to talk to her in private. She must have been good for him, though, because whenever they were together, he looked peaceful, relaxed, you know? Sorry to say that about your *wife*, but that's how it looked to me, at least. Oi, blue tips? Blue tips?'

'Look, help me out here. Okay, she isn't my wife. But do you have any idea where she is? I'm desperate.'

He looked at me properly for the first time. 'I wouldn't tell you, even if I knew,' he said. 'What would you do? Kill her?'

'No,' I said.

'Gary was my friend,' Paul said, suddenly vehement. His hands, with their strange blue fingertips, fluttered violently around his face and then mine. I backed off. The nurse was coming our way.

'Calm down, Paul,' I said. 'I didn't mean anything by that. I just want to know where she is.'

'Yes, so you can *kill* her. I tell you where she is and she winds up on the news, dead. Well, no. Understand? *No*.'

The nurse intervened: 'Paul, no need to shout. What's got your back up?'

Time to make myself scarce.

I found a place to hide. The gents' toilets. I locked myself in a cubicle and pressed my fingers into my eyes until weird blooms of colour unfolded inside my head. Hours passed, silence fell incrementally: cars leaving the car park; the shuffle of feet coming in for a piss, shuffling away towards bed; the cleaners with their vacuums; the security guards on their patrols, soft footfalls and murmurs in the corridor. Lights out.

At around midnight I levered myself upright and gritted my teeth against the sudden rush of pins and needles that turned both my legs into blocks of numb nothingness. The smell of smoke and something else – bleach maybe, madness possibly – was deep in my clothes. The most insane place to be on Earth must be the inside of a toilet cubicle in an institute devoted to mental health. I saw pictures and read messages carved on the walls that ought to exist nowhere other than the inside of criminal minds, or those of horror writers. I was cold, hungry and depressed. But then I thought about Rebecca, and remembered how lucky I was. Nothing that shat on me in life could give me proper cause for complaint. Nothing.

The corridor was quiet. I made it to the entrance hall without incident, and slipped the lock of the door into the reception area. There was a signing-in book tucked under the counter, which still, alluringly, smelled of Sonya's perfume. I took a Maglite torch out of my pocket and waded through the pages, realising that it was a fruitless task but not knowing what else I could do. The chances of Kara signing her real name were pretty slim, let alone her including an address, but you never knew; maybe the troubled air here might have affected her thinking.

Scanning the entries for August, I found no mention of Gary Cullen's name in the *To Visit* column. He was unlucky in September, too, and, flicking back further, also in July and June.

I closed the book and returned it to the shelf beneath

the counter, before sneaking over to the long rank of four-drawer filing cabinets. Thankfully, none of them was locked. I established that the files were arranged in alphabetical order, and quickly found a label reading: *CULLEN, Gary Terence*. Lots of stuff about his criminal past. Lots of medication references. Lots of chaff. And one ear of wheat among it. A photograph, black and white, from some Christmas party on the ward. Gary with his arm around a woman. The woman? She was *the* woman in my eyes: it was definitely Kara Geenan, although her hair was different, longer. On the back was a handwritten caption: *Gary Cullen and Olivia Rawle get into the spirit of Xmas*. I stuffed the photo in my pocket and quickly flicked through the other stuff in the file, but there was nothing of note.

I shut the drawer and was thinking about leaving when something tapped me at the back of my brain and whispered: *What if?* I pulled open a few more drawers. *RAWLE, Olivia*. There was nothing in her file save a piece of paper with a phone number on it. Frustrated, and swearing lightly, I checked between her file and those of *RANKIN, Elizabeth Lucy* and *RAYMOND, Colette* but nothing had slipped out.

Torch beams picked out patterns on the ceiling: the nightwatchmen approaching.

I pocketed the phone number and sidled out of the reception booth. The main doors were locked, so I set off a fire alarm and melted into the shadows until the place was milling with patients and staff, in a barely restrained mosh of hysteria. The security guards had as much say-so in proceedings as a newborn has in what it should be named. When the doors were opened, I drifted along with the crowd until we were outside, then I peeled off towards the cypress trees and the field, and the car and some sort of resolution.

* * *

Later, much later, in the sanctity of my room at the Bed &
Breakfast, in the dark, I called that number.

A recorded message. Her voice so near that if I turned my
head she could be lying on this bed next to me.

She said: *Show yourself, Sorrell.*

14

There's a little part of Aigburth Vale where people used to congregate in the summer. The triangle of land at the corner of Aigburth Road and Ashfield Road, just south of Sefton Park, used to become waterlogged sometimes, providing an extremely unpleasant swimming pool for the local kids – abutting, as it did, the public toilets situated under the raised part of the road. The toilets were closed now, and many of the buildings that had contributed to the flooding were gone, leaving a patch of wasteland. It was here that I now parked the car.

I remembered sitting here in a deckchair one summer afternoon, having taken a sicky from the security job I was then enduring. I had a mate who lived nearby but we didn't like the park. In the summer it stank of dog shit and you were in danger of being mugged for a wallet full of fresh air, so I preferred the banter on the street. We were listening to the cricket on the radio and watching the kids play football, or asking the neighbours if they could wash their cars for fifty pence. There was a lot of cheeking going on, but it was good-humoured, the sun softening everybody's edges.

Towards evening, a radio announcement told of a young girl who had been raped and strangled, her body discovered that afternoon on a patch of land near St Michael's Hamlets, no more than a mile from where we were then sitting. Everyone went inside, silently and finally, as if a switch had been thrown. Nobody said a word, not even the children as they trooped home after their parents or older siblings. I think a couple of families moved away from Liverpool not long after that.

As I crossed the A561, I wondered if the same kind of thing had happened after Georgina Millen's body had been discovered. Just on the left there was a little track, a path that nevertheless possessed the sign Otterspool Road, which took you through Otterspool Park to the promenade and various beauty spots by the river. Under the road sign was the bracketed, unpleasant word *Unadopted*. The girl had been discovered just beyond the gate that prevents vehicles from using the track, her broken body hidden from the main road by the first bend. Her head had been removed. I ducked under the barrier and tiptoed through the mud. I didn't have to look too hard, because there was an old bunch of flowers pinned to a tree, all colour drained out of them, and hiding their faces like shameful children. I scuffed about in the mud, wondering what I'd hoped to find here, considering that forensics would have taken every last fleck of gnat shit away for scrutiny. But I knew I wasn't really here in the hope of finding a miracle shred of evidence; I just needed the smell of him, I needed to be able to see what he had seen. Somehow that comforted me, made me feel closer to him. And once I was closer to him, he didn't seem so out of reach.

I was about to go back to the car when I noticed something

attached to another tree, a sheet of white paper, about twenty feet or so deeper into the park. Before I reached it, I knew it was a photocopy of a picture. It was one of the copies that the woman at Stodge had taken of me the other night. He'd been there all along, drinking champagne with the swingers, watching me flap around looking for him. That knowledge turned my balls to ice and my breath came quicker, misting around me like ghosts trying to rub me out of existence.

I took the picture down and there was a photograph Pritt-Sticked to the back of it, along with a message: *Hello again.*

I didn't need to look at the date stamp on the photo to know it was freshly developed. It was a colour picture taken from an upper-floor window, showing a large road filled with semi-detached houses. There were cars in some of the driveways and purple wheelie bins parked out on the road waiting to be emptied.

I should have gone straight to the police with it, but my prints were all over it now, and anyway, the police were on my shit list. I can persuade myself pretty quickly about some things, but this was too personal now. This was too much *me* and *him*.

I broke down for a little while back at the car. I lost it a bit. I couldn't think of the dead girls without thinking of my own and I hoped if Sarah had suffered at all, that it hadn't lasted for long. I called Melanie at her home and she answered me breathlessly. She'd just got back from playing badminton and she was about to jump in the shower. I imagined her naked, smiling at me down the phone, her lithe little body hot from exercise. I almost blurted out that I loved her. Need was rising in me so quickly that I didn't know how to begin to identify it. Instead, I said I was hoping to see her again very soon.

'Be careful,' she said. 'Hey, listen, I'm going to have to go away for a little while, to Devon. My dad's not well. My mobile might not be up to it – the signal out there is pretty weak – but you can try to call me if you want to.'

If I want to.

'What about Mengele?' I asked.

'I can either take him with me, or get Fiona to look after him, from the surgery. She's good with cats.'

'If I'd known that, I'd have dragged you up here with me.'

'Aw, that's sweet. If I'd have known that, I might have let you.'

'This Fiona,' I said, 'is she as good as you?'

'In every respect.'

'Not every respect,' I said.

She said, 'Hurry home, Joel.'

I switched off the phone with a feeling that we'd just made a quantum jump forward. Our conversation had really contained nothing more than the usual jousting we got up to, but it had been underscored with a faint line of desperation. Two hundred miles was drawing it all to the surface. I wanted her; there: I'd admitted it to myself at last. No more stepping back from the line, but time to stride over it.

'I want you. Melanie, I want you.' Christ, that sounded good.

I noodled about the roads for a while, driving without any destination in mind, just trying to put Melanie in a warm safe place of my mind while I loosened up the rest of the dross that was stopping me from thinking clearly. Eventually I found a pub. I parked and went inside. It was one of those places where the bar staff give you your change on a little saucer, in the hope that you might leave a tip. I ordered a pint and a bag of nuts. Above me, on a separate deck, people, with kids mostly, were having their dinner. I checked out the menu: simple stuff – pies, burgers, fish and chips – at far from simple prices. Fucking complex prices. Everybody was drinking bottles of Bud or bottles of Breezer. I sat in a corner with my drink and watched the staff take the meaning of apathy to a new level.

The photograph felt warm between my fingers. I imagined him holding it, then pinning it to the post on a misty morning, knowing that eventually I would get around to finding it. I wondered how he felt now. I wondered if he was getting anxious, waiting for me to find him – desperate to work his inhuman magic on me. He was giving himself to me either because he was impatient and wanted to finish things, or because he thought I was too thick to track him down without a few assists.

The wheelie bins. The cars. The houses. I spotted a ginger cat on a wall, now that I was relaxed and had more time to study the full picture. A City FM sticker in a bedroom window. At the bottom left of the photograph, almost cut out of the picture, was a road sign, but I couldn't make it out. The sign was encrusted with filth and years of exhaust fumes, graffiti filling in any gaps. I took out my Swiss Army knife and, conscious that I looked the kind of saddo twat I always promised myself I would avoid becoming, I picked out its tiny magnifying glass and held the photograph up to the light. My face burned as a couple of sweet-looking girls turned my way and laughed out loud. I was a pair of tweezers and a stamp album away from becoming an Untouchable – one level up from a leper, or a serial killer.

...IE AVENUE L9.

How hard could it be? I put the knife away and took out my *A-Z.*

'What else have you got in there, mate?' A voice carried to me from the next table, where a couple of blokes were fighting over a woman in an Abercrombie top. 'A bleeding flask and sandwiches?'

He had that kind of seriously overhanging jut of forehead that screams of an IQ so low you could use it to scoop up worm shit. 'No,' I said, speaking slowly so that he wouldn't have to move his lips to follow me, 'but I've got something for you.'

I reached into my pocket and dug around for a while. Then I pulled out my fingers in the shape of a V and flourished them at him. The girl shrieked. I went back to my map and flipped to the pages containing Allerton, while he tried to engage me with some more of his gentle Scouse wit. I spent another thirty minutes and the best part of a tenner on another pint and a bowl of chips before I found what I was looking for.

I got myself outside and slid behind the wheel of the rental car, started her up. And then I was thinking about Rebecca. Not abstract thoughts of the warmth and humour that had cocooned us in the years after we met, but the blunt edge of her death, recalled in dirty, bleached detail. The claws of that death dug into my shoulders from time to time, but I rarely looked up to scrutinise the face of what occasionally had come home to roost. Now I did. Every so often, you have to, to remind you of who you are, where you came from and, grim knowledge though it maybe is sometimes, where you're heading. I looked up into its unblinking black eyes and it placed me back in the Saab when the car was a little younger, its engine sound a little smoother and sexier. I'd been out all day, but had called Becs at lunchtime to find out if I needed to bring anything home for dinner.

'Grab some steaks,' she had said. 'Sarah's at the school disco. We'll listen to some music, and you can try out some moves on me.'

On the seat next to me was a bag of CDs from HMV. As usual, I'd shelled out on too many – there was a Stina Nordenstam album, I remember, and a Jeff Buckley live in concert, a couple of old Pixies albums that had seen me through my college days and which I thought I now needed in the more up-to-date format, some early Simple Minds before they wanted to conquer America. Some Curve, because I liked their barely controlled hysteria. Other stuff, too. And to make me feel less guilty about indulging in such a blow-out, I'd bought Becs a CD, too. Zbigniew Preisner's 'Requiem for my Friend', because she loved the *Three Colours* trilogy, and I felt it was a thoughtful present, something to distract her from my featherweight wallet, sure, but something soothing we could both listen to with the lights out.

In the end, it was just me listening to it with the lights out. Because, when I got home, the front door was off its hinges and someone had painted the hallway radiator red. On one corner of it was a pulpy mass of bone, tissue and hair. Splashes of blood were up the wall and across the hallway carpet. I followed the smears of blood into the living room, which smelled of spilled whisky and cigar smoke. Whoever had killed Rebecca had thrown her on to the sofa. Her breasts were exposed, scooped out of her bra. They were latticed with slashes. Her knickers were torn and still clinging to her left ankle. There was blood on them too. There was blood everywhere. Her head had a great pile of gore dangling from it. I approached her, thinking how I shouldn't be likening my wife to a Portuguese Man-of-fucking-War.

I stood and looked down at my wife, the bag of steak growing warm in my fist. Whoever had killed Rebecca had stubbed his cigar out in her eye sockets.

Brodie Avenue was a large thoroughfare that bisected Allerton, so large that I had completely missed it as I scoured the tiny surrounding roads. By the time I got there, it was turning dark and I was shaking, so it took longer than I was expecting to match the buildings in the photograph with those on the street. Maybe it was because the cat had fucked off. More likely it was because I couldn't focus properly, with my memories burning up what was left of my mind.

But at last, I had it. Behind me, above a row of shops, was the flat where, presumably, this guy Phythian had lived, or still lived, when he wasn't trying to put holes in me during his trips down to the capital.

I judged the window as being one of two immediately above a hairdresser and a Chinese takeaway respectively. When I tried the bell to the flat, there was no answer, which was no huge surprise. I tested the door's strength by leaning against it with my backside, while I pretended to do up my shoe. It rattled in its frame, about as secure as a spun-sugar nappy. I waited for a couple of cars to drive by, and an old man to come out of the Chinese with his bag of chicken chow mein, and then I slipped the lock with a credit card.

I smelled it straight away. It's difficult to describe, but there's only one thing in the world that makes a smell like it. Death doesn't wear perfume.

I waited on the stairwell, holding my breath, listening for sounds of occupancy. But I wasn't really, since I knew the place was empty. I was just putting off something that

I knew was going to slowly unveil itself in my dreams for the rest of my life. It wasn't as if it would be alone in there.

Up the stairs, weary as a climber making his push for the summit of Everest. The carpet's pattern was like an object lesson in vomit. I had to retrieve my handkerchief from my pocket as I reached the landing. Light from the main road spilled through the window, thought turned into something granular and uncertain by the net curtains.

How could the smell have gone unnoticed? But then a harsh blast of garlic and onions and sesame oil shot past me from the kitchens downstairs, and I understood. I inched forward to the room at the front of the flat and stopped when I saw, through the crack in the half-closed door, a figure standing very still in the centre of it. Its face was edged with light, wet light as greasy-looking as a woman wearing too much slap. There was no point in saying anything, because whoever it was, she was long past hearing me.

I got into the room and closed the curtains. When I threw the light switch, I didn't look directly at her; instead I took my time, at first concentrating on the shadow that she cast. At least it's not summer, I told myself, more times than was necessary. There was something about her shadow that just wasn't right, but I was too pumped up to understand. Until I looked at her directly. I took in what was left of her for maybe a second, if that, then I turned off the light and sat in an armchair, just me and her in the darkness. Me and her and the ghosts of violence thickening in my mind.

15

I can't say for sure whose head it is,' I said, 'but I think it might be Kara Geenan's, the real Kara Geenan, not the psycho I'm trying to find. Or else Georgina Millen's, the girl they found on Otterspool Road five years ago.'

But for a second in there I'd even convinced myself it was Sarah – I'd wanted it to have been Sarah – as crazy and unlikely as that would have been. I didn't want to consider how close I had come to punching that failed face in, once I was sure that it was not my daughter. Her mouth had carried enough of a smile to make me feel she was mocking me. It was a pinched smile, the kind of smile you might see on an old dear as she fends off a tramp begging for coppers. The thin reek of preservative fluid almost shut out the smell of decay.

'You have to give me the address, Joel,' Ian Mawker was saying. In the background I could hear the skitter of nails against a keyboard, the voice of someone asking who had ordered the coffee without. I could also hear the hunger in Mawker's voice. He was too long without a big collar, and he was going to be all over this like snot on a kid's blanket.

'Ian,' I said, 'I need you to give me some space.'

'We'll fuck you over in more ways than you can imagine, if you keep this back any longer.'

But that was going to happen anyway, once the smoke had cleared. I was now so deep in shit, I needed a snorkel. It didn't matter what I did any more, since Mawker and the rest were going to use my bollocks for catapult practice no matter what choice I made now.

'All right,' I said. 'Just do me a favour, then. Have someone watching Melanie Henriksen's house for me.'

'Who?'

'Woman friend of mine. She's away at the moment, but she'll be back, maybe in a couple of days. I'd feel better if you could keep an eye on her.'

'All right,' Mawker said wearily. 'What's the address?'

I gave her Melanie's details, and he sighed again. 'No, fuckwit, the body. Where's the fucking body?'

After that, I put the phone down and found that I was rubbing my other hand over and over against the side of my jeans. It was getting late as I dumped the car back at the rental place and posted the keys through the door. I had forty minutes to kill before the train was due to depart, so I killed them – and a couple of million brain cells – in the bar on the station concourse, along with a few men in suits who were drinking as though programmed to do so by a hacker who only knew a code that contained the word *Grolsch*. The beer on its own wouldn't take away the shakes, so I conscripted a double vodka to help out.

She was gone from the neck down, her head rammed on to a fence post that had been secured in the centre of the room by a porridge of mortar and blood. I had tried to find the rest of her but there was nothing else in the bedsit bar a raft of unsigned Mother's Day cards arranged on every available surface. I didn't look too hard, though, it has to be said.

The fucker had applied lipstick and mascara to the face, but the make-up wasn't staying where it ought to. There was the heavy, chemical smell of embalming fluid or varnish, or both. She looked like a clown in a steam room. Now I think of it, although she was grinning, she looked sad. Sadder than sad.

There were a couple of other drunks on the train with me when we got underway, half an hour late because the train driver had called in sick. Yeah, right. He was plum deep in his missus, if he had any sense. Nobody in their right mind wants to ride the last train back to London. Well, nobody except me, because I'd had my fill of Liverpool. Any shred of hope I'd clung to that it might fill my heart with love and warmth from fondly-remembered days of growing up there had evaporated like dog piss off a hot radiator.

I'd begged the barman to sell me a couple of miniatures before leaving the pub. I sucked on them now as the train eased away from the platform, my fellow drunks eyeing me enviously; the nervous, sober passengers wishing all these pissheads would fall asleep or that they themselves had had the common sense and decency to get tanked up beforehand, too.

I drifted in and out of sleep all the way back to London. I dreamed a little: foggy, confused dreams powered by alcohol, in which I had been crushed into the corner of a room in a bleak Liverpool bedsit. The only light came from the pulse of a neon sign through a naked window, sickly yellow blows that lit up thousands of masks dangling from the ceiling on differing lengths of string. You couldn't have moved in that room because of them. The only problem was that the masks were still attached to the faces they were trying to conceal. The linoleum was tigered with blood. All I could hear was the patter as red rain fell from the masks on to the floor. I couldn't look away, because my eyelids had been clipped off, or else stapled to my forehead. I felt as though my eyes were bulging in their effort to see the masks, to take in every grain of detail; and that if I didn't, mine would be the next face up there, spinning for ever along with the others, waiting for something unspeakable to come and try it on for size.

I woke up with Sarah's name vying for space with the bile and spittle in my mouth. We had come to a stop ten miles shy of Euston, and it was gone one-fifteen in the morning. I'd been on that train for nearly four and a half hours. Wind buffeted the carriages, making them lurch. Beyond the window, darkness spread like an infection. A woman in the seat behind me said 'He'll not have waited for us. We'll have to take a cab, and what then?'

Eventually the driver felt like sharing the bad news with us. There had been a fight on a platform at Euston, a big one, and someone had been pushed under a train. All incoming passengers were being diverted to St Pancras. Naturally, it was going to take time for this to happen. Sleep pulled me down again.

A cold morning as autumn dwindled, frost making the streets seem clean. The newly laid carpet in the hallway and living room still had that slightly rubbery smell. The radiator had been cleaned, the old paint scraped off it. I was considering taking it off the wall and throwing it away, but I was scared that there would still be blood that I had missed on the wall behind it.

I called upstairs to Sarah and asked her what she wanted for her breakfast. No reply.

The sofa in the living room was gone, chopped up and burnt to cinders in the garden, replaced by wooden chairs until I got round to buying something new. I'd taken down all the pictures of Becs because I couldn't hack it, walking into the house every day to have her looking at me and to find myself thinking her eyes aren't brown; they're black and full of ash.

Everywhere I went in that house, I smelled cigar smoke.

Two months since I had discovered her body. A month since they picked up the scumbag who had killed her. Graeme Tann, his name was, and he worked as a cleaner and handyman at the gym where Rebecca attended her Pilates classes. When they opened up his locker, they found about a thousand Polaroid photographs of Rebecca, some of which he'd taken through a vent that opened into the female changing rooms. He'd been stalking her for the best part of two years, it transpired. I'd even seen him a couple of times when I picked Rebecca up from the gym, standing out on the steps, smoking his cheap, Nicaraguan cigars, enjoying the evening air.

He had attacked Rebecca in a sexual way, that much was obvious, but there were no semen deposits, no signs of his having introduced any part of his body to hers. At his flat in Oval they found stoppered test tubes containing his sperm, dozens of them, with the names of girls he'd masturbated over and the dates of his ejaculation written on the labels in jagged handwriting. He'd been at it for years, collecting his fantasies in this way, but Rebecca had been the first one he had visited physical harm upon. When they asked him about this, he had said that she reminded him of a kitten he owned as a child. It had been such a cute, attractive kitten that he had felt the compulsion to batter it to death. He didn't feel that anything so comely should be allowed to exist, to highlight the ugliness in others. When he hit Rebecca, and caused her nose to bleed, he felt better, but he couldn't stop until he had removed her attractiveness completely. He needed to ruin her, to dehumanise her, before he could feel normal again.

I remember feeling utterly emasculated in terms of being a husband, a father, a law enforcer, a man. In any or all of those guises, I had failed my wife and my daughter. They asked me, the guys down at the nick where he was being held, if I wanted to spend some time with him, one night. I did, I did so very much want that. And I went along, too. But I grew so weak with rage and loss, and the need to do something to him to try to correct the balance again, that I couldn't go through with it. I could barely even walk, never mind clench my hands into fists. I was a foal, ten minutes old. I was water. In this way, I also failed myself.

So that day, a month later, I had gone up to Sarah's room to see if she wanted to go out for breakfast. I went out for breakfast quite a lot, and I spent as much time out of that house as possible. I found myself stopping outside estate agents with increasing regularity. Maybe if I'd put the house on the market immediately, Sarah wouldn't have run away.

Her bed hadn't been slept in. There was no note. Some of her clothes were gone, as was her school rucksack and the savings from her cashbox, about twenty-five pounds. She had been supportive to me in the days after Rebecca's murder. She had greeted the stony cold of shock with remarkable stoicism. She had stroked my hair as I lay trembling in bed. I had leaned hard on her, and she'd seemed able to bear my weight. I didn't for one moment consider that she was only thirteen and that I ought to be doing more for her. I told her to stay at her friends' houses as much as she wanted, so I myself could spend more time in the pub looking for Rebecca's reflection in my vodka glasses.

I almost slapped her across the face one night, when I came home drunk, and she was sitting on the stairs in her nightie, looking shockingly like her mother with that sad, soft expression on her face. She asked me: 'Dad, did you kill her?'

I almost slapped her because there was some truth in what she said. I almost slapped her because, in a small way, I *did* kill her. I killed her by failing to see. The fact that there were no clues, no prior warning of what was to happen, didn't mean anything to me. For two years he had been watching her, taking his fetid little pictures, wanking himself stupid over her naked body. Little eyes burning into her, tracing the curves of her flesh, drawing a map for his knife to follow. His hungry eyes, I should have noticed them, at least. But I didn't. All I saw when I picked her up from the leisure centre was the paperwork I had to get through, the jobs that were lined up. I saw everything but his intent, little eyes.

Instead of slapping Sarah, I screamed at her until we were both crying, holding each other so tightly, so closely that for a lunatic moment I was certain we had fused, and would never be able to pull ourselves free again.

Sarah's room smelled of her, nothing else. That baby-woman smell that drives you wild with compassion and love. Her skin, her scalp, her sex. These days, I remember only the cigar smoke. Sarah's smell has become lost to me. Sometimes I question whether I had a daughter, at all.

Maybe she was never anything more than a dream. But that hug we shared, that violent, desperate hug, I remember well. It's as if I still bear the imprint of her body on my tender, pathetic flesh. It's what keeps me going.

The carriage jolted and swayed as the train picked up speed. As we came through the busy convergence of criss-crossed lines at the mouth of the great train shed at St Pancras, I was rattled out of sleep for good. My eyes were reflected, red and swollen, in the window. A hangover was sucking the core out of me, making me feel hollow, spineless, like a cheap tin of pink salmon with its crumbling grey backbone removed. When the train came to a halt, I found it difficult to peel myself out of the seat. I waited till everyone else had shifted, and the platform was clear, before levering myself upright and shuffling down the aisle. I rescued a half-empty Coke can from the magazine holder behind one seat, and took the warm syrup down in a single gulp. The sugar rush hit me as I stepped on to the platform, dragging my eyes all the way open. A guard leaning against the ticket barrier stared pointedly at his watch and tapped a foot against its mate, waiting for me to show him my ticket. I heard a slumping noise and looked up to see a shape move across an opaque section of the shed roof, a hundred feet or so above me. Then the flare of the floodlights stung so hard that I had to bend over and blink that sting away.

St Pancras? There was no point in going round to Melanie's, as she was still in Devon. And, anyway, how attractive would I have appeared to her, hungover, dirty, my breath as iffy as a cadaver's cock? I flicked through the stained, tattered pages of the address book in my mind, came up with Lorraine Tokuzo, and reckoned I could do a lot worse. Lorraine lived in a place called Ice Wharf, on

New Wharf Road. She ran a modest business out of the Essex Road, an antiques-dealing partnership concentrating on old doors and chimney pots. She was something of an expert on them and could charge a fair whack for a house visit, to assess joists and flues and offer advice about how to jazz up a roof. She'd checked my own stack out for free, years ago, but that's between her and me.

I hurried through the streets, chicaning round the arguing hookers, suddenly busting for a piss, and buzzed her number.

'Tizzit?'

'Lorraine? It's Joel. Joel Sorrell.'

I pressed my hand against the grille, managing to cut off most of the profanities, and when she had finished I asked her if she was going to let me in, or was I going to have to piss all over her nice, clean entrance.

'When did you ever do otherwise?' she yelled, but the lock released and I went in, wondering what the hell did I do to cheese this one off?

I was still mulling it over when the lift doors opened and there she was, hanging out of her doorway like a fantastic Christmas decoration that someone forgot to put away. She hadn't fastened her pyjamas up too well and too many bits of her were lounging out of the fabric, throwing darts into the bullseye of my memory, saying, hey, look at what you gave up, Bucko.

'I thought I read about you in the papers,' she said. 'Didn't I read you were killed somewhere?'

'I'd hazard a guess that it was probably someone else,' I replied.

'Pity,' she said, inevitably. 'Come in, then. You know where the lav is.'

While I was relieving myself, I glanced around the

233

bathroom, trying to remember. She must have redecorated, because there were no lightbulbs that lit up in my mind. I looked in the cabinet for a couple of Anadin, but there was nothing there but some contraceptive pessaries and a couple of jars containing stuff for parts of the body that just didn't exist on people who didn't read *Cosmopolitan* or *Vogue*.

She had put on a pale-blue towelling bathrobe and was now making coffee. The bathrobe, like her PJs, was undone, spilling her everywhere. It didn't look as though she was doing this on purpose, but with Lorraine you could never tell. Fragments of our relationship – our three-month fling – seeped through to me from the fog of memory. She had been the first woman I'd gone out with after Rebecca was murdered. I was bruised and moody, not too attentive, drinking too much, perhaps a little snappy – hell, pretty much what I was like the whole time, anyway. I'd asked her out while in a hotel bar in Russell Square. She was there with some antiques convention, and I was there to get caned. I had started laying on the charm with a trowel, but decided that wasn't enough and nipped out to the plant-hire place for a cement mixer. Lorraine had found my ceaseless pursuit of her rather amusing. If she'd recognised it for what it was – desperation, the need to know if I was still attractive to the opposite sex, a need to eclipse the ashes that used to be Rebecca's eyes with something else, something alive – she'd have probably given me a jagged piece of her mind, and that would have been it. But she agreed to go for a drink with me, and then we went back to her room and we fucked every which way and then some, and soon on most nights I was sitting on the edge of a bed, nursing something on the rocks, while I watched her dunking herself into her bra and putting on her make-up. For weeks I had a mantra repeating in my head, and it was only towards the end that I decided to pay some attention to it and listen to what it was chanting at me, and it was this: *This isn't right, this isn't right.*

It could have been, of course, at a different time. But I was still in recovery, and not doing very well at it. I was laid out in a bed, on a drip, gradually coming back from the edge in a ward where there should have been no visitors allowed. The sign at the end of my bed said *Do Not Resuscitate.*

One night, watching her steer her tight, white bum into a tight, white thong, she said: 'Malc and Jenny want us to go round for dinner on Saturday – is that all right, babe?'

I tossed my glass at the wall and picked up my coat. 'I've had enough,' I said. 'I'm getting out.'

' That's what I'd done to cheese this one off: saved her from messing her life up. But they never see it that way, do they?

And, anyway, Malc was a twat.

'What's up with you?' she said now. 'You look like you've been doubling for Droopy.'

'Cheers,' I said.

'How do you have your coffee?' she said, knowing full well. 'Milk, no sugar, two drops of strychnine?'

'On the button,' I said.

She still looked good, five years on, better than I must have looked to her. Her hair was longer but it was as black and glossy as ever, the kind of hair, thick hair, that never gets tangled. Sly hazel eyes. A cute, slightly jutting lower jaw, a bit Reese Witherspoon-ish. She had recently been on holiday, or was putting in the hours on a sunbed, because her body was a deep, even brown. The tops of her breasts had the kind of healthy gleam to them that made your mouth go dry. She smelled good, her flat was sumptuous, she made a mean cup of coffee and, as I remembered, she gave remarkable blowjobs. Pretty shallow plus points, I grant you, but enough to start me wondering whether I was destined only to keep stepping on the dog shit all my life.

'It's good to see you,' I said.

'Fuck off,' she said. 'Drink your coffee and then fuck right off.'

'I was wondering if I could kip here.'

'No,' she said, and her voice sounded just the right side of Dalek.

'I don't want to get in with you. I'll take the sofa.'

'Joel!'

'Please,' I said. Everything was descending, the crap of my past tumbling down on me, and the death that had dogged me these last few days was capering just beyond her front door, looking for a way in so that it might wrap itself around my throat and draw tight. 'Just a couple of hours. I'll be gone before you get up. I need... I really need...' But I couldn't finish the sentence, because there were too many different ways to end it.

Maybe she recognised that manifold need behind my eyes, because her face softened. She left me for a few minutes and came back with a couple of blankets and a pillow.

'Do you want to tell me what's up?' she asked.

I shook my head. If I started now, I might never stop.

'Okay. Go to sleep. Help yourself to what's in the fridge when you wake up.' Her voice soft, warm. 'You fucking bastard.'

16

I could hardly afford it, but I needed the tonic it provided. I booked myself in for a day's membership at One Aldwych, and took the lift down to the basement. There I picked up my robe and slippers and went through to the changing rooms. I handed my clothes over in a bag and asked that they be washed, dried and pressed, then I put my wallet and watch in a locker and went for a swim.

They've got a cracking pool here: lots of blue tiles, soft music and underwater lighting; cascades of H_2O pouring down the walls. No bugger comes here during the week, so, if you're lucky, you can get it all to yourself, especially if you come in the morning just as most of the desk jockeys are sitting down to their voice messages, a cup of tea made by someone who can't make tea, and their first Rennie of the day.

I did a few laps then got out and had a shower, before stepping into the sauna. A couple of ladles of water on the coals, five minutes on the hourglass, and I tried to relax with the morning's newspaper.

But the words wouldn't settle.

I had tried calling Melanie when I rose that morning, but she had been right about the signal: I couldn't get through. A call to the vet's was no good either; the place didn't open for another hour and, anyway, they wouldn't be able to help me at all. I was impatient to see her, and I was jealous of the entire county of Devon. She was breathing its air, somewhere. Walking its streets. Eating its cream teas.

Mawker wasn't answering his mobile, either. I had taken a pot of yogurt from Lorraine's fridge, and left her a note saying thanks and sorry. I thought about leaving her my phone number, in the vain hope she might want to be friends again, but decided against it. You can't just be friends if you've had a passionate past that burnt itself out so completely. There's nothing but ash to build it on. So I left.

Sweat poured off me, speckling the front page. I put the paper down and closed my eyes but images of Melanie swam out of the darkness. I saw her face for an instant, dangling amid the sea of masks from my dream, and snatched at breath. Fuck this treatment, sometimes it's impossible to relax. It's especially difficult to relax when you've actually got the time to do it. It's even more difficult to relax when you don't deserve it, or haven't earned it, or your head is too freshly stained with the kind of things that make relaxation something that might never be achieved again.

I had to leave.

I walked out of the sauna and straight into a man, a big man with a chest about as wide as I was long. He pushed me into the steam room next-door, and sat me down. He sat next to me, near the door. I could hardly make out his face through the clouds, but I could tell he was ugly. Maybe even ugly enough to scare pigs from a shit pit.

'Jesus Christ,' I said, 'can I not have an hour to myself?'

'Nice here, isn't it?' the big man said. He inhaled deeply. 'Good for my sinuses, this menthol stuff they pump in here. I broke my nose playing rugby five years ago. I ought to have an op but I'm scared of the anaesthetic. They want to put a drill up there, and dig through all this bone and tissue that's built up over the years, but I couldn't face it.' He looked like a horror film star who's forgotten to have his make-up removed.

'Go and tell it to your prop forward while he rims you off,' I said. 'Do I look like I give a shit?'

He slapped me, almost casually, across the back of the head and I folded over on to the floor.

'Mawker wants a word with you.'

'Tell Mawker to crawl back inside the rat that shat him out.'

'You've got a dirty mouth,' he said.

'There's no big secret about it,' I said. 'You can have one too, if you try hard enough.'

'You should show a little respect to your fellow human beings,' he said.

'Is that what you are?' I said, getting to my feet. Dark shapes were assembling beyond the glass door. 'A human being? You're having me on.'

'I'll have you mashed into my dog's dinner bowl if you carry on lipping me,' he said. 'Now get outside.'

I considered legging it, but I wasn't going to get far down the Strand in my fluffy little slippers. Mawker was standing by the pool with two more heavies at his shoulder, trying to look like Pacino in *Godfather III*, and looking more like Kermit from *Sesame Street*.

'At ease,' I said.

'Sorrell,' he said, 'you're coming down to the nick with us, for questioning.'

239

'Don't be a cunt all your life,' I said, and Boris Karloff gave me another tap round the ear. 'Mawker,' I said, 'if you want a chat, fair enough, but call off your girlfriend here. And Bert and Ernie, too, while you're at it.'

Mawker said, 'I could do you, Sorrell. I could be on you like a horny teenager on the school bike. You're no different from the scum we collar every day of the week. Private investigator... bloody hell, a bit of flat-footing and you think that gives you the right to play Inch High.'

'You've just reminded me,' I said. 'We had a bike at Bruche, do you remember? Phyllis, her name was, but everyone called her Syph. 'Cept you, of course. Weren't you the sad, Bambi-eyed fuck whenever she walked in? It was like watching a peckish lioness who suddenly finds a calf come wandering into her manor.'

'That's my wife you're talking about,' he said.

'Ex-wife, I'll bet – and she's been your ex for a long time. Put a tenner on it. Put fifty on it.'

'You piece of shit, Sorrell,' but it was all air, and it came out of him in a long rush, deflating him. He didn't have a streak of the cold, hard stuff in him; didn't even have a pinch of it. He looked suddenly old, and I thought, *You and me both, mate*. I almost felt sorry for him. Almost.

And then he was coming back at me, but his words were slow, his face crumpled. He wasn't comfortable with this level of nastiness. Which was a surprise because you had to have the mouth if you wanted to get on in the Force. You didn't gain your pips for saying please and thank you.

Anyone else and I would have waded in, but from him, a man who was trying to play my game and struggling at it, the words hit home and stayed with me, like painful splinters just beneath the skin. All he had to do was say their names, and that was me finished.

'Okay,' I said. 'Okay.'

'You shouldn't throw so many fucking stones, Joel,' he said. 'There's always someone who'll pick a couple up and throw them back.'

'Don't take me in,' I said.

'Give me something to work with,' he replied.

'The girl?' I said. 'Melanie. The woman I was with when you had me tailed, is she back yet?'

'How the fuck should I know?'

'I asked you to look after her.'

'Forget her,' he said. 'It's me you should be cosying up to. I don't look after your diary for you, sweetheart.'

'I couldn't phone her, because she went to Devon. But if she's back, then I have to go and check on her,' I said. 'I don't want her to get into any trouble.'

'It's you who's in trouble, sunshine. You went away without my say-so, and I want to know what you did on your holidays.'

'I gave you the head in that flat, Mawker. What else do you want from me?'

'Who is she?'

'I told you, I don't fucking know.'

'How did you know she was… This would go down better at the nick. Come on.'

'Look, I'll do you some Jackanory, but let's all nip up to Maida Vale first. Just to put my mind at rest, hey? If she's not back, then I'll leave a note and you can leave one of your glove puppets there, to make me feel better.'

'What prevented you earlier? Having your dick massaged by some floozy wearing a hotel uniform seem more important then, did it?'

241

'What stopped me? Only the thought that you were doing what you promised me you'd fucking do.'

'We've had police in the area,' Mawker insisted, 'and everything looks tickety-boo. Very Maida Vale. People fart in Maida Vale and Neighbourhood Watch makes a report. Now book the fucker, Les.'

'Ian–'

'Oh, *Ian* is it now?' said Mawker. He was clearly enjoying himself. 'Get him into the fucking car.'

'You take me in, clearly I am not going to give you anything. I'll clam up, no matter what you do. Even if you set this mong and your two boyfriends on me.' I saw his face change, soften a little, and I went at the seam with a chisel. 'Come on, Ian, give me this. Please. It'll take us half an hour.'

'And then you spill?'

'I'll tell you everything I know. I'll chatter away into your ear until you're begging me to stop.'

'You'd better, Sorrell, you little wank stain. I'm getting dumped on from above, and the brass have got some serious big arses on them.'

The lights reflecting off the surface of the pool made little creamy ripples on the ceiling. Lapping water, the music gentle and jazzy, we stood there and took it all in while the cogs in Mawker's head turned. It wouldn't have seemed out of place, somehow, if we'd all started swaying to the music. Kicked off on some soft-shoe shuffle routine.

'Okay,' he said, 'get dressed. Les will help you. We'll wait upstairs.'

Reception gave me my unwashed clobber back and I put it on, feeling grimy and unrested. In the foyer, the three bears were giggling over the prices in the cocktail menu.

'What's up with your face?' Mawker asked, as we joined

them. 'You got your own way, didn't you?'

I strolled past him to the doors. An unmarked police car was parked on a double yellow. Some stiff opened the hotel doors for us and we headed over to the Vectra, Bert and Ernie flanking me, Mawker behind, Boris Karloff making for the driver's seat. We drove up High Holborn and got on to the Euston Road heading west. Mawker suggested we tool round Regent's Park, seeing it was a nice day, and I chewed my cheek, wishing Boris would step on it a little. We eventually got up to St John's Wood and pootled through the streets to Maida Vale. There were quite a few people out, stunned into action by the bright sunshine, although I thought the shades and T-shirts that some were wearing were a bit optimistic. At the garden centre, people were lugging giant bags of ericaceous compost into their car boots. Bungle started twatting on about Acers, and Boris chipped in with how his old mum was having to create some raised beds to grow rhododendrons, because her soil was too alkaline.

'For fuck's sake,' I said, 'let's all can *Gardener's Question Time* and show some fucking discipline, hey?'

Nobody said a word to that. I wished they had. I really wanted to lay into someone, and my tongue was aching to sharpen itself against one of these dumbfucks' whetstone heads.

As we got close to Melanie's place, the tension wound itself up inside the car and Mawker opened a window. We piled out on to the street and I barged through the gate, deaf now to the filth's command to *Hold back, we'll take it from here*. I was putting the key in the lock when the door swung open, and it was as if my guts had attached themselves to the door knocker just as it moved away from me. I felt myself unravelling all over the fucking welcome mat. She's dead. Dead, and there's me poncing about in a sauna like some health-farm fanny.

Don't touch a thing, somebody said, but forensics would be too late to find any iota of evidence to nail this cunt. A fibre from his clothes was hardly going to give us a map to his centre of operations. I went in, despite the swearing, and started calling her name, over and over, until the syllables mashed into each other and it became something nonsensical, almost unreal. The living room was untouched, the mezzanine sleeping area nicely fluffed up, with Mengele on top of the folded blankets, looking down at me bleary-eyed and disdainful. I almost asked the little bastard where she was.

The kitchen. The kitchen was fucked.

'He took her in here, guv,' Boris said, and I almost chinned the twat.

'Well, congratulations on that brilliant piece of deduction,' I said, trying to gather up the red mist and keep it in a safe place inside my head. 'Any other searing insights you'd like to share with us?'

Pots and plates all over the place, one of her beautiful kitchen chairs reduced to sticks of firewood, a cracked bottle of olive oil, a sheen of the stuff on the work surface, pooling out over the floor. Mengele's food bowls had also disgorged their contents; our feet crunched through the Fishbitz as if it were some misplaced gravel for a driveway. One of the panes of glass on the French windows was starred. At its centre, a smear of dried blood, a couple of strands of dark hair. Jesus Christ, I felt Rebecca behind me, plucking at the sleeve of my jacket, trying to say something to me. Something like *Looks familiar?*

'Les, get on the blower, call some back-up round here,' Mawker instructed. 'The rest of us might as well go for a cosy pint, while we share the wealth of your knowledge.'

I stared at him as I worked hard on my fist, relaxing it. If I hit him, that was me finished. I couldn't help Melanie while I was staring at the different species of dried jizz on a police-cell blanket.

'There's nothing you can do here,' he reasoned. 'We'll talk about what's what, and then we'll see what forensics can dig up here. If she's been kidnapped, there'll be a call through. There'll be a ransom demand, something like that. There always is.'

'He's going to kill her,' I said, trying to keep a lid on it.

'If he was going to kill her, he wouldn't put himself out, by dragging her off to some other place first, would he?' Boris looked at his boss, like some dim Igor seeking praise.

'Les is right,' Mawker said. 'Let's go and have a drink and think about how we're going to play this.'

'You can play this up your arse,' I said, 'if you can fit it in, alongside all the other things you've been told to jam up it over the years.' I backed away slowly and curled a finger round the handle of the French windows. If I bolted now, that was it; I'd be looking at an arrest for impeding police investigations, and other stuff too probably – anything Mawker could get to stick. But I knew that if I played cat's cradle with their red tape, I'd never get a chance to catch him. He'd be dead before I got to him, and I wanted it to be my face that was right in his when he breathed his last lungful. I wasn't the most effective weapon in the arsenal, but I was willing to have a crack – unlike these clowns. You could shave your face with a Rowntree's jelly more effectively than these berks felt collars.

'What's the nearest pub?' Mawker asked and, when he turned to the others, I took off. I skidded and lurched down the decorative spiral staircase to the basement garden and launched myself at the wall. Behind me, I could hear curses and yelps: what happens when a flat foot meets a puddle of oil on a very smooth floor. I was over the wall, through the opposite garden and into Edbrook Road before they had a chance to call after me, let alone give pursuit. I ran hard, knowing they'd be piling back to the car, until I reached the pub on Barnwood Close. There I stopped for a moment under the entrance arch to regain my breath, keeping a nervy eye on the main road. Then I went inside and ordered a pint. My mobile had run down, so I got a handful of change from the barman and, jamming the receiver of the bar's public phone under my chin, sorted out a pile of twenty-pence pieces.

I rang the vets to find out if Melanie had been in touch with them at all, and why the hell Mengele was still kicking back at Melanie's place. Fiona answered. She didn't know what I was talking about, which meant that Melanie must have been jumped not long after I had talked to her. He might have been already in the house, *while* she talked to me. Jesus.

I took a long swig of the lager and closed my eyes, wishing I had my address book with me. A number gradually formed in the dark. Quickly, I dialled it.

'"Keepsies" here, Dave speaking, how may I–'

'Keith there?' I asked.

'I'm afraid Keith is with a client at the moment, sir.'

'Go and get him. Please.'

'I'm sorry, sir, but he's busy. If you call back la–'

'No, I won't call back later. You'll get him *now*. You sound like a bright lad, so I won't need to repeat myself. Do as I say, or the next time you pick the phone up, it'll be with a bloody stump. Now move.'

Much under-the-breath cursing, fading away, dusty footsteps through the corridors. The sound of traffic on the road outside. And then more footsteps. Keith fading in: '... think to ask who it was? You nipplebrain... Hello?'

'Keith. Joel.'

'Joel? Jeez, mate, I'm dealing with a customer here.'

'I'm sorry. Look, did anyone get in touch with you? A woman, name of Melanie. Melanie Henriksen?'

'No. What kind of space is she after?'

'None,' I said. 'I told her to give you a bell if she got into any trouble, while I was away. I was stupid. I should have been more careful.'

'Rewind, Joel. What's going on?'

I fed another couple of twenties into the coin slot.

'I put her in trouble without meaning to,' I said. 'Heaps of shit.'

'Look, if you need help, let me know,' he said. He understood I was stuck in something bad, without having to hear the whole spiel. 'And remember you can come round any time.'

I thanked him and rang off, rubbing my face hard to try to get the blood circulating properly. I'd just been spouting nonsense, so I had to get a grip. I shouldn't be singing the blues down the blower to some poor dolt who didn't need to hear it. I had to get some information. I drummed my fingers on the counter and took another big swallow of my pint. Mawker and his retards must have given up on me by now, and were doubtless Keystone Copping it back to base. I was in trouble there, but things had developed to a point where I was prepared to do a stretch for fucking them over, especially if Melanie had come to any harm. This was my party now, all the way, and the plods weren't invited.

I asked the bartender for a phone book and he trotted off. When he came back, I called Lava Java and asked for Errol. He wasn't there but I sweet-talked the girl who'd answered into giving me his mobile number. Another girl answered that phone, shouting over the thud of music in the background. Or in the foreground, more like.

'Ez, it's for you. Some guy.'

'Yo,' said Errol.

'Errol, it's Joel. Remember? From the flat the other night. How's your hand?'

'Soon as it's better I'm coming to bust your face with it, shithouse.'

'I'm sorry,' I said. 'I had no idea it was going to get that nasty. Nobody could have predicted that.'

'Yeah, well,' he said, and tailed off. Maybe the hard talk was for the benefit of his passenger. I could imagine her cooing over his muscles. Hell, *I'd* coo over his muscles. He made Schwarzenegger look anorexic.

'I was expecting a call from you,' I said.

'Got nothing to say,' he replied, and turned up the volume. I was running low on coins.

'Listen, Errol, did you find out anything about him?' There was no need to expand on that, since I doubted he had left Errol's thoughts any more than he had left mine.

'I talked to a few people,' he said. ''Bout that tat on his throat. Talked to a few of the needles that come into Lava Java, see if they know anything about cobra tats.'

'Nice idea,' I said, wishing he'd hurry it up.

'Talked to this guy who, it turns out, did it, 'parently. How cool is that? Got a parlour in Camden. Name of this headcase is Cullen.'

'I know that, Errol. Gary Cullen.'

'Yeah, well, it took this guy – Phil Hibbert's his name – a while to do the tat, because very sensitive area the throat. Phil said he shouldn't have done it really, not ethically pukka, but he needed the dough. And they got talking. The psycho was a speed freak, by all accounts. Anyway, this guy Cullen had paid up-front for the tat but was in bad shape financially. Spiralling, bad style. Burgling to finance his habit, but having to keep a wife and two terrors happy. Desperate. Upping the ante. Mugging. Bag-snatching. Asking around for a shooter.'

'This guy Phil told you all this?' The name Gary Cullen was burning up in my thoughts. The bump on the back of my head flared, too. My swede was giving him a right old salute. But he was gone now, which meant that I was back on Phythian. Phythian, a ghost, a shadow – someone who existed only as a name, and a false one at that.

'Yeah, well, I leaned on him a bit,' he said. 'Told him that if he didn't talk to me, he'd have a face full of tats that I'd be doing for him free, like.'

'Go on, Errol.'

'So, things get so bad, his wife threatens him that she'll leave, take the kids with her, if he doesn't straighten himself out. Last Phil saw of him, the last session he was having, he said he was going to get professional help. Signed himself up with some kind of counselling service. Therapy. Voodoo? Hypno? Barefoot shit, something like that, you know. Said it was somewhere out East.'

'Somewhere out East? Errol, you would have been just as helpful by telling me to fuck off.'

'Fuck off.'

'No idea where this place is? I mean, Christ, Errol. How East? Canning Town? Margate? Fucking Pyongyang?'

'Phil didn't say. I'm sure he would have done, if he knew. I was going to draw a knob on his forehead with those needles of his.' Giggling in the background. 'Anyone would have talked, faced with that.'

'What about this tattoo parlour? This place run by Hibbert. Where is it?'

'Camden, I just told you.'

'*Where* in Camden?'

'No idea.'

'Okay, Errol. Thanks, mate. Thanks a lot.'

'Don't mate me, guy. No friend of mine put me through what you put me through.'

'It won't happen again.'

'Too right. Hey, any time you fancy coming round the Lava Java for a drink, don't hesitate to decide not to.'

Dead line.

I needed to collect Mengele, so I had to go back to Melanie's place. I checked the area out hard before I approached her house. The place was busy with police. Cordons were being put up and teams of PCs were dispersing to speak to the neighbours. I doubted they'd be specifically on the look-out for me, which was fair enough; who'd have thought I'd be so stunningly stupid to come back? But nor was I about to stride up to the front door and ask for my cat back.

I went round to Edbrook Road and started making the sounds my cat likes to hear. Top of the list was can-opener-meets-tin-of-tuna, but I didn't have the tools for that, so I plumped for basic 'Ch-ch-ch' noises. I was at it for five minutes before I saw him, on a wall about thirty feet to my left, watching me with the ultra-pitiful gaze that certain animals seem to have perfected. Soon, cats will have evolved into a position where they will be able to open tin cans, or put a maggot on a hook and go fishing, and then they'll dispense with us altogether. But I was glad that time wasn't now. I'd missed the little shit. I stroked his dense fur and chucked him under the chin.

I was in bad trouble now, every option open to me less than ideal. I could go back to my flat and spend every night wide awake on the edge of my bed, waiting with a gun for Phythian, who probably wouldn't do me the favour of turning up. Or I could lean on another friend and put him or her in jeopardy. Or I could dump Mengele and hit the streets, rough it till this was all played out. The last way was clearly the only way, despite my feeling that I must have lost the direct attention of Phythian during my jaunt up north. Decided, I lifted Mengele into the only carrying position he will tolerate: draped around my shoulders like a scarf. He growled at me a little, and I almost thanked him for it. I was getting off cheaply, because I'd be first up against the wall, come the feline revolution.

I scurried across the road and got into a cat-friendly cab. The Harrow Road was a nightmare, but that kept my mind from wandering on to what might have happened to Melanie. I had to keep hold of the possibility that she was alive, that Kara and Phythian had only done this because they wanted to lure me in, to make me expose myself. If that was true, then that was fine, because I wanted that too.

Keith was happy to take Mengele off my hands. He said he needed a mouser although, from his concerned searching of my face, I could see that he was just being charitable. I gave him a twenty and told him about the Fishbitz and the tuna, and tiger prawns, how he wouldn't eat anything else, and left him to it. In the few minutes I'd been inside with him, the sky had closed up around the city and turned the air thick. The first spots of rain were dropping, real fat bastards. Some storm was riding in.

I rushed back to my flat and picked up the Saab. Lights switched on, wipers working, I toiled along the Edgware Road to Marble Arch, by which time the remnants of the light had collapsed to form a narrow tunnel in my rear-view mirror. Everything seemed possessed with subtle electricity, with a secret, vibrant colour. It was beautiful, all of it, from the gloss on the scraggy pavements to the cheap neon signs, and the people bent into the wind with their shopping bags. Somewhere, among all these people, he was struggling in the teeth of the storm just like everyone else. It empowered me, thinking of him tamed by the weather, as vulnerable as anybody else. He was no different, really. He got scared, he got pissed, he got injured. We all carried our wounds with us, and he was the same.

I took the first left that I could manage, and jinked left and then right, running parallel to Oxford Street till I hit Great Titchfield Street. I parked in my res zone, as close as I could get to Berners Street, and switched off the engine. The lights were instantly spoiled by the play of rain on the windscreen; detail became something that might never have mattered. *Find her*, I thought, thinking of Kara Geenan, her strange aloof manner, her crocodile ways, *and you find him*. And I knew that when I found him I would end it. I wouldn't wait for any explanations: there wouldn't be a pause for pity or second thoughts. I would rub him out as quickly and as hard as I could, or I'd be slab meat myself.

I got out into the rain and crossed Oxford Street. In Dean Street people were using the downpour as an excuse

252

to take an early dinner. The windows of the Crown and Two Chairmen were fogged up with condensation. Outside, sitting up against the wall, a girl in a sleeping bag was trying to keep her puppy from getting wet.

'Do you need help?' I said. 'And if you did, would you know where to get it?'

'Get lost,' she said.

'Do you know Gary Cullen? He's got a tattoo on his throat, of a cobra.'

Dismissive shake of the head. I stopped on the threshold of the pub and felt in my pocket for a coin. I was just handing it over when I stopped and got my wallet out instead. I gave her a tenner. All I had by now, bar a fistful of shrapnel. She gazed at me as if I was looking for something extra, but I just smiled and told her to keep well. I didn't need money where I was going. You can't take it with you.

17

'Less than three hours, but you can paint me black and call me Mabel if you think I'm getting on it sober. I don't do sober on planes. I just don't. I'll be three sheets to the wind, and then I'll get another sheet and peg that one up too, just to make sure...'

The word *gobshite* came to mind, but I kept grinning because it kept my teeth tight together. If I stopped, I might try to chew his boring bloody heart out.

His name was Muirhead and I don't know what he'd done to piss his chin off, but it looked as though it had left him for another man. He had one of those deeply offensive thick bottom lips, liver-coloured and always wet. It flapped around, staying right out of touch with the top lip, like that of a camel eating a toffee. What he wore could have been chosen from a catalogue called *Things Not to Wear*: a checked granddad shirt smothered by a tight-fitting green tartan waistcoat, trailing off at a pair of charcoal trousers with a neon-bright pinstripe. And a pair of fucking sandals. With socks.

He had one of those braying voices that increases in

stridency whenever someone else tries to say something, pummelling them into silence. Whatever school he'd attended had been seen right with the readies from his pater's wallet, I'd put my mortgage on it. I grinned away, like a dumb grinning thing. He was getting them in, after all.

But it wasn't Muirhead I was interested in. There was a girl standing next to him, someone whose name I hadn't caught properly when Bertie Wooster introduced us. Something like Ria or Tia. Something '–ia' anyway. She was well out of his league, or he was out of hers, but neither of them seemed too bothered by it. I doubted he'd be whisking her off to see his relatives down at the country pile in Surrey any time soon. She leaned on him for another rum and Coke, and I drained my pint just in time for him to waggle his twenty at my empty glass and raise his eyebrows.

'So where are you off to?' I said.

'Perth,' he said. 'But the Perth in Australia, not the one in Scotland.' He started cackling at this, and –ia and me swapped a look. Encouraging, I thought. I wanted to talk to her, but she looked timid, suspicious of everyone. I didn't want to show her how keen I was. I chewed some invisible nails and bided my time. If I rushed this now, then Melanie might end up dead and I couldn't deal with that, so softlee, softlee, catchee monkey...

'And your flight is when?'

'Eleven-thirty. Thiefrow. Malaysian Air. Now you know everything about me. Shall we dance?'

He'd been putting the gin away like an enthusiastic trainee at the Beefeater warehouse, but he didn't yet look as if it was getting to him. That said, he must have been half-cut to be crashing every round of drinks for a couple of complete strangers.

'Mia going with you?' I asked, gambling on the consonant.

'*Nia*,' she said.

'That's what I said,' I said.

'No,' said Muirhead, passing me my lager, 'but I was hoping she might give me a send-off, if you know what I mean.'

What remained of Nia's slashed left eyebrow went north, crinkling her forehead. The light caught in her buzz cut, the shortness of which made her eyes look huge. She resembled Sinead O'Connor, but without the polish. I then knew that he didn't have a chance, but I didn't want her exit scene to come before his. I had to start knocking nicely on her front door.

'Would you mind, awfully, holding my drink for me, old man?' Muirhead said, passing me his gin and tonic and reaching into a waistcoat pocket for his cigarettes. He put his free hand around Nia's shoulder. She shrank a little, and flashed me an aghast look, but she didn't fend him off. I dropped his glass and it shattered on the floor.

'God, man,' he said, 'what's wrong with you?'

'Nothing. You said to awfully hold your drink, so I did.'

Nia started laughing. Muirhead turned on her, and I was impressed: I'd never seen a concave chin jut out before. 'You drink my bloody rum and yet you find that funny? Put that down and let's go.'

'Excuse me?' Nia said.

'Either drink that or leave it. We're going.'

Nia shook her head, slowly enough for him to understand. 'I'm going nowhere with you. What made you think I would?'

'You drank my rum.'

'You offered it to me.'

'You were flirting with me all night, you bitch. If you don't come with me, I'll give you such a slap–'

'That's enough,' I said, and stepped in between them. He

257

smelled of the kind of aftershave that was a distillation of Barbour jackets. He looked as if he might wear a shirt and tie whenever he had his parents round. 'There's the door. It's closing time for you,' I said.

'Is that a threat?'

'It's a fact. Your plane leaves in three hours. You shouldn't miss it. My daughter would hate you to miss it, too.'

'She's not your bloody daughter,' he blustered, as Nia stepped up behind me and put her hand on my shoulder. He didn't look too sure about it, though.

'You didn't even know her name.'

I said, 'I'm aphasic. I have trouble with my worms sometimes.' I moved closer to him, tired to my bones of this Land Rover-frotting individual, and showed him just enough of the Glock to make him decide pretty quickly that he didn't want to argue the toss any more. He took off.

'We'd better go,' I said.

'Oh, fuck, not you and all.'

'Don't worry about me. It's just that I reckon there'll be coppers crawling all through this pub in ten minutes. Listen,' I said, 'let's you and me have a bet. If I'm right, you owe me five minutes of chat. If I'm wrong, you can have my coat to go home in, because it's bucketing down out there.'

'Five minutes of chat?' she said. 'What's that a euphemism for?' But she was smiling. I smiled back, and gestured for her to follow me.

We stood across the road from the Dog and Duck, trying to shy away from the worst of the rain in a doorway that smelled of stale urine, with a mush of nightclub fliers underfoot. Melanie and the need to find her had bloated in my head like a super-tumour, and I felt my palms grow slick with sweat. I just wanted to grab this aloof bitch and scream questions at her until her skin blistered off. But I bit down on it. I sucked it in. Six minutes later a couple of squad cars turned up, followed by a police van. Armed plod scurried into the pub; the place started emptying like a bag of rats chucked into the canal.

'I'm impressed,' Nia said. 'What did you do? Call them yourself?'

'Muirhead,' I said. 'He overreacted. Now, about this chat.'

'Go on, then.' She tilted her face up to me. She could only have been seventeen, eighteen tops. A few years older than Sarah. I almost asked her if she knew her, but then I tore my mind back to the here and now. I must have sounded harsher than I meant to, then, because the humour went from her voice and she stood up straight.

'Phil Hibbert did that for you, didn't he?' It was a long shot, but I had nothing else. The hooded cobra on her wrist, in the classic strike attitude, was enough like Gary Cullen's to make me interested enough to ask this question, at least.

'Yeah,' she said. She wouldn't look at me now. Instead, she glared up and down the street like a sullen kid being told off for spitting. She probably had me down as a plain-clothes – a very plain-clothes – copper about to nick her for the eighth of resin in her pocket. She said, 'So?'

I thought about all the things I could ask her, to try to tease some information out of her, but it all came down to one question. She either knew the answer or she didn't. I tried to get rid of the need in my voice. 'Look,' I said, 'do you know Gary Cullen?'

I gave Nia my jacket anyway, in the end. I had to tuck the Glock away under my T-shirt and felt woefully exposed, wandering around with a bit of hardware that I wasn't used to gradually being revealed by the wet. But it was the least I could do: I didn't want her going off thinking I was a complete wanker. It might mean that at least one person in London might put a tick against my name.

I pounded along Old Compton Street, glad that I was in Soho because nobody was going to give me a funny look because I'd dressed for the beach in the middle of winter. The pubs were spilling out on to the streets and people were now heading for clubs or kebab houses. There was the odd scuffle. Someone in a top-floor window told someone in the street to 'Cock off home, Randy'. I saw some names go into the Groucho, and some names go into Soho House. Some more names came round the corner from Shaftesbury Avenue, maybe having just left Teatro. Jude Law – was that his name? – and that guy McGregor who I'd once seen eating two apples for breakfast on his way to Belsize Park tube, before he did *Star Wars*. I didn't give them a second look, despite my celebrity checklist looking healthier than it ever had done. The only name I had on my mind was Melanie Henriksen. It was good that it was a long name, because it filled my head completely. Anything shorter and some other stuff might have squeezed in around the edges, started shouting at me for some attention. Anything else got my attention tonight, and she'd be dead. I could feel it in my water.

'Hold on,' I implored her quietly, as the rain plastered my hair to my head and trickled down the back of my jeans. My boots were already waterlogged. Butch Boots, they were called. Yeah, right. Maybe they were when I bought them a decade ago, but now I'd have had more protection from a pair of crêpe slippers. As I ran, I thought: *Hold on, hold on, hold on*.

Tuzie's was a crappy little strip joint on Brewer Street.

Like there are any classy strip joints? Maybe there are, but I haven't seen any. And not in this neck – this arse – of the woods. I was scrabbling through my wallet, trying to find a fake warrant card – if I couldn't I'd have to get the shooter out and beggar the consequences – when I recognised the doorman. In this game it's a good thing if you can cultivate a few friendships among doormen, and Henry here was okay. I'd helped him a couple of years before, tracked down a bent business partner of his who'd stung him for a couple of grand, legging it with the business loan after they'd rented premises they wanted to turn into a gym in the East End. People tend to go out on a limb for you if you do that sort of thing for them, even if it is what earns you your daily crust.

'All right, Henry? Not seen you for a while.'

'Mr Sorrell. Yes, it's been a while. You dressed unwisely tonight, it would appear.'

'I gave my jacket to a damsel in distress,' I said.

'Not your old leather number? I'd have paid you good money for that old beauty.'

'No, the other one – some tatty thing I bought from Oxfam for threepence ha'penny, years back. From now on, mortal men shall know me as Joel One Jacket.'

'Get inside,' he said, standing clear of the entrance. 'If they start pinching you to buy a drink, give them this and it's on me.' He handed me a raffle ticket with a stamp on the back. He has very small, very well-manicured hands, Henry Herschell. In fact, all of him is pretty small and well turned out. He can't weigh more than nine stone, but I've seen him lift more than twice that in the gym. Fewer people will mess with a guy who doesn't look as if he should be a doormen than they will with the Errols of this world. Which only goes to show you that there a quite a few wise punters around.

Henry is also a master of Tessenjutsu. That pretty-coloured fabric poking out of his top pocket isn't a hankie, it's a fan. And he can kill you with it. If he can do that with a fan, imagine how tasty he'd be with a big stick.

I thanked him and headed down the steps into the club. At the bottom I was greeted by another bouncer in a dark-green suit and matching teeth. He was going to frisk me, but I showed him the ticket and he let me through. The girl at the cloakroom desk was flicking through a copy of *Condé Nast Traveller*; she snapped her gum when I said 'Hi.'

Lucky me, I'd stumbled into the last place on Earth where you could hear Neil Diamond songs without the benefit of restraints. Up on the pole, a woman was down to her leopardskins, trying to look sexy while that dull, gravel-voiced twat whinged on about telling some lies if you'd only pour him a drink. I wish somebody would, a big one to keep his mouth occupied for a long time.

I sat in a booth and waited for the waitress to come over. The place was deader than an abattoir conveyor belt at down-tools. I flashed her Henry's ticket and she went away again. When she came back, she put a wine glass and half a bottle of fancy-named vinegar on the table.

'What's your name?' I said.

'What do you want it to be, darling?' she said, with all the passion of a doll with a draw-cord sticking out of its back.

'Harold,' I said.

'Cute,' she said, and turned to leave.

'Hang on,' I said, and she did a slow-motion twirl, embellishing it with a big sigh. 'Will Jasmine be on tonight?'

'Jazz? Yes,' Harold said. 'She'll be on at half-twelve.'

'Will you give her a message?'

'It'll cost you.'

'Henry said it would be all right.'

'Henry isn't my boss.'

I ground my teeth together because it was more polite than grinding them against her fucking forehead. I dug for my wallet and showed her the warrant card. It was the kind of dog-eared thing that you might find at the bottom of an infant's school satchel. An infant could have done a better job on it, but it was all I had on me. She swallowed it though.

'Okay,' she said. 'What are you, plain-clothes?'

'Looks like it, doesn't it, Harold?'

'You might have made an effort, coming to a place like this. Management doesn't like jeans.'

'Neil Diamond does,' I said. 'Take your eyes out and give them a good wash. You work in a toilet with a dance floor.'

She shook her head as if deciding I wasn't worth the bother and I scribbled a note on a piece of paper. I folded it up and handed it to her. She unfolded it.

'"The cobra's had its throat cut". What does *that* mean?'

'If it was meant for you, Harold, you'd know. Now, will you fucking well give it to her, or do I have to take you down the nick for obstruction?'

She huffed off and disappeared behind the big purple curtains at the rear of the dais. I sat and watched the turns and drank my drink, acid reflux pistoning up into my throat whenever I belched. The crackle of a needle hitting the groove, the hackneyed songs and the buck and weave of undernourished bodies winding around the pole. In its weird, greasy reflection, I saw my face warped and bent into something alien. Maybe that was how I really looked. And then a bush shaved into the shape of an infinity symbol dinked down in front of the pole, and Melanie was another few seconds closer to death. Or another few seconds beyond it.

A couple of faces poked out from behind the curtain, couched in darkness beyond the range of the spotlight. They disappeared again. I relaxed back in the seat, accepting that I wasn't going to get a summons until she'd swung around the pole a few times, getting goosepimples. She came on a few minutes late, introduced as Jazz Maggs by a limping spiv with greased-back hair and a face like an old woman's elbow. She did her thing, and it was all right if you're into that. She made an effort, at least, putting on a smile that didn't look borrowed from something standing in a John Lewis window. And Neil Diamond had been replaced by *The Girl with the Sun in Her Hair* by John Barry, which was an improvement, in my book. The goggles on the front row chafed their helmets on the dais as they reached forward to slip fivers into her garter. She finished with one last twirl round the pole, and a wiggle of her arse as she disappeared behind the curtain. The spiv came on stage with an opened tin of baked beans and a catapult and asked everyone to put their hands together for Rhonda Valley but, before I saw who Rhonda was, Harold was standing in front of me again, telling me that I was wanted backstage.

There wasn't an awful lot going on back there. Clothes, for one thing. Half a dozen naked women sat in front of make-up mirrors under faulty strip-lighting, smoking or pouring brandy into plastic beakers. They didn't spare me a flicker of interest as I moved past them to the end of the room, where Jazz Maggs was sitting, pushing her feet into a pair of leather, thigh-length boots. She wore a crimson thong and nothing else. Her boobs had been lightly oiled and they gleamed under the harsh light, firm as chilled blancmange, but up close she had tiredness lines under the warpaint. Her nails were varnished unevenly, and they'd been chewed into submission. She'd tied her black hair into a ponytail too tightly, so the skin around her eyes was taut, giving her a surprised look. Her voice was tobacco-scarred.

'What's with all the secret messages, then?' she asked. 'Help me with the zip on this – it's fucked.'

I wrestled with the fastener till it stumbled over the curve of her calf muscle, then she took over.

'Gary Cullen is dead,' I said. 'He killed himself.'

'I know that,' she said. 'You're a bit slow to be going round offering counselling. What do you want?'

'He was seeing someone recently,' I said.

'Yeah, me,' Jasmine said. 'He wasn't getting none off his missus and he had a bit of dosh to splash around, so me and him, we had a good time for a while. How did you find out?'

'Friend of Gary's. Girl called Nia told me.'

'Nia? Nice girl, but you couldn't nail her mouth shut.'

'Did his wife know? About you two?'

Shod, she sat back on the plastic chair and lit a cigarette, pulling on it as though it were the only way to stay alive.

'If she did, he never said. I'm not one for wrecking marriages, but that one had hit the rocks before I was on the scene.'

'Gary was on the rocks, too,' I said. 'Amphetamines. He had a couple of kids to look after too.'

'Why are you telling me this? It's nothing to do with me.' She ground out the cigarette and lit a fresh one.

'He tried to kill me. The same night he killed himself. He killed himself, I think, because he couldn't kill me. Because, if he hadn't, I'd have been able to squeeze some info out of him as to who put him up to it. I reckon he was forced into something he wouldn't normally have done. I reckon someone reassured him that his family would be well looked

265

after if he failed to kill me and then topped himself.'

'What?' she scoffed. 'You're saying he was brainwashed?'

'It's just a theory,' I said. 'I haven't any hard facts.'

'You've got some hard nerve trying to get me involved,' she said. 'You *are* involved. End of story.'

The spiv hopped over and gave her a grin full of rot.

'On again in five minutes, Jazz,' he said. 'What shall we spin?'

'Robert Plant,' she said. '"Big Log".'

'Right you are, love,' he said, and shrank away. I hadn't taken my eyes off her. She must have been used to that, in her line of work, but now it seemed to be unnerving her.

'Do you ever blink?' she said. 'Get an eyeful, why don't you?'

'I'll put a fiver down your knickers if that'll make you feel better,' I said.

'You can leave through that door,' she said, cocking her head towards the fire escape. She put out her fag and stood up in front of the mirror, teasing back invisible strands of hair.

'When I said that Gary was seeing someone, I didn't mean you,' I said.

'I thought not.'

'He was seeing someone for therapy.'

'Was he?'

'Yes,' I said, 'according to his tattooist, he was. And whoever he was seeing was giving him money for some reason.'

'Don't know what you're talking about.'

'I reckon you do,' I said. 'I reckon you know who this therapist is. Gary comes round here and makes your knees tremble against the bog wall, all hugs and smiles like he's got no cares in the world, I think you'd be forgiven for asking him what kind of happy juice he was drinking and where he found it. I reckon he told you.'

'You reckon a lot. Good at maths, are you?'

'Not really. But I know when something adds up, and this doesn't. I'm right, aren't I? He told you.'

'If he did, then I've forgotten. He's gone. Try to move on with your life. It's what he would have wanted.'

'I wonder if his wife is able to move on,' I said.

'Why don't you ask her? She works here. You probably walked past her on the door.' She finished touching up her lipstick and put a hand against my chest, pushed me gently out of the way. 'Some copper you turned out to be,' she said. 'I'll draw you a map, shall I, so you don't get lost on your way back? Now, if you don't mind, I'm flashing my rack for five minutes, and then I've got a nice warm bath waiting for me when I get home.'

Back at the cloakroom, the woman snapping her gum had gone, replaced by the new shift, another equally disenchanted specimen who looked as though if she sucked a lemon, the lemon would pull a face. Henry was getting ready to leave, too. He was shrugging himself into a greatcoat. I beckoned him over.

'Enjoy the show?' he asked.

'It was okay,' I said, 'but there wasn't much of a plot.'

'You caught them on a tame night,' he said. 'Sometimes they have acts up on that stage that would make your balls curl up and die.'

'Spare me,' I said. 'But I'll tap you for a bit of knowledge before you go. That lass on the coats, not this one, the one before – I need her address.'

* * *

267

Wood Green is an unwelcoming place at 9 a.m., but I'd have settled for that. Now it was 3 a.m. on Tuesday night... Wednesday morning. The exposed guts of Shopping City straddling the main drag and the multiplex cinema just beyond it, introduced in an attempt to tart the place up, have all the charm of a dog eating its own puppies. If you're not in a motor as you tool up the main drag, then at least make sure that you're tooled up. I was. And I was fucking freezing.

By the time I'd got back to the car and found the front near-side tyre down, I was ready to kick a few windows in. I didn't have a spare in the boot. That said, I was a bit too pissed to be driving, so instead picked up a lift off one of the minicab desperates hanging around Charing Cross Road by flashing my warrant card at him. But after a few of his questions, as we got up Green Lanes to Turnpike Lane, he got wary and told me to get the fuck out of his cab. I did as he asked and then, as he was powering away, gave my own face a slap: if I'd flashed him the Glock instead, I'm pretty sure that would have guaranteed me a ride to the doorstep of the house I was on my way to. My brains were as slow-moving as slob ice. I wanted a cup of tea and a hot bath and Melanie Henriksen brushing her hot mouth against my neck, asking me to come inside, just for a little while.

I hung around the tube station, hoping for another cab, but the streets were dead and it was getting later and colder. I started walking.

It took me half an hour to get to Shopping City and it was like finding yourself in that part of the enchanted wood where the eyes are all fixed on you. I gave it some swagger and hoped that the sight of someone in their T-shirt in temperatures that were hovering just above zero would convince any would-be muggers that I was a lunatic not to be messed about with. I saw a gang of kids, in windcheaters and trainers the size of breezeblocks, standing around a black BMW with tinted windows at Wood Green tube station. But they didn't do anything; they just watched me walk by. My heart, despite the fact that I was John Wayne-ing my socks off, felt like a kangaroo on a trampoline.

Another ten minutes and I was turning into Sylvan Avenue. The house was a semi-detached job with a pebble-dashed façade and an unkempt lawn. In the centre of it was a bright yellow plastic pedal car. There was a light on in the downstairs window, turning the net curtains a filthy ochre. Two buttons on the doorbell indicated that the house had been split into a couple of flats. My hand, as I reached out to press the lower button, was pale as boiled chicken, the fingernails blueish. I sensed the curtain to my left tremor but I didn't turn to look. A minute later, the letterbox flapped open and a waft of takeaway curry belched out at me. My mouth filled with juices. I hadn't eaten since that morning.

'What do you want?' A female voice, tired, but its edge had been planed off with, I suspected, a couple of large jiggers from the jollies bottle. 'It's four o'bleeding clock. I'll have the police round.'

'I *am* the police,' I said, and showed the flap my crayon and cardboard pass.

'Bollocks you're the police.'

The flap dropped and I slammed my hand against the door. 'All right,' I said, 'I'm not the police. My name's Joel Sorrell. I knew Gary.'

A beat. The flap yawned open. 'I'm very happy for you,' came the voice, more circumspect now, maybe a little unnerved. 'What do you want me to do about it?'

'Let me in, Carol. I want to talk about him.'

'He's yesterday's news. We've done our grieving and we're getting on very nicely now, thank you very much. There's nothing to talk about.' Another pause, and then she said: 'How do you know my frigging name?'

I told her I was an acquaintance of Henry's and that I'd been at the club earlier that evening. The flap closed again and the door opened a crack, the security chain lengthening across the shadow of her face, giving her a dull, metallic grin.

'Henry's all right,' she said, more softly. 'You'd better not be shitting me.'

'I'm not. You can call him now, if you don't believe me. He gave me your address.'

'Whatever,' she said. 'What is it you want to know about Gary? I don't have to tell you anything, you know?'

'I know. Look, can I come in? I lost my jacket and I'm losing the feeling in my fingers.'

She didn't say anything for a few seconds, then she pushed the door to and released the chain. She didn't wait for me. I found her in the living room sitting by an electric fire with one bar on. The lamp I'd seen from outside illuminated just one cosy little corner: a tiny hill of cigarette ends in a stolen pub ashtray; a bottle of Grant's with a Spurs mug to drink it out of; a couple of tinfoil cartons containing the remnants of a chicken tikka dinner. A copy of *What's on TV*. The rest of the living room was uninviting. Paper was peeling away from a damp section of the wall. A corner of a carpet the colour of lightly toasted bread was mottled with mould. Some toys had been perfunctorily cleared away, but the tidying hadn't extended to the plastic plates of congealing instant mashed potato and ketchup on an upturned cardboard box beneath the window.

Carol Cullen sat in her director's chair and motioned me over to the only other seating space in the room: a child's bean bag decorated with scenes from *Pokémon*.

'Kids asleep?' I asked, trying not to look too ridiculous as I sat on it. I edged closer to the fire and wished she'd put the other bar on.

'I'd be surprised,' she said tartly, 'after the racket you caused.' She was chewing gum, still. Bizarrely, I found myself wondering if it was the same wad she'd been jawing at Tuzie's. Her face was long and thin enough to do shifts as a spatula.

'I'm sorry,' I said.

'Drink?' She picked up the bottle and poured herself another dose. There was another mug by my foot. I picked it up and had a sniff.

'Just Ribena,' she said, and did the honours.

I'm not a big fan of whisky, but that mugful was the best drink I'd had in ages. I felt stiffness seeping out of my joints, the pain of the cold lifting from my shoulders and back, life flooding into my wooden hands.

'Are you going to start chatting soon, then?' she asked. 'This isn't a refuge for the homeless.'

'I want to know where the person is who's paying for you to stay in this five-star get-up,' I said. That drew the salt out of her. She suddenly appeared hunted, as if she was a child caught putting a whoopee cushion on the vicar's chair. She answered by lighting a cigarette and instantly putting it out in the ashtray.

'It's not for ever,' she said. 'Just till I get back on my own two feet. Then we'll be moving on.'

I chanced my arm. 'I know it's Kara Geenan,' I said. The name made the holes in her face grow wider. 'She had Gary

271

hypnotised, or else she drugged him up with his favourite cocktail–'

'That's not fair! Gary was trying to come off the whiz. He was–'

'Whatever she did, it doesn't matter. Because somehow she got him to come and have a crack at me. And when that didn't work, he killed himself. And I think he knew that, when he was gone, you and the little ones would be looked after. He saw his own death – was forced or tricked into seeing his own death – as providing some kind of key to a door for you, a new future. And here you are.'

'Nobody said nothing to me about a killing,' she said, trying not to lean too hard on the last word, so that it came out in a frightened whisper like that of a well-brought-up child trying out some four-letter curse for the first time. 'Gary said he was going to do a job for someone, and it would mean us getting out of the miseries for a change. He never talked about suicide. Never.'

'Well, he wouldn't. He was conned into it, wasn't he, by this Geenan woman? She runs hypnotherapy courses, and counselling for druggies. Only she does it on the quiet, right? So she can use her poor, desperate clients to do some dirty work for her, if needs be. Which is why she isn't in the *Yellow Pages*.'

'I don't know where she is.'

'Bollocks.' Me trying to come the hard man, while sitting on a midget *Pokémon* beanbag. Carol was buying it, though. She went to refill her glass, but saw that she hadn't touched the last tot. She put the bottle down.

'If she finds out it was me–'

'She's not going to do a blind thing. I'm going to nail the bitch tonight, if you'll pull your finger out. Nobody need know about you or your little stash of dirty bills, but if you won't play Cluedo, there'll be more coppers in this room than you'll find in bumbags at a car boot sale.'

'You wouldn't, you bastard. Would you? For me and the kids, Gary was a good man.'

'Yeah,' I said. 'I was thinking that, too, as he pulled a big knife on me the other night.'

'The kids,' she said again, but I just waited.

'She's out East somewhere,' she said at last, and capped the statement by draining her mug.

'Narrow that down for me a tad, will you? I could knock on all the doors between Homerton and Hoxton Square, but by the time I found her I'd be pointing at her with a wet stump.'

'Spitalfields,' she said. 'I think that's right.'

'Better,' I said. 'Now all we need is an address, and the next time you see me it won't be in court.'

'I don't know.'

'Oh, come on.'

'I *don't*.' Her eyes flared, spittle flying from between her lips. She wasn't having me on. So that was that. I helped myself to another mug of whisky and thanked her anyway.

'You won't screw me over, will you?' she asked. I didn't answer. She needed a bit of excitement in her life. On my way out, I helped myself to one of Gary's jackets that were draped over the banister. She wouldn't notice, and I was doing her a favour. I reckoned that everything in this house that belonged to Gary would be burned or left on the doormat at the local Oxfam shop, before the end of the day.

I was close. I was so fucking close to her I could smell her, but not quite close enough. I checked my watch: coming up to 5 a.m. Still dark outside, an unpleasant urban dark,

273

fume-filled and uneasy as if the fevered dreams of the people sleeping beneath it were just hanging there, unable to escape. I felt the weight of it pressing down on me as I made my way back to the main road and lucked on to a night bus. As I drew closer to the city centre, the handful of shift-workers dozing in their seats around me grew restive, their breathing troubled, as if they could sense it too. London's heart was being choked by its own excesses, palpitating with its ceaseless need for violence, as if it were the drug that kept it fast and loose: feeling alive when it was anything but. Nobody lived in London who didn't look over their shoulder now and again. The pressure you felt here wasn't anything to do with traffic jams or the nine-to-five. It was the barely suppressed question: *Will I be next?* I was asking that question now. As the bus roared along Camden Road, and I buzzed the driver to stop, I wondered if I'd ever really asked myself any other.

18

There used to be a good little bookshop up towards Camden Lock. Compendium, it was called. You could buy all these weird literary 'zines and books about fetishes, American paperback editions, lots of odd stuff: highbrow texts and sleaze so low it must have been just this side of criminal. And then it closed down to make way for something abysmal, just another cliché shop in the row of overpriced clichés that Camden High Street was turning into. Even the people who came here at the weekend for the market became different. They dressed in shabby-chic clothing or peasant gear, or as Goths, but you knew when they went home they'd get back into their jeans and Travis T-shirts. There's a Wagamama in Camden now. That says it all.

It was just shy of six when I reached the top of Camden High Street, just where it morphs into Chalk Farm. A couple of clubbers in gear that at 2 a.m. would have looked rad now merely made the people wearing it look raddled. They were eating slices of pizza they'd bought from God knows where, while walking silently back to twelve hours of kip. One of those motorised roadsweeps was redistributing the litter more evenly across the roads and pavements, and a garbage-disposal truck was emptying bins that nobody bothered to use.

There was a newsagent's just opening, and a café that looked as if it had never closed. It would have been nice to buy a paper and read it over a coffee, but my mind wasn't up to anything that wasn't Melanie Henriksen. I knew that if I didn't sort something out before the morning was over, then I'd collapse, unable to wake up again until long after she'd been plugged and left to cool.

I compromised by swapping the last of my shrapnel for a takeaway espresso, which I guzzled while crossing the road to the tattoo parlour opposite the warren of stalls and boutiques that make up Camden Market. Hib's Tats, the place was called. *Tattoos* announced another sign in the window, in dead neon over three boards of photos depicting the sore, red-edged patterns that people had acquired in Phil Hibbert's needle-and-ink surgery minutes before those pictures were taken. Above the display window was a black space, curtains drawn.

The coffee had slapped me around a bit, so I kicked at the door and jammed the heel of my hand down on the buzzer, until the black space of Hibbert's bedroom window became a nicotine-coloured space and the window opened.

'Fucking lay off it, will you? Crack of fucking dawn.' How the words got past that expanse of beard, I'd need a degree in physics to work out.

'Phil Hibbert,' I said.

'Correct. Well done. Now get to fuck.'

'Open up. It's the police.'

'My arse.'

'Do you want to open this door, or do I break it down? Makes no odds to me.'

276

'Fucker.' But he shut the window and a few minutes later a light came on in the hallway, and I heard him stomping down the stairs.

He was swearing again before he'd even got the door open, but that all faded away when he saw the gun I was pointing at his guts.

'That's right,' I said. 'Get your teeth married and let's get indoors before my finger gets too cold and needs a work-out.'

We went into the shop front, where his catalogues were stacked with pictures of butterflies and dragons and tribal symbols. There was the smell of nervous sweat and dead cigarettes in the walls. Plastic chairs were arrayed around this waiting room, and there was even a small table covered in magazines: copies of *New Woman* and *FHM* from the late 1990s.

'Let's go into your surgery,' I said.

'You look like shit,' he said.

'What's your frame of reference, pubis?' I said. 'That remark might hurt if you meant anything to me. As it is, I haven't met you before in my puff, and I don't expect to again. Unless you fancy going face-to-face with me in court. So let's get this over with, so we can get back to where we were before, hmm? Me outside, breathing fresh air, and you in your pit, feeling up your so-called dick. And both of us a lot happier.'

I sat on the edge of his treatment table. His tattoo gear was nowhere to be seen. Maybe he kept it in a little black briefcase and got it out with a nasty little flourish, like Laurence Olivier in *Marathon Man*.

'Who are you? What do you want? There's no need to play hard bastards.'

'I'm a private detective,' I said with a start, noticing one of my business cards pinned to a cork board filled with local adverts on the wall behind his head. 'What I want is for you to do me a very great favour.'

'Get on with it.'

'Just what I wanted to hear.' My stomach rumbled. 'Look, you don't have anything to eat, do you?'

'For you, after that graceful entry? You can eat the winnets off my arsehole.'

'Come on,' I said, 'I'm starving.'

He reached around the back of a desk and pulled out a packet of biscuits, which he handed over, reluctantly. I could have thrown the gun away and asked him to marry me there and then, if it weren't for the beard. I devoured a couple and, as the sugar kicked in, my eyes sprang apart as if I'd been dunked in ice-cold water.

'Okay,' I said, feeling better, the need for sleep retreating for a while. 'Okay, this is what's happened. You had a visit from a friend of mine. Bloke called Errol, he could fit me and you into his trouser pockets – yeah, I see you know who I'm talking about. Now, I know he shook you down pretty vigorously, but Errol, he's thicker than two poodles. What he forgot to ask you about our pal Gary Cullen was, where was he going for this treatment of his?'

'Spitalfields,' Hibbert said, quicker than a kid in class trying to win a gold star.

'I know that,' I said. 'If you could bung me an address, then I could leave you in peace. As opposed to leaving you in pieces.'

He didn't hang around admiring my wit. He said, 'Spitalfields Market. Basement of the Elegant House. It's some kind of airy-fairy gaff sells scented candles, soap with bits in it, herbs. You know the stuff. Gary told me he used to come out of there smelling like a whore's drawers.'

Fatigue slammed down on me. I don't know if it was because I felt I was suddenly in charge of how things might turn out, that for the first time I had the upper hand over Kara Geenan, but my body seemed to give in a little, to flag under the weight of adrenaline that was spewing through my veins. I sat down in his dentist's chair and the light swam around my head. I saw him move across the plane of my vision, his beard like some dirty cloud spoiling the view. The gun was heavy in my hand, so I put it down and took off Gary Cullen's jacket. The light was turning into liquid, drops of brilliant water that wouldn't fall and just kept rilling around on the ceiling. Hibbert rolled up my sleeve and wiped the biceps of my left arm with alcohol. From somewhere he produced what looked like a pen with a lead attached to it. His beard parted and I fixed on its pink, wet centre.

'I don't...' I said.

A tongue flickered from the end of the needle, black and bifid. I felt its heat against my skin, and then all I knew was the buzzing, and his beard turned into a swarm of flies and I could see nothing beyond that.

I woke up and the light was gone. No, not gone. Different. It didn't have the watery edge of before. I sat up and a blanket fell away from me. I reached for the gun and it wasn't there. I pulled my sleeve up and I was slightly disappointed to find the skin had not been broken. Sunlight painted a square of gold on the drab wall of the parlour. Late sunlight. Very late. I felt my guts clench and I stood up groggily, reaching out for a hand or a rail that wasn't there.

Stumbling across the room, I got to the parlour to find

Hibbert in there, his needle working on a red-haired woman. She was having a spider's web across her breasts.

'Look,' she said, when she saw me, 'tit for tat!'

I ignored her. You would, too. 'Hibbert, what the fuck did you do?' I said. My voice felt gummed up and untrustworthy.

'I did nothing. You blacked out. It was like someone reached inside you and pulled your plug. You must have been burning the candle at both ends with a flame-thrower.'

'I'm in a rush,' I said. 'I shouldn't have–'

'I know, but you sparked out and there was no kicking you awake. I tried, believe me.'

'Where's my gun?'

His beard moved; I could imagine his jaw hardening beneath it. 'I don't think you should... I took it off you.'

'Yes,' I said, 'it looks that way, doesn't it? So give it back.'

'Guns,' he said. 'People who use guns...'

'There's a killer loose,' I said. 'He's killed at least three people. And he's got someone I care about and if I don't find him, he'll kill her too. If he hasn't already. And there's no way I want to go up against him with nothing more deadly than the piss in my dick.'

The woman laughed. Hibbert withdrew his needle and gave her a look. She quietened down and he went back to work. In the shade of the hallway, his own tattoos writhed around his arms as if they'd been imbued with life.

'So call the police,' he said.

My eyes filled up with red. When they cleared again, I had my hand wrapped around his chin mullet, and I was smacking his head down against the bone in my knee. The woman was sitting back on the chair, lifting her boob up for a closer look. I felt awake and refreshed. While I was putting dents into his head, I thanked him for lending me his blanket. He was making noises, the same noise over and again.

'Now where's the gun?' I said. And then I realised that the noise he'd been making for the past few minutes was the answer.

'...thedeskthedesk...' he was wailing.

I let go of his beard and he dropped to his knees. Blood from his nose was making the beard look more and more like something mankind should never have evolved. I retrieved the gun from the desk drawer and stepped over him. 'Shave it off,' I suggested. 'You can always tattoo it back on.'

Melanie Henriksen was sitting in a high-backed wooden chair. She was naked. Her flesh was white except for the deep gash of red that opened her torso. The tiny, caramel-brown mole that sat midway along her right clavicle looked as enticing as it had when I'd left her at her doorstep the other night. It was the best way of identifying her, since whoever had killed her had stolen her head.

No.

I had to keep hold of the hope that she was alive. I sat in the back of the taxi, fuming silently at the traffic on the City Road and trying not to allow the black tidings of my thoughts to gain a foothold. The old guy who was driving was on his phone now, talking about Chelsea versus Everton. He waved a woman in a Corsa on to the main road from an adjacent street. I realised I was squeezing my fist too tightly when I saw four tiny crescents of blood across my palm. The next time the taxi stopped, I opened my door and then I opened his door.

'What the bleed–'

He was on the ground, his hand still wrapped around his phone, and it was all I could do not to stamp him into the tarmac.

Rein it in, I thought. *Use it on someone who deserves it.*

I got behind the wheel and took the car up on to the pavement, sent the needle up to a number that started people screaming. Car horns blared at me, just drivers full of hot air wishing they had the stupidity gland that allowed me to do what I was doing. No police on the City Road, thank fuck. Not for now, anyway.

I'm a good driver. I've never had an accident, never had any points on my licence. When I was a kid, I was a member of the Tufty Club.

A woman coming out of a second-hand clothes shop, pushing a buggy. Kid in it wearing one of those humiliating jester's hats, the kind that make them grow up into granny-batterers. Hard right, just avoiding her, and half on to the road again, skinning the cab against the passenger doors of London's patient motorists. Guy on the radio saying that in the capital, you lucky people, we're looking at some very early spring weather coming our way, just for a short while. Now here's three in a row from Céline Dion.

Cyclist. Hard left, back on to the pavement. Take out a couple of saplings and a litter bin. Plastic tables outside a grotty café become pretty, but impractical, sky furniture. I save the locals from buying bruised or unripe fruit from the greengrocer's by ploughing through his stall. I'm standing on the pedal and leaning on the horn. It feels as though my arse hasn't touched the seat since I got behind the wheel. All I need now is a couple of blokes carrying a huge pane of glass to walk out in front of me, and I've got the set. If the traffic doesn't ease up soon, I'm going to kill someone and that must not happen. That will not happen.

Down on London Wall, the traffic did become less of a bitch. I pushed the taxi at fifty to Bishopsgate, and turned north. Opposite Liverpool Street station, I took a right and parked along Brushfield Street. I got out of the car and hurried towards the old Spitalfields Market. The unseasonal spring weather we were just being promised wasn't here yet; the sunshine earlier hadn't possessed the muscle to last the entire day. Rain was coming in hard from the west, black fists of cloud rising in readiness to hammer the city once again. By the time I reached the archway leading into the market, the first spits were coming. The sky felt close. The colour in the Christmas decorations hanging from the entrance had turned to lead, and darkness was being trowelled thickly on everything. I tried to swallow, but the wetness had gone from my throat. I sucked in some deep breaths and tried to think rationally.

I ducked into a phone booth and rang Jimmy Two. Jimmy Two, as mentioned earlier, is a mate of mine, the younger brother of Jimmy One, a nasty piece of work who's in Wandsworth doing a stretch for armed robbery. I've no idea what their surname is. Jimmy Two is all right, though. He has a garage out on the Cally Road, but he loves my motor more than I do and he promised to pop round to Berners Street to slip a new tyre on her within the hour. I told him that if he could get the car over to me in E1, I'd keep him in whisky for the next six months. No problem, said Jimmy Two. I almost asked him if he wanted to come in with me on what I was about to do, but that would have been pushing it a bit. And, anyway, the clock was ticking.

Spitalfields Market was pretty much dead. It only really came to life at the weekends, when the stalls and the shops were filled with people looking to buy lamps and mirrors and candles, or kicking back at the lunch areas or having a beer. There were a couple of games of football taking place on the five-a-side pitches, though, so the occasional shout, cheer or insult echoed around the enclosure. I turned right and walked past a shop that sold cast-iron beds. Next-door was a second-hand bookshop. And next to that was the Elegant House. I hung back, although it appeared that the shop was empty. A fat padlock was looped through the front-door handles. A sign above the lock read: *Closed for three weeks. Holiday.*

In the windows were displays for calligraphy pens and coloured inks in tiny, attractive bottles. Orange fake-fur cushion covers were piled up behind them, along with vases made out of twisted glass in electric blue. The smell of the soap seeped out of the cracks in the door, a heady mix of lavender and sandalwood. It was a beautiful display. I waited for another vociferous outburst from the artificial pitches, then put the butt of the gun through the window. Quickly, I hacked out as much of the glass from the window frame as I could and ducked into the shop. The smell of the soap was much stronger now, and I had to fight the urge to sneeze. I stood in the gloom for a while, hunched over, listening out for any noise to signal that there was someone in here, but nothing happened. There were stairs leading to a basement office. A sign at the top said *KayGee Karma*, with an arrow in red felt-tip pen pointing downwards. I followed it.

At the bottom of the stairs there was a small seating area and, behind a partition, a desk with a couple of books on it, and a stool on either side. On one of the white walls was a picture of a heron standing by a river, with a fish speared on its beak. Beneath it was some certificate of authenticity regarding Kara Geenan's proficiency as a hypnotherapist. I ought to get her to do me a warrant card, it was so good. I checked the drawers of the desk but they were locked. There was a door behind the desk. I went to open it but it was locked. Down here, the sounds I was making died pretty quickly, so I thought fuck it, fuck it, and kicked the bastard in. A frightened human smell sprang out at me, backed up by the sour reek of organic waste. I scrabbled for a light and threw the switch.

A pale bulb shone at the centre of the ceiling, illuminating some kind of storeroom containing tons of junk: broken brushes and dustpans, old posters rolled up and secured with elastic bands, chipped plant pots, a deckchair speckled with cigarette burns. There was a tall metallic cabinet filled with receipts and invoices. To the rear of the storeroom, where the light bulb was having trouble penetrating the dark, something was moving under a large mound of hessian sacking.

I switched off the safety on the Glock and edged forward, tiptoeing around the mounds of furniture and bric-a-brac. I couldn't breathe, but then I realised that was because I wasn't trying any more. She was speaking, and I heard her voice but, in the moment before I recognised it, I didn't want to recognise it. I wanted to shoot her in the head without pulling back the sacking. And then I wanted to run away, run until I'd worn the soles off my boots, run until I ran out of land. Do her and go, I urged myself. You don't want to see her, not if she's speaking like that.

'Anything,' she was saying in a broken, dispirited voice. 'I'll do anything. I'll do anything. Just don't kill me.'

I tugged off the sack and it was bad, but you manage. You have to deal with it. You might say 'I can't bear it', or 'I can't go on', but then you do, despite it all. You have no choice. What's behind the closed door bothers you only for as long as it's closed. I untied the bloody string around her wrists and helped her to her feet. I took off my jacket and wrapped it around her shoulders. Shit and piss drizzled off her naked thighs. The bleach that had turned her hair white had burned into her forehead and neck. Her mouth was bruised and dry, like a sliver of dried aubergine, and her eyes wouldn't fasten on anything. She was shaking. So was I.

I was leading her out of the room, masking her with my hand against the glare of the lights, when I heard a single footstep gritting on the broken glass in the shop upstairs.

'Wait here,' I said.

'Joel?'

'It's okay, Melanie,' I said. 'Just wait here for me. I'll be gone a minute, that's all.'

I sat her on a chair, then I went up the stairs as fast as I could, going into a roll at the top and swinging my arm round towards the shape that was coming at me from the front of the shop. I knew it wasn't the police as they'd have said something by now, so I fired at the legs. Nothing happened. Hibbert – he'd emptied the clip, the prick, the fucking, fucking prick.

'Fucking prick,' I cried, and hurled the gun at the shadow. It sidestepped it easily and waded in. Something flashed by the side of my face, connecting hard, and I went down. It felt like a hammer, or a cast-iron candlestick, but I didn't have time to play Guess What? I scuttled backwards on my arse as fast as I could, feeling my mouth fill with blood, trying to blink away the darkness that was trying to close in. A slow sweep of headlights through the window showed me enough of her face to tell me who it was.

'Kara,' I tried to say, but my jaw felt too loose and the

words turned into a wet sigh of pain. She came on, swinging the weapon in her fist, and I was running out of scuttling space. The most dangerous thing my hand fell upon was an inflatable cushion for the bath. But then the room filled with white light and the sound of thunder. I heard a bullet zing off the wall and shatter a mirror about a foot above my head. Geenan threw herself at the broken window. Another huge crash, another bullet thunking into the heavy wooden frame.

I pushed myself upright. Melanie was slumped over the top riser, her arm outstretched. I went to her and took the gun out of her hand.

'Where did you get this?' I asked her.

She moved her head in the direction of the stairs. 'Desk,' she breathed, 'if you know where the keys are kept.'

'I'll be back,' I said.

I could hear her footsteps, already distant, moving fast, very fast, across the concrete. Kara could run. Yeah, well, so could I. There are few things I can do better.

I took a potshot at her, to keep her on her toes, just as she was careering around the corner of Steward Street into the new development that had been built in the pocket of land directly behind the market. Office buildings, bland and grey, the kind of place you just can't wait to get out of bed for in the morning. And there would be plenty of people getting out of bed now, double-quick, at the sound of all this gunfire. I had to get closure on this little bitch before the Sweeney turned up.

I reached the corner just in time to see her disappear into the building site. I got after her fast, never taking my eyes off her point of entry. She flitted between two Portakabins, and I squeezed off another round. The gun was big and heavy and the shot went well wide, but I wasn't too bothered. It was a nice feeling, knowing that she was the one being hunted for a change. The far end of the building site was protected by a tall, white wooden fence that enclosed the rear half of the perimeter. There was no way she was climbing that unless she had a pocket stepladder concealed down her strides. The only way she could get out was if she ran straight down my throat.

I skipped down the side of the Portakabin and spotted her by a stack of pallets loaded with white ceramic toilets wrapped in shrink-wrapped plastic. She was standing with her hands behind her back, head down. It looked as though she knew she was on a loser and had decided to play nice.

Yeah, right.

I approached her with the gun pointing straight between her breasts. Any funny stuff and I was going to blow her chest wide open and sod the overtime she owed me. But, as I got nearer, I found she was crying.

'Give it a rest, Kara,' I said. 'What are you expecting me to do? Melt?' I stepped closer. 'Come on,' I said, 'I will fucking shoot you if you fuck about with me. I want to know where this cunt is who's trying to rub me out. And I want to know what's in it for you.'

She wasn't crying; she was chanting. Some weird mantra that I couldn't get a hold of. It looped in the thick air between us, feeding off her fear and my suspicion, sounding like a familiar name that I'd forgotten about for years. The name of someone precious to me who had been so long gone they had almost escaped my thoughts.

'What?' I said, and leaned in closer. Her voice deepened and grew softer, becoming something lyrical that ought to be listened to while accompanied by music. The noises she was making were as alien as a foreign language, yet as known to me as the sound of my own breath as I lay in bed at night. Other notes came into the lilting of her voice, turning it warmer, more trustworthy, the kind of voice that your mother has.

Her hands came out from behind her back. They were holding a beautiful crown made of some astonishing silver metal that absorbed all of the light and made it appear liquid. Glittering seeds swam all around the circumference, blazing here and there like polished jewels. It drew the light and colour from my eyes.

'Can I wear that?' I asked, and a great mouthful of spit and blood washed across my chin. I couldn't see her eyes behind the crown. Her face was a black nonsense. And then it all went wrong. The noises from her mouth stopped sounding like aural honey and were spiked by awful jags of rage. I stumbled back as the crown spoiled in her fingers, turning into a rusted length of thick iron with a vicious claw on the end. The whoop of the police siren twisted through the air like a fantastic creature taking flight for its dinner. I staggered some more and a couple of large staples in the plastic wrap punched through the skin of my outstretched hand.

I swore and went down, a headache ripping through me. I found myself trying to work out what was hurting more, and awarding points for pain quotient. Headache = 7 points; staples in hand = 6 points; mullered jaw = 9 points. Any advance on 9 points? You, madam, with the fucking crowbar, got a 10 on you?

I rolled away as the jemmy came down. My face went straight into a hill of sand, and I came up spitting grains. I shot her through the stomach and she staggered back, dropping the crowbar. Blood, a lot of blood, fell with it, giving the day-shift's cement an interesting tinge.

'Fuck,' I yelled. I didn't want to do that. I went after her but she was gamely staying one step ahead, the pain and the shock, like me, trying to catch up with her. Death was strolling somewhere behind us, picking its teeth. It didn't need to hurry. It had as long as it took.

She got to the works entrance and staggered through it. A lorry clipped her and she went down hard. Her foot snagged in the lorry's rear wheel, as it braked and slewed across the road. She was dragged under the wheel and vanished for a moment, as she was fed through the axle. When she came out again, she was all mangled to fuck and back. I got to her as her last breaths turned to scarlet froth on her lips. Her body was split up the side and what looked like yellowish cheese was piling out of her; her guts were grey ropes unravelling on the road. There was no point trying to get them back inside. Her left leg was bent backwards and hiked up so far that if she turned her head a little, she could have bitten her own heel. The lorry driver was wailing like a seal who'd lost its pups.

'Where is he?' I yelled at her.

'I was just trying to protect him,' she said. Her eyes twitched spastically. 'I never wanted him to take it this far. My kid brother, I never...'

I wasn't going to get much else out of her. She was in her own cocoon of random thoughts now, as the switches were being flicked off all through her body, shutting down.

I was intending to put one through her brain, but there was no need. She was beyond suffering. I envied her that.

19

She'd tried it on me before, I realised that now, right at the very start of things. At the coffee shop in Soho. Maybe I'd been too tired or too drunk to notice, to respond, to go under but, thinking back, her voice had been the same: soft, persistent, deeper than you might expect from such a willowy woman. I hadn't cracked, then. Well, not in the way she'd expected me to.

I hurried back to the Elegant House and wrapped Melanie in a large fur rug. She'd gone back down the stairs and was sprawled over the desk, trying to collect the books in her arms. I carried her out on to the street. She was mumbling something into my ear, but I didn't pay attention because I was trying hard to think of what I'd done to deserve this kind of grief.

Jimmy Two had left the car where he said he would, parked on a little one-way avenue called Wilkes Street that runs parallel to the main drag. I made a mental note to drop round a couple of big bottles of Grant's for him. As I nosed out on to Commercial Street, three police cars and a riot van drew up on Lamb Street, and a slew of officers piled into the marketplace. We bypassed an ambulance heading for the accident scene. I was confident the lorry driver hadn't stagged me; he'd had his face in his hands the whole time. He was blaming himself for this one, at least until they told him about the bullet that helped her on her way.

I checked on Melanie every time I came up against a traffic light, or a tangle of cars stalled at a junction. Her face was very pale, apart from the scorch marks left by the bleach. I spoke to her, and I don't know if what I said got through to her, but she seemed to respond to my voice, rocking her head slightly, moving her busted mouth, frowning. I was going to take her straight to hospital, but the more I thought about that, the less I fancied it. St Bart's was crawling with police by the time I reached it and I worried that everyone from the Spitalfields incident was going to turn up there, rather than cross the river to Guy's. I blinked first in that particular little game of chicken, and took off up to Holborn Viaduct. I couldn't see any major injuries on Melanie's body. She was in shock and she was exhausted, but she hadn't been seriously harmed. She needed rest: that seemed like the picture to me. There was only one place to go.

I parked the car and fed a few pound coins into the meter, wishing for the first time that I didn't have such an easily identifiable motor. Surely Mawker would have his peelers looking out for it? Well, that was just tough. I was so strung out that I didn't trust myself not to start firing at him and his goons, when they inevitably came my way. It didn't matter so much to me what happened now that I was sure Melanie was safe. I helped her out of the car and we staggered over to the door of the apartment block. I leaned on the buzzer but there was no answer. She must have gone to work. Essex Road, right. I was about to drag Melanie back to the car, when the main door opened and Lorraine Tokuzo was standing there in a bicycle helmet, struggling to get her Marin outside.

'You didn't need to bring me a present,' she said, assessing Melanie. 'I put you up out of the goodness of my heart.'

I could have cried, but that wasn't going to help anyone. She secured the bike, with a combination lock, in the entrance hall before helping me get Melanie into the lift. Going up, Lorraine studied my face as if she couldn't quite place who I was. I must have looked rough compared to the guy who'd crashed at her pad a few nights before. I hadn't had a shave for days. My Diesels could have performed stunt jeans in *Zombie Denim-Wearers*. I smelled like something you could grow mushrooms out of. And my jaw looked as if it had just gone fifteen rounds with a peckish Mike Tyson.

I drained the best part of a litre of orange juice from Lorraine's fridge, while she put Melanie to bed. She didn't say anything to me after she came out of the bedroom; her face was pinched tight shut, like an old woman's purse. She was at the door and picking up speed, when I called her name.

'I'm sorry about this,' I said.

'So am I,' she said. 'I don't want trouble here. Just sort it out, whatever's going on, and sort it out quick. Then you can explain it to me.'

Thunk. Door shut.

Through the window I watched as she cycled slowly off towards York Way, her long, tanned legs subtly gleaming in the morning sunlight. I was distracted from memories of those legs – in other positions, in other times – by Melanie who was babbling again. I poured her a glass of water. In the bathroom I dug a tube of lignocaine out of the medicine cabinet, along with a couple of soluble codeine pills that I had missed on my last visit. Melanie had thrown off the duvet and was writhing like a cut worm on the sheets, sweating them up. I put the glass down and sat at her side, gently grasped her close. Slowly she came out of it, becoming still beneath the motion of my hand as it stroked the acid-white shock of her hair.

'Did she do this to you?' I asked her gently, too gently for her to hear. 'Or was it him?'

Images of the head I'd found in that Liverpool bedsit grinned out of the black museum in my mind. The blonde, matted hair rising free of the puckered scalp, as if it were trying to escape. The crude slashes of make-up. I rubbed the cream into the blistered areas of Melanie's forehead and her chafed wrists, and got her to swallow some of the dosed water. Her eyes were all over the place as she fought to stay awake.

She said, 'She was so nice. She knocked on my door. She said her car had broken down. Her eyes…'

She said, 'He was in the car. He pulled me in. A kid. Strong.'

She said, 'The woman turned to him in the car, told him he could play with me for a while. He told me he didn't know what would hurt you more. If he killed me or if he just hurt me. He asked me for advice. He said: "What do you think would cause him most pain?"'

She said, 'He stroked my hair and leaned over. "Not in that colour, love," he said.'

I pulled the duvet up around her naked body and waited until sleep smoothed away the lines from her face. Then I got up, returned to the living room and, in absolute silence, lost my mind for a few moments. When I came to, my knuckles were white and I'd gouged nail marks in the soft leather of Lorraine's sofa. Slowly, I came back. I calmed down.

I took a long, searingly hot shower and carefully hacked off the week-old growth on my face, grimacing whenever I moved my jaw to accommodate the blade. At least it didn't feel as though any bones were broken, but it was going to swell up till I looked like the bastard offspring of Desperate Dan and Jimmy Hill.

I threw my clothes in the washing machine and eased myself into Lorraine's ratty, but much-loved, towelling bathrobe. Then I fixed myself a tuna sandwich and bolted it down with some fresh coffee. I took a handful of painkillers and lay back on the sofa. Then I thought, nuts to that, and crawled into bed alongside Melanie. I fell asleep smelling the magical, warm scent from her skin.

You couldn't change that, I thought. You and your bottle of bleach, you fucker. You couldn't chase that out of her.

Erased. Rubbed out. Retired. Topped. Whacked. Blown away…

No, you're not getting away with any of that playground talk. What you did… what you did, Joel, is that you fucking *killed* someone today.

That was the first thing I thought of as I opened my eyes. It didn't seem to mean much that she wanted *me* dead for some reason that was currently beyond me. I had pointed the gun at her and shot her through the guts. I had killed a person. A human being. My first. Somewhere, maybe, a father and a mother were sitting together watching television, wondering if their daughter was going to call them soon. And she wasn't. She wasn't going to call them soon. She wasn't going to call them ever again.

On my right, Melanie was in deep sleep. To my left, Lorraine was lying on top of the duvet, but covered with a blanket, her eyes open and fastened on the play of light from the city, curving across the cool blue shadows of the ceiling.

Melanie rolled over and her eyes opened. She then went very still but said, very clearly: 'Ghosts between the shelves.' Then she shut her eyes again, and it was difficult to believe that she had ever been anything but fast asleep.

Lorraine must have felt me tense up, because her hand came over to take mine. Her hand was warm. Its warmth flooded into the cold iron of my own, and induced it to soften.

I said, 'Will you look after her?'

'Who is she?' she asked. Our voices sounded calm and breezy, like any ordinary couple indulging in a little pillow talk before sleep.

'Melanie's my vet. Well, my cat's vet. She got dragged into some bother.'

'That I can see,' Lorraine said. 'Me too, hey, if I'm not careful?'

'No,' I said, 'I won't let that happen. That was the first and last time.'

'Okay,' she said. 'I'll keep an eye on her, but you should take her to see a doctor.'

'I will, when I've finished.' She was going to ask me another question, but I wasn't sure how I could answer it. I didn't even really know what it was that needed finishing. Maybe it was me: maybe that was the answer.

I said, 'Give her plenty to drink. Water. She's pretty dehydrated.'

I let go of Lorraine's hand, even though I wanted nothing

more than to keep hold of it, to roll over and have her engulf me in warmth for a while, to lie there and absorb all her heat and understanding into me. I was a loner, and I preferred my own company, but nobody can stay sane like that. Even the most aloof, isolated individual needs a hug now and then. We wither and die without such contact. That was me then, stuck in bed between two beautiful women, and lonelier now than the kid who's just been sick on the back seat of the bus.

I left them in the bedroom and gathered together my gear. The jeans were still a bit damp, but it didn't matter. I felt like a new person, by wearing fresh, clean clothes for a change. I checked my watch: it was a quarter to six in the evening. God knows what day it was. Wednesday, I think. On the floor by the bathroom was the rug that I'd wrapped Melanie in. Next to it were the books she'd rescued from KayGee Karma. I picked one of them up and studied the cover. *Mind Medicine: Hypnosis for All* by some barefoot-hippy quack called Dr Saffron Twohy. Why did Melanie want this so much? It seemed a bizarre comforter even for someone in her state. Maybe she had been made a convert to Kara's methods and fancied it as a career change – I don't think. I was dumping the book in the bin when I noticed the little sticker on the spine. Inside the front cover was a stamp for St Pancras Library. Okay, so what was Kara doing in Spitalfields with a copy of a book from a library in King's Cross? Couldn't get it at the library on Commercial Road? Possibly. Possibly.

I threw on my jacket and went outside.

I walked up to the car and then stopped. I had the urge to get in, gun the engine and put her in gear, fuck off out of it. Drive until I ran out of petrol, then settle down, marry a woman I didn't love, find a job in an office working for someone who would look at his watch whenever 5 p.m. came around and people started to leave work, enter the weekly pub quiz and call out the answers in a loud voice. Start wearing cardigans and learn the Latin names for all the plants in the garden. It would be just what I deserved.

Instead, I wandered up to the Euston Road, wishing that I'd reached her before the lorry slammed the life out of her, saving her from the pain I'd exploded in her stomach. She probably wouldn't have told me where he was, but maybe she would. In extremis, she might have whispered his whereabouts. In return for another bullet. Now I was back at square one. I knew his Liverpool retreat, but he wasn't going back there. He wanted me dead, but he could take all the time he wanted. He knew my face.

He knew my face.

I forced my brain to pick away at memory's seam, sealed over as it was by all the vodka and beer I'd swilled down me during the past decade. I had disturbed some monster in Liverpool that wanted to silence me for some crime that I'd committed. But I couldn't think what that was. For want of something better to do, I called Mawker. I was feeling sick and fed up. I wanted to talk to someone who I felt superior to, and there weren't many of those around.

Mawker came on in the middle of bawling someone out: '...see your face again, you idiot! Who is this?'

'Ian,' I said. I was almost happy to hear his voice. 'It's Joel.'

'Sorrell? Where the fuck are you? I'm going to come down on you like a fucking plane whose wings just fell off.'

'I can't tell you where I am.'

'This Geenan woman turned up this morning, dead as my cock. Know anything about it?'

'Not really,' I said.

'She'd been shot. And then she'd been turned into pizza by a big truck.'

'Sounds as if that might sting for a while.'

Mawker's voice went into Radio 2 purring mode. I wondered if he'd learned how to do that at Bruche. 'Talk to me, Joel. We want this nutcase just as much as you do.'

'I doubt that,' I said.

'Look, there's another dead woman. Not the same MO as Liptrott and the Liverpool lass, but the same knife, we found out. Had her throat slit a couple of weeks ago in a back alley in Holborn. Fucking rush hour, and no fucker saw a thing. This guy is fast, but he moves like a ghost. He wouldn't leave footprints in diarrhoea. The linens have given him a name already: the Wallpaper Man. He blends in something fucking frightening.'

'The Holborn girl will have been classmates with Georgina Millen and Kara Geenan,' I said. 'Bank on it.'

'Our Kara Geenan?' he asked. I could imagine the puzzlement drawing lines all over his face.

'No,' I said. I then gave him the details of the school in Penketh. Told him that maybe it would be a good idea to track down the other members of the class. Keep an eye on them. 'I can't come in yet,' I said. 'He wants me.'

'We gathered that,' said Mawker. 'That could be to our advantage. We can offer you cover. If he makes a move for you, we'll have him.'

'I'd rather do this alone.'

'Look, Sorrell,' the voice changing again, losing its even tone, 'if one more person dies at the hands of this cunt, you'll go down. If *you* die at the hands of this cunt, you'll go down. I fucking guarantee it.' Then he said, 'Don't be a

299

hero, Joel. It isn't going to help you get any more work if you're lying on a gurney having your head sawn open.'

I called Mike Brinksman then and let him off his leash, thanking him for being patient. He barely said two words to me, and one of those was some incoherent bark of gratitude. I had no choice. In another few days he'd have gone after the story, anyway. Everyone seemed to be closing in, but nobody was any the wiser as to who the guy was or where he was hiding. Now it looked as if he'd won. The only way I could get something out of this whole shitty mess was to go back to living my life. Move back into the flat. Get out on the streets. Show myself. And hope that he made a mistake when he came for me. Hope that this wallpaper man had a bit of damp in him.

I got to the library about ten minutes before closing time. A security guard on reception was leafing through the sports pages of his newspaper. Behind the double doors of the library, there was one girl in tight jeans and a cropped sweater, checking out a huge cairn of poetry anthologies, chatting to the guy with the stamp who didn't believe she was going to read all of them in the few weeks before they were due back.

'All right?' the guy greeted me, as I walked past the desk. I nodded.

I had the rest of the library to myself, and I made a beeline for the medicine section. I don't know what I expected to find there. Maybe some kind of elaborate messaging system on the *Alternative Remedies* shelf. Maybe a contact of hers. What had seemed promising back at Lorraine's place now seemed like just another dead end. It was a book, that was all.

He knew my face.

How, exactly? How did he know my face?

The guy on the desk was asking the nice-looking girl in the jeans how old she was.

'Get away,' he said, 'you don't look a day over seventeen.' Might have been flattering, I thought, if she was in her sixties, but I glanced at her and saw she was lapping it up. She was guessing his age now.

'Nope,' he said. 'I'm actually four years old.'

Well, with that chat-up technique, it wouldn't surprise me. I traced a finger across the spines while he then explained he was a 'leapling', born in 1992, a Leap Year. Fascinating. The girl giggled and jiggled. Good luck to him, I thought. Hopefully he'd score and pull out a four-year-old's cock. That'd wipe the smile off her face.

I scanned the shelves, wondering how many hands had held these volumes, how many pairs of eyes had pored over the words, and closed in boredom. How many of them had Kara cribbed from, in order to entrap Gary Cullen with her words of wisdom and calm?

It had been years since I set foot in a library. I could never be bothered with them. I preferred to buy my books in pristine condition, rather than flick through something that might have been handled by some ogre with mange. I liked the idea of having a little library of my own: some separate room that I could lose myself in, dipping into favourite books, using them as reference points to remind myself of different times, places, or women. Maybe one day. There was nothing wrong with reading the same book twice, I thought. Books tend to receive bad treatment that way. Every other art form gets a look in more than once. You didn't buy the latest Oasis CD just to put it on the player only once. If you'd loved *Eyes Wide Shut*, you bought it when it came out on DVD. And every time you walked past that Rothko print, you gave it another glance. Books, well, most people read them the one time and then they went to the charity shop or ended up forgotten on a shelf gathering dust.

I was turning my attention to the philosophy section, thinking, hang on, I *did* play the latest Oasis CD only once: it was shite. When I checked my watch again, it was twenty-five to seven. I glanced back at the double doors and saw that they had been closed. The guy behind the desk had buggered off, forgotten about me. I thought I heard someone in the row next to mine, a fellow prisoner perhaps, but when I rounded the far end of the shelves, there was nobody. I strolled over to the doors and fuck it, I was locked in. Great.

I put the book down on the desk and gave the glass inserts a hefty knock with my watch strap. The security guard was nowhere to be seen. Fine, fire escape then.

The lights went out.

Again, I thought I heard someone moving among the shelves, a little whisper of fabric. 'Hello?' I said. 'I think we're locked in.'

I made my way over to the rows of shelves again, thinking it might be a senior citizen, or a kid turned nervy because of the dark, but again there was nobody there. I had to be alone. The guy had missed me, even though he must surely have checked the place was empty before he locked up. I was surprised nobody had made an announcement that the place was about to shut. Maybe his thoughts had been elsewhere, tangled up with that bookworm's tight jeans, for example. Maybe she'd decided she liked his inane banter and had gone off for a beer with him. I couldn't blame him.

I went back to the desk and picked up the book, then made for the rear of the library where the fire escape was located. I'd come back tomorrow and talk to the staff, see if they knew anything about Kara. I was halfway there when the shadows thickened and I felt the air tremble just by my cheek. *Ghosts between the shelves*, I thought. There was a sensation of cold, and then extreme heat. I backed off, feeling fluid coursing down my face, and I started panicking because I thought, shit, if I get blood on this book there'll be a hell of a fine. The shadow came again, quiet and lethally fast, and I kept stepping backwards, trying to keep more than an arm's length between us. I felt the blade again, felt its slipstream wash across my throat as it slashed through the space between us.

He knew my face.

I threw the book at the shadow and took off for the door, trying to get the gun out from my jeans, but of course it was back in the flat, nicely wrapped up in a towel, waiting to go back to Keepsies. I felt another shift in air pressure and I was only saved from having my back carved open by the thickness of my jacket, which split open by at least a yard. I crashed against the bar of the fire escape and we were suddenly outside. I resolved never to go anywhere without a gun in future, and bollocks to the risks. Carry a gun and you were more likely to get shot. Fair enough, but I could live with those odds right now, right this minute.

I ran across the road towards the train station. The concourse in front was, as usual, filled with weaving drunks, ugly prostitutes, pretty prostitutes and backpackers staring grimly at maps of the London Underground. I pushed my way through this meat market, nicking glances behind me and feeling panic build up in my guts like a Bernard Herrmann score. People were backing off when they saw me. I raised a hand to my cheek, and it came away sopping with blood. My hand looked as though I'd shoved a red mitten on it. I wasn't going to be able to blend in, then, or hope to spot him under cover of my fellow pedestrians.

I stopped and backed up against the glass screen of a bus shelter. The road in front of me was choked with traffic: taxis, buses, and couriers on motorbikes navigating a route around the larger vehicles. People streamed along the pavements in all directions. Pretty much everybody gave me and my flapping cheek the once over and then treated me with a super-wide berth. He could have been any one of them. I wondered if he knew about Kara yet. Perhaps he'd gone back to the Elegant House to pick up Melanie, and been confounded by the police barricades. If I was lucky, he was feeling confused and threatened, unlikely to be thinking straight. And, if I was right and he relied on Kara as a child often relies on its big sister, then he was in unfamiliar territory for the first time. He was out on his own. He was wounded and dangerous, but then so was I.

I pressed my handkerchief against the gaping lips of the gash. I finally had my long-term wish: a big, manly scar like Action Man's. I decided I wasn't that keen on the idea any more, but it was too late now. Best, in future, not to wish too hard for what you want, I admonished myself.

The cut was beyond painful. I felt a little queasy when my finger slipped deep into the wound and through it I felt, or thought I felt, my teeth, but then a blast of cold air spanked me awake and I started moving again. It looked as if we had lost each other, when what we wanted most was each other rendered into millions of pieces. I needed to have him alive, though, just for long enough to find out what his monumental beef with me was – a beef so big it needed its own farm.

Just when I was about to give it up and get myself down to casualty for a six-hour wait on an uncomfortable plastic chair, I saw him. He slipped through a tear in a fence leading on to a building site next to St Pancras, where immense red Bachy Soletanche piledrivers were pounding the last ghosts of Agar Town from the gouged earth. I watched him for a few seconds as he made his way to the forecourt of what had once been St Pancras Chambers, which for decades had been little more than a glorified filing cabinet in which British Rail could lose their complaints letters.

I followed him, trying not to make too much noise on a ground strewn with plastic wrap and scaffolding, and it was me now trying to be like Grasshopper, trying not to tear the rice paper. There was a hammer hanging by its claw off the back of a JCB, along with a large donkey jacket and a hard hat that had been left behind at the end of the working day. I put the hammer in the jacket pocket and slung it on. I then jammed on the hard hat and moved towards where the scaffold rose against the face of the hotel entrance.

He was moving up through a lattice of struts, couplers and braces. He moved like a spider, skating over the obstructions as if they were nothing more than sketches on paper. He had made this journey many times, I realised. I thought of lairs and traps and slow death. A few lights were on in the ground floor of the venerable old building, and I could see movement inside, possibly workers desperately fitting out the hotel rooms to meet some impossible deadline. There was a sign, *Draper Security*, and I thought that if he was able to get past the guards on a regular basis, then either Draper was an appalling security firm or this guy *was* wallpaper after all.

Phythian disappeared through an open window on one of

the upper floors, and I followed at a distance, trying to make sure that I wouldn't stumble on top of him as I clambered inside, all knees and elbows and oaths. I pushed past a veil of brick netting and began to climb. Duckboards scattered with pebbles of glass and gritty chunks of plaster. Muffled footsteps. Somewhere in the distance I could hear a music playing behind the babble of a DJ on the radio.

I monkeyed on, clenching my jaw as I came face-to-face with two men just behind a window, drinking tea and staring out at the view. I averted my injured cheek. They nodded at me. I nodded back. Hard hats and hammers was clearly the way to go here, if you wanted to be inconspicuous. And maybe six inches of builder's arse-crack for good measure.

I reached the same open window and swung inside. Dark here. A pale shape emerged from the gloom: a doorway. The light switches were decorous brass affairs, but I didn't dare throw them. I inched open the door and peered out into the corridor. I thought I could hear the kiss of leather on stone and to my right, maybe fifteen metres away, the slow blur of something dark trembling against the grainy shadows, gradually rising. A stairwell? I took the claw hammer out of my pocket and gripped the handle, relishing the way the rubber filled my fist. Numbness was creeping across my cheeks as the blood there turned gummy; dull pain was already nesting in my lower jaw from Kara Geenan's jemmy. I was going to have a face like a scoutmaster's arse come morning.

I moved on through the corridors. The air was syrupy in here, as if it had not been refreshed by an open window for decades. There was a clean, new smell of furniture freshly unveiled from shrink-wrapped plastic, and the hot, sweet aroma of sawdust. But there was also an old smell of damp and diesel. You couldn't give a place like this just a lick of paint and expect its grimy history to be eradicated. The walls here were soaked with the sweat of hundreds of thousands of people. Ghosts clung jealously.

The light changed. A deep fart from a train reverberated through the walls: of course, the platforms of St Pancras International must be just on the other side. Keeping close to the wall, I started up the stairs. A landing maybe two dozen risers up sat below two huge, ornate arched windows covered with anti-pigeon netting. I could make out figures on the platforms below, the snout of a Eurostar idling in front of the buffers. A black wedge of night hung beneath the great arch of the train shed at its northernmost point. I felt secure there, so close to the mundane, to the everyday. Somehow it wouldn't matter how weird or dangerous things turned out, as long as I kept in mind the passengers down there, with their magazines and elasticated underwear and their six-inchers from Subway.

A soft, snicking sound drew my attention back to the unremarkable stairwell, what I guessed would have been a means of access for the servants when the building had been known as the Midland Grand. I climbed half a dozen steps to a door that would have led me on to the first floor, had it been unlocked. I doubted Phythian had keys for the place, but I couldn't be sure. I had to keep going. The second-floor door was shut, but it opened when I turned the handle. I was greeted with a sigh of rotting wallpaper and ancient dust, despite all the clean new rooms waiting for their new beds and shower units. Recesses were punched into the darkness on either side of a long corridor running parallel to the Euston Road. It was hard, forcing myself out on to that corridor with all its potential booby traps and tripwires. Every shadow contained his silent form, waiting for me to draw level before he dropped on me and finished off the job. I wondered if any murders had been committed in this building over the years, and whose blood in the floorboards my own might soon mingle with. But I got myself through the doorway and walked down the centre of the corridor, one step at a time. All I had to do was think of those dead girls. All I had to do was imagine Sarah struggling under his damaging hands. It was easy once I thought of that.

Halfway along, the beam of a torch sliced across the carpet at the corridor's far end and I ducked left through a door into a sub-corridor which served three large rooms that must have comprised an extravagant suite at one time. The first room had an open fireplace and enormous windows that reached just a few feet above the floor to a few feet beneath the ceiling. The drone of traffic rose up from the main drag. I caught a glimpse of the BT Tower, off to the left, before the torch swung into the mini-corridor and I had to start moving again. I tried to match the rhythm of the security guard's footsteps, approaching him as he approached me, but on opposite sides of the dividing wall. I had to gamble that he wouldn't move into any of the three rooms on his right; if he did, I'd be caught in his beam. I could try to butch it out, claim I was a builder who had left some tools behind, but it wouldn't look good. All the grunt work was finished here. Now it was the turn of the painters and decorators.

I was bypassing a door to my left, keeping my eye on the torch beam as it gradually intensified, its angle of attack rising as it met the hand that wielded it, when he did decide to move into the next room in the suite, directly in front of me, despite being able to see that there was nothing in there. I glimpsed him, not ten feet away, and stepped neatly to my right just as he turned the beam my way; I watched it fall across the space I'd just occupied. Again I followed his lead, matching his measured tread, my heart leaping like a bare-footed punk in a mosh-pit full of broken glass, and I heard him sniff loudly as we bypassed each other, separated by a mere inch or two of wall.

I gathered pace once I had jinked back on to the main corridor, knowing that he would be out of the suite before I reached the far end. He might not train the torch back along the route he'd already covered before arriving at the servants' stairway, but then again he might. I was steeling myself to face the wash of light, to hear a strident voice calling after me, but it never came. Instead I found myself turning on to the main landing of the second floor of St Pancras Chambers. The sweeping staircase before me made the stairwell back home look like something borrowed from a Barbie doll's house. Other corridors peeled off this floor, leading to suites and storerooms and function areas. They all seemed to contain yet more beams of light pushing through the darkness, so I skipped up another floor, hoping that Phythian was shy of security guards, too, and had done the same.

I thought I saw something move, like a shadow that flirts with the periphery of your vision, at the end of the corridor opposite the top of the stairwell. I moved into it fast, because the landing was better illuminated than the corridors, thanks to the huge windows sucking in the lights from the main roads surrounding King's Cross. Some of the rooms along this arm abutted the roof of the train shed. They were filled with damaged filing cabinets and desks, and they seemed to have been overlooked. In one, a table groaned under the weight of a prehistoric manual typewriter, so these rooms must have been used by hotel staff, presumably as their administrative offices. Perhaps no guest would tolerate a view of the train-shed roof, or the constant clamour that went on beneath it, so maybe these rooms would end up being part of the staff headquarters, and therefore didn't need to be improved as urgently as the others.

The last room on the left was the WC. A stained, cracked toilet bowl gaped as if in shock at some of the things it had witnessed over the years. Flyblown mirrors hung over sinks that bore the tracks of hard water dribbling from loose taps over a long period. The window above the urinals was open. A gangway beyond led to a metal stairway that criss-crossed the rising vault of the train shed, leading to its apex a hundred feet above the ground. The weather gods, in their wisdom, had decided that a session of sleet was in order; it now slanted in across the roof of the shed, propelled by a bitter wind. Sleet is the most miserable weather going: it can't be arsed to wait till it's cold enough to become snow, and it's not wet enough to be proper rain. Every time you see it, your mouth goes south and your eyes garner the kind of weighed-down, pained look that often accompanies stomach cramps. I made a mental note to send that DJ who had promised pleasant weather something unpleasant in the post, then ducked through.

I clambered on to the gantry and hurried across towards the shed itself. Spotlights picking out the clock tower provided a little ambient light for the shed roof, like a gleaming finger stroking the outermost curve. Outlined against this, Phythian was making his way up to one of the catwalks that led the entire length of the shed, extending to the furthermost point overhanging the converging tracks that, as soon as they had crossed a narrow bridge over York

Street, split into numerous routes diverging out of the city.

How desperate was this clown? Was he so intent on evading capture that he'd taken to living on rooftops like a fucking pigeon? I watched him until he disappeared beyond the crest of the arch, heading towards the opposite side of the shed. I followed, glad of the donkey jacket, but I could still feel the cold searing through me, sleet stinging my face. When I got to the brow of the roof, where he had slipped out of sight, I was able to see him a couple of hundred feet away, crouching down on his haunches and staring out at the night sky. Liverpool lay in that direction: a home and a hell for the both of us. He remained as still as a bit of architecture, a gargoyle waiting for time and the weather to erode him.

I kept my hand inside the jacket as I approached, loosely clasped around the hammer. I couldn't see the blade on him, but he wouldn't have dropped it. It was with him like an extension, an extra finger for his hand, and every bit as familiar. I thought of the way Barry Liptrott had been carved apart, and any doubt I had that this kid wasn't insane flew apart in my mind like tissue paper fed to a flame. Twenty feet away I spotted the remnants of a meal scattered next to a sleeping bag nailed into the framework enclosing the panels that comprised most of the roof. He was totally still, his hands empty, planted firmly on either side of his body. Dark shapes moved faintly underneath us like fish swimming at the bottom of a brackish pond.

'Hey,' I said, trying to come over all authoritative, but sounding like a boy at bollock-drop. I should have brought a clipboard. 'Hey, this place is off limits to the public. You're trespassing. We could have you arrested.'

I wasn't going to get an answer from him. That was okay.

We both had plenty of time on our hands. I dumped the site-foreman voice and squeezed the handle of the hammer. I thought about how, only the day before, I was determined not to listen to his side of things. That I would simply jump in and do him before he could have a chance against me. But now he was right in front of me – a big, solid shape, yet somehow still possessing the stature of a child – I found my resolve fragmenting. He was what? Eighteen? He had a whole lifetime in front of him. And then the frozen, lizard-like part of my brain must have thawed a little, and I thought, he's going down for life for multiple murder, so you might as well fuck him over anyway.

'Come on,' I said. 'It's cold. Let's get inside. It's over.'

Quietly, but just audible above the slashing sleet, he said: 'It isn't over till I say so.'

He knew my face.

He knew my face, because I knew his. Some famished thing in the back of my head extended a claw that was holding the school photograph Don Banbury had shown me. Gemma Blythe smiling out of it, looking tired, looking like a teacher whose class is getting on top of her. Gemma, her voice broken and hoarse with tears, saying, *Don't leave me, Joel. How will I get by without my Sorry Boy? Don't leave me, please. What about my babies? WHAT ABOUT MY BABIES?*

'You… Gemma?' I said, but he rolled on to his back and flipped his legs over his head – agile, frighteningly agile for his size – before I could get the rest of it out. His feet were bare. I saw the knife only after it had ricocheted off the hard hat I was wearing, and slithered away down the curve of the roof. Now he was upon me and I was staggering back, trying to keep my footing on what was to me uncharted territory, and slippery with it, all the time trying to get the hammer clear of the pocket. The claw had become caught in the heavy, wet fabric.

I jammed my arm up in between us and, though he was total calmness, economy of movement, focus, there was also madness in his eyes. I knew it would be dangerous to do so, but if I could unlock that frenzy, try to bait his rage, then I might survive.

He was trying to get at my throat with his teeth.

'I know you,' I said. He laughed, not even expecting that himself; a rope bridge of saliva connected our faces for a couple of seconds. Everything slowed down: I saw each and every arrow of sleet lash into us, every wet explosion of it on our skin in acid-bright detail. The powder-white arc of light from the floods turned the outer edges of him into frost, left his centre an impenetrable black thing. I said, 'I've wiped your arse.'

The eye is the only part of the human body that does not alter in size throughout a person's life. It possesses exactly the same dimensions from the first breath to the last. I knew this fucker's eyes – eyes now close enough for me to lick them.

'I didn't kill her,' I said. 'She took her own life. I was well out of it by then. I had no idea. You want someone to blame, dig her up and stick your knife through what's left of her. She's to blame. She took her own life, and she took your life too.'

He breathed on me and I almost folded with pity, with the horrific threat of love. I realised that, if things had turned out differently, I might have loved him. I remembered him as a baby, lalling happily in his cot, smiling up at me, his eyes brimming with complete trust. The smell of his scalp. The tiny hands, the fingers grabbing my hair, sometimes reaching out to touch my nose or my mouth with barely creditable tenderness and precision. There had been nothing evident in him then to turn him this way. No stains, regrets, grudges. All that was in him was the warmth of love and a blissfully simple routine of sleep and nourishment and play, and wondrous things viewed with large laughing eyes. He had been a happy baby, so what had gone wrong?

I had gone wrong. His mother had gone wrong.

I could almost smell milk on his mouth. His teeth didn't yet know what a filling was.

My woeful boots slipped on the glass panels and I went down, my other leg twisting awkwardly under me, the knee popping as if it had just opened a bottle of champagne. He actually winced at the sound. I screamed as I landed on my back, and the violence of it threw him off me. I rolled as he sprang back towards me, already on his feet. Again I tried for the hammer. It shifted a little, tearing the lining of the pocket. Sleet filled my eyes, slapped me awake.

I lifted an arm, but could only partially parry the kick he aimed at my nuts. I felt the jag of pain cut through my groin. I was off-balance again. This time I tripped on one of the gangway rails and sprawled on to my back. I started sliding and the sky rolled like a few half twists on a kaleidoscope. I rammed my fingers into the roof's curve but was rewarded only with a couple of torn fingernails. Another tug on the hammer and it ripped free, but I almost lost it as my arm jerked back. I tightened my grip and brought the claw down hard, felt myself jerk to a halt as it bit into one of the rubber seals edging the roof panels.

Christ, what was wrong with me? I thought I was all right. I thought I could move okay, still pretty fit for a guy in his mid-thirties. I was no Premiership footballer, but then I wasn't exactly a Sunday afternoon toe-poke either. Phythian was making me look like the last spaz to get picked for the school netball team.

I levered myself upright and scrabbled back to an even footing, my kneecap feeling as if it had been replaced by an eggshell filled with molten lead. He'd retrieved his knife, and my cheek burned in recognition. I peeled off the hard hat and flung it at him. He volleyed it back over my head, showing me exactly what balance meant.

We did the scorpion dance for a few beats, and the sleet eased off. I knew he knew he could take me, but he knew I wasn't as easy as his other stiffs. There was no wallpaper up here. The light seemed to be intensifying. The wind too. I looked up and there was a police helicopter taking time out to watch the big fight. Someone was saying something through a loudhailer, but they might as well have been reciting The Lord's Prayer in Welsh through a mouthful of blancmange, for all it meant.

He came again. I ducked right but he followed it, anticipating my moves. He slashed out with the knife and its tip lightly nicked a part of my forehead above my left eye. Blood drizzled into it immediately and I backed off again, blinking madly. The arc of his arm movement helped bring his foot round, and he was raising it high, aiming for my throat. I was losing balance again, but for once I was grateful. His strategy was designed for someone who knew how to stay on his feet. As a result, he missed by a fair whack. I shifted my weight and brought my hand down hard as his foot sailed by my midriff. The claw of the hammer disappeared into the meat of his right ankle and I went down, my momentum dragging him with me. He didn't make a sound. He slashed at me again as he jackknifed over my prostrate body, and the blade parted the

315

fabric of the jacket over my heart and scored a line along my left forearm that was almost a caress. Then he plummeted over the edge of the roof and I tightened my grip on the handle as his weight yanked against it suddenly, massively. It was all I could do to slam my free hand hard against the rim of the shed roof, to prevent me joining him as human soup on platform number 7.

'She died because you left her,' he said, his voice incredibly calm, all things considered. 'She was like a slow puncture after you left. She had no chance. No fucking chance. And me... I needed someone. I needed a dad. When you went, you ripped something out of me and took it with you. You stole something from me, you bastard. You fucking bastard.'

The spotlight from the police helicopter was fixed on my hand. I had never seen the sinews and muscles distended like that, as if in extreme reaction to an electric shock. The skin of my fist was so taut and white that it looked as if it must soon tear. The handle of the hammer seemed fused to my fingers. Even so, it was slipping, a millimetre at a time. I edged forward, my free arm already shaking at the strain that was being asked of it, cramp shooting up and down my muscles as I gripped the lip of the roof. My foot found the sleeping bag and tucked itself underneath it, secured behind one of the nails that fastened it down. That helped, but not much.

I looked down over the edge at him, dangling. I wanted to get my other hand down there, too, to grab him, and haul him up, but my balance was shot. If I moved, we were both fucked. Someone on the platform was screaming. The claw in his foot moved, pulling away from the meat slightly. Not long now. I told him about his mother, not knowing if he could hear me through the wind and the yells below him, and the clatter of the helicopter. It didn't matter, because it wasn't really for him. It was for me. I was still talking long after the claw had sucked itself free and my hand felt supernaturally light, as though, had I not been holding the hammer, it might have floated off into the night. I was still talking, whispering, crying, when the footsteps stopped behind me and firm hands landed on my shoulders. They felt so light, despite their rough grip. There was no longer anything there to weigh me down.

20

Two boys died that night. And I killed them both.

I was in hospital for a week. Both the anterior and posterior cruciate ligaments in my knee were ruptured. My jaw had a hairline fracture. I needed seventeen stitches in my cheek and three in my forehead. Two of the fingers in my left hand had been dislocated, and I had pulled the muscles in my arm every which way. The ligament in my groin was badly bruised. And my right wrist was broken. Phythian had fallen a hundred feet (a hundred and five feet one inch, according to the tabloids) straight through the roof of an empty train just in from Leeds. He was dead. To me, lying there, hurting when I pissed, he seemed better off.

Mawker came to see me, on the second day.

'Another hospital visit? People are going to talk.'

'I could... Fuck me, Sorrell, I *should* arrest you right now.'

'There's a bottle of vodka in my bedside cabinet,' I said, 'hidden under a bag of magazines. Why don't you get it out and let's give both our mouths some time off?'

He looked at me hard. 'At least I've still got a mouth,' he said. And then, with a dismissive sigh, he retrieved the Skyy.

I took mine neat, he mixed a splash of orange squash in with his, the heathen.

'What a sorry, fucking mess,' he said, and he could have been talking about his drink. Or about my face. 'You should be more careful who you shack up with.'

'Thanks for that, Elizabeth fucking Taylor.'

He told me that Phythian, whose real name was Steven Blythe (Steven, yes, yes, I now remembered), had been living at St Pancras for weeks, on the train-shed roof, under the platforms, in the bowels of the Renaissance hotel, or in its neighbouring acres of construction sites and the unknowable territories deep underground, where the tunnels of the Northern Line roamed.

Mawker's counterpart in Merseyside had worked with him on Phythian's – on Blythe's – bedsit. The head that I had stumbled upon wasn't Georgina Millen's, as I had supposed. A DNA test nailed it as Gemma Blythe's. That head that, once upon a time, I'd had in my lap. I'd had that mouth – that pulped and varnished and freeze-dried mouth – all over me at one time or another during our six-month romance. And Steven had missed her so much he had dug it up and given it pride of place in his crummy Liverpool bedsit. It must have been more of an incentive than any photograph of me.

Georgina Millen's head, and the rest of her, remained missing. It would turn up, though. They always did, eventually.

Steven Blythe had me down as the reason his mother had killed herself. Because I'd meant something to her, but I hadn't reciprocated. He was unbalanced enough to decide that nothing else mattered. We hadn't been right for each other, but all he saw was my rejection of her, and therefore my rejection of him. And all those people had been killed or damaged in his need to resurrect her, and put me where she had gone. He was trying to wipe out the people on that photograph, the kids who had been in her last class at school before she got the sack. It had all been training, in the lead-up to nailing me. Kara Geenan had been feeding him scraps, amateurs and no-hopers like Liptrott, giving him a sense of worth while trying to have me killed at the hands of her drugged-out drones, in order to spare him. So I suppose she *was* protecting him, after a fashion. Although, in the end, his desire was too great. She no longer had control over him. She no longer had the influence that had so obviously once been there. He had come of age and wanted to mark that fact, to celebrate it.

I have no idea – nobody does – as to what Kara's real name was. Maybe it was Olivia Rawle. Maybe it was something Blythe. If she *was* his big sister, then she certainly wasn't around when I had been on the scene.

All the police had found on him, other than the knife, was one of Gemma's diaries from the year in which she killed herself, and a battered black journal filled with notes he had made about her, and about me. His dark little promises and oaths. The police let me have a look, and I read the first few lines – *It might be sunny outside, but to us there's shadows and rain all over the fucking place. Me ma came in just now and asked us what I wanted for me tea. I goes shepherd's pie, peas, chips, bread and butter. She said right, buckethead, that's your starters sorted, what do you want for your mains? Least, I wish that's what happened. I can make them come to me, the daydreams, if I close me eyes and I'm alone in a silent room.* – and quickly handed it back. That kind of thing is interesting only to ghouls and psychiatrists. It was over now for me and him.

The photograph was in there, too, with the faces of the three girls he had killed obscured by the adhesive gold stars that teachers give out to kids who've done well in class. Their crime was to have reported Gemma to the headmaster after she came in smelling of booze one morning, and fell asleep at her desk. She had been given her marching orders not long after. So the boy had got a revenge of some sort, out of it all, even if it wasn't the blue-riband event he wanted.

Mawker didn't stay long. After giving me his information, he told me to keep my beak out of his seed tray, or he'd make it his ambition to be sacked from the Force for police harassment of me.

I hadn't thought about Gemma for fifteen years. Well, maybe I had, but not while I was awake. Not while I could avoid it. That was one very black mark against my name, one that I had tried to turn into a white-chalked tick against the word EXPERIENCE. But who was I kidding? It was a fuck-up, plain and simple, but at least I'd learned that early enough to save myself. We were kids then, we knew no better, and I got out. Only one of thousands, hundreds of thousands, who have done the same thing.

I had plenty of time to think now. I tried hard, but I couldn't remember much about Gemma Blythe. I had met her at some party in Hatton, a tiny little place near Daresbury, while I was at college. She had already been teaching at primary school for a year, having graduated from teacher training in Nottingham the previous summer. I remember getting pissed and striding up to her, thinking she was all right, and sticking my tongue down her throat in a spur-of-the-moment bit of madness. We went out together a bit after that. Cinema, pub, walks in the park, and suddenly things were serious. Well, they were for her. The only serious things in my life were playing football, buying records by The Cure and trying to develop my abs into a six-pack.

Women, or rather shagging, made it into the top five – but relationships? I always used to think that I met the girls I liked the most at the wrong time. When I wasn't ready for them, or them for me. That was the reason things didn't work out. *Wrong*. Things didn't work out because we were fundamentally mismatched. It was like trying to marry a Lego brick to a jigsaw piece. It was never going to happen. At the time, I'd been what, seventeen? She was twenty-two but seemed older, perhaps because of her kid. Hard work for a single mum. But I thought I'd hit pay dirt: my first woman. My first grown-up woman. Time to shut the drawer marked *Girls* and delve into the one marked *Adult Relationships*. What a bollockhead I was.

Things hadn't changed too much meanwhile. I'd long given up on the hope of a chiselled gut, and I'd rather listen to people in a cave making sounds with a pair of emu bones rattled against a bucket than to *A Forest*. But the relationship problem remained. Rebecca had been killed, but things weren't going brilliantly there beforehand, partly because she said she couldn't get access to my head. It was best that she didn't: *I* don't like what's in there very much, so it was for her own protection, but she seemed to think such familiarity was an intrinsic part of any long-term hook-up. And now I had yet another dark file of secrets to lock in that sad cabinet in the basement of my brain; another barrier between me and the world, and all the sweet, loving people who moved through it.

Talking of which, the day before I got out:

'You're looking better,' I lied.

'I wish I could say the same for you.'

I reached out to touch her hand, but she withdrew it. That was painful for any number of reasons, not least because she looked so fragile. Her days of being locked naked in the storeroom, without a scrap or a drop, had eaten away at her. She had lost, was still losing, pounds. The skin around her hairline had peeled away, leaving it pink and tender. She had since dyed her hair black, which only served to highlight the ravaged flesh. Her mouth was dry, her eyes puffed up; shadows filled the hollows of her cheeks with grey cross-hatchings. She couldn't, or wouldn't, meet my eye.

'I came to say goodbye,' she said. I made to protest but she held up a hand. Her voice was tired and resigned, and I wondered how long it might be, if ever, before it regained some of its sass and sexiness. 'I can't do it. I can't stay. The city... it's too big now, too many people. Too many people I don't know and don't know about. I'm going home.'

Home was now Salcombe, Devon. She was selling her flat and returning to the family-run veterinarian practice.

'Maybe I could come to see you, when you feel all right. I'd like to–'

'No,' she said, and stood up. She turned to leave, but quickly leaned over me and gently brushed her lip against my cheek.

Three hours after she had gone, I could still smell her perfume poised in the air near my bed.

It took an age, racked as I was with aches in parts of the body that science had yet to discover, and it also took a while to get used to the crutches, but I picked up Mengele, lean as a whip after his time scampering through the labyrinthine passages at Keepsies, and tottered back to the flat in Homer Street, feeling as if I'd been away for years. I picked up the Eiger of post behind the door and started cleaning the flat. The pain was too great to get much done, however, so I sat on the sofa with a cup of tea and sifted through those depressingly brown, formal envelopes. There was one envelope stiffer than the rest, with a pleasingly handwritten address. I tore it open and a cream card slipped into my hand, an invitation to a photography exhibition by Neville Whitby. It was that same evening. I hadn't RSVP'd, but I doubted it would matter if I just turned up. I fancied an hour or two in the real world, even if *my* real world wouldn't have a canapé within about three thousand miles of it.

I had a long bath, and a couple of martinis to put me in the mood. Then I treated Mengele to a tin of tuna and left him to patrol the assault course of the flat, while I went out and hailed a cab on Crawford Street.

By a coincidence that I wasn't too happy about, the exhibition was in a place called the Spitz Gallery, on Commercial Road, part of Spitalfields Market. It seemed a completely different place to the one I had left just over a week before, although I noticed the police cordon around the Elegant House was still in effect.

Neville greeted me warmly – there were only a handful of other guests so far – and we talked. The tabloids loved the story of my escapades and had come back for seconds and thirds. The hospital had needed to put security on my ward to prevent hacks trying to take pictures of me and offering me huge sums of money for my side of the events. The money would have been good, but I'd have rather chewed my own face off than pocket a penny of it. I just wanted to forget. I wanted anything and everything associated with the last few weeks scoured from my head, like a stain scrubbed from a sink. In time, I thought it might happen, but on every occasion I imagined this, Gemma Blythe's impaled head would swim out of my thoughts and give me a smile with its greasy, cherry-coloured, corrugated mouth.

'What's going on here, then?' I asked Neville. 'You gone all Tate Gallery on me?'

'Remember that night,' he said, 'when I found you licking the pavement in Archway? After I packed you off to hospital, I went back to the squat just in time for the mother and father of all barnies to kick off. There were crusties chucking stones at the police, and the police piling in with horses and shields and batons. Pure theatre, it was. I must have shot fifteen rolls. Anyway, a couple of galleries saw my pictures in the papers and one thing led to another, and here you go.' He was smiling like the Joker with wind. 'I'm up for an award next week. For photo-journalism. News Picture of the Year. Editor of the *Independent* asked me to go to Syria.'

'What did you say?'

'I said fuck off. I said "*You* go to Syria".'

I had a couple of glasses of wine and felt myself slowly relaxing. It had felt for a while as though I might never know what relaxation felt like again. It seemed the past fortnight had seen me only in different postures of stress and pain. More guests arrived. A couple of them looked at me as if I was someone who shouldn't really be there, but nobody said anything. I wouldn't say anything to a man who had a foot-long scar on his face, either.

I decided to have a look at the pictures and get home to bed before a real crowd formed. I didn't want to risk being jostled. Enough people had arrived and were milling in what was quite a small space to have me sweating up already. I decided I would get out of the city as soon as I had mended sufficiently. I needed some time off, time to mend properly, and try to deal with the upset of losing Melanie. A quiet coastline and a rented caravan. Me and Mengele and a bottle of vodka. A bit of fishing. A lot of sleep.

All of the photographs were in matt black and white. Some of them had been manipulated in the darkroom to give the sky a more forbidding look. The physicality spilling out of the images was impressive, and the inherent threat of violence oppressive. The heat and the smoke and the noise of the throng around me was already getting to be too much. I thrashed about, trying to see Neville in order to say goodbye, but he was lost among such numbers.

I shambled through the crowd on my crutches, towards the exit, and found myself having to take a detour past another wall decked with pictures. I said no as politely as I could to a woman with a wine bottle, and twisted violently aside when it looked as though she was determined to freshen my glass anyway.

That put me just an inch away from the photograph. In the foreground, a lone police helmet. In front of him, a dozen baying protestors in grungy clothing, all dreadlocks, beards and piercings. A girl was standing off to the side of the main pack, flipping the finger at the police. She wore a cropped top bearing the number 69. A bolt of silver gleamed in her navel. She wore torn hipsters and trainers. The noise and heat were suddenly sucked away down a long corridor that I doubted I'd be able to find my way out of for a long time.

'Sarah,' I said, as she disintegrated before my eyes. 'Sarah, I found you.'

READ ON FOR AN EXCLUSIVE

JOEL SORRELL
SHORT STORY

DO NOT RESUSCITATE

There's a monster in St Josephine's hospital, Paddington, by all accounts. I haven't been back there since Sarah's birth, but I know Jen, one of the midwives. Her ex, Graham, and I sometimes took in a football match at Craven Cottage back when Fulham were flailing around the third division and the crowd could be counted in the tens. But what can you do? It's a mate. It's football. After a fashion. You go to be nice, to fit in. You go because to not go leads you back to a corner of a room where things that ought to remain still continue to flex and twitch like a spider sensing dinner. So we'd watch Fulham get tonked by Torquay or Mansfield or Northampton or whatever small fish was finning around the depths of the English football league back then, and at full time we'd have a pint or two at the Golden Lion on the Fulham High Street before heading back to their pad in Barnes for a proper homemade curry that Jen and my wife – my girlfriend at the time – Rebecca, would have been crafting all afternoon while they drank cava and listened to 80s music. I quite miss that. The curry, I mean. Not the football.

After Jen and Graham split up – this would have been back in the early Noughties (he wanted children, she didn't) – she fell into the rabbit hole of work and didn't resurface for what felt like years. Friends took her out for drinks and dinner, but she found it difficult to make connections that had come so easily previously. She felt like a potential source of disappointment to everyone she met. Nobody matched up to Graham, with whom she'd felt a special, rare compatibility shattered only because of their differing bloodline desires. Our friendship kind of petered out after that, partly because they were in Barnes – diametrically opposite to our first London flat in Wood Green – but more importantly because Becks and I were on the cusp of committing to each other, an acknowledgment that this was really it and we didn't want to feel jinxed in any way.

I met Jen on a cold February afternoon. Wind was thrusting up Praed Street like a fist, making all bow before it. I was sitting in a coffee shop watching these comma men and women and wondering how many of them were monsters, or had been monstrous. Or were capable of monstrosity. The things we'd do if we could get away with it. What divides us? What prevents those who merely entertain the dark thoughts from those who make them concrete? Are we any less monstrous for having those thoughts in the first place? I touched the scar on my cheek, only just healing properly two months on, and tried to not think about the monster who had delivered it. I really needed a break from the monsters.

Jen came in like a piece of that wind torn off at the edge, her hand fretting at her hair though it was so short it remained unspoilt by the weather. She was wearing long brown suede boots over faded jeans, a white blouse and a short tan leather jacket. I kissed her cheek and squeezed her shoulder. She looked nice. The short hair and the high cheekbones were as I remembered. She seemed hunted, though that might just have been the gale, or my imagination. Everyone I meet doing this job seems to wear a version of that look. The lost, the desperate, the last-gaspers. I'm sure I wear it myself half the time. I thought to myself, *she's in her early forties now.* The clock was ticking and she didn't even hear it. She had put it under the pillow. She had turned it to face the wall.

'Sounds like a police matter,' I managed to say, through my tightening throat, over my squirming guts, once she'd given me the gist of it. 'I can give you the number of a pukka guy at New Scotland Yard. Name of Ian Mawker. I say "pukka", but he has all the charm of an undescended testicle. He's tenacious though, and he'll look into it.'

'I'm asking *you*, Joel,' she said, and I heard the fracture in her voice. It was the sound of someone who has been tightrope-walking over an abyss for too long. 'It's just a suspicion of mine and I haven't mentioned it to anybody at work yet. I can't go to the police.'

'Why not?'

'Because–' She checked in her bag for something that was not there. She closed her eyes and worms of moisture glistened at the join. Agony trembled just beneath the skin. 'Because I'm involved with the guy I think is doing this.'

Doing this. You really don't want to know. Suffice to say there every department of a hospital that poses the risk of death: A&E, for example. Oncology. Neonatal. In a way that, say, ophthalmology doesn't. These substations are where the bodies – or the parts of bodies – end up prior to their delivery to the morgue, or the incinerator. Jen was involved with a guy called Renfrew who was a hospital porter. Part of his job description involved the transferral of dead matter – bodies, limbs, stillbirths, what-have-you – from ward to morgue or incinerator depending on the what and the why. Only, this matter was not arriving, or not all of it was. He was saving titbits and taking them home with him, or so Jen believed.

'You see him do this?' I asked.

'No,' she said. 'But in the delivery rooms things were going missing. Placentae. Blood bags. A child, almost, once.'

'A child?'

'Yes. You might have read about it in the news. Gael Miller. The security doors failed. Power loss. Nobody knows how or why, but while the power was out – there wasn't that big a panic in the delivery rooms because it wasn't hugely busy and we had back up – someone took a baby. But whoever did it must have been disturbed, because Gael was found an hour later in the rubbish bin of the gents toilets.'

'It wasn't just an opportunist thing? A freak off the street?'

'No. I mean yes, it was opportunist. But it wasn't an outsider. How much of a coincidence would it be for a chancer to be lurking around the doors at the exact time the power knocked off?'

'It could have been set up. Someone could have seen to it that the power was cut.'

'No. There was no sabotage involved. It was a genuine failure. But someone took advantage of it. Someone waiting for the chance.'

'Your man.'

'I think so.'

'So the police must have been involved there.'

'Yes, but they didn't make any arrests. Like you, they

reckoned it was an opportunist and made most of their enquiries outside of the hospital.'

'What about the other departments? Paediatrics? A&E? Gynaecology? Anything going on there?'

'Stuff is vanishing all over the place.'

'Stuff. What kind of stuff, exactly?'

She sighed, closed her eyes, steepled her fingers and rested her forehead against them. 'Little pieces of children,' she said. I stared at her. My coffee had gone cold. Hers too. I wanted something much stronger. I thought about what I was going to ask her for quite a while, weighing up the tact of it, wondering if it was too upsetting. And then I went ahead and asked her anyway.

'This guy. This Renfrew. You're still seeing him?'

She went grey, as if my asking her had somehow solidified the horror of it in her mind. She nodded quickly, eyes closed, lips clamped. 'I don't want to lose my job. I don't want to go to prison because of him. They'll think I'm complicit, won't they?'

'Tell me about him.'

Carl Renfrew. Born without his left arm. Somehow he'd gone on to become a black belt in taekwondo. I was mulling over that so much that I almost missed out on the rest of it.

She'd fallen for him after she heard he'd rescued a kitten from the canal and shaken the water from its lungs, massaged it back to life. Though she worked in midwifery, there was, she said, little to no tenderness in her workmates. That might well be a failing in her, she admitted, a lack of empathy or a tendency to be overcritical. But she felt what she felt. The kitten episode turned her head. She found that

Carl could gee her up if she'd had a bad day. He could draw a smile from her when she was broadsided by tragedy, a death in the delivery room. He was simple – in the best sense of the word – uncluttered, undemanding, and unexpected. This last she'd thought was an advantage, at first. She liked being surprised by him. He might reel off a line from an obscure Nicaraguan poet he liked, or take her to the zoo one day to see the peccary he had adopted, or make her a beautiful bouillabaisse from scratch, delighting her with his one-handed knife skills. If he could chop an onion like that, with just five fingers, imagine...

But then the simple things about him grew to be less endearing, more unsettling. He would switch off in the middle of a meal and she would have to endure silence for ten minutes or more until he suddenly snapped back, sometimes finishing off the sentence at the exact spot he'd drifted away from earlier. She would catch him endlessly sharpening a cook's knife on a whetstone with a faraway look in his eyes, and at such times she would fear for his safety, and her own. When he kissed her, sometimes, she said she felt as though he was tasting her.

She told him she needed some time to herself, that she didn't feel ready to commit to a long-term relationship; her work involved hard, long hours and she couldn't reciprocate the effort he was devoting. She had been scared beyond all reason when she told him this – it hit her like a lorry – and she knew in the asking for it that she didn't want a little time to think, she meant to drive a stake into the heart of whatever it was they had.

* * *

I got home around seven. I fed Mengele and tossed a screwed-up bus ticket into my boot for him to retrieve until he got fed up and went off to lick my stack of *Empire* magazines. I checked my answerphone messages but I never give my number to anybody so there weren't any.

I thought about what Jen had told me and felt my insides slop around heavily against each other. Jesus Christ. Some people. I retrieved the Grey Goose from the freezer and poured myself a shot. I watched the glass frost over and downed the vodka in one. Booze on an empty stomach. Not a good idea. But hey, now there was vodka in there so it was no longer empty. So it was okay to have another.

You get to thinking, after a while of walking with them, that monsters are made, created like golems from dust and clay and tears (by their parents more often than not): moulded by time, and a drip-feed of resentment and violence. The inevitable counter-measure to it all. The retaliatory strike. And some are. And I reckon those are the ones that can be saved, if they want to be. You can come back from most kinds of bad. It's still in our nature to forgive and, if not necessarily forget, then move on in some way.

But there are some monsters that are shot through with… I won't say 'evil', I don't believe in it. There's *something* that runs through them, some noisome strain that has been there since that moment in the womb when the dots of their hearts fluttered into action. And they are ice. They are mask people. They are mirrors. Any emotion they display seems to have been learned, or copied. It doesn't reach their eyes. Everything about them might gleam – their clothes, their hair, their teeth, their skin – but hit their eyes and you could be looking at something with all the lustre of dust. Occasionally, on cold, regretful days when the light fails to reach the pavements and people scuff around in a gleaming kind of dusk, soggy, spent, curved by fatigue, you'll hear the determined stride of a man or woman who seems utterly disconnected from their surroundings. There's no effect. They are dolls of their own imagining bent into shape, forced into an approximation of what it is to be human, to be normal – whatever *that* means.

I don't know what it is in them that shifts them towards violence. Everything is deflected, though. Everyone else is to blame. And there are reasons galore, usually jaw-droppingly banal, like the guy who took a meat-cleaver into a roller-rink in Altrincham and tried to hack the feet off a girl he had once been involved with. When he was asked later why he did it, he said that he'd always been irritated by the way she failed to tie up her laces properly.

I came to sitting on the floor with the glass warm and sticky in my fist and an album of photographs I'd vowed I'd never peruse again open on my lap. Me and her. Me and her. The three of us. The two of us.

I put the photographs away, trying – failing – to not see my wife's broken body, no matter how many photographs I had of her smiling or laughing or loving us.

I showered and went to bed, appalled to see that it was nearly 7 a.m. I couldn't remember the last time I'd been able to sleep without the help of alcohol, which meant it wasn't really sleep at all. My face in the mirror looked like congealed porridge. I suffered unremembered bad dreams despite only sleeping for an hour, and took another shower, as hot as I could bear it, but it would not drum out the feeling of being pursued, or somehow dismantled.

At Casey's on Crawford Street I grabbed a bacon roll and managed just one bite before I had to throw it away. Coffee didn't help. All I could think of was my daughter, wrinkled and warm, swaddled in towels, wadded into the crook of my arm – no weight at all – and Rebecca being helped up from the bed to take a shower, sweaty, crumpled, and looking more beautiful than any woman I've ever seen in my life.

And something moving around in the ward outside, something blind and hungry and massive, with the scent of my child in its twitching nostrils.

It was cold. St Josephine's was not far. I put my head down and walked.

I thought I'd forgotten most of what happened that day – or those days; Rebecca was in labour for something like 72 hours. A deficiency of prostaglandins, apparently, which meant her contractions weren't occurring when they ought to. I remember one of the midwives was a New Zealander. I remember taking a hit of Rebecca's gas and air. Little else. But as soon as I walked through the swing door entrance of Praed Street, I recognised the smell and the pattern of the floor tiles and I had to sit down suddenly because I was close to tears. It's one of the few places where you can have a cry and nobody will intrude; it's kind of expected. As opposed to a butcher's, say. I pulled myself together and walked up to the delivery rooms. Security was pretty tight; I had to give my name at two checkpoints where members of staff opened locked doors from the inside. When I called that morning I'd been put through to the consultant obstetrician, a tall guy with iron-coloured hair that gleamed and put me in mind of smart American salesmen from the 1950s.

'Dr. Fellowes? You weren't here fourteen years ago,' I said.

'Mr. Sorrell,' he said, holding out his hand. I shook it. It was warm, dry and firm; a good handshake. 'Call me Seb. Fourteen years ago I was Senior House Officer at a hospital in Manchester. Where were you?'

'Joel,' I said, jerking a thumb in my own direction. 'I was in here, waiting for my daughter to be born.'

'I suppose it's a little late for congratulations.'

'A little. But thanks anyway.'

I heard a long, low groan – bestial, you might describe it – from one of the delivery rooms, and further memories came back: Rebecca on all fours, slicked with sweat, sucking on the gas and air tube, begging me to get this damn thing out.

He followed my worried gaze to the door; blades of his hair swung across his eyes.

'Follow me. I can give you five minutes of my time.'

I followed him to a small office, sparsely decorated. He closed the door. On the wall was a board covered with greetings cards; grateful messages from new mums and dads. He rolled up his short sleeves and spread his hands. 'How can I help you?'

There was no way I'd be able to get back in here without his say so. I had to tell the truth. I asked him about the allegations Jen had made. He shrugged. 'We've had our security compromised in recent weeks, yes, and it was serious. But that's all been cleared up now. As you saw yourself, our doors are impregnable, we have new closed circuit cameras working 24/7 and we have new security staff.'

'Have they been vetted?'

'Yes, of course.'

'How about all staff?'

'Yes. All staff in the hospital, never mind neo-natal, have to be checked and cleared. Excuse me…' he was frowning, he seemed confused. 'You're from the police, right?'

'After a fashion.'

'I'm sorry?'

I spread my hands, like him. 'I used to be in the police force, when I was younger. But I'm no good with authority. No matter what Sarge used to tell me to do, it always came out sounding like: "Kick me till I bleed".'

'I don't understand. We had a full enquiry. We had the police here before, when little Gael went missing...'

'Was she harmed in any way?'

'He. *He*. Gael is a boy.'

'Was he harmed in any way?'

'No. No he wasn't. Thank God.'

Dr. Fellowes demeanour had changed. His face had darkened, his body language was no longer as expansive. 'Do you know how many babies I've helped to deliver, Mr. Sorrell?'

'Joel. I'd imagine a fair few. More than I've had hot dinner ladies at least.'

'Four thousand, give or take. I've performed over 500 Chorionic villus samplings and over 800 amniocentesis procedures with an associated loss of less than nought point five per cent. I'm good at what I do.'

'I don't doubt it, doctor. Nobody is pointing the forceps of blame at you.'

'And my team.'

'I believe you.'

'Then what is it you know, or think you know, that the police don't?'

'You have an employee here who came to me–'

'Name?'

'–in strictest confidence because she didn't want the police involved. She told me that there might be someone on the payroll at the hospital, not necessarily directly under you, but someone who has access.'

'A cleaner?'

'Perhaps. Perhaps someone who has access but who shouldn't.'

He mulled this over, shifting the blade of hair back behind his ear as he did so. 'But now you're talking about a team.'

'Am I?'

'I already told you that the doors here won't open from the outside unless you have the code. And the code changes every day.'

'Who decides the code?'

'A computer. It's randomised.'

I felt frustration gnawing at me; we seemed to be drifting further from where I wanted to be. 'I'd need to speak to some people, if that's all right with you.'

'Mr. Sorrell. Joel. This sounds like a police matter. I'm uncomfortable allowing a… what is it you do exactly?'

'I'm a Private Investigator. I have a licence.'

'I had no idea that line of work was regulated.'

I sighed. 'It isn't. Look. We can call the police, but they've already been here. They've taken statements. No arrests were made regarding Gael's attempted abduction. All I want to do is talk to a few people – your tech guy, the cleaners, a porter or two – and I'm gone. Just to give peace of mind to one of your colleagues who doesn't trust the police, that's all. Would you rather have a twitchy member of staff on your hands failing to concentrate on an important job, or someone who has been reassured by an old friend that everything's on the up and up?'

'The "up and up". That's an American thing, isn't it? Don't you get sick of that? That invasion of ridiculous phrases?'

'I've not really given it much thought. It's hardly at the level of "awesome sauce", is it?'

He winced, and I knew I had him. 'I suppose not. Look, we're relatively quiet today, so far. Can you do what you need to do this morning? And I'll have to post a staff member alongside you at all times. You understand, don't you?'

'Of course,' I said. 'I'd expect nothing less.'

Bizarrely, he asked Jen to accompany me. She looked so pink and nervous when she scurried back from his office that I thought he must have sussed her straight away as his mole, but he'd been distracted while he delegated the task, flicking through medical charts, barely making eye contact.

'He called you a plod-lite,' she said, giggling nervously.

'Charming,' I said. 'Where's Carl?'

'He's not in yet. Anyway, you should talk to some other people first. Make it seem less obvious.' She plucked at the elbow of my jacket, tugging me towards an open door at the far end of the suite of delivery rooms. Cartoon light flickered and spilled to the glossy floor outside. This was a combined technical support office and security hub; one side of the room was devoted to closed circuit camera screens, the other host to a desk with a computer and a server and an enormous bag of tortilla chips. A guy in a suit and glasses with matte grey frames was tapping at a keyboard, his brow furrowed as he stared at a streaming page of, what looked to me, unintelligible code.

'This is Andy Sowden, IT wizard.'

We shook hands. His skin was soft and cool. He wore the kind of anaemic tinge to his flesh that suggested most of his light came from a monitor. Handshake-wise, it was like being lightly fondled by an empty Marigold glove.

'I understand the doors can only be opened by a randomly-generated code. Is that done here?'

Sowden raised his eyebrows at me and nodded, as if it was some kind of trick question.

'What happens then?'

'It's circulated on a need-to-know basis. The only people who have access to the code are employees, Mums-to-be and their wingmen.'

'Wingmen?'

'Well, you know… husbands, boyfriends, birthing cheer-leaders.'

I didn't like his glib little labels. I didn't like his micro-expressions. I didn't like him, I decided. But he was no Burke and Hare trainee. I couldn't be sure about that, obviously, but sometimes you can just tell. You look into a pair of eyes and you see too little going on behind them, or too much. This guy spent his downtime fannying around with his Raspberry Pi or flaming people on PC versus Mac forums. I doubt he'd ever seen the inside of a proper boozer in his life.

'Do you have the code too?'

'I am employed here. So yes.'

'All employees get the code?'

'Well, no. Just this department. Reception sees who's coming and going too, and we have CCTV.'

'Reception isn't always staffed though, is it?' I asked.

'If we're busy, or quiet, there can be times when the desk is unstaffed, yes. But you'd be better off asking Reception about that. I am but a lowly ones and zeroes kind of guy.'

Jen took me to the reception desk. A woman behind a door begged for Jesus. Another woman behind another door swore to God. One nurse was sitting behind the desk writing notes in a large book.

'Hi Jen,' she said without looking up. 'Who's your new bodyguard?'

'It's someone who's come to follow up on the Gael case,' Jen said. 'Kind of a security consultant.'

'Jolly good,' she said, finishing off her work with a flourish and closing the book. She looked up at us with tired, very green eyes. You could tell she couldn't give a flying fanny fart who I was. She was coming to the end of her shift. Her mind was on bed.

After she'd gone I turned to Jen. She had been chewing her lip constantly for the past ten minutes. Her mouth was reddening.

'Lot of tired people in here,' I said. 'People miss a lot when they're on their last legs.'

We swept around the ward and I asked questions that were batted back to me politely, all the while keeping my eye on the door and waiting for Renfrew to walk through it with a baby between his teeth. After a while, the scrubbed floors and damning light began to scour away at my good nature and I felt a headache begin to grow, like two sticks pushing into the backs of my eyes. The memories of being here with Rebecca were anxious and gnawing. Much of what I'd forgotten was coming back. Going for a walk with her in Hyde Park to try to induce labour. Sitting under the shade of a tree with sandwiches – I remember I had prawn and mayonnaise and she was grumpy because she wasn't allowed shellfish – and a frosted bottle of Sicilian lemonade. We talked about names. We had decided we didn't want to know the sex of our child before it was born.

So how about Vermilion Antagonistes for a girl and Braggadocio Clapperboard for a boy?

How tragic that Daddy suffered a horrible death just before birth, Rebecca said.

'Maybe he's off sick today,' I said.

'He was fine this morning,' Jen said.

'It comes on fast sometimes.'

'He would have texted me, or called in. He's good like that.'

'So call him.'

'I tried,' she said. 'He's not picking up. I think he's on to me.'

She was pale with fright, her eyes unable to lock with mine. 'Christ, Joel,' she said. 'I don't know what to do.'

I said: 'Where does he live?'

She said: 'You won't hurt him.' It wasn't a question.

Renfrew lived out Clapton way in a house on Wattisfield Road that overlooked Millfields cricket pitch. When I got there it was beginning to rain, despite clear, soft blue skies just a little further south. I parked on the street, a little way from the building, and waited. A monkey puzzle tree grew in his front yard. A wad of circulars stuck out from the letterbox like an impudent white tongue. A woman dressed for sunshine in a lemon-yellow dress pushed a buggy across the grass, the backs of her legs streaked with mud.

I watched Renfrew's windows for a while but there was no movement beyond them. I wondered if he might well have seen Jen's texts to me and decided it was time to get out of Dodge. I got out of the car and walked over to his front door. I rang the bell once and I heard it echo through the building. Bare floorboards, I thought. And no footsteps falling upon them.

I walked round to the back of the house, slipping through a tired, sagging side gate, and saw a cat bowl, freshly-filled, on the patio near the door. I tried the handle. Open. Keys dangling from the handle on the inside. I stepped through into the kitchen. A smell of garlic and harissa: last night's dinner still hanging in the air. Breakfast remnants. Renfrew ate well in the morning: fruit, yogurt and muesli. Green tea. More keys on a table. Along with a passport. A door leading to the cellar. Locked.

I moved through the house and the creak of my feet on the boards went with me. The rooms were small and unremarkable, utilitarian. There were no photographs on the surfaces, no prints on the walls. It seemed like a house that was hardly ever used: a sleeping station rather than a place where warm memories were made. But then who cared about their house when long shiftwork hours were the focus of your day?

I went upstairs. Some of Jen's products in a wash bag on the cistern. In the bedroom, on a double bed, was a large suitcase. I stared at it for a while, and at the indentation next to it. I felt the skin on my scar prickle as if cold air had just flooded the room. I raised my hand to touch it and it was that action that saved my life.

A looped bicycle chain whipped over my head and snapped back against the edge of my hand, tightening suddenly. I felt myself forced back against a hard body. Panic descended, but all I could think was... how is he doing this with just one arm? I did my best to make some space, forcing my hand against the links, knowing it would be agony, but knowing too that the chain could not slice through my skin in the way a piano wire would. I earned enough room to be able to turn my head to the left. Out of the corner of my eye I could see that the man who must be Renfrew had the other end of his chain in his teeth. I got angry then. No way was

I going to allow myself to be garrotted by a fucking one-armed man. No way was I going down in *Ripley's Believe It Or Not* as the guy who was strangled by a mouth. I'd never live it down.

I closed my eyes and jerked my head back, smacking my skull into his nose. His grip on the chain loosened. I stamped my boot down hard on his instep, then turned within the circle of his arm and hit him in the chest as hard as I could. I felt bones snap – his ribs or my fingers I couldn't yet know for sure – and we both cried out. I could taste blood in the back of my throat. My hand throbbed where the links had chewed at it. He shook the chain out and it rattled on the bare floor. He seemed to like the theatre of that because he kept doing it. I tried to keep to his left so he wouldn't be able to swing it at me with much of an arc.

'You going somewhere, Carl?' I asked. I sprayed blood on that aspirant 's'; I'd bitten my tongue pretty bad.

'How do you know me?'

'I'm a friend of a friend. She wanted me to come and see if you were okay.'

'Bollocks,' he said.

He came at me with the chain and I sidestepped him, but he twisted and caught me full in the face with a roundhouse kick. My mistake was to try to stay upright. He tossed the chain to one side and in that moment I knew that he knew he had me. I was positioned to defend another kick, but instead he punched me above my left eyebrow and followed it with a head-butt. I was trying to say something, trying to say how that wasn't very jujitsu of him, but the darkness smothered my words.

* * *

I can't have been out for long because when I revived my tongue was still bleeding. I was lying at the foot of a set of stone steps – I could just make out their shape in the thin edge of light sneaking under the foot of the door – on a cold cement floor. I hobbled up the steps and tried the handle. Locked. I pressed my ear against the wood and heard Carl coming down the stairs with his suitcase.

'You won't get far, you fucking freak!' I shouted. 'We're on to you!' But I doubt he heard me. And even if he did, so what? He was gone. He could be at the airport in an hour. He could be lost on the network of rails in less time than that. Yes he had quite an unusual identifying feature, but there was something about him, the way he crept up on me on those bald floorboards, like Grasshopper on rice paper. He could lose himself, all right. He was smoke and shadow.

I flicked on the light and looked around the cellar. Unlike some cellars I knew, used as a dumping ground for the debris a family collects over time, this one had been kept tidy. Interlocking foam mats covered the floor in red and black squares. A punch bag hung from a chain attached to the ceiling. Free weights were arranged in one corner. Next to that was a filing cabinet. Next to that was a small fridge freezer.

I shuffled over to the furniture, trying to work out if anything was broken. My fingers were sore but I could move them. My left eye was puffing shut, and the back of my head was throbbing where it had met with the gristle in the centre of Renfrew's face. But I was mostly functional. In the filing cabinet were folders containing bills, bank statements, documents regarding Renfrew's car, various papers concerning his job. I found a large envelope stuffed with cards from landmark anniversaries, separated from each other with elastic bands. Eighteen, twenty-one, thirty.

You passed your driving test! Congratulations on your new job! We're sorry to see you go! In another envelope was a bunch of notes and cards and letters from old girlfriends. *I love you. I hate you. I miss you.* I sifted through them, feeling ugly at the enjoyment I was receiving from seeing his seamy past laid bare before me. It was a kind of revenge. Pathetic, but then I'm not the most noble of men.

I dug out my phone. No signal. I felt a sudden piercing panic as I imagined Renfrew setting fire to those fliers in the door with me trapped down here, but murder would only intensify the search for him, if any were to be ordered, which I doubted. I closed the filing cabinet and reached for the fridge door. If he had any booze down here then not only would it make the wait bearable, pleasurable even, but I would take out a full page advertisement in *The Times* apologising to Renfrew for everything. I should have known, though that a green tea-drinking martial arts expert would be unlikely to own anything so unhealthy as a beer fridge. The shelves were packed with health drinks – pomegranate juice, carrot juice, kefir, a range of smoothies, a couple of protein shakes. I slammed the door in disgust and tried the freezer.

I was sitting on the other side of the room without knowing how I got there. The freezer door was still open, as was the first drawer I'd pulled out. I was trying to convince myself that what I'd seen wasn't what I'd seen.

A pair of eyes. Tiny organs on ice. A hand, like something snapped from a doll.

Gone seven o'clock in the evening, my arse numb from sitting on the floor. I was rooting around in a toolbox for something that might help me get the door open when I heard footsteps on the gravel drive, and a key in the lock. Carl returning, seeing sense. I doubted that. And anyway, these footsteps were lighter. I heard them go upstairs. After about twenty minutes they returned to the kitchen. I heard a cutlery drawer rattle open. Then a key in the cellar door.

'Hello Jen,' I said.

'I'm finished,' she said. She was holding a long butcher's knife in her hand.

'No, no. We can find him. Or at the very least, we can get you safe. But I doubt he'll be ba–'

She sat on the bottom step. The knife gritted against its edge and she looked down at it, as if surprised to see it there. 'No,' she said. 'This was not how it was meant to go.'

'I don't understand.'

She looked up at me and there was accusation in her eyes. Anger too. She levelled the point of the knife at me and her lips thinned. 'You were meant to kill him.'

'What?'

'You heard me. That business between you and the guy. You and the guy on the roof at St Pancras. I read all about that in the newspaper. It was on TV. You were ruthless.'

'That guy was ruthless. Carl wasn't a killer. He's sick, but he's no killer.'

'But you are.'

'Jesus Christ, Jen. What the fuck are you talking about? What I did, I did in self defence.'

'I know what he's like. I know what he's capable of. I thought you could finish him for–' She stopped short and put her hand to her face. There was a green tinge to her skin but it might have been this weird subterranean false light, and the pressure of my black eye.

'For… what? You?'

She sighed. 'Yes.'

'Why?'

'You're the private investigator. You work it out.'

We stared at each other. Her eyelids were drooping and she kept licking her lips. She had positioned the knife blade flat against her arm, the point dimpling the blue shadows at her wrist.

'What have you taken?' I asked.

'Thirty diazepam tablets,' she said. 'I told you, I'm finished.'

Something heavy and thick was moving through me, like cold, like sickness. Dread.

'Why did you and Graham split up, why did you really split up, all those years ago?' I asked. My voice was suddenly small and uncertain in this enclosed space, cowed by the enormity of what was opening in my thoughts. 'You told me it was because he wanted children and you didn't.'

She smiled. Her eyes were closed now. When she talked her voice was gluey with fatigue. 'He wanted children and I... couldn't,' she said.

'You couldn't? Did he know that?'

'Eventually.'

'Why not?'

'I had a hysterectomy when I was seventeen. I suffered from endometriosis.'

'And you never told him?'

'I loved him, Joel. To tell him was to see him walk away.'

I had been backing away from her, beginning to understand the shape of my dread. Perhaps I had known all along, ever since the moment she came into the café from the wind-blasted Praed Street, maybe earlier, when I'd seen the way Graham watched the children playing in the park, all those years ago. I felt my thigh collide gently with the edge of a wooden chest. I sat down on it. I was trembling all over. It felt as if my bones were trembling.

'Why did you do it, Jen? You tried to kidnap a child.'

'And I couldn't go through with it. That's when I realised I had to find another way.'

'The freezer… the freezer…' I couldn't say anything else. I didn't know what to do.

'I wanted to make a baby,' she said, as if I was the world's most stupid person. And I felt it, in that moment.

'What's the knife for?' I asked.

'Don't worry. It's not for you. It's in case I'm sick. But I think it will all be okay. I'm going to sleep now.'

I followed her at a distance while she moved up through the house. At one point I thought she was going to collapse on the stairs, but she composed herself and made it to the bedroom. She dropped the knife on the floor. She reached around to unzip her skirt, but thought better of it, or no longer had the strength for it. She got on the bed. She fell asleep.

I watched her. I don't know why. At one point, after about ten minutes, she was copiously sick. But the drug was deep in her by then and she did not revive. I watched her for an hour, until the skin of her lips was blue, until the tremor in her eyelids was stilled.

I watched the monster until I was sure.

ACKNOWLEDGMENTS

Love and thanks to Mum and Dad, as ever. I owe it all to you. Thanks to the friends who read early drafts of this novel: Richard Coady, Mark Morris, Nicholas Royle, Michael Smith and the late, great Graham Joyce. Thanks to Robert Kirby for his faith in the book, Maxim Jakubowski for enthusiasm and support, and Peter Lavery for supreme editing skills. Thanks too to John Schoenfelder for help and advice. I'm deeply grateful to Miranda Jewess at Titan for breathing life into Joel Sorrell and giving him a future. Special thanks to Rhonda, who read this first, showed unwavering support for it and helped to find it a home.

JOEL SORRELL WILL RETURN IN

SONATA OF THE DEAD

JULY 2016

ABOUT THE AUTHOR

Conrad Williams is the author of seven novels, four novellas and a collection of short stories. *One* was the winner of the August Derleth award for Best Novel (British Fantasy Awards 2010), while *The Unblemished* won the International Horror Guild Award for Best Novel in 2007 (he beat the shortlisted Stephen King on both occasions). He won the British Fantasy Award for Best Newcomer in 1993, and another British Fantasy Award for Best Novella (*The Scalding Rooms*) in 2008. He lives in Manchester.

AUTHOR Q&A

What inspired you to write this novel?

In the early Noughties I heard of an anthology Maxim Jakubowski was putting together with M. Christian, a *Blade Runner*-ish book called *Future Cops*. I came up with an idea for a story called 'Footprint on Nowhere Beach.' My protagonist was a guy called Rad Hallah. I had an enormous amount of fun writing that story, and was considering writing more in the world I'd created, but in the end I thought it would be easier to write something set in the here and now. Rad Hallah was slightly too exotic a name and so he became Joel Sorrell. Although he's pretty much no different from that original story. I was living in London when I first had the idea for *Dust and Desire*. I was at St Pancras and I was thinking, pretty much as The Four-Year-Old does, that everything you needed was here. You could live here. The story grew from that, and also was inspired by some colourful characters I remembered from my life in Warrington: bouncers and bodybuilders and what they might get up to.

Joel is a very damaged character, but also darkly humorous. How did he introduce himself to you?

The characters that matter to me in crime and thriller fiction are all flawed in some way. The unnamed Detective Sergeant in Derek Raymond's *Factory* novels is profane and obstinate, Will Graham possesses traits of the thing he wants to defeat, James Bond is a blunt tool, a womanising bastard, Scylla in *Marathon Man* and *Brothers* is an expert killing machine crumbling under the sense of his own mortality. Dave Robicheaux is a recovering alcoholic. I wasn't a very rebellious teenager, so Joel's puerile sense of humour and disdain of authority is pretty much me dealing with some thirty-year-old frustrations.

The Four-Year-Old is a very disturbing antagonist. Do you think that serial killers make for the best perpetrators?

The reading public's appetite for serial killers doesn't look like abating. But I wanted to come up with a killer who has an agenda beyond what the voices in his head are telling him. I wanted his reasoning to be the kind of thing a reader might think about and decide, well actually, he's got a point. I'm not looking for sympathy for my devil, but I certainly felt for him. What he's doing, in his eyes, is a noble thing, the right thing.

What kind of research did you do while writing this novel?

Lots of stuff form the unnecessarily picky (what kind of cheap cars would be on offer to hire from a Liverpool car rental company?) to the nerdy and pointless (what kind of ships operated out of the Liverpool docks a hundred years ago?) to the mundane (wandering around St Pancras looking for hiding places and seeing what shops were in business). I also had to look into exercise routines and weight-lifting. I think the vast majority of research is unecessary actually. But it's fun to do. I could have made everything up and I doubted it would have mattered.

Joel is driven by the search for his missing daughter. Do you think that crime protagonists need to have a dark past?

No, but it helps me. I wanted to write about a punished character, someone with a nightmarish history, a knottier, chewier kind of character with no black and white sides but lots of edges, lots of shades of grey. Someone who is driven, and good at what he does, but is fallible, knows moments of weakness and fear, but has to go on because his daughter is out there.

Do you think that your background in horror has influenced the Joel Sorrell books?

Without doubt. I think there's much to be said about the crime/ horror fusion that has been going on probably since Thomas Harris's *Red Dragon* appeared in 1982. You only have to look at how the covers of crime and thriller novels have developed over the past thirty years. You could put a horror novel alongside a crime novel and have a tough time deciding which was which. And there really isn't much difference. Crime is horror. I want to push Joel into some dark, dark territory. The only real difference is that I'm not entertaining any supernatural strands in these books.

If you could have written any other crime novel, which would it be and why?

It's an odd subject, because my idea of crime might be someone else's idea of horror and vice versa. I don't see much of a difference, as I've said. I like the books that have a transgressive feel about them. Recent favourites include Michael Connelly's *The Poet*, Louise Welsh's *The Cutting Room*, *The Eros Hunter* by Russell Celyn Jones and *Others of My Kind* by James Sallis. But I would have to choose either *Red Dragon* by Thomas Harris or *I Was Dora Suarez* by Derek Raymond. Both are the kind of book you put down with fingernail indentations on the cover.

Who are your favourite crime writers and why?
Derek Raymond, James Sallis, James Lee Burke, Thomas Harris. Joel Lane, who was best known for his supernatural stories, but was moving into crime fiction before his untimely death. For reasons I've already touched upon, but also because they write beautifully, from the heart, and tell great stories.

Who would be present at your fictional character dinner party?
James Bond, Ignatius O'Reilly, Danny Torrance, Clarice Starling, Agaton Sax, Thomas 'Babe' Levy.

Where and how do you write? Do you have any unconventional habits?
At the moment I'm lucky enough to have my own study. This might change as my three boys grow ever bigger. Sometimes I'll nip out to the coffee shop in the village if I have to get a chunk of work done fast (fewer distractions). I have to wash my hands before I sit down to write (some would say I really ought to be washing them afterwards too, if not during). And I like to listen to lyricless music (so classical, jazz, soundtracks, ambient). I like

to write longhand with a nice fountain pen containing some funky ink colour, or directly into a dedicated writing application (Scrivener and Ulysses are current favourites).

Do you prefer print or e-books?
Print. I own a Kindle because I thought it would be handy to carry lots of books away with me on holiday, but I almost never use it. I prefer the heft and texture of a block of paper between my fingers.

What is the most beautiful book you own?
There's a limited edition of Clive Barker's *Weaveworld* from Earthling Publications, which is rather beautiful. And an illustrated edition of *Nineteen Eighty-Four* I'm fond of. But I think the book that means the most to me is a copy of *Treasure Island* (Paul Hamlyn, 1967) with a gorgeous deep green cover. It contains some hair-raising illustrations by Josef Hochman. My dad gave it to me for my second birthday. It's getting a bit tatty now, but it's the one book I own that constantly turns my head.

How many Joel Sorrell books will there be and are you writing any other books?
I'd love to write many more Joel novels. I always wanted to create a series character, and I think he has legs, although part of me wants to do something unspeakably cruel to him in *Hell is Empty*, which will be the third book in the series. I'm also working on a ghost story set in France, informed by events that took place in 1944. It's kind of *The Shining* meets *Eye of the Needle*.

Can you give us the one-line pitch for the next Joel Sorrell novel, Sonata of the Dead?

Members of a secretive militant writers group are being murdered and Joel Sorrell must infiltrate it to find out why when he discovers that his daughter is involved in their activities and next on the killer's list.